INTERTWINED

ERIC SUDDOTH

RISING SMOKE PUBLISHING

Cover design by Leah Joyce

Rising Smoke Publishing
ISBN 978-1-949869-11-8

For my thoughts are not your thoughts,
Neither are your ways my ways, declares the Lord.
For as the heavens are higher than the earth,
so are my ways higher than your ways
and my thoughts than your thoughts.
Isaiah 55:8-9

PREFACE

"Mary, Mary, can you hear me? Mary?" he gasped, trying to catch his breath after a mad chase through the woods.

Her blank sapphire blue eyes caught a glimpse of his mysterious maple-colored ones before they rolled back into her head. She had lost consciousness again.

"Mary, you are going to be okay," the dark stranger said as he leaned over and whispered in her newly pierced ear. "You are going to be okay." He clutched her drenched, quivering small frame against his. He could feel the life-giving air enter and leave her lungs and breathed a sigh of relief. "Nice to meet you, Mary. My name is Josiah." He spoke gently, as if his words would break her delicate exterior. He brushed his leathery charcoal hands through her wet sandy blond hair, letting the drips splash onto her soaking wet University of Mississippi t-shirt that clung to her eleven-year-old skinny body. "Mary is a very pretty name for a very pretty girl," he said innocently.

Her eyes shot open with a twinge of fear. The limpness in her arms and legs fled as she raised her chest up with fight or flight instinct. "No, stop!" She tried to scream, but only a gurgling groan escaped her thin colorless lips. *Please don't hurt me,* she thought as she flashed back to *Dateline* specials of child predators that her parents had made her watch. "Please."

"Child, it's okay," Josiah said as he attempted to reassure her. "Mary, you don't have to be afraid."

Wiggling and squirming in panic-stricken anxiety, Mary tried to get away from the older man's tight grip, but she was too weak. He continued to hold her tightly. "It's okay, Mary. I'm not going to hurt you. The ambulance is on its way."

"The what?" she whispered, looking down and noticing her wet clothes. Turning her head slowly in a circle, she found herself in a

1

familiar location. She looked up and saw a ceiling of clouds overhead with some treetops not too far away.

Josiah slightly released his grip, but not enough to let go. He wanted her to feel safe, not caged like a wild animal. "I've got you."

She looked up into his eyes and stared intently as he returned the favor, looking into hers. They watched each other in silence for a couple of minutes, as if to reintroduce themselves, scratching the first frightening introduction from their memory. There was something different about his eyes, she thought. There was an immediate connection that transcended understanding. She didn't know anything about him, yet in the same breath, she felt like she knew him better than anyone else. His eyes held the wisdom of age with a few wrinkles laced around the edges; yet they were soft and unobtrusive.

Her arms began to feel light as she sunk deeper into his lap, leaning her dizzy head on his muscular shoulder. In an instant, all the fright left her, followed by a feeling of warm peace radiating around her cool body. She closed her eyes. "Thank you...Josiah."

Josiah's smile stretched across his face as he began to slowly rock. He wasn't sure what to do, but he did know the power in a touch, his touch. He loosened his hold and allowed his hands to rub up and down her bony back. "You're going to be okay, Mary," he kept repeating as if trying to convince himself of that notion. "You're going to be just fine."

He stared up into the heavens and started humming softly. The rhythm of the river tides lapping onto the rocky shore fit perfectly into his hymn. Tearfully, he bowed his head and watched as she took a few deep breaths before closing his eyes and muttering a heartfelt prayer. He still wore his smile that had remarkably grown brighter. The silence was broken by the sound of sirens in the distance, while he scanned the landscape suspiciously looking for the person who caused this near-death event. He knew that person wasn't far away. He knew for certain that he was being watched.

"He's not ready for you yet, Mary. He has something in store for you."

CHAPTER 1

Tuesdays in the Sutton family meant chicken for supper. Charlie, the chicken fiend and youngest in the Sutton clan, got to choose supper on Tuesdays, just as seafood lover and mother, Claire got to do so on Mondays. The marinara-obsessed and father Dan held the Wednesday slot, and twins, vegetarian Amelia and unpredictable Scarlett were in charge of Thursdays and Fridays, respectively. Last Tuesday was chicken teriyaki, the Tuesday before that was chicken parmesan, and the one before that was great grandma's original double-crisped fried chicken.

Claire, the queen of the Sutton household, stood over her stainless-steel sink, running the chilled water for the pot of red ripened potatoes. Her kitchen had fingerprints of Martha Stewart in the country style draperies, the personality of Rachel Ray in the orange handled Furi Gusto-Grips knives, the bam of Emeril Lagasse in the cast iron cookware, and the friendliness of Paula Deen in the robin egg blue mixing bowls. Her kitchen was a makeshift altar to her cooking gurus whom she aspired to emulate. Instead of lighting candles, she would light her blue flamed gas stove in their honor.

Turning the water on low, she couldn't help but stare into the peaceful backyard, which was usually filled with shouting kids playing baseball or capture-the-flag on their jungle gym playhouse. This was the life that was better than Claire's most lofty and aspiring imagination – being a stay-at-home mother of three precious children and married to the handsome attorney and love of her life. They lived in a lavish plantation style four-bedroom home, and behind a row of elm trees in their backyard a glimpse of the Shantoee River could be seen when the wind blew the tree limbs at the right angle. Her life was better than a dream.

Many summer evenings were spent casting their lines into the peaceful river, only to hear Amelia rant about the killing of innocent fish.

"What did God put them he'e fo?" six-year-old Charlie would ask without enunciating the "letter r" in each of his words. As the only son, he could usually be found standing inches from his hero, his dad, holding onto his Snoopy fishing pole that was barely taller than he was.

"What do you think aquariums are for?" Amelia would refute as she sat fifteen feet behind the rest of the family on a tree stump trying not to get hooked by a stray cast.

"Dad, what's an aquawium?" Charlie asked innocently.

"It's a place to keep fish," Dan answered without taking his eyes off of his bobber that flowed slowly downstream. "Remember when we went to Sea World last year?"

"Yeah! That was fun!" Charlie exclaimed.

"Weren't those some beautiful creatures?" Amelia asked.

"Uh huh," Charlie nodded in agreement.

"Well, when you eat them, they can't swim anymore. They're dead," Amelia commented with a solemn facial expression.

Charlie's lip quivered in disappointment.

"Don't worry bro, you can watch 'em and have fun. Then enjoy 'em even more for supper. There will always be another fish to watch the next day," added Scarlett, the oldest of the siblings by two measly minutes, which she reminded Amelia of weekly with birthright arrogance.

"Po' fishie," Charlie said looking into the bucket of fish they had caught. "But you weally do taste good."

"Right on," Scarlett high-fived him as Amelia grunted in disgust. "Let 'em swim in your tummy."

Amelia walked into the shrine of great chefs and stood beside her mother, who stood staring out the same window at the hypnotizing blades of grass. "What did Charlie pick tonight?" Amelia asked her mother.

Entranced with her daydream of lightning bug-filled summer nights, Claire didn't acknowledge Amelia or even the pot of water running over the rim in the sink.

"Earth to mother," she said, stopping the water and snapping her fingers inches from Claire's nose.

"Oh, sorry. I was just looking out the window and lost track of time, I guess. Isn't it beautiful today?" She placed the pot on the stove to let the water warm to a boil as she got out the chicken with various spices and two chunky white cloves of garlic.

"Garlic chicken?"

"Yeah, we haven't had this in a while, and he wanted something different."

"Why don't we do veggie chicken sometime and see if they notice it?"

Claire poured some olive oil into a cast iron pan to heat up. "Your night is Thursday. If you want veggie chicken, we can do it then."

"I'll pass on that. If we serve it on Thursday night, they'll know it's veggie and Scarlett won't even try it."

"You never know. She might," Claire added as she smeared some garlic flour over the chicken breasts.

"I know her quite well. She would never do that for me; she's too stubborn."

"And you're not?" Claire grinned as Amelia smiled devilishly in surrender. "Speaking of Scarlett, where is she?"

"Don't know," Amelia said, shrugging her shoulders as she left the kitchen.

Claire went to the stainless-steel refrigerator which housed a collage of Charlie's letter magnets and family calendar. Claire traced her finger over the dates until she came to March 8 and noticed soccer practice – 3:45 p.m. glowing in neon pink ink. She opened the door and got a few uncut vegetables to make Amelia's nightly apple and pecan garden salad.

It's only 5:27, so she is probably walking home.

CHAPTER 2

Chase, the emergency medical technician, stepped out of the ambulance. The red light was still spinning wildly, but thankfully the squeal of the siren had been turned off. He ran over to Josiah still swaying the girl snugly in his arms and knelt like a catcher behind the plate. Chase looked to be in his mid-forties with short black hair and patches of gray around his ears. His expression was emotionless, but he was trained for this type of situation. He knew to not show fear because people don't want their rescuer to go limp in the tough times. Josiah released his hold, allowing Chase access to the drowsy child.

"What happened here?" Chased asked.

"I was walking down that path," Josiah answered, pointing to the wooded area about fifty feet behind them, "when I heard a scream. I ran and saw Mary floating down the river. She was trying to stay afloat, but I guess the heavy rain last night caused the river to be stronger than it usually is because she was having a hard time."

Chase laid Mary on the ground and checked her breathing and heart rate, which appeared to be stable. "Get me some blankets," Chase yelled to the other EMT, who was still in the back of the ambulance getting medical supplies.

The white metal doors swung open and a slumped gawky kid, who looked fifteen but was probably in his early twenties, tripped out carrying a couple of blankets with an oxygen tank trailing behind.

Chase quickly put the plastic mask on Mary, wrapping the oxygen tubes behind her ears. The equipment began filling her lungs with the air she was gasping for ten minutes earlier. "You said her name was Mary?" he asked Josiah.

"Yes," he answered.

"Mary, my name is Chase. If you can, please open your eyes."

Her left eye strained to open while the right remained sealed shut.

Chase placed his hand in hers. "Mary, squeeze my hand."

Her hands quivered in movement. It wasn't a squeeze, but it was good enough for now. She had experienced a great shock. She was freezing, and all her body wanted to do was to sleep it off.

They wrapped her four foot seven-inch frame in the red blanket to escape the cold. Even though the temperature was in the low seventies and the sun's dazzling rays still shone overhead, the water was much colder. In addition, the agonizing feeling of the frigid liquid filling one's lungs would cause anyone to go into shock.

"She was lucky," Tucker, the pimple-faced EMT, stated as he towered empty-handed over the small huddled group.

"I guess one could say that, but I don't believe in luck," Josiah replied as he stood up, wrapping a blanket around his lean, six-foot body.

"I mean, you just happened to be walking down here the moment she was in the water. And how did she get in the river?" Tucker asked, scratching his head in deep thought.

"I didn't ask that." Josiah stopped and stared down at the picturesque river. "I just asked for her name." He was engulfed with the idea that something so beautiful could also be so unsympathetically violent. Remorsefully, he knew the oxymoron too well.

Chase continued to administer his medical procedures, writing her vitals on his clipboard, check-marking the appropriate steps, and crossing off the needless information. He looked down and noticed that her right eye was beginning to open a little.

"Hello, Mary. How do you feel?"

She blinked her eyes as if waking up from a drug-induced nap. "I feel…" she started with a chilled stutter, "I feel wet."

Josiah smiled as he knelt beside her. "Mary, I think he wants to know if you feel good or bad."

She stared up at him in confusion and reached for the mask that was pumping in oxygen.

9

"We need to keep this on you for a little while longer. Just relax," Chase said as he tucked the blanket around her arms. "Mary, can you tell me what happened?"

She turned her face from Josiah to Chase with another confused look.

"Why do you keep calling me Mary? No one calls me Mary, except when I'm in trouble," she frowned.

The small group of men each chuckled at her whimsy. "You're not in trouble. We're just here to help. What do you like to be called?"

"Scarlett."

CHAPTER 3

"That is a beautiful name," Chase said as he brushed her hair back from her forehead like he would do to one of his own daughters.

"My full name is Mary Scarlett Sutton," she said in one long breath. "I live less than a mile from here."

"Do you know where here is?" Tucker asked, trying to get in on the action.

She looked up at him in annoyance. "Bethany, Mississippi."

"Good. When is your birthday?" Chase asked as he filled in the paperwork.

"April 2, 1998," she piped out nonchalantly. "Can I take this off now?" Her hand quickly removed the mask before Chase could answer. "It's pressing on my cheeks."

"Yeah, I think you can," Chase answered, jotting down a note without noticing her struggle with the maze of tubes attached to the mask.

Josiah carefully helped her with the mask. "Good to see you doing better, Mary. I mean, Scarlett."

"You can call me Mary; I'm used to it. I get in trouble a lot."

Josiah smiled at her honesty, clutching the mask in his hands until Tucker grabbed the breathing apparatus.

"I need to make a call," Tucker said walking away, grabbing his cellular phone from his holster.

"Kids. What would they do without cell phones?" Chase smirked.

"My dad won't get me one," Scarlett interjected. "He says I don't need it."

"He's right, but it was handy for Josiah here to have one. If he didn't call immediately, we may not have been here yet. But it seems like Josiah knew exactly what to do."

Scarlett leaned up, her arms escaping the blankets to give a strong hug to Josiah. "Thank you!"

11

"You're very welcome."

"I need a little more information," Chase said as he started asking her some basic questions. Many she could answer, but for others, she suggested they ask her parents. Josiah tilted his head up and noticed the clouds quickly passing by. The wind was beginning to pick back up, so he threw the blanket over her shoulders. Mary smiled in appreciation and continued to answer all the questions she could.

"How did you get in the river?" Chase asked.

"I guess the truth is going to come out," she breathed out in surrender. "Promise me you will not leave me when my parents get here."

"I promise," Josiah assured her as Chase looked up, uncomfortable with the request.

"I was walking home from soccer practice when I decided to take a short cut over Mr. Maple's bridge. Do you know the place I'm talking about?"

They each shook their heads no.

"Well, it's a rope bridge with wooden boards on the bottom like in the *Indiana Jones* movies. My parents always tell me not to walk over that rickety bridge and to use the sturdier one. But I wanted to get home quicker, and that bridge saves me about five minutes." She looked around for a glance of disapproval, but all she saw was Josiah's smile.

"Go on, Mary, we're listening," Josiah added.

"Well, I've walked over his bridge many times before, and I never had any trouble. There are a few boards that are missing or loose, but I have them memorized." She stopped and rolled her eyes. "Or so I thought."

"So, did a piece of wood break?" Chase asked.

"I was jumping over one of the loose boards when I guess I landed too hard and broke it. I was falling backwards, and I broke the loose board as well. I grabbed onto the rope that was used as a handle,

12

but I couldn't hang on long enough to pull myself up. The rope is old, and it was hurting my hands, so I fell about twenty feet into the river."

"Do you know how far you drifted down the river?" Chase asked, scribbling frantically.

"I don't remember," she said. "I just remember going under and thinking that I was going to die." She looked up at Josiah with an appreciative smile. "That is until you rescued me."

"You stay here. I'm going to call your parents," Chase said.

"Do you have to?" she pleaded with terrified eyes.

Chase got up and walked toward Tucker, who was returning from his phone call. "I need to use your phone to call her parents."

"Better use the handset in the ambulance. There's no reception down here. I walked all over and couldn't get a single bar on my phone."

The two looked down at Tucker's cell phone and saw that there were no bars then turned their attention to the mysterious stranger. "And he says he doesn't believe in luck."

CHAPTER 4

Charlie sat at the fully dressed dinner table, his mouth watering as the mountain of fried chicken laid in the middle. There were also bowls of butter-smothered mashed potatoes, sweet golden corn, and a basket of buttermilk biscuits arranged from end to end. He looked up at the grandfather clock that stood in the corner of the formal dining room which had struck 7 p.m. six minutes earlier. The golden reflective pendulum swung back and forth, grinding the gears and turning the wheels to help keep the massive piece of cherry wood in perfect time. Every time the pendulum swung, Charlie saw his sad, hungry face in its reflection.

Staring at the five empty plates and crystal glasses, his heart began to race faster. The smells swirled around the room, creating a potpourri of his favorite meal. He considered sneaking a biscuit and nibbling, but he knew he wasn't allowed to eat until everyone was at the table – family rule.

The rumbling in his stomach began to overpower the ticks of the grandfather clock. With each second that passed, his growling became louder and louder until the sound became deafening to his young ears. He patiently scanned the room, looking for shadows along the hallway, the sound of footsteps coming, or the smell of the ranch dressing for the first course of their meal. His senses didn't pick up anything on their radars. The coast was clear.

He quietly jumped down from his chair and tiptoed across the mahogany oak floor to the far end of the table that housed the delectable biscuits. He unwrapped the linen around the golden treasures and saw a wave of steam rise from the goodies. The warmth took his breath away, or it could have been the smell of the butter-crusted bread, or just the cherished image of food within reach.

With trembling hands, he clamped onto a biscuit. He suspiciously looked around the room one final time. His eyes darted from corner to corner, trying to conclude if it was safe for him to proceed back to his seat and enjoy the stolen treasure.

He looked down at his hand and saw the heavenly manna, and he couldn't wait. He lifted his hand and took a large bite. His tongue leapt to the roof of his mouth at the taste of his desiring. It was delicious! He breathed in a large sigh of relief and continued walking back to his seat.

He chewed for what felt like minutes, but he knew that he practically swallowed the entire biscuit whole. The biscuit only whet his appetite as he licked his lips and fingers clean, trying to hide any evidence that he had broken the family tradition. *But it's after seven*, he told himself. *Supper always begins at 6:30, and it's after seven.* Deep down, Scarlett was his favorite sister. But right now, he was furious because she had taken away the limelight on his night! Again!

He looked around the room, hoping to hear someone coming toward the dining room, but there wasn't a sound. Just ticks and tocks, over and over.

He looked up at the table and noticed that he had left the biscuits uncovered. He quickly jumped up to bury them under the linen, only to stop when he heard the telephone ringing.

"Hello? Yes, this is Mr. Sutton."

CHAPTER 5

Dan hung up the phone and hugged his wife. "She's fine. She will be home in a few minutes."

Claire was shaking in her husband's arms as tears of relief were dripping onto Dan's white Brooks Brothers shirt. "Charlie, your sister is coming home," Claire yelled as she tugged Amelia up from the couch into the huddle.

The three stood in a silent embrace, except for the sound of Claire's runny nose every time she took a breath. They heard running footsteps coming from the hallway as Charlie ran in to join their family cluster of arms. "She's on her way? Can we eat when she gets here?"

Amelia patted her brother on his head and untangled herself from the emotional scene. "I'll fix you a plate. Is that okay, Mom?"

"Sure, go ahead," Claire said, smiling as they walked away, yet still clinging onto Dan – her support.

"She's fine, honey," Dan whispered in her ear as he kissed her forehead. "The ambulance is bringing her home."

"The ambulance? They had to call an ambulance?" Claire asked, her voice rising with fear.

"Stay calm. Someone was there to rescue her."

"Rescue? What happened? Where?" she asked, panic taking hold once again. "Who saved her?"

"I don't know. They just told me that she's fine, just a little shaken up, and they will be here in a few minutes." He wiped the tears away from her eyes and cheek. He was relieved, but he was trying to keep his emotions in check. The wait had been agonizing since they'd called the soccer coach to hear that soccer practice had ended more than an hour earlier at the school that was only a fifteen-minute walk from their house.

They called most of her teammates' parents, and none of them had had anything to say, except for seeing her start to walk home with

16

Lucy. A couple expressed remorse for not picking her up and bringing her home since it was only a few minutes out of their way. It was sad that during a crisis, the terrified parents had to console other parents for not taking care of their child. "She always walks home. There was nothing you could do," they reassured the others. "She probably would have said no because she likes her alone time. Her walks are probably the only time she gets to be by herself."

During the wait, Claire had been making excuses as to why Scarlett wasn't home. Each one sounded perfectly believable, except Scarlett wouldn't have done any of them. She knew better than to stop at someone's house or library without calling to tell them. During a time of worry, excuses were sometimes all that people cling to, yet they were always the easiest to break down and prove false.

Claire stood at the open door and stared out the glass, waiting for the ambulance to pull in their driveway and see their little girl come bouncing up the walkway. "She's okay, Claire."

"I know. I just want to see her."

"You will," he said as he stood beside her, his heart pounding as he, too, watched for the first sign of the ambulance.

"You couldn't even wait?" Amelia shouted at Charlie from the dining room. "Mom always covers the biscuits with the linen."

"But I was hungry," he whimpered like a scorned puppy.

"But Scarlett was missing. Isn't that more important than a biscuit?"

Charlie looked down at his feet in remorse. He mainly felt regret for getting caught.

"Kids!" Dan shouted, "she's home!"

CHAPTER 6

Holding hands, Dan and Claire led the pack, followed closely by Amelia and Charlie as the ambulance drove up their winding driveway. They stood anxiously. Charlie's hunger pains diminished, Claire's tears began again, and even Dan and Amelia were starting to show signs of wet eyes.

The ambulance pulled up a few feet from the pack, and they immediately went to the back and waited for the doors to part. Chase opened the doors from the inside, and there laid Scarlett wrapped in a red blanket, hair still damp, with terrified-wide eyes.

"I'm sorry. I am so sorry," Scarlett blurted out as Claire jumped into the ambulance and hugged her daughter.

"Don't worry. Don't worry about a thing," Claire said as they both began to cry.

"Can I see her?" Charlie said, trying to peek into the ambulance.

"If everyone will please stand back, she can come out," Chase said, clearing the way for Scarlett and her mother.

"Why is your hair wet?" Amelia asked as she hugged her sister.

Charlie snuck around the action to investigate the ambulance. "Cool!" he whispered to himself as he scanned the interior filled with gadgets and gizmos. He was mesmerized – as if he was seeing Santa's workshop.

Scarlett looked at her parents, then at Chase, who winked at her with encouragement. "I took a shortcut home and fell in the river," she said sheepishly.

"Did you go on Mr. Maple's bridge?" Claire asked, her voice rising to a shriek.

"Yes," Scarlett grimaced, waiting for the tongue lashing to begin. She was thankful that Chase hadn't left yet, thinking that after her parents' scolding she may need to be bandaged from head to toe.

"You know Mom and Dad don't like that bridge. Why would you do that?" Amelia asked.

"I don't know. I was just trying to get home quicker," Scarlett answered, dumbly. "I am so sorry."

"How many times have we warned you about that old bridge?" her father questioned. "How many?"

"I know. I know. I'm sorry," Scarlett blurted out as tears began to form.

Claire wrapped her arms around Scarlett. "I know you are, but…" she stopped what she was going to say when she saw the look on Scarlett's face. "But nothing. You are home. Safe and sound."

"Did someone save you?" Charlie asked, rejoining the group.

"Yes, Josiah," Scarlett answered.

"Who is Josiah?" Dan responded as he hugged his family together.

"I, I don't know," Scarlett answered looking up at Chase.

"I didn't get a last name, because I thought you knew him when you said his name," Chase said in shock.

"Well, we've got to find him," Claire mentioned.

"When he walked away, he told me that he would see me tomorrow," Scarlett said, thinking back in her memory. "I didn't think anything about it, but I have never seen that man before in my life. I guess I'll find out more about him tomorrow if I see him."

"Thank you so much for your help," Dan said, shaking Chase's hand almost pulling for his wallet as if Chase was a bellhop at a hotel dropping off their bags. Except Chase dropped off something more valuable than luggage. The rest of the family clutched onto Scarlett as they started walking to the house.

"We need to get you out of those wet clothes and into a nice hot bath," Claire said, rubbing her daughter's wet hair. "And promise us you will never go on that bridge again."

"I promise," Scarlett said with a hint of a smile.

"What's so funny?" Amelia asked.

"Well, I don't think anyone will be using the bridge for a while," Scarlett said, tucking her chin in shame. "I messed it up pretty good."

"Do I have to wait for her to get done with her bath before I can eat?" Charlie asked with a mischievous smile.

"Come on, kiddo. I'm starving too," Dan replied as he picked up Charlie and ran up the porch steps.

"Men only think about their stomachs," Amelia scoffed prompting snickers from the other Sutton females.

"That they do," Claire echoed, clutching both of her girls and kissing each on their foreheads as they slowly climbed the porch steps as a pack. "That they do."

CHAPTER 7

Josiah pulled out a folded, matted down piece of paper with 294 Sycamore Lane scribbled on it. At least he thought it said 294 since it had smeared due to the river water. He stood on the sidewalk in front of a two-story colonial home and looked around at the surrounding houses. He glanced over at the mailbox that had 294 embossed in gold numbers down the white wooden post with Stapleton in elegant cursive writing. *This must be the place*, he thought.

He opened the gate of the 1950s style white picket fence and admired the landscaping with its towering rosebushes climbing up the waterspouts, oodles of marigolds lining the walkway to the front door, and at least ten African violets in hanging plastic pots on the southern style front porch that circled the entire house. He rang the doorbell and heard a woman's voice responding, "Coming, I'm coming."

The porch light came on as the door swung open revealing a woman in her late sixties with platinum curly hair, dressed in a long blue skirt a few inches above her ankle and a multicolored flowery blouse. She wore a silver lily brooch pinned on her right chest. "May I help you?" she asked behind the screen door, straining her eyes to see.

"Good evening, ma'am. I'm Josiah, your new tenant," he warmly greeted.

"Oh, I've been wondering about you. I received your luggage a few days ago, but not you," she laughed.

"Yes, well I wanted to make sure it got here before I did. I would hate to have to wear the same clothes day after day, especially starting a new job," he said with a smile, still standing awkwardly on the front porch.

"Lord help me. Where are my manners? Please do come in," she said, finally opening the screen door to welcome her guest. "My name is Ethel Stapleton, but you probably already know that. Are you hungry or thirsty? Let me show you around. I haven't had a tenant in quite

21

some time. People these days just do not want to stay with an old lady like me, I guess. People prefer to stay in these large apartment complexes and go about their business. They get no connection in those, no family lifestyles. I mean, when I was a young lady there were no large apartment buildings in Bethany. It was just homes like this, and you could rent a room. How fast things change."

Josiah politely listened and nodded his head in agreement but couldn't get a word in edgewise.

"But look at me ramble about younger generations. I mean, you are younger than me, though not by much."

He again smiled politely as she froze in regret. "I hope I didn't offend you. I just mean, well, I don't know what I mean come to think of it," she said, chuckling in an air of embarrassment. "Let me show you to your room, and you can come down when you feel like it. It's early and I can't miss any of my shows, even though they don't make television like they used to. Now you see everything you don't need to see. They say things that modest folk don't even dare to think, and they just don't have any reservations at all. I mean, I was watching that Dr. Phil the other day and was shocked at what they were discussing in the early afternoon. I just turned off the television and picked up my Bible and read for five minutes before I slouched over and fell asleep right in my chair," she said, giggling like a schoolgirl. "Can you tell I haven't had a guest in some time? I'm practically talking your ear off. Lucky for you, you've got two."

They started up the stairs as Josiah admired the many black and white photographs on the wall of people in their finest dress. "Like the pictures? I can tell you all about them when you have a spare night," she commented. "Didn't bring any belongings with you? That's strange, but I guess there are stranger things in life. If you need anything, we have a local drugstore a block away. They close at six, but they open at eight in the morning, and I can get you anything you need. I don't mind it at all. And if you have a favorite thing to eat, just tell me. I love to cook and bake."

They reached the top of the stairs and turned left down the hall. She opened the first door on the left. "This is your bathroom. I hope it suits you."

He poked his head in and noticed the yellow shower curtain and pink wallpaper. "Very nice, ma'am. Very nice."

She turned off the light, closed the door, and proceeded farther up the way. She came to another door on the right. "This is a spare bedroom for when guests come, but I haven't had any in quite some time. So if you need some more space, go right ahead. You are family here."

"Thank you. Thank you, ma'am."

"You are so polite. I miss that in today's society. Nowadays people just don't talk anymore. They do the texting thing and that social computer gathering, but they don't actually say anything. I saw on *Rachael Ray* that they don't even spell out words, just a few letters. How would they know what just random letters mean? I mean, who knows anymore? It's all gone downhill if you ask me." She glanced up at him still smiling and nodding.

"I'm going to like you. So polite, so friendly. I could just eat you up." They continued a few more feet until they reached the last door. "This is your bedroom." She opened the door and flipped on the light. It wasn't anything extravagant, but it would do. "I will let you get settled in and if you want, I have plenty of leftovers. I always have leftovers. You never know when someone will just drop by. But I don't mind. I mean, if people just drop by that must mean something special. Don't you think?"

"Yes, I believe so," he smiled as she stood by his door.

"I can start warming up the meatloaf and vegetables if you wish," she said, praying that he'd say yes.

23

"Mrs. Stapleton, I would love it. It's been a long day, and I missed lunch."

Her smile stretched across her face wider than the great state of Texas. "Just give me a few minutes, and it will be ready." She turned to leave and then turned back around as quick as a yo-yo. "And you don't have to call me Mrs. Stapleton. Ethel will do just fine."

"Thank you, Mrs. St--, I mean Ethel," he said with a slip of the tongue.

"You are too polite," she said, shaking her head as she left. "Just too charming."

Josiah examined the room and took in the flowery bedspread, the dark blue curtains, and the beige shag carpet. He was extremely pleased with the setting. He looked in the corner and noticed his luggage that had been shipped earlier. He was going to start unpacking but thought it could wait.

He opened the nightstand drawer, found a tablet of paper, and pulled it out. He sat down on the edge of the bed, which wasn't too firm or soft. He took out a pen from his shirt pocket and started scribbling.

Dear Home,

I have found her and everything is working out as planned. I will be in contact with you later.

Josiah

He laid the notepad on the nightstand and got ready to go downstairs for his first home-cooked meal in years. He paced around the room and smiled, thinking that this was going to be just fine.

He went to the door and turned back to look at the notepad laying beside the alarm clock. The letters started to disappear from the paper as if they were never there.

CHAPTER 8

"Goodbye, Mom," the Sutton kids yelled in unison as they ran out the door.

"Everyone got their lunch?" Dan yelled from upstairs where he was putting on his tie.

"See you this afternoon," Claire waved from the front door as the kids made their way down the driveway to wait for the school bus.

Charlie and Amelia were bickering as usual. "What are we having for supper tonight?"

"Is that all you think about, food?" Amelia scolded.

"I like food," Charlie said, shrugging his shoulders, bewildered as to why she didn't have the same thought.

"Probably a veggie burger, or tofu stir fry, or broccoli casserole," Scarlett suggested in an unflattering tone.

"You just have to wait and see! Wow, the anticipation is weighing heavy, I bet," Amelia said, waving her hands in the air dramatically.

"No, not really," Charlie smirked, examining a caterpillar he'd found.

"Well, it's not my night to pick anyways," Amelia corrected.

"That's right," Charlie giggled, eyeing the creature a little closer. "Spaghetti."

"So, how are you feeling this morning?" Amelia asked.

"Oh, I'm good," Scarlett answered, catching sight of the school bus up the road.

The bus stopped, and the three got onto a full bus, since their stop was usually the last one. "My sister almost drowned yesterday," Charlie shouted to the bus driver, Mr. Hasselburg, and the rest of the bus.

"Amelia or Scarlett?" Mr. Hasselburg asked in shock.

"Who do you think?" Amelia said, rolling her eyes as if the answer was obvious.

25

"Scarlett, did you cross that old bridge? Don't you know that it was made before I was your age? It isn't safe!"

"I know, Mr. Hasselburg," she grunted, making her way to her seat. "I know."

The bus ride was full of questions for Scarlett, who didn't mind because she loved attention. Those who didn't really know Scarlett might have even wondered if she purposefully jumped in the river just so she could get more attention.

Scarlett liked attention. She enjoyed being the talk at soccer practice, the personality in the classroom, the comedian in the cafeteria, but it wasn't something she lived for. Some people were extroverts and some were introverts. Scarlett and Amelia may have been identical twins by appearance, but they were completely opposite everywhere else.

Amelia was more introspective and a true thinker, whereas Scarlett was not. They were both intelligent, but Amelia was more driven by academics. Amelia wanted to become a physician to heal the sick while Scarlett wanted to be a soccer phenom or zookeeper, changing from week to week. Amelia didn't intend to be the cynical sister, but Scarlett was just so peppy, that it came off that way when the two were in the same vicinity. Simply put, whatever Amelia wanted, Scarlett didn't and vice versa. Yet, at the core of their sisterhood, their love was thicker than blood. There was no denying their bond, even though no one in the outside world would believe them. They liked it that way, though, existing as a living conundrum.

"So, did you really almost die?" Chapman Littleton, the school bully, asked.

"What type of question is that?" Amelia reared up in defense.

"I mean, did you see the light?" he beamed ghoulishly.

"I didn't see the light, but I might have if Josiah didn't save me."

26

"Josiah? I don't know of any Josiah. Has anyone here ever heard of Josiah?" Chapman announced as if taking a poll on Scarlett's honesty.

Everyone on the bus shook their heads no, including Charlie, which caused Amelia to smack him on the back of his head.

"Ouch! Why did you do that?" Charlie asked, rubbing the soreness away.

"For siding with Chapman," Amelia answered snidely. "And I didn't hit you that hard."

Scarlett smiled at her sister and took charge of the situation. "I don't know him either. He was just a man who rescued me from the river after I fell through the bridge."

"We live in a small town. If there is really a Josiah, someone would have seen him before," Chapman concluded, nodding confidently to his dim-witted wingman beside him.

The bus entered the grounds of Nathanial Community School, which was named after the mayor of Bethany in 1954. It was a small school with kindergarten through twelfth grade, and each grade consisted of about twenty-five students. Bethany was a very small town, but it had a big heart. Some people felt that when they stepped into Bethany it was like stepping back in time. People in Bethany had the Internet, spotty cell phone reception, and all the modern conveniences, but the town also had a small, homey feel as well.

The kids stepped off the bus and headed to the front doors which were being held open by one of the school's staff.

"Good morning, Mary," the door greeter said.

Scarlett looked up, shocked at the familiar voice, and grinned. "Josiah!"

CHAPTER 9

"Have you always worked here?" Scarlett asked confusedly.

"No, today is my first day," Josiah answered as the other students proceeded through the doors.

Scarlett scanned Josiah's outfit from head to toe and realized that he wasn't dressed in normal teacher attire. He wore a pair of khaki carpenter pants, apparently new since they still had the crease down the legs. He also wore faded brown work boots and a short-sleeved flannel shirt.

"What are you doing here?" she asked.

"I am one of the janitors."

Scarlett nodded, agreeing with his choice of clothing. "So, are you nervous? I'm always nervous on my first day of school."

Josiah smiled politely. "I've been doing this job for a while. Nerves don't get to me anymore."

Scarlett stood fumbling with her backpack straps as the school bell rang, warning kids that they had a few minutes to get to their first class. "You better go Miss Mary. You don't want to be late for class."

"Oh, I don't mind. I'm usually late twice a week anyways," her mischievous, but infectious smile beamed with childish innocence. "Mrs. Claybrook has gotten used to me walking in a minute or two behind."

"Miss Mary, you've got to follow the rules. There isn't always going to be someone so lenient to let you slide," he responded with a tone of encouragement. "You never know what you might miss if you're late."

"I'll try," Scarlett said as she walked away, looking behind her every few steps. She watched Josiah, still at the door, letting in the few straggling students. She waved when he eventually looked at her, and he returned the gesture. She continued her journey down the hall, passing the elementary section of the school. She poked her head in

28

Mrs. Edwards' class, Charlie's first-grade teacher, to find him telling his best bud, Emanuel, about the excitement of the night before.

"She was all wet and cold." Charlie stopped to take his backpack off and then proceeded. "And then…we got to eat fried chicken."

"Wow. I like fried chicken," Emanuel responded, more interested in the mention of food than Scarlett's near-death experience.

"Me too," Charlie grinned with uncontainable happiness.

Scarlett smiled at their six-year old conversation; Emanuel and Charlie were a perfect pair. Each had a lead stomach that could never be filled, yet each only weighed about forty-two pounds soaking wet. She kept walking down the hall until she came to a small group from her class standing outside their room.

"Who was that?" Amelia asked.

"That's Josiah," Scarlett answered as she whipped her head to look at Chapman, who had recently doubted that he was a real person. "Told ya."

"Well, how do we know his name is really Josiah? You could have just pretended to be talking to him to prove your point."

"Chapman, how ignorant can you be?" Amelia asked in warrior-like defense. "I mean, you can be pretty stupid sometimes, but really? Are you that dumb?"

"If you weren't a girl, I would hit you," Chapman said, rearing back his arm as if about to throw a punch.

"Well, if you wouldn't cry and tell on me, I would hit *you*," Scarlett said, stepping in front of her sister to take the punch if he was brave enough, knowing he wasn't.

When they were in the third grade, Amelia got picked on quite a bit from students because she was smart. Even at that age she didn't socialize in their cliques. At first Scarlett would watch from a distance on the swing set, slide, or the basketball court, but one day Chapman went a little too far.

She had been swinging beside her friend, Nicole, and noticed something bad going on where Amelia usually sat during recess. She had taken one last swing and flew out of the seat, landing perfectly on the ground to begin her sprint across the playground.

"Come on, brainy, why are you over here by yourself? Your own sister doesn't want to be around you," Chapman teased in a baby voice as the small group around him laughed hysterically like a pack of idiotic hyenas. Every pack needed a leader, and Chapman was their ringleader. Sadly, intelligence didn't factor very high in their qualifications for a captain.

"I just, I just like to, to read," Amelia quietly answered. "Will you please just leave me alone?" She scooted closer to the wall, trying to back away from the situation and nuzzle herself into her pages.

Chapman grabbed the book from her tiny hands. "So, what do brainiacs read for fun?" He looked down at the book. "What's *To Kill a Mockingbird*? Are you some kind of animal killer? I didn't see that in you, Amelia," he said with a grotesque expression.

Amelia jumped up, but being a foot shorter than Chapman, she couldn't reach his hand clutching her book over his head. "Give it back!"

"Jump for it! Come on, can't your nerdy legs jump?" he laughed as he stood on his tiptoes, reaching his hands higher in the sky.

Amelia was jumping as high as she could, but it wasn't high enough.

"Nerds can't jump. Nerds can't jump," Chapman started chanting as the small sheep-like group joined in.

Amelia looked like a marionette dangling from his hands. The invisible strings were tied to her feeble hands and shaky knees. Every time she jumped, her legs and arms flared as his hands raised a little higher.

Scarlett had seen the show Chapman was performing at her sister's expense, propelling her legs to go into overdrive. No one had seen her coming, as everyone was witnessing the spectacle. She was within a few yards when she heard them chanting. She saw her sister's head bobbing up and down in the middle of the circle.

"No, but I can!" Scarlett had screamed, piercing through the circle and pushing aside anyone who was in her way. She jumped higher than she ever had before, moving like a hawk diving in for a kill as she swooped over Chapman's head. She stole the book from his grasp, and for good measure, planted a right jab to his cheek, as she twirled down.

The circle quickly dispersed with only Amelia and Scarlett staring down at the crying, bleeding Chapman, who was clutching the left side of his face. "I think you broke something."

"It's only your head," Scarlett scoffed. "You weren't using it in the first place!"

The two sisters turned to leave Chapman, who was curled in a fetal position. "Now you know you have to do my math homework for doing that," Scarlett whispered in her sister's ear.

"I know," Amelia said, smiling as she hugged her book to her chest as they started walking back to the swings. "Hey, I was already doing your math homework for eating my pork chop for me last night. I'll do your science project."

Scarlett started laughing, forgetting about the night before. "Amelia, I don't know how we are twins. You are too nice for your own good sometimes."

CHAPTER 10

Viktor Ivanov was a sixty-one-year-old Russian immigrant who had come to Ellis Island with his family when he was three years old. They had fled the effects of the war and had wanted a place to call their home that didn't come with the price of freedom. They had lived in New York in a small Russian community in Brooklyn but moved away after a few years. New York was not as cold as Russia, but it still had harsh winters, and the Ivanov family had wanted to find a place where they would not be reminded of their past; seeking a mild climate, they had decided to move to Mississippi. It wasn't that they had been ashamed of their ancestry, they'd just wanted a new start, and sometimes new starts demanded a new location. What better locality than Bethany?

Viktor's father, Lev, had picked up odd and end jobs in manufacturing companies, construction sites, and in the fishing industry. After about ten years of scraping by, he had gotten a job as a janitor in the local hospital. He'd loved his job, and he'd loved the people, but most of all, he'd loved that his life was stable.

Viktor had seen the turnaround in his father with this new job and decided to follow in his footsteps. When he graduated from Nathanial Community School, he turned around the next day and applied as a janitor at the same school he had attended for the last few years. Everyone had loved Viktor's dedication while he was a student, so as soon as there was an opening, he'd gotten the job. In the last forty years, Viktor had worked himself up to be the head janitor in the school.

"Josiah right? My name is Viktor Ivanov," he said in a mixture of Russian and southern accents while stretching out his hand. Everyone in Bethany had their own impersonations of Viktor's speech, and he was pleased with their attempts, even though he would always laugh and say, "I don't hear my accent. I think I sound just like you."

32

"Nice to meet you, Mr. Ivanov," Josiah responded with a firm grip.

"Just call me Vik."

"Yes sir."

"Not sir. Vik."

"Sorry."

"There is nothing to be sorry about," Vik smiled as he slapped him on the back. "Let's get to work."

"What do you want me to do?" Josiah asked.

"Let's mow. We had a heavy rain here a few days ago, and the grass is really coming up fast."

As they walked to the garage, neither one spoke very much, just casual small talk here and there.

"Have you ever driven a tractor before?" Vik asked as Josiah stared in wonder at the array of machinery and equipment.

"To be honest, when I mowed in the past it was with a push mower," Josiah answered as he followed Vik through the showroom of lawn care tools.

"Well, today's your lucky day. I will start you off in the open area for you to get the hang of it."

"I will do my best," Josiah said, lifting his chin.

"I know you will," Vik nodded approvingly. "I know you will."

Vik showed Josiah all the levers and pedals. He commented on the various speeds, the varying cuts of grass, and the things not to touch or do while mowing. After a two-minute lesson, it was time to bite the bullet and ride Bertha, Vik's nickname for his John Deere mowing machine. Vik rode the tractor to the open area in front of the school and cut a strip of grass. Josiah watched Vik closely: the way he gripped the steering wheel, the pressure he had on the gas pedal, even the sideways glances to make sure he was going straight. Vik was a pro, and Josiah only hoped to be decent.

Vik put the tractor in park. "Your turn. Just be kind to Bertha, and she'll be kind to you."

Josiah jumped up on the green monster and took a deep breath. *You can do this,* he heard a voice inside him say. He released the park lever and pressed on the gas and he was off, clipping away. After a hundred feet it was time to turn. He gripped the wheel and tugged to the left, and the tractor followed. His heart was starting to slow and a smile began to build on his face. He looked over at Vik who gave him a thumb's up before he turned to head to the garage.

Josiah guided the machine over the lawn, bouncing up and down on the padded seat. He wore a smile the entire time as he mowed the grass, realizing that he'd had tougher assignments than this in the past, and this one would succeed like all the others. As he mowed, he discovered this was a perfect time to think and plan. There was no noise besides the mower to interrupt his thoughts; nothing to preoccupy him from focusing on his main assignment. Being a janitor was just an alias to accomplish his purpose. It was an only a character he played in order to complete the mission.

All systems are go.

CHAPTER 11

The cafeteria food at Nathanial Community was just like any other school food. The students somewhat enjoyed spaghetti yesterday, so today, the lunch lady magicians used the leftover meat and fixed chili. They never left the leftovers unused. Lucky for the Sutton kids, their mom packed their lunches, except for rare occasions when something actually tempted their taste buds.

Scarlett sat at one of the dozen rectangular tables surrounded by all her closest friends: the basketball queen Jackie Nevell, the beauty contestant Samantha Whu, the future pop singer Whitney Fredrick, drama queen Nora Sellers, and the new girl Lucy Nialliv, with Amelia at the far end, not paying attention to the conversation as usual.

"Well, I cannot believe you survived that fall. I mean, it must be at least fifty feet with all those hard rocks below," Nora cried, breaking down in a spastic fit of self-induced emotions.

"Nora, chill. It's only about fifteen feet, and there aren't any rocks near the surface," Jackie stated while rolling her eyes around in her head.

"Did you think you were going to die?" Whitney asked. "Because if you did, I had the perfect song to sing at your funeral."

"That's a reassuring thought," Amelia butted in, not looking up from Jane Austen's *Pride and Prejudice*.

Whitney huffed and took a large bite out of her turkey sandwich.

"Yeah, but Josiah saved me," Scarlett answered calmly. "I was under water and I couldn't get my head up. I thought I was as good as dead."

"Wow. You were saved by a mysterious stranger," Lucy cut in, trying to make a place for herself at the table.

"What? How did you look when he pulled you out?" Samantha asked.

"I don't know. I guess wet," Scarlett answered, annoyed with the question.

Samantha gasped in horror. "I would have asked him to throw me back in. I bet your hair was a mess, your clothes all wet. And God forbid your makeup was probably smearing."

"If we wore any," Amelia once again approached the conversation, only to turn back into her world of Mr. Darcy.

"You don't wear makeup?" Samantha laughed believing that Amelia was certainly joking.

"Nope," she said, popping a barbeque potato chip in her mouth.

"Never?" Samantha asked deadly serious, as if the lack of makeup was more devastating than Scarlett's near-death experience.

"I wear a little on Halloween," Scarlett chimed in nonchalantly.

"Face paint is not makeup," Samantha corrected. "Makeup hides your blemishes and makes your best features shine," she beamed, quickly pulling out a mirror from her purse to check her lip gloss.

"I guess I don't have any blemishes to hide," Scarlett said, shrugging her shoulders and glancing over at the new girl Lucy.

"You wish you didn't," Whitney commented with a cough.

"Thanks," Scarlett sarcastically smiled, grabbing an apple wedge from Whitney's lunch.

"Don't listen to her. I don't wear it either," Nora whispered in Scarlett's ear, too ashamed to say it so everyone could hear.

Scarlett took a sip of her skim milk and noticed through the field of plastic chairs and tables, Josiah was sitting by himself. She smiled his way, but he kept his lonely eyes glued to his bowl of chili. She got up without telling anyone at her table and marched to his table. "Hi, Josiah. Having a good lunch?"

"Why yes, I am," he smiled as he laid down his spoon on his lime green lunch tray that looked to have been made in the 1970s. "I haven't had a good bowl of chili in some time."

Scarlett scrunched her nose at his opinion of good. "So, how's everything going so far?"

"Pretty well. Everyone has been really nice so far. This is a nice school."

Scarlett scanned the 1970s cafeteria art deco with teachers that seemed to be from the 1870s huddled around a nearby table. "Yeah, I guess so."

"You guess so?" Josiah asked quizzically.

"Well, it's not so nice when you have to come here and don't get paid for it," Scarlett said with a fake smile.

Josiah belted out a hearty laugh. "You are a sharp girl."

"I like sharp more than what other people sometimes call me," she smiled.

"Mary, you keep your smarts. You never know when you are going to need your quick wit."

"I will," she said, still standing awkwardly, watching him eat his lackluster lunch. "Well, I better finish up. Math is next and I need all the strength I can get to get through that class."

"Math. Does Mr. Fleming teach that in room 212?"

"Yes, he does. You are pretty sharp yourself, Josiah."

"I try," he said as she walked away. *More than you know, Mary. More than you know.*

CHAPTER 12

"Mom! Mom!" Scarlett screamed as she came barrelling through the front door.

"What is it?" Claire asked.

"You are never going to guess who I saw today at school," Scarlett said with gleeful enthusiasm.

"Do you want me to guess?" Claire asked walking back into the kitchen where she was putting up groceries in the pantry.

"Nah, I'll tell you," Scarlett said, simmering her excitement like an ultra-cool hipster. "It was Josiah."

"Really, what a small town we live in. What was he doing there?"

Amelia stepped into the kitchen, hopping up on a barstool and grabbing a whole wheat cracker out of the canister.

"He's working there," Scarlett answered.

"He's vorking for Vik," Amelia commented in a thick Russian accent.

"Bill no longer works there?" Claire asked, rearranging her canned goods to have her pantry looking well-organized and pristine.

"Guess not. It's a small school. They don't need too many janitors," Scarlett commented.

Claire circled around Scarlett to put up the skim milk and cheese. "Well, I think we need to have Josiah over for supper one night."

"Really?" Scarlett beamed. "He is really nice."

"Well, that's good, but he saved your life. I just want to show him our appreciation."

"Oh, yeah, that too," Scarlett laughed.

"That too?" Amelia snickered. "I thought you would never have gotten that off your mind. In every class we were in, Scarlett had to tell the story to the teacher."

"It got us out of class work for about ten minutes in each class. That adds up throughout the day."

"Yeah, but it just means more homework for tonight," Amelia scoffed.

"I didn't think of that," Scarlett sighed.

"You never see the whole picture, only what is happening right now and to you," Amelia said rolling her eyes.

"Yeah, but that is what you are here for. To guide me, oh wise younger sister."

Amelia spoke with an air of intellectual superiority, "I bet you would miss the forest for the trees."

"Amelia, what are you talking about?" Scarlett asked, dismissing her sister's arrogance. "How can anyone miss a forest?"

"Geez," Amelia uttered under her breath.

Claire stopped busying herself around the kitchen and turned to hug both her girls.

"What's that for?" Amelia asked.

"I just love you. That's all," Claire lovingly said.

"We love you, too," Scarlett said, squeezing in closer, grabbing her sister's arm to bring her into the bear hug a little more.

"Yeah, we love you too, Mom," Amelia finally choked out, thinking that by saying it quickly, the hug would conclude quicker.

Claire let go of her two lovely daughters and wiped a lonely tear away. "You all get out of here, and I will holler at you when dinner is ready. Your dad will be home early today, so quit eating those crackers, Amelia."

Amelia jumped from the stool and headed to her bedroom to start her homework, while Scarlett stayed beside her mother.

"What?" Claire asked as Scarlett stared at her. "You're freaking me out now."

"Nothing. I just really love you," Scarlett said tenderly. Claire turned and kissed her daughter on her forehead. "Do you need any help?" Scarlett asked.

"If you want," Claire said, shocked that she wasn't having to force Scarlett to help around the house.

"If I didn't want to, I wouldn't have asked," Scarlett snickered.

"You're a good kid. You know that?"

"Nah, I just don't feel like doing my reading assignment yet."

"Well then, will you please get out the rigatoni from the cupboard?"

Scarlett found the box of rigatoni noodles and realized it was Wednesday – her dad's night to pick supper. "Why does Dad only come home early on Wednesdays?"

"Why do you think?" They both laughed as they enjoyed each other's company.

"What're you laughing at?" Charlie asked, poking his head in the room.

"Nothing," Scarlett turned.

"Okay, bye," he casually said trotting out the backdoor with a blue bath towel tied around his neck as a cape to enjoy an hour of playing outside and saving the world from evil villains.

"Why did you have to show him that?" Claire said, jabbing Scarlett on her cheeks. "He has already gotten holes in two towels by getting them caught in the tree limbs."

"I gotta stay the cool big sister, don't I?" Scarlett said with a smile.

"He's got two cool big sisters," Claire commented in the tone of a Hallmark card.

"Well, I never expected him to be able to jump so high. That little dude is all legs."

CHAPTER 13

"Is that you, Josiah?" Mrs. Stapleton shouted with a hint of operatic soprano, as she stood stirring her chicken and dumplings, hoping that the sinkers on the bottom were not sticking.

"Yes, ma'am."

"Good, I didn't want just anyone barging in on me. I can't leave the stove now, because they are about tough enough to start sticking, and we don't want that. No sirree. Once they start sticking, they all start to clump and there is no going back."

"Smells good, Mrs. Stapleton," Josiah grinned as he inhaled the tasty aroma.

"Josiah, what did I tell you to call me?" she bantered without glancing away from her bubbling pot of broth.

"Sorry, ma'am."

"Well, don't just stand there, get washed up, and by the time you get finished, hopefully I will be as well."

Josiah made his way up to his room, once again examining the pictures hanging along the wall. It seemed like the first stair had the most recent picture, and with each step, the pictures got older and older, until it appeared they were five generations old. He caught a whiff of the cooking, and his stomach caused his legs to move up the stairs to change his clothes.

He jumped in the shower to remove all the grass clippings that had been imbedded in his short black hair. He stood under the jets and let the water cascade down his dark skin, enjoying the hot steam as it relaxed his sore muscles. He had performed many jobs in his past, but he had not performed as much manual labor as he did today in an extremely long time, and tomorrow was another day.

Drying off, he quickly put on a fresh pair of clothes and made his way down to the kitchen, allowing the aroma of chicken to direct his path. "This looks great," he said.

41

"You don't look so bad yourself," she quipped.

Josiah slightly blushed but quickly started helping Ethel set the dinner table.

"How was your day, ma'am?"

"It was a nice day," she smiled as she grabbed a brown paper bag that was lying on the counter. "I went to the store and got you a few things. I hope you don't mind, but my husband always wore cologne and I didn't smell any on you as you left for work this morning."

"Thank you, but you shouldn't have."

"It's no bother. Every man needs some cologne," she remarked.

"I sure needed it today." He opened the bag, took out the bottle, and smelled the masculine aroma. "This is nice. If you don't mind, will you excuse me while I put some on?"

"Whatever you want, and when you return, dinner will be ready."

Josiah quickly went to the next room and splashed on some of the cologne and instantly felt invigorated. He closed his eyes and inhaled the scent, his scent. He'd had a long day, but now it was time to relax for a little while.

"So, what did you do after the store?" Josiah asked as he walked into the dining room set with place settings one would have on holidays or special occasions. Fresh cut flowers were centered on the table with linens encasing the newly polished silverware.

"Oh, we can talk in a minute. Sit down and let's say grace," she said. The two sat across from one another and quietly bowed their heads. "Dear Lord, thank you for all the blessings you give us each day, and thank you for our new friendship. Amen."

"Amen," he echoed.

They each picked up their forks and started to enjoy their meal and conversation. "Tell me, Josiah, I don't know very much about you. Where are you from? Do you have any family? And I hope not to sound bold, but how old are you? You black people age so well."

He smiled politely as she quickly tried to take back the last thing she said. "Oh, dear me, that didn't come out right. I'm sorry, Josiah, but you," she tried to say as he quickly shook his head with a grin, letting her know that he understood what she meant and wasn't offended. She chuckled to herself as she took her first bite, enjoying the dumplings.

Finishing his bite, he kindly smiled and proceeded to answer the round of machine gun fired questions. "I'm from up north." He laughed to himself at his thought. *At least that is what most people think.*

"Oh, like Chicago?"

"Around there, but a little farther north. I don't have any parents or family, but I have some really good friends that I consider family." Taking another bite of the dumplings, he added, "This is heavenly."

"I'm glad you like it. So, no family at all?"

"No, but the man who raised me was very kind. He is like my father, but I don't get to see him much. I speak to him all the time, but I miss him dearly when I don't get to see him."

"Maybe he can come visit sometime," she said.

"Probably not. But some other people that he raised may come by and visit. I see them every once in a while. We are like family."

"That is good," she said as she quickly changed the subject. "Sorry to be so blunt, but how old are you?"

"I am much older than I look, but I feel young. I think that is the important thing," he said with a smile.

"I wish I had your genes. I'm in my sixties, and I look like I'm in my seventies."

Josiah quickly shook his head in disagreement. "No ma'am. You are very lovely. Age is just a number, but life is an attitude."

"'Life is an attitude'. I like that," she smiled with youthful essence as she stabbed another dumpling. "Weight is also a number, but I don't worry about that number as much," she said, laughing at her own joke. He busted out laughing as he patted his firm stomach.

"I bet your family loves your cooking," he said taking a drink to quench his thirst.

"At one time, but now I usually just cook for myself," she said with a sad tone. "Do you want any seconds?" her voice heightened in hospitality.

"I probably shouldn't," he said, patting his belly again. "But it is just too good to pass up."

"I knew I liked you," she said as she scooped another plateful for him and another for her. "From the first moment I met you, I knew I would like you," she said as she once again changed the subject like a close-knit family member. "So, are you married or have you ever been?"

"No, I never was. In my line of work there just was never a good time to settle down."

"A janitor?" she quizzed in surprise, almost dropping her dumpling off her fork.

"Oh, I've had many jobs," he quickly responded quickly.

"What were you before you came here?"

"Oh, I have been around the world. Name it and I have probably done it. I don't want to sound boastful, but I have led an interesting life."

"Were you ever a soldier?" she asked. "My husband was a soldier."

"As a matter of fact, I was."

"God bless you," she said. "Leo was a good man, but sometimes even good men die too young." She stopped to take a sip of her iced tea as Josiah listened with willing ears. "He was so proud wearing that uniform, and he looked so handsome. But then Vietnam happened, and my love went off to defend our country. We were newlyweds and never had time to have any children. Even though we were only married a few months, I loved him more than anything else. There has never been a man that could fill his shoes."

44

"I know how you feel. A third of my team fell, and not a day goes by that I don't think about them."

They locked eyes for what seemed like half an eternity. Sitting in silence, Ethel began to feel a great sense of compassion and connection with her new tenant. She felt an unfamiliar warmth from Josiah that she had always dreamed about. It was the feeling she believed a mother would have for a son. "Eat up, dear, I have extra."

"Thank you," Josiah replied, helping himself to more. He took another bite and realized that Ethel was going to sit and watch him enjoy every dumpling. He felt a connection with Ethel, but unlike her, it was a connection like most of his previous jobs. He had done his research on Ethel Stapleton. He didn't hear anything new tonight that he hadn't already known.

CHAPTER 14

They sat on the couch with full stomachs and relaxed after dinner. Picking up her cross-stitching from the basket next to her, Ethel started threading her needle to start working on her latest project. "Will you flip the channel to something good?" she asked.

Josiah got up, stretched his long, nimble legs, and flipped it to an old movie channel. "I think I am going to go for a walk. If I don't keep moving, I am going to get fat with all your good cooking."

"You go right ahead and do whatever you feel like. I, on the other hand, enjoy getting old and fat. I may not have too many more years left on this great planet of ours, and I plan on enjoying it."

"Oh, Ethel, you have many more years ahead of you. Believe me," he winked playfully.

Exiting out the door, he stopped to admire the new red flower Ethel had potted in the afternoon. He wasn't sure what it was, since he was not an avid gardener, but its fragrance was delightful. He walked down the footpath and noticed that Ethel had one of the greenest thumbs he had ever seen, and he had seen a lot of them. The landscape was flourishing with a burst of rainbow colors splattered over the entire yard. It was a sight to behold, and he took a moment to simply enjoy it.

The sun was slowly fading beyond the horizon, and a half moon was starting to take its place. He stared into the colored sky; the orange was colliding with the night blue, forming a swirling beauty of colors. Tiny specks of light were poking their way through the cloudless sky, causing Josiah to stand amazed at how such huge balls of fire appeared so small and insignificant millions of light years away.

The warm day was turning into a tolerably cool evening with a light breeze from the gulf flowing through his shirt sleeve. This was his second night in this town, and there was still so much he hadn't seen.

He had seen the forest yesterday during the chase, but he hadn't had a chance to casually stroll on the sidewalk.

The town was peacefully quiet with no cars moving through its streets. It appeared to him that everyone must have been at home, eating a nice meal with their loved ones. He came to the end of Sycamore Street and turned onto Broadway where more houses with picket fences aligned the street. Despite their similarities, each house was distinct. Each home had its own character, whether it was dark or light brick, brightly colored or more neutral siding, wooden shutters with slates or solid slabs, solid wood doors or only partially-stained glass.

As he walked by a few of the homes, he saw families huddled around their tables, experiencing each other's company, and he hoped they realized how lucky they were to be in a loving home. Other places he had been lately were totally different. The towns were fast-paced and self-centered symbols of lost hope. He felt good here. He felt like he was going to like Bethany.

Broadway forked with Main Street, so he turned left because he wasn't ready to return home just yet. He walked the lonely streets, but he didn't feel alone. He wore a smile as if he was greeting the neighbors, even though there weren't any. Soon, the homes faded into little shops and civic buildings. A few marble statues stood in front of the library with names he had never heard of but assumed to be historical figures of this quaint town.

Taking his time, he would occasionally stop and look in the shops through the glass at the treasures that each one sold. He didn't need anything, but he wasn't in a rush to return home, so he just took a seat on a park bench under the newly lit streetlamp. He sat staring across the street when an odd feeling came over him. He looked up and down the street, but there was nothing to alarm him. Yet he couldn't shake the feeling.

47

He got up, thinking that maybe he was just tired and started to head home, when he started to feel the eeriness more intensely. The wind started to pick up, making the light chill turn cold. He made his way back to the corner of Main and Broadway when one of the streetlamps started to flicker. He walked under it and stared in wonder at the light flashing like Morse code until it burst.

Shards of glass came raining down on him, and he quickly clasped his ears and hid his face. He shook his head to get all the pieces off of him as he started walking up the street. Strangely, every time he came near a streetlamp, it would flicker, but unlike the first one he didn't stop. As he passed, the light would instantly stop and then turn back on.

He knew that he shouldn't be afraid; it was probably a coincidence, but he couldn't force his mind to believe that. He'd turned onto Sycamore when he instantly felt better. He looked up and saw his home just six houses down. He started walking toward it, but something was nagging him to look behind.

After a few seconds, he finally turned his head to see something he hadn't seen all night.

It was someone else's shadow under a streetlamp.

CHAPTER 15

The bell sounded, signaling the end of the first period. Scarlett and her clique left the world of prehistoric history and began walking toward the room of atoms and molecules with all the other seventh graders while Amelia departed to go with the ninth graders to biology class, which was across the hall from Scarlett's chemistry. Amelia had had the option to skip a few grades when she was younger, but she didn't feel like moving ahead without her sister. She didn't fit in with people her own age in the second grade, so she figured she definitely wouldn't fit in with fourth graders. As a result, Amelia had about half of her classes with her sister and the rest of the seventh graders, but the other half were with older grades.

"Did you see Luke's post last night?" Nora asked, speaking of the heartthrob's post on Facebook.

"Yes," all the girls chimed in with a squeal of excitement – well almost all of them.

"No," Amelia said unconcerned as she trudged behind.

"Amelia, how will you know what is going on if you don't have a Facebook account?" Whitney asked, shaking her head.

"Um, I watch the news," Amelia answered wide-eyed.

"Well, did the news tell you that Luke and Joni broke up?" Whitney devilishly smiled.

"No, but I bet you didn't hear about what happened in Chile yesterday."

"No, and I don't know anyone who lives in Africa," Whitney said, rolling her eyes as she stopped at her locker to get her chemistry book.

"An earthquake happened..." Amelia said, reciprocating the eye rolls. "And it's South America, you twit."

"Amelia, quit being rude," Scarlett said in annoyance. "Why do you always look down on us because we're not as smart as you?"

"I have other reasons to look down on them besides their IQ," she smiled.

Scarlett and her friends waited behind and spent the last few minutes of their break socializing. Luke walked past without Joni on his arm, and all the girls' knees went weak. He was handsome but didn't flaunt it. He didn't try to gain attention; it just came natural with his wavy blond hair, emerald eyes, and rosy cheeks with only a right dimple sinking in when he smiled.

"Poor Joni," Lucy said, speaking too soon by the dead stares she received from the other girls. "Sorry."

They all watched like a pack of lions feasting their eyes on a lonely gazelle. "Hey, Scarlett. Hey, Amelia," Luke said as he strolled past.

"Hey," was all Scarlett could spit out in shock before she slammed her head in Whitney's locker. She sunk behind the group mortified. "Did he see that?"

"Gotta go to biology," Amelia said without acknowledging her sister's fear. She turned and walked a little farther up the hall to her next class, leaving the drama behind her.

"I hope not," Jackie said sympathetically. "I would literally die if he did."

"Thanks," Scarlett grimaced at the lack of confidence-building words.

"Oh, he didn't see anything," Lucy snuck in encouragingly.

Scarlett recovered a little self-respect, poking her head out of the group. Luke had already entered the classroom, and there wasn't any eruption of laughter. She waited a few seconds to let her knees settle and noticed Josiah mopping right in front of her classroom, poking his head in her next class.

The group of girls left the locker area and entered their next classroom. "Give me a second. I'll see you in class," Scarlett said as she waltzed up to Josiah, startling him as she poked him on his shoulder. "Looking at something?"

"Well, Miss Mary, you rattled my cage," Josiah said honestly.

"I did what?"

"Oh, it's just an expression," he answered, waving his hand signaling never mind.

"My mom and dad wanted to know if you had plans for supper Friday night. It's my night to choose the meal, so we're going to have something really good."

"You don't have to do that, Mary," he said as he continued to mop.

"We want to," she said, beaming with youthful exuberance.

He paused his mop and stared up at the ceiling as if his calendar was posted up on the tiles. "Sounds great. Can I bring a guest?"

"Sure. Why not?"

The bell rung for the start of the next class period as Scarlett instantly jumped into the classroom. "I'm here Mrs. Pitts. I'm not late. See, I'm in the room."

"Mary, Mary, Mary," Josiah said shaking his head as he commenced his mopping. He went from side to side, catching glances of both the Sutton girls in their prime, a scientist and a social butterfly.

CHAPTER 16

"Charlie, get out of the fridge and set the table," Claire requested, checking on the chicken quesadillas that were oozing with cheese and peppers.

"Done," Charlie quickly remarked.

"Then take this," she said, handing him a pitcher of sweet tea. "And don't drop it." Charlie stood statuesque in the middle of the kitchen watching his mom's every move. "Don't just stand there, take it in the dining room," she commanded as stress started to fill her insides.

"You didn't say that," he said huffing as he left the kitchen carefully gripping the pitcher tightly with both hands.

"What's wrong, little bro?" Scarlett asked as she almost collided with him in the hall.

"Nothing," he mumbled as he watched the tea slosh around with only a few drops escaping the rim.

"Whatever," she said perturbed, but quickly moved by him and peeked her head in the kitchen to smell one of her favorite dishes. "Yum."

"Where's your sister?" Claire asked, ignoring her compliment.

"Upstairs sleeping," Scarlett answered, inching closer to the stove hoping to get a nibble before dinner.

"Stop that," Claire barked, smacking Scarlett with a nearby wooden spoon. "You can wait like everyone else. Go get your sister. They will be here any minute," she commanded, suddenly hearing the chimes of the doorbell. "See. They are here."

"Yeah, yeah, you just got lucky," Scarlett grinned as she quickly grabbed a few pieces of diced peppers before her mom could stop her.

"Maybe," Claire smiled as she blew a few strands of her disheveled hair out of her face.

Dan welcomed Josiah and his guest, Ethel, as he complimented her attire, a pink ruffled dress with pearl accessories on her ears, neck, and wrist.

"Thank you for inviting me. I have seen you around town, but sadly I have never really met you Mr. Sutton," Ethel said as she changed Dan's handshake into a hug. "Going out on a Friday night...well, it just reminds me of my younger days."

"We're glad you came," Dan smiled as Claire whipped off her apron and quickly entered the room. "This is my wife, Claire," he said as he spun around trying to find something. "Kids, come here," he yelled as Charlie and Scarlett surprised him. "This is Charlie and Scarlett, and we have another girl, Amelia, who will be down shortly."

"Nice to meet you, Charlie. I'm Josiah," he said, shaking the little boy's hand. "And this is Mrs. Ethel Stapleton."

"Well, aren't you a handsome little thing?" Ethel mused. "Just the handsomest."

"Yeah," he smiled without a bashful bone in his skinny body.

The room laughed while Charlie stared around unsure if they were laughing at him or with him.

"Dinner is ready, so if you follow Scarlett, we will be right there," Claire said. "Dan, can you come help me?"

Claire and Dan went into the kitchen to get their platters of Tex-Mex cuisine. "I was expecting something different in Josiah," Claire said, watching Dan for a similar expression.

"Didn't expect him to be black?" Dan said, wincing at her.

"I don't know. I just..." she stammered her words, then realized what he was implying. "No, it wasn't that at all. I just had a different image of him in my head. Grab the bowls of salsa and pico de gallo."

They walked into the room and found Amelia finally making an appearance sitting beside Ethel. Claire gave each person the option of cheese or chicken quesadilla, with Amelia being the only one taking the plain cheese.

"What do you call this?" Ethel asked, lifting the fried tortilla with her fork.

"It's a quesadilla," Scarlett answered. "It was my night to pick the meal."

"Good choice," Josiah commented with a wink.

Claire and Dan sat down as Charlie took a large bite of his quesadilla. "Do you mind if we say grace?" Ethel asked, and Charlie's eyes quickly magnetized onto her as if he had been caught red-handed in the cookie jar.

"I think that is a good idea," Claire said as she held out her hands for Dan and Charlie to grab, causing a domino effect of handholding around the table. "Will you do us the honor?"

"I am more than happy to," Ethel grinned. "Dear Lord, thank you for new friendships and new tastes. Thank you for all you always do and will do. Amen."

"Amen," Charlie repeated with his mouth full of cheese, finally swallowing it down with a relieved smile. "Amen."

Everyone started to cut away at their meal, enjoying the delicious course. "Josiah, we just want to say thank you for rescuing Scarlett the other day," Dan said a little choked up.

"Anyone would have done it," Josiah replied humbly.

"What did you do, Josiah?" Ethel asked. "Do we have a hero in our midst?"

"I don't know about that," Josiah answered, quickly fumbling with the food on his plate.

"He is. He saved me from drowning a few days ago," Scarlett said with her mouth half-full of chips and salsa.

"Poor girl, what happened?" Ethel remarked, setting her fork down to give the youngster her undivided attention.

"I really don't remember too much anymore, except for Josiah being there," Scarlett answered popping another tortilla chip into her mouth.

"Shock can do that to some people," Amelia commented in a matter-of-fact tone.

"Where did this happen?" Ethel asked.

"In the river behind our house. There's an old bridge up the way back there, and it seems like it broke and she fell through," Dan answered since he was the only one with an empty mouth.

Ethel gasped in horror. "Good thing Josiah was around," she said patting Scarlett's hand then turning to Josiah. "How did you find her?"

Josiah stared at Ethel then slowly looked at everyone before laying his fork down and taking a drink of his tea. "I was taking a walk in the woods and out of nowhere I heard this faint scream. I ran, following the screams that came and went, and I saw a small arm reaching from the water into the air. I jumped in and pulled her out."

"It just happens so fast sometimes. Someone was looking out for you," Ethel said shaking her head at the notion of Scarlett being so close to death.

"I think so," Scarlett agreed, looking up to Josiah and giving him his customary wink.

CHAPTER 17

"This is a beautiful home," Ethel said getting up from the dinner table with everyone else. "Truly beautiful. I love the wallpaper in this room. And everything is just so, so, thought out."

"Well, Claire did it all," Dan said proudly.

"You are very talented, Claire. Very talented." Ethel beamed like a proud mother.

"Thank you, Mrs. Stapleton. We like it," Claire said picking up the empty plates as Ethel began to help. "Please, you are our guest. Don't do that, Mrs. Stapleton. We've got it."

"Oh, honey, I've been doing this all my life. I can't stop now," Ethel smiled as she tried to grab another plate.

"Mrs. Stapleton, please, come in the living room with us," Dan requested as he slid the plate out of her grasp. "Please."

"Yeah, come with us," Charlie motioned down the hall. "I want to show you something."

"Well, how can I resist that precious boy of yours?" Ethel asked, beaming at Claire with love and happiness.

"You learn," Amelia snapped as Claire shot her a dirty look when Ethel wasn't looking.

They journeyed into the living room, with Claire only a few minutes behind. "So, Mr. Sutton, what do you do for a living?" Ethel asked, admiring the breathtaking black baby grand piano in the corner.

"I'm an attorney," Dan answered with pride. He always loved the feeling of saying that he was an attorney. It never got old to him.

"Interesting," Ethel said. "What type of law do you practice?"

"I handle corporate cases mostly. I used to do family law, but I didn't enjoy it. They can get very messy."

"And corporate cases don't?" Claire scoffed, remembering the many stressful nights he'd had in the past few years.

"It's a different type of messy," Dan said, correcting himself.

56

"Well, I sometimes wish you didn't socialize with criminals," Claire said rubbing his shoulders.

"They're not all criminals," Dan answered politely in front of their guests.

"And someone has to do it, Mrs. Sutton," Josiah commented. "Innocent before proven guilty."

"I don't believe that," Ethel remarked flatly. "Some people are guilty and the whole world knows it."

"How can you say that?" Dan asked shocked.

"But it's true. It is sad when there are criminals that get off because their defense attorney is better than the prosecution," Ethel said solemnly. "Just sad."

"That's the justice system," Dan remarked professionally. "It's not perfect, but it's much better than most."

"Dad, have you ever gotten a criminal off?" Scarlett asked as Charlie and Amelia quickly fixed their attention on him.

"It's complicated," Dan said, feeling himself getting backed into a corner.

"You have, haven't you?" Amelia bolstered up in enthusiasm. "Tell us!"

Dan sat silently weighing the scales that he tried to balance every day. "That's enough," Claire said, playing spousal referee. "Let's talk about something else."

"I think this is interesting," Amelia said, ignoring her mother's request. "Probably the most interesting conversation we've had all night."

"I think it's best to listen to your mother," Josiah said with a voice of reason in the room.

"Josiah, I think you'd better get me home. It's getting late, and I don't want us to wear out our welcome," Ethel remarked, feeling the mood shift in the room.

"Please stay," Claire said, cordially speaking up. "You don't have to run out on us now."

"When you're my age, late comes earlier and earlier, my dear," Ethel laughed. "And at my age, I ain't doing any running." She smiled looking down at Charlie who nodded his head in agreement. "I can't remember the last time I ran. Oh dear, look at me showing my age," she started to giggle. "It was lovely of you all having us over for dinner. Just too lovely."

"Well, please come and visit us again," Dan said while showing his guests to the door.

"Why don't you come and have lunch with us on Sunday?" Ethel said returning the hospitable gesture. "You can come to church with us and then come over for a nice lunch."

"I don't know," Claire winced as she looked up at Dan. "I don't know what we have going on."

"Well, at least come to church with me and Josiah, and then you can decide afterwards," Ethel said with some friendly pressuring.

Claire and Dan stood silent, trying to find an excuse between them, yet nothing was found except Scarlett breaking to the front of the group. "We'll be there."

"Great!" Ethel exclaimed as she and Josiah bid their farewells and made their way to her car. "See you Sunday."

"Can't wait," Dan grumbled with a fake smile.

"It's only one Sunday," Claire whispered in his ear as she waved goodbye to their guests from the front porch. "You can handle one church service."

CHAPTER 18

Claire busied herself around the kitchen, cleaning up and stuffing the cheese-crusted plates into the dishwasher for the machine to work its magic. She huffed at the work of cleaning up the mess, forgetting the hassle that women would have had to endure fifty years ago.

"Charlie, are you washing up?" she yelled. "I don't hear any running water."

"He's still watching TV," Amelia answered while sweeping the kitchen floor. She circled around the room, assembling a pile of food fragments in the center that resembled some work of modern art with the blotches of cheese and peppers. "Do we have to go on Sunday?"

Claire poured the dishwashing liquid into the dishwasher, inhaling the lemony scent. "What do you have against church? When I was your age we went all the time."

"I just don't know if I believe in it or not," Amelia said casually.

"Amelia!" Claire said turning around stunned.

Amelia froze at her mother's reaction to her honesty before finding her inner strength. "I just don't see how someone can believe in it."

"Well, belief doesn't need an explanation. That is why it is called faith," Claire recited from a Bible lesson she had learned as a young girl.

"Faith? Try telling that to my biology teacher," Amelia said as she scooped up the dirt and dumped it into the trash. "'Night."

"I'll check up on you later," Claire said, standing over the sink, staring out the window up at the moon. It was beautiful, so large and bright, with the sky filling with stars. How can she not believe? Where did I go wrong?" she asked herself out loud.

"What was that?" Dan asked as he came from running the water for Charlie's bath.

"It was something that Amelia said," she stated, stopping in thought and shaking her head in frustration. "Why don't we go to church anymore?"

"Why don't we go to church?" Dan echoed with a confused look on his face. "Well, it's the kids' day to sleep late. I play some golf with the men from work and you stay at home and relax. It's the perfect day."

"Is it really?" Claire asked, digging deeper to find the roots of their reluctance.

"Did Mrs. Stapleton get to you?" Dan asked, walking over to his wife and hugging her, allowing her to feel his strength. "She is just an old lady, and that is the only thing she has to hold on to."

"What do you hold on to?" Claire said looking into his eyes.

"You," Dan whispered, staring into her eyes and kissing her tender lips like they were newlyweds. "Always and forever you."

"Me too," she agreed as she leaned in for another kiss. "But I think church will do us all some good."

Letting out a breath, he surrendered. "Whatever you wish, my love."

"I like the sound of that," she said planting another kiss on the love of her life.

"What sounds good? 'Whatever you wish' or 'my love'?" Dan smirked as he started rubbing her back.

"Get a room," Scarlett interjected, placing her dirty glass in the sink. She quickly covered her mouth and tiptoed out of the kitchen realizing that the dishwasher was going.

"Didn't I ask for your glass ten minutes ago?" Claire scolded.

"Sorry, Mom. I love you. Or should I say, 'Sorry, my love'?" Scarlett said laughing with a cheesy dramatic voice mocking her father.

"Get out of here," Dan laughed as he chased Scarlett out of the kitchen before stopping to turn to his wife. "We'll continue this later."

CHAPTER 19

Stacks of manila folders stuffed with legal-sized papers laid all over his cluttered desk, resembling the skyscrapers of New York City. Dan sat behind the towering paper city and tossed a folder open to begin the last few hours of billable time for the day, as he heard his son sloshing around in the bathtub.

He unlocked his desk cabinet and found his two friends, Jack and Daniel. He unscrewed the bottle and poured the soothing liquid into his shot glass. Gripping the golden drink, he let the burn slide down his clenched throat, opening him up to see past what was right and wrong and to see only the needs of his client, Pharm Laboratories, Inc. Letting out a breath, he slammed the glass on the hard wood.

Pharm Laboratories, Inc. was an up and rising cancer drug research facility that developed a pill that allowed a more powerful dose of chemotherapy that ultimately sped up the cancer remission process. Dan hadn't been the wisest in his chemistry class, barely passing with the help of his nerdy lab partner, Bridgett, who'd had a crush on him since the second grade. Dan stared at the medical advancements of this "miracle pill" as *Time* was calling it, when it made their cover story a few months ago.

After carefully dissecting the scientific language, Dan discovered that the patient took Pharm's pill, which acted like a magnet to the cancer. The patient waited ten to fifteen minutes for the medicine to find the cancer and then the chemotherapy started. In laymen's terms, the pill left a trail for the chemotherapy to follow to the exact spot of the cancer. This allowed the chemotherapy to be more precise to the cancer area and left the other parts of the body unaffected. This also decreased the timeframe of the chemotherapy.

He slid his hand to the employee file of Dr. Karen Anderson. She'd received her masters' in biochemistry at Brown University, then her doctorate at Northwestern University with an emphasis in oncology research. She was always in the top of her class, and Pharm Laboratories, Inc. snapped her up before any of the more prestigious pharmaceutical companies even received her resume. It was as if Todd Clements, CEO of Pharm, had been watching her from the time she'd won her fourth-grade science fair.

Dr. Karen Anderson had reached her pinnacle at the young age of thirty-three when she discovered the missing link in cancer treatment. Many researchers worked their entire lives, gaining only a little ground in their advancements, yet Karen did it in fewer than ten years. Some were calling her the modern-day Madame Curie, which was a backhanded compliment. Even though Madame Curie discovered the effects of radiation, she also died from her continual research.

Dan flipped through the novel of legal documents recognizing this was what he craved. This was the law that he dreamed about at night. All drugs have side effects. The people who used this pill were told about the possible outcomes, yet what other choice did they have? They were given the option of leaving it up to the body's resources or beginning a new proven procedure that could eradicate their illness.

If it worked, praise God.

If it didn't, sue, sue, sue!

CHAPTER 20

"Go, Scarlett! Go!" yelled Mrs. Cabot, the girls' soccer coach for Nathanial Community, as she ran alongside the field, chasing the ball like she was an opponent. Mrs. Cabot was the stereotypical soccer coach with her blue and gold tracksuit to cover her tall lean body, a black whistle dangling beside an emblazoned Nike logo, and a bleached white Adidas hat with her blond ponytail exiting through the back.

Scarlett was in her soccer zone, passing number 19, a little redhead with bony knees, only to psych out number 4 by pretending to go left and turning right at the last second. She kicked the ball to her teammate, Madeline, who was open in the left side of the field. She dribbled the ball, allowing Scarlett to sprint in a mad dash up to the goal. Madeline kicked the ball through the swarm of girls directly to Scarlett who instantly kicked the ball. The goalie jumped, missing the ball by two feet. The ball hit nothing but white net.

"Way to go!" Dan cheered with the rest of the standing crowd. He blew his proudest and loudest whistle as Charlie stood beside him trying to do the same but only blowing out a machine-gun spray of spit.

Scarlett was the best soccer player on the team, even though she was one of the youngest. She had the agility of an antelope and the speed of a cheetah. She had the fierce competitiveness of a lion, yet the humility of a lamb. They were winning five to two. Scarlett scored two of the goals, and she could have easily scored them all, yet she allowed some of her teammates the thrill of seeing their ball fly past the goalie. Amelia looked down at her stopwatch and noticed that they only had a little less than two minutes left in the game.

"Can I head back to the car?" she yawned watching the game clock tick down the seconds. "I just finished my book, and I have another one in there."

Claire looked down confused. "There's not much time left, is there?"

"No, one minute and thirty-seven seconds," Amelia answered.

"Well, just wait here. We will be leaving shortly," Claire said keeping her eyes glued to Scarlett.

Amelia huffed as she rolled her eyes. "You know we never leave right after the game. The team has a huddle. Then they pass out the MVP ball. Then they get their snacks. Then they talk about their next practice, then their next game. Mom, we still have thirty minutes."

Claire, unwilling to have a debate with her twelve-year-old, who would probably beat her, waved her off like an annoying fruit fly.

"Thanks. I'll just wait in the car. I'm a little tired," Amelia said as she started to make her way to the grassy parking lot.

"Miss Amelia, how are you?" a familiar voice asked from behind.

She turned, somewhat startled. "Oh, Josiah. I'm good. Just going to get another book."

"What is the next one?" Josiah sounded interested.

"I don't remember. I just always keep an extra book around in case I finish the main one I am reading."

A whistle blew, causing Josiah to look up and Amelia to roll her eyes, knowing that the other coach was probably trying to prolong the game to try to figure out a plan to get three goals in the next minute. "Stupid," she remarked.

"Why aren't you playing?" Josiah asked.

"Me?" she asked with a laugh. "Scarlett's the sporty one." She stopped to calculate her next statement. "I'm the, um, not."

Josiah chuckled at the strangeness of her last statement. "You're not? Why not?"

"I'm just not interested in running, or kicking, or getting sweaty."

"Are you a girly girl?"

She appeared annoyed at the question. "I'm not that either. I guess I'm not one you can categorize in stereotypical fashion."

64

Aware of her tone, Josiah quickly wanted to diffuse any tension. "It takes a brave woman to be like that. Don't ever cave to anyone else. Be yourself."

She gazed up at him in admiration, tapping her finger to her chin. "Thank you, Josiah."

"You're welcome, Miss Amelia."

The referee's whistle blew again, signaling the end of the time out. "I've got to go get my book."

"Be careful," he said.

She looked at him in confusion. "I will. The car is just right over there."

She started walking and heard another whistle blow. It caused her to stomp her feet and turn around in anger. She wasn't too far from the field, so she saw everything that was going on. Lucy was angry after apparently getting a technical and threw a tantrum on the field. "Stupid," Amelia muttered under her breath as Lucy kicked the ball as hard as she could in Amelia's direction.

The ball was rolling fast across the grass. "Stop that ball!" Scarlett yelled as she started to follow its straight path toward the parking lot. "Amelia, stop it!"

Amelia watched the ball come toward her and stuck out her foot, only for the ball to bounce over and enter the parking lot. Scarlett ran by her. "Thanks for the help," Scarlett mocked.

"No problem. I tried," Amelia said, shrugging her shoulders.

Scarlett kept running through the cars, trying to catch the steadily moving ball, which oddly missed any of the parked cars. The ball was beginning to lose momentum as it stopped in the driving lane of the parking lot.

"Finally!" Scarlett burst out as she sped toward the still ball. She was about to leave the last parked car and run into the lane when Josiah grabbed her arm.

"Scarlett!" he shouted as a car sped by, running over and popping the soccer ball. "Watch where you're going! He could have hit you."

The car stopped and a gentleman in a blue suit stepped out of his sleek red M6 Coupe BMW with its 500-horsepower engine still running. He was a young man, probably in his thirties, well-built with black styled hair. Scarlett was entranced by his radiant smile. "I'm so sorry! I didn't even see the ball."

Josiah stood still clutching Scarlett's arm as if holding her back. "Sure you didn't," Josiah whispered to himself.

The stranger whipped out his wallet and held up a hundred-dollar bill. "How much do I owe you?"

CHAPTER 21

Dear Home,

I have been keeping a close watch on the girl, and I am learning a little more about her family. I hope to gain more of their trust so I can watch her more closely. I think the attempt on her life earlier today, which she believes was a coincidence, helped me out more than I thought it would. Two near-death experiences in one week — good thing I was here to rescue her.

I met the others. You only warned me about one, but I saw another one today, and I think I saw someone the other night. Call me naïve, but I guess I didn't figure that this case was going to be like this. Hopefully your confidence will reward itself. Overall, everything is going decent so far, but I may need some help later, or at least just a visit from a friendly face.

Mrs. Stapleton is just the way you described her. I didn't mention that I knew one of her prior tenants, but maybe I will eventually. Who knows? If she allows me to speak more, I may accidentally tell too much about myself. I guess secrecy is the key in our field of work.

I'd better get ready for bed because I have a busy day tomorrow. By the way, did you know janitors work after all the school events here? You didn't tell me that I may have to work seven days a week. That may cause a problem, but if you get it approved by the boss, I will continue this pace.

He sat on the edge of his bed, allowing his mind to settle from all the swirling details. He only wanted to tell the important bits of information. Scanning his memory of the last few days, he believed that he had hit all the high notes.

The words dissipated off the page as soon as he scribbled his signature, just like before. He got up from the bed, throwing his mysterious pen and notepad on the bed, and walked over to the window. Pushing the curtain to the side, he stood in the light of the moon, examining the outside. The old oak tree in Mrs. Stapleton's front yard was moving its limbs in the wind. The owl that had sung throughout the previous night must have moved because it was refreshingly silent. He scanned across the street at the Lamberts' home, but the only light was on the front porch. Nothing was happening, but it was an hour before midnight. It seemed like nothing ever happened in the dark in Bethany.

That is what frightened him.

CHAPTER 22

Stained glass windows the color of a sunset cascaded a spectrum of rainbow colors throughout the sanctuary of the small chapel hidden behind a wall of towering trees. A melody from the freshly-tuned upright piano filled the space with a soothing and inviting tone, as if it was inviting everyone to come and listen. It was played simply, but sometimes simple was received better than theatrical.

A narrow center aisle separated the two rows of twelve solid dark cedar pews that could each sit eight adults comfortably. There were no cushions on the pews, just the hard wood, except for the occasional seat cushion brought in from parishioners' homes. It was a quaint chapel, small in size, but large in friendliness and love. A relaxing swoosh was heard overhead as the two large ceiling fans brought refreshing cool air down to the worshippers. A few said that the church was steamy because they were on fire for God, but the majority of the congregation simply stated that they lived in the South and the South was hot.

Josiah stared up at the wood ceiling and pictured the tall white steeple directly overhead. A smile stretched across his face as he sat in silence beside Mrs. Stapleton, who was kindly introducing him to anyone who walked by. He nodded or shook hands when approached, but he stayed respectfully quiet. Gazing ahead above the choir loft that housed twelve chairs was a wooden cross nailed to the back wall above the still waters of the baptistery.

Worshippers were gathering in the sanctuary, starting to sporadically fill the emptiness, maintaining a friendly dialogue about their kids' softball games or aching muscles caused by yard work the day before. Mrs. Stapleton, dressed in her finest yellow dress, listened attentively to every conversation in the room, even the ones that didn't involve her.

"That there," she said pointing five rows ahead to the pulpit, "is Reverend McArthur. He's a good man, and his wife has the voice of an angel."

"Mm-hmm," Josiah replied politely.

"Oh, Geraldine, I want to introduce you to Josiah," Ethel said as a woman in her late seventies in wobbly high heels and an Easter sun hat carefully walked over a few pews, clasping each one for balance and support.

"Nice to meet you, Josiah," Geraldine said with a raspy voice as if she had endured years of sandpaper being rubbed on her vocal cords.

"It's my pleasure," Josiah said as he stood, helping Geraldine to her seat in the pew in front of them.

"Such chivalry. They don't make them like you anymore," Geraldine said sincerely, locking her shaky elbow with his sturdy one.

The piano music continued to play as the bells started to chime, echoing through the sanctuary ten times. "I guess the Suttons aren't coming," Mrs. Stapleton said as she peered over her shoulder to see the doors being closed by the ushers.

"You never know," Josiah reassured her. "They still may come."

"Good morning, and God bless you for coming to worship with us today. It is truly a gift from God when we have another day of life to enjoy the countless blessings that He bestows on each and every one of us," Reverend McArthur announced behind his mahogany podium.

"Amen," many voices said in a blend of peaceful chaos. "Praise God," others echoed around the room.

"Let us pray," Reverend McArthur said as the church bowed their heads. He approached the throne of God in his prayer with humility and deep conviction and passion. Murmurs of "Yes, Jesus" were said faintly in agreement throughout his prayer. He finished his prayer and a door closed, signally to the entire church of eighty-five people that someone was late.

70

Mrs. Stapleton immediately turned her head. "Come, sit with us," she said, immediately motioning the newest attendees to her pew like an air traffic controller without the lighted wands.

"Sorry we're late," Claire whispered as Josiah and Mrs. Stapleton scooted down the pew.

"Don't worry about it, child. Late or not, you are here now," Mrs. Stapleton said gathering her purse and Bible.

"I'll sit behind you," a familiar man's voice said causing Josiah to turn in his direction.

"No, you and your girl can fit up here," Mrs. Stapleton said as they readjusted themselves in the pew.

Josiah sat at the far left end of the pew, then Mrs. Stapleton, the Sutton family, and the newest addition of a father and his daughter. The row was filled with a mixture of strangers and friends with a common thread. Josiah knew each one, and each one knew Josiah. Questions began to swirl through Josiah's head faster than his brain could process them. He took a deep breath and closed his eyes. When he opened them he focused his attention on the wooden cross on the wall. He had always thought it was strange how an execution device that inflicted so much pain could bring so much peace to the faithful.

Help me, Lord, Josiah said to himself.

He removed his eyes from the fixture and scanned down the pew. Mrs. Stapleton was beaming with a proud smile, Charlie was drawing, Claire was watching his sketching, Amelia was eyeing the room suspiciously, Dan was sitting like a statue, and Scarlett was passing a note to the girl beside her. The girl, Lucy from her school, read the note and immediately glanced up at the preacher and made a small childish giggle, instantly nodding in agreement.

"Shhh," Lucy's father said who patted her leg to get her to quiet down.

Josiah watched as Lucy's father laid his hands neatly in his lap, letting them rest on his designer pants. Josiah moved his eyes up his pastel pink shirt and multicolored bowtie, perfectly tied. His face was smooth and clean shaven with no hint of stubble or razor burn. His smile was stretched wide, showing off his cosmetic porcelains that were customized by the best dentists that money could buy. In his occupation, first impressions make or break the man, and his always made him.

Josiah continued to stare in his direction, only for the gentleman to turn his head calmly in his direction, catching Josiah off guard.

We meet once again. How many soccer balls did you get yesterday?

CHAPTER 23

"It was very nice to meet you, Josiah," Geraldine said, smiling as Josiah helped her down the cement steps in front of the church.

Josiah smiled kindly, shading his eyes from the blinding sun. Geraldine was rambling about the beautiful weather they were having, yet his eyes were straining to watch another situation. Lucy's father was speaking with Dan beside his sporty new BMW.

"James, that is a nice car," Dan said with an envious eye.

"It gets me where I need to go. And gets me there fast," James said, quickly stopping as he remembered the occurrence of the day before in the soccer field parking lot. "Maybe a little too fast. I am sorry about yesterday. I didn't see her."

"She shouldn't have been running through the parking lot chasing that ball without looking. But it's all good, she's okay. She just was a little startled, but hard lessons are good," Dan said affirmingly.

"Well, that lesson was a little too close for comfort," James said with a grimace.

Josiah continued to keep a close watch from the comfort of the church steps. Every now and then someone would get in his way, but nothing that a little head bob couldn't stop. The conversation between James and Dan wasn't anything interesting, or alerting, but it caused an anxious feeling to pierce through Josiah's body.

"Are you ready for lunch?" Mrs. Stapleton asked as she exited the church with Reverend McArthur. Josiah quickly turned his head in her direction, leaving the eavesdropping for another time.

"For your home cooking, I couldn't be more ready," Reverend McArthur said, grinning as his stomach growled, causing his face to redden.

"Wonderful. We will also be having the beautiful family that sat beside me, the Suttons," Mrs. Stapleton said.

"I'm not an imposition?" Reverend McArthur asked.

73

"Imposition? I asked you, Reverend," Mrs. Stapleton smiled.

"I just wanted to make sure."

The three started to make their way to their vehicles when Josiah spotted Dan shaking James' hand. "I will call you later tonight," Dan said.

"I'll be waiting," James stated as he opened his car door. "Lucy, it's time to go."

Lucy parted company with Scarlett and headed in her father's direction. "See you tomorrow at school."

"Bye," Scarlett waved as she walked over to their Toyota Highlander.

James revved his engine and pulled out of his parking spot, inching forward about to pass Josiah, Mrs. Stapleton, and Reverend McArthur. Rolling down his window, he politely waved with a scheming smile. "Good day, Josiah."

CHAPTER 24

Fried chicken, mashed potatoes and gravy, corn on the cob, buttermilk biscuits, and strawberry shortcake – the lunch couldn't have been any better. Ethel served her guests like they were family gathering around the table at Thanksgiving.

"Mrs. Stapleton, you really outdid yourself," Reverend McArthur said, placing the linen napkin on his lap. The table was cramped with people, barely leaving enough elbow room.

"Oh, no, it was nothing really," Ethel said pleasantly. She was enjoying the community of everyone, and she wasn't going to let tiredness win.

"You must have woken up early to get all this done before church," Reverend McArthur commented, eyeing the food like six-year-old Charlie.

"Please, enough about that, let's enjoy the meal," Ethel said smiling.

"I heard her at five this morning," Josiah whispered to Reverend McArthur, who nodded his head.

Pouring the lemonade for Dan, Ethel heard the faint whisper. "What did you say, Josiah?"

"Oh, I was just telling the Reverend how much I enjoyed his message this morning," Josiah said with a playful wink.

Ethel eyed him with skepticism. "Really? However, it was a lovely message, as always."

"It was just what the Lord wanted me to say, so I shouldn't get the compliment," Reverend McArthur said meekly.

"But you were the one who said it, so why not tell you that you did a good job?" Amelia burst out.

"Amelia, be considerate," Claire rebuked.

"It's not a bother," Reverend McArthur responded in a laugh leaning down in her direction. "I believe I shouldn't get the credit

75

because I am just a messenger. It is my job to preach. I didn't say anything that I came up with; rather, God gave me the words. When people tell me that my message was good, I just want to relay to them that God deserves all the praise, not me. I am just delivering a message."

"Like a postal carrier?" Amelia asked.

"You could say that," he nodded. "When you get a greeting card or a present in the mail, do you tell the postal worker that you enjoyed the card he sent you or the person who sent it to you?"

"I know Mom doesn't like it when she gets mail," Charlie said jumping in.

"Probably not, dear. Bills are never fun," Ethel said rubbing his rosy cheeks.

"I may thank them for the card they delivered, but I usually call my grandma and tell her thanks," Scarlett answered, ignoring Amelia's deep breath as her sign of annoyance.

"Exactly. We need to thank God for the message that is heard, not me," Reverend McArthur mused, pointing at Scarlett with affirmation.

"I never thought of it that way," Claire said as she handed down her glass for some lemonade.

"Good analogy, Amelia," Reverend McArthur said, raising his lemonade to her as a toast.

Ethel eventually finished her hostess duties and sat down to enjoy her hard work. They said grace and then started to devour the many delicacies. "Mr. Sutton," Ethel said as she started to butter her biscuit, "I couldn't help but notice that you were speaking with..." she stopped to remember his name. "Oh, goodness me, my memory. Who was the gentleman you were speaking with after church?"

"James Nialliv," Dan said, wiping the corner of his mouth with his napkin.

76

"Yes, Mr. Nialliv. Nice fellow. He just moved here from, oh, dear me. My memory is not as good as it used to be," Ethel said with a hearty laugh.

"I think he told me that he moved here from California," Dan answered.

"Yes, I do believe that is correct. How do you know him?" Ethel asked before scooping a forkful of mashed potatoes into her mouth.

Dan quickly took a sip of his water, "Through work."

"Oh, is he an attorney at your firm?" Ethel asked.

"No, he works for one of my clients," Dan answered. "This chicken is delicious. Very juicy," he complemented, hoping that their discussion wouldn't turn into the legal banter from the other night.

"So, you're an attorney," Reverend McArthur stated. "Interesting work."

"It can be sometimes," Dan answered nonchalantly with a polite smile. He knew most people perceived attorneys to be conniving, tongue twisting, ambulance chasers; yet, when they realized that most attorneys were not like the ones on television, they lost their interest.

"Anything interesting right now?" Ethel asked as she nibbled on her chicken leg, wishing her own legs were as small and firm. Charlie, however, ignored their conversation and continued to inhale the biscuits like they were Dorito chips.

"One could say that it's interesting, but I don't like to talk about work too much," Dan said kindly, hoping to change the conversation topic away from him to something else. "Thank you, Josiah, for watching out for my little girl yesterday."

"Dad, I'm not little," Scarlett quickly rebutted, dropping her fork on her plate and causing a loud clink against her dish.

"Scarlett, please," Claire quickly interjected.

"Glad I was there, Mary," Josiah said winking at Scarlett.

"This better not become a habit of saving our daughter," Claire responded with a struggled laugh. "Thank you, Josiah."

"You're welcome, but anyone would have done it."

"Done what?" Ethel asked confused.

"Josiah saved my life again yesterday," Scarlett said.

"How?" Ethel speedily questioned with a tone of fright.

"I was chasing a ball at the soccer game, and a car almost hit me."
"It killed the ball," Charlie stated, chuckling with a mouth full of potatoes.

"Manners, son," Dan edged in.

"Lucy kicked the ball like crazy, and her dad was coming to pick her up and then Josiah grabbed my elbow before I could get flattened like the ball did," Scarlett said matter-of-factly.

"Wow," Reverend McArthur said laying down his fork. "That is a miracle."

"No, just the right place at the right time," Amelia said confidently, dismissing the absurd notion of anything unscientific.

The table sat uncomfortably for a minute with the sound of forks scraping the bottoms of their empty plates. "Does anyone want any more before I bring out dessert?" Ethel asked.

Everyone agreed that they were finished and saving room for the cake that Ethel told them about before lunch. It was an old recipe that had been passed down four generations, each time to the oldest child.

"So, where does James work? What does he do?" Ethel asked as she started cutting the cake.

Dan looked over at his wife and then at Ethel. He didn't want to say too much, but he didn't want to be rude either. "Well, he works as a consultant for Pharm Laboratories, Inc.," Dan answered. "Can you cut me a small piece? I'm getting full."

CHAPTER 25

"Come on. Pick up. Pick up," Dan chanted as he strolled in his backyard, walking aimlessly around the jungle gym that Charlie practically lived on in the summertime.

"This is Dr. Anderson. Leave a message," a frigid feminine voice said through the telephone. Her voicemail sounded uptight and distant, which was nothing like the Dr. Karen that Dan knew.

"Karen, I just got off the phone with James, and there have been some new developments with the incidents. I don't want to alarm you, but another case has been documented in the San Francisco area. The way these reports are coming, we may need to do something sooner than we expected. I don't know how long we can keep sweeping this damning evidence under the rug. Just give me a call." He was about to end the call when emotion surged within him. He debated for a split second what he should or should not say. "I miss..." he started to say when her voice mail interrupted.

"Press two to listen to the message, press three to..." He hung up before the automated operator could go through its recorded routine.

He stuck his Blackberry into his shirt packet and stared up into the tree limbs that blocked his view of the stars. He wondered if God was protecting him from leaving the message he wanted to. Nothing had happened yet, but he could tell by the long glances that something could if he initiated. Dr. Karen was a beautiful specimen who worked out almost as much as she worked in her lab. Her long blond hair dangled freely on her shoulders, scented with lavender and jasmine. The scent tickled his nose every time he caught the aroma. It was just another reason she made him smile.

He hadn't trekked on dangerous territory yet, but he was well past the thirty-ninth parallel. Walking over to the swings, he childishly sat on the yellow plastic seat, allowing his legs to regain their strength. He sat with his feet shuffling the woodchips, digging holes and watching his leather shoes disappear. *Was his life like his shoes? Was he on the verge of digging a hole allowing himself to jump in, only to be swallowed alive with the aftermath?*

"Honey, is everything alright?" Claire asked as she stepped out of the kitchen onto the back porch. He looked up at his beautiful wife, mother of his three precious children, supporter of all his dreams and knew that his love was standing in front of him. She was always there to ask if everything was alright.

"Yes, I'm fine," he said getting up from the swing and walking toward the porch to escape the night. "Just enjoying the peace and quiet."

"Lovely night. Wish nights could always be like this," she said wrapping her arms around herself. "Good thing we live in the South where it seldom gets cold."

"Yeah, it is nice."

"We are so lucky."

"We are," he smiled. "We really are."

A cellphone suddenly started to ring. "Doesn't sound too quiet to me," she said as she turned to go back inside, still basking in the thought of their good fortune.

Dan slid his phone from his shirt pocket and examined his Blackberry screen, "Incoming call – Dr. Karen Anderson." The screen caused him to stop in his tracks. He looked up at his loving home then back down to his ringing phone. He had a decision to make, but he wasn't ready to make it.

"Hello, Karen."

CHAPTER 26

Josiah stood outside of Mr. Turk's classroom window, soaping down the glass and scrubbing the bird mess away to a streak-free clean. Mr. Turk was standing in the front of the class, pointing on a map with his arthritic finger. Josiah stared confusedly at the map, trying to figure out if Mr. Turk's crooked limb was pointing to Georgia or South Carolina. He scanned across the room, examining the blank stares on the majority of the class, while Amelia beamed with interest.

The history classroom was stereotypically set up – five rows and columns of chairs, housing twenty-five students comfortably. Posters of Benjamin Franklin, John F. Kennedy, Martin Luther King, Jr., and other great Americans were sporadically tacked on the yellowing walls, which reeked of remnants of lead paint from the 1970s. Mr. Turk was dressed in his usual ankle-length blue pleated slacks with striped beige socks, and a pair of black Velcro walking shoes. The front pocket of his red and white checkered shirt housed a plastic pocket protector. He may not have had fashion sense, but retirement was only seven months away.

"On April 12, 1861, the United States Civil War began when General Beauregard opened fired on Fort Sumter, a small island in the Charleston Harbor," Mr. Turk droned with a monotone voice that even insomniacs could fall asleep to. He stood behind his desk, holding his lecture notes inches from his nose, with his squinting eyes straining through his thick black-rimmed glasses that had been out of fashion since the 1960s.

"Amelia," Scarlett whispered from the next aisle.

"Shhh…" Amelia quipped back, undisturbed.

"Amelia," she said a little louder than the first time.

Amelia didn't move, except for her hand continuing to take notes from the lecture.

Scarlett grabbed a clean sheet of paper from her notepad and rolled it up into a tight little ball. She aimed her ball as if Amelia's head was the basket. Slickly, she looked up at Mr. Turk, oblivious to the rest of the students who were all paying attention to Scarlett. She aimed her ball again and then took her shot. The paper bounced off Amelia's head and landed beside her foot.

Amelia didn't acknowledge the attention attempt.

"Amelia," Scarlett said in a normal tone, with a hint of annoyance, aware that Mr. Turk always turned off his hearing aid during his lectures.

"What?" Amelia said, whipping her head around and staring angrily at her sister.

"I just wanted to give you another sheet of paper. It looked like you were almost done with that one," she said, pointing down at the rolled-up paper ball.

Amelia sarcastically laughed, rolling her eyes as she turned back to give Mr. Turk her undivided attention. "Did I miss anything?" Amelia asked Dru, the boy sitting next to her.

He raised his head up from his book, wiping a drop of drool away from the corner of his mouth. He shrugged his shoulders in uncertainty, only to drop his head for another few minutes of sleep.

Lucy tapped Scarlett's shoulder. "What's up with your sister?"

"Teacher's pet," Scarlett responded, both embarrassed and proud of her sister. Amelia never bent for anyone.

Josiah stood by the window, chuckling to himself at the commotion. He didn't know why; it could have been Amelia's spunk or Scarlett's careless attitude, but he thought he was going to like his current job more than some of his recent ones. If only his job didn't include disposing of dead rats found in the boy's locker room, it would be almost perfect.

Almost.

CHAPTER 27

"My legs hurt," Lucy said as she and Scarlett walked home from soccer practice in their white shorts stained with grass. "I hate Cabot's sprints."

The walk was mainly through the semi-empty city streets of Bethany. It was after five and the majority of the business and municipal buildings had already closed. They passed Bobby's Hobbies, which many people assumed was a front for some illegal cock fighting or knockoff purse distributor, because hardly anyone went into the store during business hours. A few storefronts down was the mouth-watering Delta's Bakery which made the best cannoli in the South, or so Scarlett had been told. All that was left hanging around the streets were walkers enjoying their early evening strolls.

"Yeah, mine do a little," Scarlett said, gulping the last of her orange Gatorade as she wiped sweat away from her forehead.

"Just a little?" Lucy asked shocked.

"Well, I try not to think about it much," Scarlett answered unfazed then quickly perking up. "Did you see who was watching us practice?"

"I saw someone. Who did you see?" Lucy said annoyed.

Scarlett blushed slightly. "Luke."

"What? I didn't see him. All I saw was that creepy custodian watching us."

"Josiah? He was just doing some yard work."

"Whatever," Lucy said annoyed. "So, was Luke watching us all, or just one player?" she giggled with a Cheshire cat grin.

"The whole team. Yeah, definitely the whole team," Scarlett sighed with a frown.

"Yeah, you're probably right," Lucy agreed. "But he did speak to you during lunch today."

"That was nothing. He probably overhead me talking about the game on Saturday."

"And heard you almost died." Lucy stopped in her tracks. "I'm so sorry about that. It was all my fault. I keep replaying my stupid kick and how close you came to being squashed. And by my dad! It was close. You could have been toast."

"Stop that. Nothing happened, and I'm fine. But he talked to all of us at the table."

"He only talked to us to see if we saw what happened," Lucy reiterated.

"Yeah, but Amelia was the closest one to see everything. It happened so fast."

"Well, maybe he came by today to watch you in case something happened to you and he never got a chance to watch you play," Lucy squealed in enthusiasm all the way to her toes.

"Quit that. He didn't come just for me."

"Where was he standing?"

"Behind the bleachers," Scarlett answered.

"So he was hiding?"

"No, he wasn't hiding," Scarlett commented, quickly defending him. "He waved at me. Would someone who was hiding wave to get attention?"

Lucy eyed Scarlett inquisitively. "Well, he didn't get my attention. Looks like he got the only person's attention he wanted."

They walked down the block in silence as a small flock of cardinals flew over their head to the nearby elm tree, taking refuge for the evening. Scarlett stared up into their residence and found a few small nests scattered throughout its massive limbs.

"I heard that some of the trees along this street were used for hanging criminals years ago," Lucy spoke, sounding both nervous and intrigued.

"What made you think of that?" Scarlett asked with a laugh.

84

"You were just staring up in the trees, and I remembered something my dad told me one time. Lots of towns in the eighteen-hundreds had hangings in their local parks beside their courthouse."

"Well, the park is farther back," Scarlett said, turning around to point to the civic building that was a few blocks behind. "So this tree couldn't have been used to kill someone."

"These homes were not built back then. We could be standing where the park was back then," Lucy rebutted.

Amelia, who was walking quietly a few feet behind them, shut her book and ended her silence. "Lucy is correct. These homes were built where the park used to be, and the last public hanging occurred in 1912, right over there," Amelia said pointing without looking behind her where a park bench sat under a tall oak tree. "Right where that bench sits is where they did it. Do you see the low thick tree limb on the right of the tree? That is where the rope was hung. Isn't history fascinating?" She sarcastically smiled at Lucy, who reflected the same gesture. Amelia rolled her eyes at the girls' interest in the grotesque sight of a man dangling to his death, and if he wasn't fortunate enough to get his neck broken in the fall, to gaze up at his twitching limbs until he used up the last bit of oxygen in his lungs.

Scarlett turned her head back toward the city park, which was three blocks away and noticed a tall black man walking their way. He looked tired, but he still had a smile on his face. "Josiah." She waved, letting the memory of the town hangings swing away from her thoughts.

"Good evening Miss Mary. Miss Amelia," he said as he made his way to where they were standing.

"Hello Josiah," Lucy said, as if she was prodding him with a stick.

"Lucy," he replied in the same manner. "Good practice today," he said politely and courteously as if he was a knight in the era of castles and dragons. "Amelia, why did you stay after today?"

"Mom wanted me to wait for Scarlett," she said, huffing at the thought of explaining her mother's reasoning for the fifth time this afternoon. "After the accident, she has been mothering her a little too much and she wanted me to stick around and watch over her."

"Mothering? I think you mean smothering," Scarlett said, grunting in teen angst. "And isn't it a little hard to watch over me when your head is stuck in a book?" Scarlett continued with a laugh.

"I saw you fall a couple of times," Amelia refuted, proving that she had the skills to multitask, unlike most people her age.

"I didn't fall. I was trying to trip the other players from scoring," Scarlett said defensively.

"Well, what I saw looked like a fall," Amelia said unflinchingly.

"I couldn't help but notice your soccer skills," Josiah commented, wedging into the conversation, trying to be a buffer between the water and oil twin sisters. "You are very good."

"I thought you were supposed to be working," Lucy quizzed as if she was his superior.

"Lucy," Scarlett snapped like a mother to her rude child.

"I was, but some people can do two things at once," he answered looking into her calloused eyes as Lucy returned the same stare.

"Oh, I bet you can," Lucy spoke in almost a slow deep groan. "I bet you can."

"It's not hard to do," Amelia chimed in facetiously. "Maybe you should try it sometime but start off with something easy."

"Like walking and talking, Amelia," Scarlett mocked. "I'm so happy to have such a smart twin to guide me through life."

CHAPTER 28

Charlie sat at the dining room table working on his science homework of analyzing and deciphering the interworking of the magical system of evaporation. He stared in his textbook at the image of a lake with three yellow fish, a red arrow pointing up to a white fluffy cloud that pointed to a gray cloud with a lightning bolt showering some raindrops into a small stream that flowed into the lake with the three yellow fish.

"Mom! Amelia!" he shouted in frustration. He thought about shouting for Scarlett, but knew that even though she was the oldest, Amelia was the smarter sister.

"What is it?" Amelia said, entering his makeshift laboratory first.

He pointed at the image in his textbook. "Is this real?"

Amelia walked around the table peering over Charlie's shoulder and smiling in amusement. "Yes, that's how it happens," she said confidently and smugly.

"Charlie, did you holler for me?" Claire said drying her hands on a blue dishrag draped over her left shoulder.

"Yeah, but Amelia got here first," he said in a matter-of-fact tone. "You can leave."

"Well, thanks for the loving words," Claire said as she turned around to head back to the kitchen, lovingly rubbing Amelia on the back before she left.

Amelia turned to leave. "Where do you think you're going?" Charlie asked as if he was her superior.

"Um," she stopped but didn't turn around in Charlie's direction. "I'm leaving as well."

"But I'm not done with you!" he shouted, throwing his pencil and hitting the back of her head.

She twirled around like a karate master about to attack her villain. "Not done with me? Is that how you say 'thank you'?" Amelia scolded.

"No, but I still don't understand this," he said, pouting once again like a normal six-year-old.

"What don't you understand?" she asked, crossing her arms to show her dominance. "You got your little elementary pictures and arrows pointing you in the correct direction."

"I understand that water comes down when it rains, but I never see drops of water fly up to the sky," he said, trying to control his fake sniffles.

"Is that what they teach you? Now I see why Scarlett is the way she is," Amelia said with a slight moan.

"Huh?" he asked confused and agitated.

"Nothing," she said coldly. "Water evaporates," she said, watching his face still look glazed. "You know, when Mom boils water there is always less than what she originally put into the pot."

"I wondered where it went," he commented.

"That is evaporation. The water turns to gas and floats in the air."

"And eventually gets into the clouds!" he bellowed enthusiastically.

"Something like that."

"Wow, I think I get it," he said waving for her to leave.

"You should be a little more thankful," Amelia said, hovering over him.

"I am."

Amelia rolled her eyes as she was walking down the hallway to get to the stairs.

"Amelia!" Charlie shouted. "Amelia!"

"Maybe if you said 'thank you' I would come back," she shouted from the stairs, stomping up each one with fury, letting him know that she wasn't returning.

"Mom!" Charlie shouted as a second resort.

"I see how it is," Claire said with a smile from the kitchen, leaving her post at the sink to return to her little boy. "You want me now? Did your tutor leave you?"

"I didn't have Tutor. Amelia left me, Mom," he answered confused. *Who's Tutor?* he thought.

"Ask away," Claire said as she kissed the top of his brown head.

"Amelia was explaining how water evaporates, but then I had another question."

"What is it?"

"Well, on this picture," he said, pointing down at the lake with the three yellow fish, "she said that water turns to gas and evaporates."

"Yes, that is right," Claire agreed with a soothing tone.

"Well, do fish evaporate?" he asked seriously. "I mean, when they have gas and fart, does that mean a part of the fish goes up to the clouds?"

Claire started to laugh, shaking her head no.

"I didn't think so," Charlie said with wide eyes. "Because that would mean that little parts of me were in the cloud too after I eat too much chicken."

Claire stared to laugh hysterically at her little Charlie. "You are too much, Charlie. I needed that," Claire said, kissing him one final time before she left the room.

She walked back into the kitchen, her eyes wet with tears. She wiped them away and noticed the cooling plate of leftovers sitting on the bar. She glanced at the clock on the microwave, 8:34 p.m. She sat beside the plate and folded her hands in prayer for a few minutes. Then she grabbed the plate and covered it with plastic wrap from the cabinet above the refrigerator. She stood still as she held the cold plate of pink salmon with a fresh lemon wedge, garlic fried potatoes, steamed broccoli, and homemade cheese biscuits. This was the first time in their marriage that Dan hadn't made it home by the time he said he would.

"Dad's still not home? Didn't he say he would be home at eight?" Scarlett asked, picking up an apple from the basket on the counter.

"Yes," Claire said with a smile. "I guess time just got away from him."

She opened the refrigerator door, feeling the cool air brush past her arm, and an unnerving chill shot up her spine. She placed the leftovers on the empty middle shelf above the lunch meat and pudding for her kids' lunches and below the jugs of milk and orange juice. She turned around and was startled by Scarlett's closeness.

"Sorry to startle you," Scarlett said, quickly stepping back.

"It's no problem," Claire said as she kissed her oldest daughter on the forehead. "I love you, Scarlett."

"I love you, too."

CHAPTER 29

The school day was long, but thankfully there wasn't any soccer practice, Scarlett thought as she walked down the lonely hallway. Her grades were faltering in English, so her parents decided a few days of extra tutoring may be helpful. Her brain was still spinning with the painfully, lengthy debate with Mrs. Matis over the controversy of gerunds.

"You just have to learn that words that look like verbs can sometimes be nouns," Mrs. Matis' nasally voice echoed in her brain.

"That's just dumb," Scarlett had retorted a little too quickly by the surprised expression on her teacher's face. Mrs. Matis, who appeared to have been able to retire since the 1970s, had more wrinkles on her face than the Michelin tire man, but suddenly, her face puckered up so much that it appeared her wrinkles had engulfed her entire face.

"I'm sorry," Mrs. Matis said unconvincingly, "but the English language is quite complicated, and since this is your *primary* language you need to learn it."

Scarlett tried to look Mrs. Matis in her eyes but had to quickly look away before she burst out laughing. "When am I ever going to need to know that living can be both a noun and a verb?"

"I don't believe that it will be brought up per se in job applications or interviews, but being well-rounded is what school is all about," Mrs. Matis commented. "And please look at me when I am talking to you."

Scarlett lifted her chin to vaguely see a pair of beady brown eyes in the cavern of folds. "Well, I am well-rounded per se in soccer," she said, plunging her tomboyish fingernails in the palms of her hands to stifle the smile that was about to explode on her face.

"If only that would suffice, Scarlett. If only," Mrs. Matis said, shaking her head judgmentally.

The memory of the afternoon tutoring/grilling session caused Scarlett's blood to begin to boil as she punched open the school's front doors and grunted wildly.

"Hold on, Miss Mary, what's wrong?" Josiah asked startled at the animal noises she was making.

"Gerunds," she commented with a groan, "and participles, and adverbs, and comma splices."

"Oh," he nodded in confusion as he continued to sweep the dirt off the front entrance.

"Oh?" she asked snidely.

"I didn't mean anything by it, Mary. You students are just much smarter than me," he smiled. "I can't remember when I learned about what you just said, but you've got to stick with it."

"I know," she surrendered. "I just wish it was easier."

"If it was easy then it wouldn't mean anything," he said taking a break from sweeping and resting his hand on the wooden broom handle. "How do you feel when you score a goal?"

A smile surged upon her face. "Awesome! It's the best feeling," she said, raising her voice in excitement.

"Is it hard to score a goal?" Josiah asked calmly with a warm smile.

"Sometimes it's pretty easy," she said, hoping not to appear arrogant.

"Well, is it sometimes pretty hard?" Josiah asked, prodding deeper.

"Yeah, depending on the team," Scarlett answered.

"What makes you feel better? Scoring against an easy team or a hard one?"

"Scoring is scoring," she answered, not getting into the depth of the philosophical question.

"Think about it, Mary. When do you get excited? Scoring your seventh goal in one game or scoring the only goal in the whole game?"

92

"Oh, I see now," she said, eyes widening in comprehension.

"It is just like in school. If it was easy then it wouldn't be appreciated as much, so even though you don't feel like it now, try to see this time as something positive," Josiah said, beaming in pride.

Scarlett rolled her lips in disgust. "I don't think I will ever get excited about prepositions."

"Probably not, but anything is possible," Josiah said as he ended his short break and continued to sweep the dirt and crunched leaves into the grass. "Be safe."

"I will. Bye, Josiah."

"Bye, Mary."

Scarlett took a few steps but suddenly stopped. A question had been nagging her since her first meeting with Josiah, but she never asked. "Josiah, can I ask you a question?" she asked as she walked back, trying to not step into his dirt piles.

"Why sure," he replied as he took another break from sweeping to give her his undivided attention.

"Why do you call me Mary?" she asked, cocking her head in bewilderment.

Josiah smiled in amusement as he looked down the pavement and noticed he had a lot more to sweep. "I just like the name," he said as he proceeded to sweep again.

"Why? I like Scarlett more."

"Why?" he asked.

"I guess because I don't know of any other Scarletts."

"Any other reasons?" he asked, trying to get her to search beyond the surface and find another reason.

"Well, probably because that is what everyone has always called me."

"That's a good enough reason," he said nodding with understanding.

"So, why do you like Mary?" she grilled playfully.

"I guess it is because I knew someone whose mother's name was Mary and I loved her dearly. Every time I hear that name, I cannot help but think of her," he said, stopping to look at her. "And you somewhat remind me of her."

"How?" she giggled. "How do I remind you of an old lady?"

Josiah smiled at her naiveté. "Not in your age, Miss Mary, but how you act. You have spunk, just like her."

"Amelia calls it something else," Scarlett said with another smile.

"And you have a kind heart."

"I guess so," she agreed shyly.

"And you have a big life ahead. I can tell. God has something big planned for your life."

"What?" she laughed unconvinced.

"It's true. God has a plan for everyone's life. Everyone is important, but some are bigger than others, and I believe He has something big for you. So, keep at it."

"I don't know about that, but if I don't do better in English, my parents are going to ground me 'til I'm as old as your friend's mom," she said with a playful frown.

"Good enough reason to try harder to me," Josiah remarked.

"Me too," Scarlett agreed, waving goodbye again to start her way home.

"Oh, Mary?"

"Yes," she said, turning around and brushing her hair out of her face.

"Is it okay that I keep calling you Mary?" he asked politely.

"Fine by me," she smiled as a thought entered her brain. "Josiah, do you want me to keep calling you that, or do you want me to call you Mr…" she started as she went blank. "I don't even know your last name, Josiah."

"Josiah is fine with me, Miss Mary. Josiah is fine by me," he said as he continued to sweep the dirt away.

"Good," Scarlett said. "I like that name. It's like Scarlett. You don't hear it much." She turned for her final time and started to head home.

The day was almost over, the area was looking clean, and Josiah's stomach was telling him that it was about time to call it a day and head home. After he put away his supplies in the janitor's closet he embarked on his journey home. The sun was slowly making its descent, but there was still a little over an hour of daylight.

He mentally replayed his conversation with Mary, hoping he had said the right phrases, made the right cues, and given the best insight he had, at least the insight he was currently allowed to tell. Sometimes one cannot tell everything one knows. Josiah knew that quite well.

When Josiah had traveled to Bethany, he'd wondered why he was going to pose as a janitor when there were many other ways to get close. *Maybe it all lies in the sweeping,* he thought. When you clean dirt off a surface, a new image appears underneath, but Josiah wasn't quite ready to reveal his true image. Most people wouldn't understand.

CHAPTER 30

The newly ironed linen tablecloths were beautifully covered with the finest porcelain plates from Haviland & Company and Baccarat crystal goblets purchased in 1896. Even though thousands of distinguished meals, enlightened conversations, and hidden rendezvous had circled these dishes, they were still as flawless as the day they were designed.

The room was filled with dramatic opulence, tasteful masterpieces of art, and five-star cuisine. One large chandelier crafted by Tiffany & Company with twelve branches hung in the center of a domed ceiling and shimmered a prism of lights over the entire room. Three-foot-wide Roman style columns were placed sporadically through the dining area with a mosaic ceiling that would have fit in one of the chapels in the Vatican.

Mirabile Dictu was one of the most prestigious and elitist restaurants in Pascagoula, Mississippi, but the name was full of irony. Even though the name in Latin meant *wonderful to tell*, the only way someone could find out about this hidden gem was from a personal invitation from one of the twelve members. It was purposely aloof, yet very few commoners ever learned of the intrigue, and if they did tell, no one would believe them.

The restaurant was birthed in 1832 when a group of twelve extravagantly wealthy men decided to host a weekly meal for their wives on the third floor of one of the member's downtown stores. They brought in the best chefs for their weekly dinner from Jackson, Nashville, Atlanta, and Birmingham. They never crossed the line to the North, because they believed the Yanks would poison them and plunder their belongings if given the opportunity.

Soon they realized the luxury of having such exquisite courses and hired Kendel Renner to be their head chef. He had studied in Europe and traveled all over the world and experienced the flavors of East

Africa, the spices of India, and the flare of the orient. No two meals were alike, and his fame and prestige within the group grew to godlike status.

Years passed and the war of Yankee aggression took center stage. The weekly gatherings ended, yet Chef Renner stayed on staff. He continued to experiment in multifaceted flavors and desperately wanted to share his new creations. He started inviting the members to come and partake of their meals on different days of the week. This allowed more privacy between the chef and the members, and some seized this treasured opportunity.

Soon, each member was coming at different times and bringing his guest, whether his wife or his mistress. Chef Renner saw the same men each week, and a few of them had a different guest each time, sometimes two in one week if they were courageous.

The group had not added any non-relative members in their history. When one member died, one of their male descendants inherited membership. Once the member passed on, their wives could only return with an invitation from one of the remaining members. Sadly, some widows never knew that their own son had gained membership, and they wouldn't know unless the son told them. The same was said for the chef; one of his male descendants became the head chef when he was too old to continue concocting superior cuisine or merely passed away.

A gentleman continued to sip his 1952 Chardonnay, enjoying the tickling of his taste buds as the succulence swirled in his mouth. He sat down his goblet next to his clean plate as he looked down at his platinum diamond studded Rolex. 12:12 p.m. *Lunch starts at noon.*

"Mrs. Happle," he said as the waitress poured some sparkling imported water from the Swiss Alps.

"Yes."

"My guest should be arriving soon. Can you tell me what the chef's specialty is for today?"

"Chef Renner does not wish to divulge that information until the plate is placed in front of the patron's nose," she smiled. "But you should already know that, sir."

"I just wanted to keep you on your toes," he smiled back.

He looked around the room, empty except for the attractive young couple two tables away. He had entered this room many times, with various invitations from various members. Each time he was allowed to come, it was an experience that titillated every nerve in his body with the calming yet eerie atmosphere that this room was only folklore for a fraction of civilians. He enjoyed secret societies and the allure of their mysterious ways. Maybe that was why he did what he did so well.

"Sorry I'm late," his guest said as the well-groomed male took a seat. "This place was not listed on my GPS."

"Didn't you get my instructions?"

"Yes, but they were so cryptic I didn't understand them. I tried calling you, but it kept going to voice mail."

"Sorry, this place does not allow cell phones."

"I know that now since the maître d' confiscated mine at the door," he laughed. "How did you learn about this place?"

"I'll tell you later; it's an interesting story, but we have other pressing matters."

The hostess came to their table holding two plates covered with stainless steel lids. She laid them down in front of her guests and lifted the lids in perfect unison. The steam mixed with aroma escaped like the air from a balloon.

"I hope you enjoy escargot, Dan," he smiled as he looked down at his plate.

"I do, James. I really do."

CHAPTER 31

Dan settled his linen in his lap as he enjoyed the contents of his plate. The flavors were hypnotic and dangerously addicting. "This is delicious," he raved as his face expressed the ecstasy of the moment.

"Yes, it is quite good," James kindly conversed, thinking that he had tasted better, but finding nothing to complain about.

"This place is dead. How do they stay open?" Dan commented after he took his eyes off his plate and looked around the quiet room.

"This place is dead for a reason. Where else could you enjoy sublime cuisine without all the ruckus?" James answered arrogantly.

As Dan continued to eat, all he could think about was the price of this meal. He was a respected attorney, living a lavish lifestyle, and fabulous meals were routine. He knew how to wine and dine his clients. He enjoyed the luxurious dinners along the gulf coast in Biloxi, the quarterly trips to New York or San Francisco, and even the personal travel to Europe. He had given tips larger than some people's paychecks, but this meal was even causing his mind to grow envious.

Dan took a sip of his perfectly chilled water. "Why did you bring me here for lunch?" he asked before quickly correcting himself. "I mean, not to sound disrespectful, because this place is quite nice, but why here?"

"Nice?" James asked, ignoring the question and focusing on such an inadequate description of the glorious Mirabile Dictu.

"Now James," he kidded. "You know me better than that. I didn't mean anything by the word, just a slip of the tongue. Why did you bring me to this place?" he asked again, accenting *place* as a word bigger than itself.

"I thought a change of scenery would be nice."

"It is a very nice, I mean, excellent choice, but is there something else going on?"

"To be honest with you, Dan, there are some changes going on," James answered, finally getting straight to business.

"Changes? Has Karen found the cause? I spoke with her yesterday, and she didn't mention anything definite."

"Spoke with her? I heard you two have been spending plenty of time together," James devilishly smiled.

Dan cleared his throat in shocked defense. "I have been spending more time with her to go over the case and all the paperwork."

"There is nothing to get defensive about," James laughed. "We need to win. Hell, I would sleep with her if that gave me a leg up on this."

Dan sat silent by the remark. He hadn't even come close to sleeping with Karen, but to be fair, the notion had crossed his mind a few times – a day.

James caught the tension in the air and quickly tried to settle the smoke. "Dan, keep doing what you are doing. We need all your input to get this taken care of and to get it swept under the rug as quickly and quietly as possible. Not a day goes by that we have not gotten some kind of negative report from another hospital."

"But you still haven't answered my question. We could have discussed this at your place. Why here?"

James looked around the room, smiling at its aura. "I wanted you to experience what I have so many times."

"That's all?"

"Yes, Dan, that's all. This is a very private society and I received an invitation yesterday to come. Since you have worked so hard on the case, I wanted to show my appreciation," James cooed, trying to reel Dan into a more comfortable state.

"The case isn't over yet. I think it is too soon to start rewarding my efforts," Dan quickly rebutted. "Not that I'm not grateful, but I tend to be more reserved in celebrating this early."

"Oh, I don't believe so, Dan," he said coolly as he turned his glass of Chardonnay. "Everything is going to work out as planned."

"I hope so," Dan remarked unconvincingly.

"And when it does, you will probably be invited here yourself," James winked.

Dan sunk back into his chair, lighting the cigar that the hostess had brought. "Are these Cubans?"

"Just enjoy yourself," James smiled as he puffed on his. "Sit back, relax, and enjoy your early rewards. Just keep it up," James said, leaning back and closing his eyes, inhaling the rich taste of his cigar. "Just keep it up."

They sat and relaxed, alone in the mysterious room, since the young couple had left while they were eating. "So who do you know that is a member here?"

James slowly shook his head as he blew out four rings of smoke, one right after the other.

"That secretive?"

"When they want you to know who they are, they will tell you," James said slyly. "But if you stick with me, all your wildest dreams are possible. All of them."

CHAPTER 32

"Thanks again for allowing me over here today. My dad has been working late a lot," Lucy said as she washed up for supper in the Sutton's kitchen sink.

"Oh, it's no problem. You are always welcome here. Dan has had to work late a lot lately," Claire said as she tossed the salad, allowing all the raspberry vinaigrette dressing to cover evenly.

"That's right, my dad works with him," Lucy said, nodding her head and drying her hands.

"Charlie, did you pick up your game in the dining room?" Claire asked.

"No, but I'll do it later," he said as he stared up at his crush, Lucy, with lovebird eyes.

"What were you playing?" Lucy asked politely.

Charlie stared up at her in a muted trance.

"Charlie, are you going to answer her?" Claire asked as she poured on a little more dressing.

"Sor…..rry," he slowly answered with a slight stutter.

"I always liked Sorry. I'll help you pick it up," Lucy said as she patted his shoulder.

"Lucy, you don't have to do that. It's Charlie's mess and he needs to pick it up himself," Claire commented as she examined the consistency of lettuce to dressing ratio.

"I don't mind. Come on, Charlie," Lucy said pushing him out of the kitchen. "Lead the way to the game. I'll be right there." She stopped and turned back to Claire, who had fixed a couple of the plates. "I'll take some of these for you."

"You don't have to, Lucy. I can get those," Claire said, trying to be hospitable to her guest.

"No, it's the least I can do," Lucy smiled as she turned toward the dining room.

"Scarlett! Amelia! Supper is almost ready!" Claire shouted as she finished the salad and started to scoop some into individual bowls.

"Coming," shouted Amelia from her bedroom.

The five of them sat around the table as Dan once again had to work late. They sat in their normal seats with Lucy sitting beside Scarlett and across from Charlie.

"Lucy, thanks for helping me bring in the food," Claire pointed out. "Usually I get help from some of my own kids."

"Mom, I was finishing my homework," Amelia refuted. "Scarlett was the one doing nothing."

"Thanks Amelia," Scarlett snapped back with a curled lip.

"Let's just enjoy the meal," Claire said, calming down the table.

"I love these tiny tomatoes," Lucy said as she popped one in her mouth from her salad.

"Me too," Charlie agreed as he placed one in his mouth, following Lucy's every movement like a lovesick puppy. But unlike Lucy, he grimaced as he swallowed, remembering that tomatoes were not his favorite.

"You shouldn't have gone to so much trouble for me, Mrs. Sutton," Lucy said as she examined the table full of food.

"Don't get too excited. It's Amelia's night," Scarlett huffed.

"Mom!" Amelia retorted.

"Scarlett, we will eat what you want tomorrow night. Tonight is Amelia's night," Claire commanded like she did every Thursday night.

"You eat meals like this every night?" Lucy asked confusedly.

"Don't you?" Charlie inquired, finally letting loose his tangled nerves.

"No, I usually have pizza," Lucy laughed as she dived into her salad. "Frozen pizza."

"Sounds great to me," Scarlett snickered. "Anything would be better than eggplant casserole," Scarlett moaned as Amelia rolled her eyes.

"You are lucky to have a mom to cook for you," Lucy said as she looked down at her plate.

The mood quickly shifted from the lighthearted banter. Claire almost dropped her fork into her lap, but quickly caught it with her pinky. "I am sorry, Lucy," Claire said as she looked over at the young girl.

"Oh, it's not your fault. I never knew my mother, but James, I mean Dad, does the best that he can," she smiled as she took a large bite of her first vegetarian casserole. "Yum! Amelia, this is good. I don't know why Scarlett doesn't like it."

"Thanks," Amelia said, perking up with newfound hope tempered with a sliver of apprehension.

"Try eating it twice a month," Scarlett whispered. "It gets old real fast. I've learned to barely chew it so I can get it down without gagging."

Scarlett scooped up some of her casserole and demonstrated the technique. With one fork full, she opened her mouth, slipped in the fork, tilted her head back, and let the vegetables slide down her throat. "See?"

Lucy giggled, causing Charlie to snicker. "What is so funny?" Claire asked with a smile.

"I don't know," Charlie answered, staring straight into Lucy's eyes.

"It's nothing, Mom," Scarlett said taking another fork full and gulping it down. But this time, she felt something different in the back of her throat. She tried to swallow, but something was lodged. She tried to cough, but nothing happened. Jumping up from the table, she clutched her throat and tried to squeeze the blockage back up.

Claire ran around the table, "Scarlett!"

CHAPTER 33

Karen's florescent office light was the only one left on at Pharm Laboratories, Inc. This was her life and she wasn't going to let her dream crash and burn with the allegations. If she was found to be at fault, what company would hire her? If she couldn't find another job, who would continue her important research? If her research stopped, what would become of the world? She couldn't let that domino effect begin. She couldn't let a few incidents ruin her reputation. She had to do everything possible to dismiss all these negativities.

She sat behind her desk, scanning through the documents that were sent in an email from James earlier that afternoon. "He sent me another one this afternoon," Karen said agitatedly.

"He told me about some of these at lunch today," Dan said, sitting somewhat relaxed with his blazer and tie off, flipping through the contents of a manila folder. "Do you have this type of information about all the complaints?" he asked laying down Roberta Martinez's health records, which had all the damning evidence highlighted in green. The fifteen-page bound report was half green.

"Not all, but a few times a week I get a FedEx box of files like that one."

Dan leaned back in his chair and stared through the glass wall that separated Karen's lab from her office. The lab had the typical beakers and tubes, but unlike Dr. Frankenstein's office, nothing was on. There were no colorful liquids bubbling, no fumes rising from the test tubes, and no crackling snaps from the electric rods. It looked like a lab on its day off.

"I just don't know," Karen let out in disgust. "I just don't know."

"Maybe we need to call it a night," Dan said as his phone began to vibrate on his belt. He looked down and dismissed the call.

"Take it."

"It will go to voicemail. I'll call back later," he said, giving her his undivided attention. "We just need to find one flaw in their claims. Something that will make them look bad. We have someone looking into their financial records to see if they were in financial crises, or if they have a shady past, or past employment issues. We are not going to rest until we have something on all of them."

"But what if it falls back on me?" she questioned in hopes that his words would erase her question from her own mind.

"It won't," he said, patting her gently on her hand. Her eyes slowly rolled up into his, and his pat quickly turned into a caress. "I promise you, it won't."

"How can you?" she started to ask until he started to move his hand up her arm.

"Don't worry your beautiful head about that. Just leave it to me," he said confidently. "Just leave it all to me." He got up and walked around her desk to get closer to her. He rested his hands on her shoulders and started to massage her tension. "Just let it go. Continue your work and leave the worrying to me."

She closed her eyes, trying to give him total control of her anxiety, when his cell phone vibrated again.

"Close your eyes. It's nothing, just another call," he said as he continued his massage, rubbing down her shoulders, moving around to her neck. He knelt, moving his lips closer to her ear as his fingertips tickled her hairline. "Just let me handle it."

"You can handle all of me," she said with an unapologetic smile.

He returned the smile and felt desire surge through his body. He felt his pulse through every nerve ending. Should he continue, he wondered He opened his eyes when he felt the vibrating conclude. It was just a voicemail.

CHAPTER 34

"Dan, it's Scarlett," Claire's voice stuttered, muffled with tears. "We...we were eating supper and then she started to laugh. She took a bite, and then she just stopped. She was gasping for air. I did my best to get it up, but it took what seemed like an hour, but probably within fifteen seconds she spit it up," she said as she breathed through her runny nose.

"I thought I was going to lose her, Dan. I thought I was going to lose my baby. I know you are working, but I need you. Please come home," she said more calmly, almost begging.

"She is doing okay. She is just a little shaken up and lying on the couch." She stopped for a few seconds. "Please come home as soon as you can. I love you," she said as she ended the phone call.

Claire sat at the dining room table as Amelia, Charlie, and Lucy sat in the living room, watching Scarlett breathe. She sat, clutching the phone in her right hand and the choking hazard in her left.

"How are you feeling, honey?" Claire asked as she walked back into the living room, grabbing Amelia's shoulder for stability as she knelt beside the couch.

"I'm okay," Scarlett feebly answered. "Just too close."

"I'm sorry, Scarlett," Charlie cried as he ran out of the room. "I don't know how..."

"Charlie," Scarlett tried to shout, but it just came out in a regular tone. "Amelia, go check on him."

"Okay," Amelia said as she kissed her sister on her cheek as she stood up.

"I don't see how he could have done it, Mrs. Sutton," Lucy said in bewilderment. "I was with him as he put up the pieces." She looked back in her memory and realized something. Her face signaled the expression of discovery. "I put the plates down and then started to help Charlie put away the game." Tears began to form. "It could have been me, Scarlett. This could be all my fault."

Claire sat on the ground, brushing Scarlett's hair with her trembling hands. "Everyone is okay, Lucy." She didn't want to think of the incident anymore. She wanted to pretend that this night had never happened. "Everyone is okay," Claire said, repeating it to herself. "Everyone is okay."

"Where's Dad?" Scarlett asked timidly, looking up at her mother.

"He's on his way home," Claire answered, hoping that he got the message and was speeding to get home.

"Good," Scarlett said as she closed her eyes.

Claire looked down at her left hand, still gripping the hazard. She didn't know what to do with it. Some part of her wanted to throw it away; another part of her wanted to put it up with the other pieces. She opened her hand, and there sitting on her lifeline was a red Sorry piece.

"Mom, will you keep brushing my hair?" Scarlett softly asked as she nestled her head into the couch pillow.

Shaking herself from her thoughts, she quickly started to brush Scarlett's long hair again. "Anything you want," Claire said. "Anything you want, my dear." She formed a fist, hoping that if she kept squeezing, the red piece would disintegrate in her hand. After a few minutes, she knew that her thought was only a lofty wish when she started to see a few drops of blood escape through her clinched fingers.

How did this happen?

CHAPTER 35

Dear Home,

They are getting too close for my own comfort. I thought I was keeping a close enough watch, but something unexpected happened earlier today. I will go into further detail when someone comes to visit, but I don't know how much I should tell here. There is no telling what they are capable of, and I don't want anyone to intercept this message.

The forces I am dealing with are stronger than I thought. I knew it was going to be a tough task, but I may have underestimated their schemes. I need some reinforcements, so I don't blow my cover. I don't think anyone suspects me yet, but it only takes one person to unravel everything.

Josiah signed his name and the words magically evaporated off the page. He lay in the center of his plush bed, trying to relax, yet it wasn't working. Jerking his head to the door, he heard a creak from the stairs. "Mrs. Stapleton?"

She opened the door after a quick knock. "Yes."

Josiah quickly jumped off the bed and headed to the door. "You have never told me about the pictures on your wall."

She looked down at her watch. "It's 8:35. Do you have time?"

"As long as you need," he smiled. He needed some company this evening.

They stepped out of the room and headed to the stairs. "This picture is of my great-great grandparents, Cledius and Maybalean Taylor." She pointed at the first black and white photo of an almost frowning couple dressed in their best attire.

"Not too happy in this picture, are they?" Josiah asked, squinting at the old photograph to make out as much detail as he could see in the fading portrait.

"I never met them, but the stories I heard about them is that this was the first time they had their picture taken and they were startled by

109

the flash and the smoke. My grandmother, who is further down the steps, said that they were the best grandparents in the world, full of love and laughter, even though they had their share of ups and downs."

"Oh, really?"

"Sad story, but they had to bury two of their sons before the age of five, a few months apart. No one knows for sure what happened, but most people believe it was probably rheumatic fever, since there was an outbreak at that time."

Josiah listened as she continued her family lineage down the stairs, telling humorous stories of pie-eating contests and skinny-dipping in the local creek in the moonlight as well as more heavy tales of lost loves and fallen soldiers.

"Your family has had quite a history," Josiah said, looking at Ethel with respect and compassion.

"I am a very blessed old woman," she said beaming, her eyes starting to droop with fatigue.

They came to the last picture, a photo that was probably taken in the 1970s. "Who is this handsome gentleman beside you?"

She squinted her eyes to see the fine-looking figure. "Oh, this is Gabe. He was my very first houseguest after my husband died in the war."

"You were a very lovely woman, and you still are," Josiah kindly remarked.

"You are too kind, Josiah," she commented as she stared at the photograph of her as a twenty-three-year-old, only to witness her reflection in the glass frame – the same smile, but with more wrinkles. "Gabe probably saved my life without knowing it."

"How?" Josiah prodded.

"Well, I was lonely. I had just gotten word that the love of my life had died a few weeks before. I had friends and family who came and stayed with me the first week, but the next week was horrible. I was so depressed and alone. People came by and visited me and spent time with me during the day, but in the evenings…well, the evenings were so dark. I didn't know what to do. I loved him more than anything else, and I didn't want to go on without him."

"So, did someone tell you to start renting out the upstairs for company?"

"No, that is the interesting part. I had come to the decision to drink a little concoction before bed and wake up in the loving arms of Humphrey. Well, after I had finished eating my supper, I sat in the living room for half an hour in silence. I thought, *What is the use of waiting?* If I was going to do it, I might as well not wait. I made my way up the stairs and started crushing the pills in my bathroom. I looked around and I had forgotten my glass of milk downstairs, so I went back to get it. As I was returning up the stairs, I heard a knock on the door. I was confused, because normally I didn't have visitors after dark. I went back downstairs and opened the door, and there he stood."

"Gabe?"

"Yes, he said that he was new in town and needed a place to stay, and he had just heard from someone in the drugstore that I might have a room for rent. He looked so tired and worn out that I couldn't say no. I fixed him a filling meal and got him ready for bed. When I finally went upstairs to go to sleep, I had forgotten about my plan. My loneliness was gone. Even though he wasn't my Humphrey, just knowing that someone was under the same roof as me made me feel a little better. When I woke up the next morning, I saw the powder I made and scraped it into the sink. Ever since then, I decided to open up my home to anyone who needed a place to rest."

"That is an interesting story," Josiah said with a smile.

"You haven't heard the real interesting part," she said as she smiled mischievously. "Gabe said that he heard from the drugstore owner, Mr. Turkelson, that I may have a room available."

111

"Yes?" he asked wondering the significance of this fellow.

"Well, Mr. Turkelson's sister, Mary Lou Freeman, lived over in Georgia and she was about to give birth to her first son, Winston. I went to the drugstore to pick up the pills, and I was the last customer for the day. As I left, Mr. Turkelson was locking up his store to get to his sister's as fast as he possibly could. He didn't even want to let me in the store, since he was already locking up, but I had made a decision to die and I wasn't going to let Mr. Turkelson's happiness stop me." She breathed a sigh of adrenalin. "So, see, Gabe wasn't told by someone at the drugstore to come to my home because the drug store was closed. How did he know?"

"I don't know," Josiah answered.

"Well, I do," she said, stopping and looking up. "I know."

CHAPTER 36

He found his family tightly curled up in the middle of his king-sized bed, like four small grapes clinging onto the vine connecting them all. He stood in the door frame and viewed the fragile scene. He didn't know what made him feel worse, knowing that there could be one less lump in his bed, or that earlier tonight he wished that he was lying next to a different pair of arms and legs.

He gripped the doorframe as if trying to make up his mind to end the feelings he was having with Karen and cling to the family he had now. Closing his eyes, he felt exhausted. He felt confused. He felt aloof. Yet deep down he didn't feel remorse for his actions.

Sneaking into his darkened room, he grabbed his pajamas and headed to the downstairs guest bathroom to wash away the smell of Karen's perfume on his white Stafford shirt. He turned on the jets to let the warm water rush through the faucets then started to unbutton his shirt for the second time tonight.

He could still feel Karen's eager fingers brush through his hair, finding a trail down his neck to his muscular chest. Stepping under the hot streams, he felt the relaxing pulsating sprays massage away the built-up tension from the night. His thoughts lingered in the moment when Karen entered back into her office wearing nothing but her white lab coat, accenting her perfectly tanned body. The mere thought made his breathing go heavy once again.

"What are you doing?" he asked aloud, shaking his mind back to the current place and time. "I am lucky, very lucky I didn't."

"Lucky you didn't what?" Claire asked as she stepped into the bathroom, closing the door behind her.

"Claire?" he asked startled, peeking his head through the shower curtain.

"Lucky you didn't, what?" Claire asked again with reddened eyes and dark circles underneath.

"Lucky I didn't lose Scarlett," he quickly answered. "I am so sorry, honey," he said ripping away the curtain to hug and console his agonizing wife. "How is she?"

Tears began to form again. "She's doing okay, but it...it was too scary," she said. "But the worst thing was I couldn't get ahold of you."

"I know. I know," he said, stepping out of the shower and letting his body drip on the daisy bathroom mat. "I promise," he started to say, but she stopped him with a kiss.

"I know," she said with a quiver in her voice.

He stood there vulnerable before the mother of his three children as the shower continued to pelt the tub. He looked into her eyes and showed a cocky smile as he kissed her passionately.

She returned the passion but suddenly came to a halt. "Not tonight," she said, gently pushing him back. "Just not tonight." She left the bathroom and headed up to her warm bed with her three snuggle bunnies, wondering if a fourth would be following.

He stared into the foggy mirror at his hairy wet chest and tight stomach as he posed for his own reflection. He had been turned down twice in one night, but sadly, he didn't know which one made him feel worse.

Karen had had to leave because of an urgent meeting with the CEO of Pharm Laboratories, Inc., and Claire had rejected him due to the tragic events of the night. Each had a reasonable and understandable cause, which he rationally agreed with, yet he couldn't help but linger in his narcissism.

He stepped back into the shower, hoping that the water would wash away his confused feelings. He stopped the water and wrapped the blue cotton towel around his waist. Stepping out of the tub, he realized that sadly all his feelings were mixing together. He stared down and watched the water funnel down the drain and realized that it may be only a matter of time before his life whirlpooled into a similar messy abyss.

114

He once again stared at his reflection, retracing where Karen's hand had grazed below his bellybutton and his devilish smile appeared.

It could cause pain, but right now it is fun. To hell with the pain.

CHAPTER 37

"Mary. Mary," Josiah said, breathing heavily as he came running up to the school's entrance. "I just heard about last night."

"Yeah, close call," Scarlett said as Amelia stood like a marble statue by her side.

"How did you already hear?" Amelia asked. "I just saw you walking to school as we drove by on Main Street."

He quickly and unflinchingly answered, "I got a cup of coffee at the diner, and someone was talking about it. You know how news spreads in a small town."

"She's news?" Amelia muttered.

"You have a good day now," Josiah said as he headed inside. "I'm running a little late this morning, but if you need anything Mary, I'm here."

"Thanks, but I think I will be okay," Scarlett answered nonchalantly.

The sun continued to rise, stretching its morning rays across the mulch-covered playground in front of the school. The last school bus had just turned into the school's parking lot to signal the start of another day.

"We're a little early today," Amelia said as she looked down at her watch. "We still have three minutes until the bell rings."

They joined the last group of students as they headed into school. "Did Josiah seem a little strange to you this morning?" Amelia asked. "Well, stranger than usual."

"Why do you do that?" Scarlett asked with a hint of frustration.

"Why do I do what?" Amelia scoffed with her hands firmly clinched on her petit hips in a defensive stance.

"You always think the worst of people."

"I do not." Amelia scoffed at the thought of thinking the worst of people. Yes, she had to admit that she had low standards for a majority of the population, but usually she had a good reason for her hypothesis. But for someone to say that she thought the worst of people was simply wrong.

"You do too! What do you think of Samantha?" Scarlett continued.

Amelia stomped her foot in aggravation. "You know what I think of Sam."

"I know, but you never think the worst of people," Scarlett mocked in a whiney voice.

"She's a ditz. And you cannot tell me that you don't think that too," Amelia whispered as they walked down the crowded hallway.

"Unlike you, I don't always vocalize my comments."

"Uh, vocalize?" Amelia stopped in shock. "Maybe the first breath of air last night was like a jolt to your brain to kick it into gear." She watched Scarlett's face frown at her uncompassionate words. "God knows you haven't used it in months." She was on the verge of losing her best friend, even though she rarely told her so.

"You really hurt sometimes," Scarlett said as she turned into her class, leaving Amelia who stood awkwardly rigid in the commotion-filled hall.

"I know," Amelia said remorsefully to herself as she turned to go into her first classroom. "Boy, do I know."

CHAPTER 38

Silence. He loved it, yet hardly experienced it like he once did. He stepped in front of the kitchen window staring out at the backyard noticing the stillness of nature. Even though the clock ticked midnight a little over an hour ago, the light from the full moon allowed him to see outside perfectly. It could also be that he had let his eyes adjust to the darkness, since he was tiptoeing in someone else's home.

He quietly roamed around the first floor, searching for any signs that would cause any alarm, yet found nothing. He scanned the family photos, the smiling faces, the goofy looks, the matching wardrobe. From the outside they masqueraded in perfect harmony, yet he knew one wore a mask, which could cause the whole machine to fall apart.

He walked down the hall and saw the stairs that led to the family's bedrooms. He had lost his sense of fear and started to comfortably stride up the stairs. He came to the first bedroom and he saw the tiny Superman nightlight against the far wall. Such a small light, yet it radiated through the whole room. He stepped into the doorframe and poked his head in the small boy's room.

The light shone on the fishing pole in one corner, his navy-blue backpack on his chair, and his rosy cheek complexion. The boy lay snuggled with his stuffed turtle clinched in his armpit, with his right leg hanging off the child-sized bed. He left the room and headed to the next; Charlie wasn't his concern.

He came to one of the girls' rooms and quietly stepped into the spotless room. Her desk was prim and proper, no loose papers or misplaced items. Her clothes, which were probably laid out for tomorrow, were neatly folded on her dresser. The window curtains were perfectly placed allowing in the right amount of light, yet strategically placed so it wasn't in her face.

He stepped into the room and stood in the corner and watched the young girl sleep. She was restful, with very little movement, except for her chest moving up and down from her breathing. He stared intently at the sleeping child. Even though the girls were identical twins, there were slight differences between them; strangely enough, when asleep, there were fewer differences. Maybe each tried to form differences from the other, and when asleep, the trying was over.

He left what he assumed was Amelia's room due to the clean surroundings to head to the next. He waltzed into the room without a care of getting caught and realized that his assumption was correct. Soccer balls were plastered as a border along the walls, a poster of Mia Hamm was pinned on her closet door, and her love-crush, David Beckham, was taped to her ceiling, so he was the last thing for her to see each day. Her clothes were strewn on the floor, wadded up paper was overflowing from the trashcan beside her desk, and a layer of dust laid on her small cassette/cd player. This was Mary's room.

Moving farther into the room, he decided to get a little closer to her. He laid on the floor beside her bed and listened to her breathe, well, snore. She snored pretty loudly, and from the strips on her nose, her family was trying to help her control her deafening nightly sounds. Lying still, he closed his eyes and rested in the comfort that her breathing was good and unblocked. He rested in the fact that nothing could happen to her when he was around her. Sadly, he knew that he couldn't always be there to protect her, no matter how hard he tried.

He hadn't been there last night.

He opened his eyes at the sound of the grandfather clock as it chimed once. He rose up and left the room, only to continue his journey through the rest of the house. Further down the hall, he found a room with the door slightly cracked. He pushed the door open a little and saw two figures sleeping on opposite sides of the bed. The room was empty of love. He felt the chasm, the coldness, the divide that went beyond the bed. He watched the couple sleep soundlessly. He wished that they would have tossed a little and maybe have rolled into one another, but for the time that he watched, he never saw any movement. Not one inch.

He turned and left their room and walked down the lonely hall. He passed the snores of Mary, the peacefulness of Amelia, and the light of Charlie. Each had their distinction, yet underneath it all, they were just kids sleeping their way to another crazy day. He headed down the stairs and barely saw his dark reflection in the mirror. He'd had years of watching from corners and walking down quiet halls undetected. Josiah was a professional in camouflage.

Even though the night was a success in being undetected, it was a failure in detecting what he wanted to find. He opened the kitchen's back door, hearing only the click of the latch. The cool spring air breezed past his arms and he felt a chill, not from the temperature, but from the thought of his duties. He exited the kitchen and quietly shut the door with his gentle touch. He looked up and saw the pure white sphere in the darkened sky. *This world needs more purity*, he thought.

He stepped across the dry lawn because it was still too early for the morning dew. He turned and stared up at the silent bedrooms as a morbid thought engulfed his mind. If he got into their house, others could get in as well.

You can do this. You've got to do it, Josiah.

CHAPTER 39

The moon was as full as it had been when he stared at it through the Sutton's window, yet now walking back to Mrs. Stapleton's home, the trees were shading him from its light. The wind had picked up slightly, and he noticed the trees swaying overhead like terrified hostages waving their hands in surrender. He walked in a state of peaceful confusion. At the bottom of his heart, he didn't think that he would find anything in their house, but he desired to find that missing piece that kept him on edge.

The owl in the nearby tree was making its normal hoots, yet to Josiah, it sounded different. He didn't hear a lovely bird, he just heard a question.

Who?

Who?

Each time the owl spoke, he knew the answer. What he didn't know was how. How was he going to stop the inevitable? The 'who' was easy; it was the 'how' that made him unable to sleep tonight.

Coming closer to the neighborhood, he saw Mrs. Stapleton's home begin to shine like a beacon, as if he was a lonely captain trying to make his way home. "Josiah." He heard a voice but couldn't see anyone nearby, only trees lining the sides of the street.

"Who's there?" he asked, straining his eyes to see through the shadows of the dancing tree limbs as he continued to slowly walk wondering who else would be out at two o'clock in the morning.

"It's me," the voice answered coldly.

Josiah came to a halt and moved off the road, walking into the black forest. "Who are you?"

"Come on, Josiah. Have you forgotten me already?" the voice asked with a hint of laughter.

"Nathanial?" he questioned with wavering uncertainty.

"Good job," a younger man said as he jumped down from a perch on a nearby oak tree. In the dark, Josiah couldn't see his blond hair or emerald eyes, but the outline of his figure proved that it was his comrade.

"You startled me," Josiah said, jumping back in shock at his falling friend.

"Startled? What is there to be startled about?"

"I know. I know. But it is different here," Josiah said unashamedly.

"Josiah," Nathanial said walking over and embracing his good friend. "You are doing a good job. You really are."

"I'm trying," he said with dwindling confidence as he clung onto his friend's blue jean jacket. "But there is a lot of pressure."

"If he didn't think you were up to it he would have sent someone else," Nathanial said with a smile, but Josiah couldn't see the toothy grin. Josiah knew Nathanial's encouraging optimism and his always faithful smile.

"I know. I know. I keep telling myself that, but down here, self-doubt is just in the air," Josiah relented.

Nathanial agreed as he rested his back against a tree. "People around here think it's Voodoo, but Voodoo has little power unless you believe in it." During one of Nathanial's previous jobs he had seen the power that Voodoo supposedly possessed, which was usually very little. Voodoo was just as effective as a sugar pill, unless just like a sugar pill, it was combined with a little belief. Then, it could cause a miracle or devastation.

"You know me better than that," Josiah said disparagingly.

"Yes, but..." Nathanial stopped. "But why are you falling into their trap?"

Josiah walked in a small circle, trying the find the best words, but none came to his mind. "Weakness?"

"You are not weak, Josiah. I saw you fight. You just need to get that same intensity. Lives are on the line here," Nathanial commanded. He had seen Josiah fight many years earlier, and he'd fought like the bravest of warriors, not caring about the enemy or their number. The only thing that mattered was the hard and honest fact that only one could be the victor, and losing was not in Josiah's vocabulary.

"Nat, this is probably the first time that I want to tell the truth and unveil my secrets. I have envisioned telling them, but..."

"But?"

"I know if I told, everything would change. Or worse, they wouldn't believe and nothing would happen." He stepped out from the wall of trees to get back to the paved road returning into the glorious moonlight. He didn't know why, but the moment his feet touched the solid black river, his knees stopped quivering with uneasiness. It was as if the road reassured him that if he stayed on the narrow path, he would reach his destination.

"That is what happens when we try to rationalize everything. You have a mission, and you've got to stick to the plan."

"But..." Josiah said hesitantly.

"No buts! Stick to the plan. You've got to stay focused. Don't get sidetracked. Don't divert from the plan," Nathanial said forcefully.

Josiah started to walk home while Nathanial stood motionless in the dark. Josiah turned around. "Do you want to come back with me? It is pretty late."

"You're not my only watch," he laughed as he sank farther into the mass of trees until his emerald eyes vanished. "I'll come and visit again."

"Promise?" Josiah asked, but there wasn't any answer.

CHAPTER 40

"Did you sleep well last night, Miss Mary?"

"Yeah, I guess so," she answered knowing she could have slept longer.

"You need to get all the rest you can. You, too, Miss Amelia," Josiah commented.

Amelia looked up at Josiah a little perturbed at the conversation. "Sleep? Is that all we can talk about?"

"What do you want to talk about?" Scarlett barked.

"I don't know, but something better than sleep," Amelia said agitatedly. She could count a dozen possible conversation starters at a drop of a hat, including stem cell research, global warming, animal drug testing, the works of Chaucer, the paintings of Picasso, the symphonies of Canon, the constant uneasiness in the Middle East, or even the staggering decline in the housing market.

"Fine then, how about the weather?" Josiah chuckled as he wiped down the table in the cafeteria.

Amelia rolled her eyes as Scarlett laughed. "He's just kidding with you, Amelia."

"I know that," Amelia said crossing her arms as if making a shield from their babbling nonsense.

"You have a good day," Josiah said as he moved on to another table to clean after the morning's breakfast.

"Why are we in here again?" Amelia asked pulling out *Metamorphosis*.

"No reason," Scarlett answered nonchalantly.

"No reason?" Lucy scoffed unconvinced. "Is it because Luke eats breakfast here each morning?"

"I followed you here for a boy?" Amelia groaned, disgusted at the thought that a boy could unknowingly have so much power.

124

"No!" Scarlett quipped quickly. "I just thought since we got to school a little early, we could wait here."

"Wait here to see Luke," Lucy giggled with a high-pitched squeal, causing Mr. Turk, who sat alone eating his oatmeal in the teacher's section, to clutch his ears because his hearing aid buzzed a deafening tone in his ears.

Amelia couldn't sit idly by anymore. "Well, I'm not going to watch you two act like imbeciles; I'm going to the library."

"Fine then," Scarlett said as she and Lucy stayed seated.

"What's up with your sister?" Lucy asked as she watched Amelia stomp away. "I mean. I don't have any sisters, but I always thought it would be cool to have one."

"I know," she smiled. "I guess since we're twins she got all the smarts and I got everything else."

The two girls peered around the room, unsuccessfully trying to find Luke's table. There weren't too many people in the room, and Luke always ate breakfast at school. They continued to look around, elongating their necks like ostriches.

"Who are you looking for?" a guy asked from behind.

"Oh, no one import..." Scarlett said as she turned around to find Luke sitting alone at the table directly behind them. "Important, but my sister."

"I just saw her leave," he said as he took a bite of his Granny Smith apple. "She didn't even notice me."

"Did she have a book in her hand?" Lucy asked.

He nodded as he took another bite of his apple. "Should've known then," Scarlett answered superiorly. "So, do you always eat by yourself?"

"Yeah," he smiled as he opened his carton of chocolate milk. "I never see you all in here this early."

"The bus got us here early this morning," Scarlett answered without a hint of a stutter from her nerves. "So, do you…" she started to say as the bell rang for the start of the day.

Luke got up and placed his apple core on his tray and gulped the last bit of his milk. "You were saying something?" he asked as he stopped by their table.

"Um, well," Scarlett said picking up her backpack and trying to think of the words that were on her tongue just a second ago. "I don't know," she bashfully smiled, while internally punching her gut for acting girly.

"Well, I'll see you later," Luke said as he threw away his trash, strutting out the doors as all the girls watched him leave.

"Bye," Scarlett whispered as Lucy got her belongings.

"What's up with you?" Lucy prodded.

"What do you mean?"

"You should have made a move."

"Lucy," Scarlett blushed with embarrassment as she waved goodbye to Josiah from across the emptying room.

"I'm serious," Lucy said encouragingly as they headed out the cafeteria. "Also, what is up with the janitor always talking with you?"

"Josiah? He's nice," Scarlett said sincerely.

"Well, I think he's weird. A child molester, probably," Lucy hissed with disdain.

"Lucy!" Scarlett gasped at the thought of Josiah being so inhumane. Josiah could possibly be one of the kindest souls she had ever met, and to hear her friend say such hurtful, outlandish, and bigoted words was almost too much for her to take.

"I'm sorry, but I still think he is weird," Lucy defended. "Don't you, even a little?"

Scarlett came to a proverbial crossroads – stand up for one friend or agree with another one. "Well, maybe," she said. As the words escaped her mouth, she quickly tasted the bitterness of regret.

126

CHAPTER 41

"Mr. Sutton, you have a call on line two," Jenna Simone said. His new college-dropout receptionist continued to flip through her *People* magazine, scoping out the latest shoe fashions of Jennifer Lopez.

Dan didn't say a word, refusing to acknowledge the intercom. He didn't even flinch. He kept his stance in front of the floor to ceiling window in his corner office on the third floor of Brock, Stallins & Boswell, LLP, one of the largest legal firms in the southeast, with offices in over a dozen cities in four states.

"Mr. Sutton?" Jenna asked again before ending her one-way conversation.

His plush office, located in the tallest business building in Bethany, which was only four floors with a different business controlling each floor, towered over the rest of the surrounding two-story buildings. Honey's Sugars, which was the town's premier bakery and other confection supplier, sweetened the first floor. Stockyard Insurance, which focused on automobile coverage, gave financial stability on the second. Lastly, Pimble's Cable, which claimed to provide Bethany and the surrounding counties with the best quality of cable television for the most affordable prices, was located on the top.

He stared as a flock of cardinals glided from above the treetops to swoop down on a display of popcorn kernels being thrown like confetti from an elderly man sitting on a wooden park bench. He watched as squirrels left their tree limbs to visit and be fed by the local Dr. Doolittle. Dan gave birth to a smile that was quickly eclipsed by the buzzing of the intercom. "Mr. Sutton, your ten o'clock is here."

"Give me a few minutes," he answered, shocking Jenna with his response after such a silent morning.

He looked down at the old man wearing a pair of tan slacks and long-sleeved plaid shirt. Dan was caught off guard at his fascination with this complete stranger. It wasn't that the older gentleman was

127

doing something exciting or even worthy of watching, but for some reason he was completely mesmerized.

Dan turned from the window and looked down at his compact calendar filled with appointments for the next week. Most attorneys would be thrilled with the number of billable hours about to come their way, but Dan's mind was thinking of other matters. His mind was on one complex professional case that had somehow tipped into his personal life. On one side he was feeling alive with a well of passion, yet on the other he felt remorse and sympathy for the sins of his own being. Attorneys were taught to play in the gray area of the law. Sadly, he knew that colorful embellished stories would always be a part of his life and livelihood.

But now the tall tales were getting a little closer to home.

CHAPTER 42

"You did what?" Dan shook in uncontrollable anger throwing the fraudulent patent paperwork down on Karen's cluttered desk.

"We had to," she answered with a mixture of assassin tenacity and childish fragility.

"You had to?" he scoffed at the incongruent answer. "You had to?" He repeated the answer again, hoping she would understand the total blunder that this would cause. "Do you know how much sh...?"

"Yes, I know we are walking on thin ice," she quickly interrupted his manic tirade.

"Walking is an understatement. You better run as if your ass is on fire melting the freaking ice!" he yelled as if he was trying to convince Scarlett that her science project better get finished by the weekend.

"You don't have to talk to me like a child," she growled with unflinching attitude. She was an intelligent scientist who was dubbed by some of her own colleagues and professors as the 'next big thing'. *How dare this elitist ambulance chaser talk to me in such a disparaging tone?*

"When you act like an idiot, I don't know how else to talk to you," he snidely undercut her at her knees.

"I am not an idiot!" she shouted, waving her perfectly manicured finger in his face. "Without me, this company would still be in the first stages of researching a drug that does what I found."

"What you found?" He stood back and laughed at the arrogance of the statement. "You found a chemical combination of false hope, laced with untimely death."

"Untimely? They have terminal cancer. What other drug do they have to pick from?" she retorted in logical defense.

"Patented ones!" Dan shouted as it was his closing argument.

She coldly stared through his navy-blue suit, piercing his soul if he had one. "That is low."

"Low? Low? I'm not aiming for low," he said as he walked around her office in a state of utter confusion. "I'm digging your early grave. That is how low this is going to go."

"Thanks for the encouraging newsflash, but I know what we are up against." She plopped down in her desk chair and leaned back, tossing her hair to alleviate some of the stress in her neck.

"Are you sure?" he asked unconvinced.

"I know more about the drug process than you do, Mr. Esquire."

"Apparently you don't, or you wouldn't have fudged the documents," he said judgingly.

She sat still for a moment as Dan sat across from her. "I need your help," she pleaded. "We..." she started again, waving her arms in the air of Pharm Laboratories, "We need your help."

He leaned back and recounted all his friends from law school that had been punished by the Bar for small offenses. He didn't want to be the first from his graduating class to be disbarred. "You need more than help."

She stood up and sauntered over behind him, tickling his neck with her delicate fingers. His eyes were straining to stay fixed in the moment, but they quickly subsided at her sensual touch. "I don't just need you," she strategically whispered in his ear, causing his ears to perk up by the touch of her tongue. "I want you."

CHAPTER 43

A scattered array of potato chip crumbs and crushed cheese puffs laid embedded in the carpet underneath a herd of giggling teenage girls. The sleepover began with the three girls, Lucy, Scarlett, and Whitney gorging themselves on Claire's homemade meat lover's pizza, as Amelia nibbled on her garden salad. Shocked at the total massacre of the Italian pie by the three tiny girls, Claire had to settle for Amelia's vegetables.

"What do you want to do next?" Scarlett asked as she ejected the latest chick flick from the living room DVD player.

"What other movies do you have?" Lucy questioned as she grabbed another handful of pretzels from the Tupperware bowl.

"I don't feel like watching another movie," Whitney whimpered. "How about you let me fix your hair, Scarlett?"

Scarlett's face twitched in a state of bewilderment. "How long have you known me?"

"Um, since the second grade, I think," Whitney said.

"Third grade," Amelia chimed in from the chair with a flashlight in her hand, projecting the light onto her latest literary work.

"Thanks A," Scarlett retorted sarcastically. "So, you have known me for years, but have you ever fixed my hair?"

"No, but..." Whitney started as Scarlett instantly cut her short.

"Have I even once ever asked you to fix my hair?" Scarlett asked, already knowing the answer.

"No, but," Whitney quietly answered, hoping to get her complete sentence out.

"So, what makes you think I want to do it tonight?" Scarlett said with a laugh.

"I don't know. It would just be fun," Whitney said depressingly as she looked at Lucy for encouragement.

"Fun?" Amelia chuckled. "Do you know Scarlett at all? She isn't your Barbie doll to primp and doll up."

"Come on, Scarlett. Let her do it just this one time," Lucy said entering into the conversation, adding a little more weight to Whitney's side of the issue. "What would it hurt?"

Scarlett looked at the two girls on the other side of the couch but felt uneasy about letting go and giving into them so easily. She would have easily brushed off Whitney, but now Lucy was siding against her. After a few seconds, she realized that the night was too short to debate this matter any longer. "Well, I guess," Scarlett subsided and stepped over into foreign territory of curls and hairspray.

"This is going to be great," Whitney squealed as Lucy joined in with the high-pitch alarm.

"Oh, jeez," Amelia said rolling her eyes and turning her attention once again to Toni Morrison's *Beloved*.

"Whatever, Amelia. You know you want to join in on the fun," Whitney said whipping around the room, grabbing her toiletry bag of hair brushes, clips, bobby-pins, and packages of body glitter, some of which escaping the bag.

Scarlett caught the falling packages as if they were a line drive to second base. "Just fix my hair. Nothing else," Scarlett said, tossing the girly glitter up for Whitney to catch, who only fumbled it like any prissy girl would.

Amelia giggled at the sight of Whitney's lack of hand-eye coordination. "Something funny in the book, Amelia?" Lucy asked with a tone of defense.

"Yes, the book is loaded with laughs," Amelia said, lying through her teeth.

"Why don't you read us what is making you laugh so much then, chuckles?" Lucy prodded as her smile shifted from gleeful to menacing.

"You wouldn't get it," Amelia quickly answered. "You just have to read the story to understand these inside jokes."

"Sure," Lucy said suspiciously. "Why don't you go up to your room? You know you don't want to be here anyway."

"Whatever gave you that impression?" Amelia quickly snapped with her overconfident flare.

"Mom's making her," Scarlett said breaking in like a taunting older sister.

"Shut it," Amelia snapped while shooting an arrow stare that would have run off even a coyote with its tail between its legs, but not Scarlett. Scarlett was tougher than a pack of wolves.

"Not so big and bad now, are you?" Scarlett prodded.

Amelia sat broken and silent, watching her blood turn her back on her. She didn't know what hurt more, having Scarlett break to peer pressure by letting them fix her hair or allowing them to change their relationship. Deep down she wanted to run away and cry, but she didn't want them to enjoy the humiliating surrendering. She stuck her nose further into her book and let the words carry her off to a distant land.

"Ouch, Whit," Scarlett whimpered.

"You have tangles, and the only way to get them out is to brush them out," Whitney said stroking her hair with a motherly firmness that even Mother Dearest wouldn't have attempted.

Lucy stood in the middle of the two sisters as she sadistically smiled at Amelia's fragmented state. She watched Amelia intently, as if to dare her to look up from her safe book, but Amelia didn't succumb to her bidding. Lucy turned and saw her new friends and joined Whitney with brush in hand. "What do you want me to do?"

"Turn on the light. I can't see what I'm doing," Whitney ordered.

"That's comforting," Scarlett sighed as Lucy jumped up and flipped the switch. Light filled the room, spilling the brightness into the Suttons' front yard.

Whitney looked over to the window and had a strange feeling come over her. "Do you ever feel like you're being watched?"

Scarlett turned her head, forgetting that Whitney had a death grip on her hair, causing another pinch of pain. "Yikes!" she screamed, mad at her own stupidity. "Who would be watching us, Whitney?"

"You never know," Lucy mysteriously answered as she went to the window and looked out into the midnight sky. "You never know."

CHAPTER 44

Lurking in the weeping willow's shadows, the sagging branches swayed against his cool cheek. He made his way from the desolate road, crossing over the well-maintained front yard. He had the yard memorized: the row of Claire's lilies, the bubbling koi pond that Charlie often fished in, even the protruding tree root that lingered although the tree had been demolished when a hurricane came through the area eight years earlier.

He had a mission to accomplish and nothing was going to stop him. Not even a sleepover.

The night was darker than usual due to clouds congregating, showing signs of a storm brewing. Walking through the yard, all he heard was the sound of his leather utility boots stepping through the freshly cut grass. As he neared the house, no lights were on, not even from Charlie's bedroom, but he was a small boy and even on Friday nights, children still had bedtimes.

He squeezed his way through the boxwood bushes aligning the house's exterior, desperately trying to dodge the thistles and thorns on a few of the shrubs. He pressed his back against the white siding and quietly moved towards the living room window. The window sat low, so he dropped to his knees and started his military crawl. He took a breath and sat under the window, listening to the laughter of the four girls.

The windows were securely sealed, yet he could faintly make out the words from the movie they were watching. He envisioned them huddled around the television watching their movie, when suddenly the movie ended and their conversation began.

He listened as Whitney expressed hopes of fixing Scarlett's hair and was shocked when she subsided to their wishes. His heart sank as he heard Scarlett dismiss her sister and his blood started to boil with the audacity of Lucy's smugness. "You little…" he started to say under his breath when suddenly a light came on overhead. He quickly scooted in his legs to his chest, still fearful of being seen.

"You never know," he heard Lucy say directly overhead, as her shadow landed on him like a stone. He knew that if she just looked down he could be seen. His cover could be blown, and the mission would never recover.

He held his breath as if his lungs filling with air would be the sound of a gang of dogs barking. He clinched his eyes as if telling himself that if he couldn't see them, then they couldn't see him. He knew that these notions were not rational, but he wasn't thinking rationally at the time. Even though he had spent his entire existence doing what he loved to do, it seemed that with each new job, there came new insecurities, new problems, and new enemies.

"Are you going to help me or not?" Whitney muffled through the glass.

"I'm coming. I'm coming," Lucy answered as the weight of her shadow dissipated off Josiah's back. "You're bossy."

"Not bossy," Whitney snickered, "just in charge of fashion matters."

Josiah uncurled his legs to straighten them onto the ground. He looked up and noticed that his head was inches from the window. He'd had a close call, but he didn't need another one. He rolled around, allowing his back to hit the ground and lay comfortably in the dirt. He closed his eyes, listening to the chatter of girls talking and laughing. Well, all of them except for Amelia.

CHAPTER 45

"Do you hear that?" Lucy asked Scarlett as they laid on the living room floor, snuggled in their sleeping bags.

Scarlett opened one of her eyes to examine the darkened room, listening intently, but hearing nothing out of the ordinary. "Hear what?"

"You don't hear that?" Lucy shot up, throwing the covers off her and starting to walk around the pitch-black room. She held her hands out like a zombie to watch out for the end table and lamp, but all she found was the door frame across the room.

"All I hear is Whitney's snoring," Amelia answered without batting an eye.

"That's Whitney?" Lucy gasped as she tried to find her spot beside Scarlett. "I thought it was an animal outside."

"No, just Whitney," Scarlett yawned. "I guess we're just used to it, since she has been snoring like that ever since we had our first sleepover."

"It did unnerve me the first time I heard it, but now I just sleep through it," Amelia said as she rolled over onto her side to get more comfortable.

"I would never expect her to sound like that," Lucy whispered with a snicker.

"Yeah, but she denies that she snores," Scarlett stated with a chuckle that she tried to hold in, but couldn't.

"She denies it?" Lucy asked, slipping her legs back into her red thermal sleeping bag.

"We've even taped her snoring and she makes excuses," Scarlett said lying with her arms wrapped over her head. "The best one was when she said it was the heater kicking on, but it was in June. No one turns their heater on in June."

"Yeah, it would have been as hot as Hell if that happened," Lucy commented with her eyes still fully awake.

"Watch your tongue," Amelia snapped.

"What? It's just a place," Lucy said sitting up again, hoping she struck a nerve with Amelia.

"There's no proof of that place, and it just isn't appropriate to say with the religious connotation behind it," Amelia ranted.

"Oh, it's real alright," Lucy whispered to Scarlett.

The room was silent except for the ceaseless snoring that seemed to fill the room. Lucy tried to sleep, but the snoring echoed in her ears louder and louder as each minute ticked by. She tapped Scarlett on the shoulder. "Are you asleep?"

Scarlett kept her eyes closed and mumbled something incoherent, but slowly started to enunciate her words. "Why aren't you asleep?"

"I keep hearing the snoring and I can't sleep," Lucy answered fully awake.

Scarlett rolled over onto her side to hear Lucy better. "It took me a while to sleep through it, but now I don't even hear it."

"I don't know if I will ever get used to it," Lucy moaned in sleepy agony.

The two girls stared at each other for a few seconds until Lucy broke the silence once again. "What's up with you and Josiah?"

"He's just a nice guy," Scarlett answered sleepily.

Lucy shook her head in disagreement. "I don't trust him."

"Well, he saved my life, so I think I can trust him," Scarlett said between yawns.

"How well do you really know him? I mean, why is he always there to save you? To me, it sounds like he is following you," Lucy said suspiciously.

"I don't know, Lucy," Scarlett said as her eyes started to feel the weight of being awake at this hour.

"Don't you think you shouldn't be so trusting to an older man? For all we know, he could be a molester." Scarlett opened her eyes and looked at her in disbelief, but the words were filtering into her ears. "You don't know where he is from. You don't know anything about him except he works at the same school you go to and he saved your life. I wouldn't trust him if I was you."

Scarlett ingested every word Lucy was saying and somehow, even though she felt safe around Josiah, she had to admit that Lucy did have a good point.

"He is just a weird old man who is trying to get to you, Scarlett. Don't trust him," Lucy said as she closed her eyes.

"He is a little different," Scarlett said, her voice subsiding in agreement to Lucy.

"Men his age don't talk to kids our age without some agenda. He has something up his sleeve," Lucy continued.

"He does only talk to Amelia and me," Scarlett said as she closed her eyes in thought.

"You two are twins; you look alike. No wonder he only talks to you two. He likes you, so he would also like Amelia."

"Will you shut up, Lucy?" Amelia shouted with uncontrollable rage causing Whitney to say something in her dream state. "Josiah is a very caring man. You're just trying to see something that isn't there for your own agenda."

"And what would my agenda be?" Lucy spit back with anger flaring from her lips.

Amelia got up from the floor and stomped her feet upstairs to her bedroom with her pillow under her arm. "See, Scarlett, the brainiac couldn't even answer my question. Don't trust him."

CHAPTER 46

Dan sat alone in the Bethany Country Club dining room, watching the rain pelt the solar-insulated windows that spanned around the room allowing the diners a perfect view of the PGA-worthy golf course as they enjoyed their four-star meals. He glanced down at his watch and noticed that James was a few minutes late. He was saddened that the game of golf had been canceled due to the inclement weather, but he was more grief-stricken with the scandals of Pharm Laboratories.

He sat in contemplation of how to start the dialogue, or if he should even mention what he knew about the fraudulent patents. He was the legal counsel for Pharm Laboratories, Inc. and they should have been up front and honest with him from the very beginning. He had dealt with different types of cases, many of which where he knew of his client's guilt and had to use his legal forte to bend the laws in the direction he wanted. He loved to play in the gray area of legality; the gray territory was his playground. It was his oasis to find when everything seemed black and white.

He knew he would have to wander into the land of gray and take up residence in that state for some time. He wasn't sure exactly when, but the situation was not going to resolve itself quickly. He didn't even have all the pieces to try to fit the corruption into a beautiful picture. Some people would look at his work as tedious legal jargon without any hint of flare.

He looked at his work as a canvas with some painting blotches. There may have been a sky or even some trees that were artistically crafted, but then somehow the artist stopped and started to create a fiasco. His duty was to highlight the singular tree and concoct other images to showcase its superiority. Or in other cases, build a forest of trees to hide the original. Most people would not call his work an art form, but most people only saw what they want to see — a man in a suit who defended the innocent and guilty alike.

"What do you think about this weather?" James asked patting Dan on the back and sticking out his hand in the most gentlemanly fashion.

Dan looked at James' attire and noticed he was sporting his Nike golf wardrobe as well. "I see you were hoping the rain would let up as well," Dan said as he, too, was showcasing his orange nylon polo and pleated khakis.

"So, do you want to do lunch and just wait this storm out?" James laughed as he looked down at the menu.

"I don't think the storm we need to talk about is going to end anytime soon," Dan answered, as James' smug smile remained intact, even as they made eye contact.

CHAPTER 47

"What type of consulting do you do, James?" Dan asked as they stood under a shelter within sight of the clubhouse, shaking off the rain from their quick jog away from the commotion. He stood listening to the rain pour out from the heavens, and the tapping reminded him of one of his relaxation sounds in his office.

"Patents, Dan, patents," James answered with angst-filled breath. "You've known that from the first time we met."

Dan took a step closer to the falling rain, until he felt the cool beads splash on his hairy arms. He stood with his back to James, shaking his head in disgust. "Did you know that they forged the patent documents?"

"Come on, Dan, don't get riled up," James said, trying to lighten the mood.

Dan turned around so he could look squarely into his friend's eyes. "Did you know?"

"Dan, it's going to be okay."

He bit his lip in unrelenting anger as he shook his head almost in a state of convulsion. "James, I will ask you only once more. Give me a straight answer or I will walk away from this project faster than another person will die from the 'cancer helping drug.' Did you know?"

The two grown men stood as if a duel was forming. They didn't have guns, but they each had their chosen weapons, willing and able to slaughter the other, their professional craft. "Yes, I knew," James finally relented with a friendly smile as he decided not to pull out his weapon first. "This is not the first time we fudged some of the paperwork to get a patent quickly."

"Not the first time?" Dan said in a tone of hysteria. "Have you ever legitimately worked on a patent?"

"You are treading on rough waters, Dan. You do what you do best, and I will do what I do best."

"And what is that, fraud?"

"You of all people should know that a little lie here and there isn't the problem in our society. Sometimes the truth is more wrong than a thousand lies." James started strolling up and down the shelter house, practicing his golf swing with the greatest of ease. "How many times have judges issued the wrong verdict because you had to follow the law? How many criminals are behind bars because of the brotherly police officers watching out for their own, even if it means overlooking some minor incident that would have been tossed out if the defense attorney knew?"

"People have died because of your patent," Dan commented.

"People were going to die without it as well," James said as he took another golf swing and envisioned his ball hitting the nearby green. "Beautiful shot." He dashed away from the cover to enter the waterfall of rain, leaving Dan to contemplate his next move. It was a decision that would impact not only his future, but possibly the future of millions of others.

CHAPTER 48

Dan sat in his platinum Lexus, dripping water on his leather seats and staring at the text message he'd received ten minutes earlier in the grocery store parking lot. He didn't need any food, but he had to pull over to try to halt his racing heartbeat.

The words on the screen radiated like a skylight, even though they were dimming from the phone's sleep timer. He read and reread the message probably twenty-five times, and each time, he felt the knife in his chest.

"You know what you'd better do if you want to work in the Southeast again."

James had power. Dan had never heard of him before he met him through Pharm Laboratories, Inc., and whenever he tried to research him, he couldn't find anything about this consulting firm, JS Consulting, LLP, on the Internet. He was just as elusive as the Mirabile Dictu. And that scared him.

Dan had always heard of secret societies of high-profiled professionals and politicians, but he thought they were merely urban legends that got glamorized through Hollywood. Sadly, the mythical dragon seemed to have wielded its ugly head into Dan's nonfictional life.

Gray Saturdays were always a mood breaker, and it seemed that gray was an understatement for outcomes of the day. He left the engine running a mild hum; he could hear music faintly playing through the stereo, but he wasn't listening. All he heard was the sound of his world shattering around his feet like a tower of porcelain plates colliding with the foreseen ground.

He loved the law and he loved his work. How could one man have the gall to beckon power at a drop of a hat as if he were a god? James' claim was so full of pride and arrogance that Dan wished for him to fall from his false pedestal of grace. He wanted him to fall and come crawl on his knees for compassion, but deep down, he knew that would not likely happen. Deep down, Dan saw the charismatic charm of James and knew that James probably had better connections than he. Despite the fact that Dan was a well-known and beloved attorney in the Southeast, he knew that his reputation couldn't stand up against forces of an unknown alliance.

Picking up the phone, he texted James as if hypnotized. He read the message, and he couldn't believe what he had typed. He hovered his finger over the send button, but he couldn't send it. He looked through the fogging glass at the smiles being worn by customers, splashing through puddles like four-year-olds. He envied their simple lives at that moment.

A water drop fell on his phone, "Great!" he yelled. "A leak. What more could happen?" He tilted his head up to examine the sunroof, but saw nothing to signal a leak. No wet spots, no new drips, no hole. He patted down the ceiling, and it was completely dry.

He glanced up in his rearview mirror and noticed something else. His eyes were red with a single tear stream running down his cheek. He looked down and saw the tear drop on the glass of his phone with a haunting message underneath.

"Message sent."

CHAPTER 49

The girls ended their sleepover late Saturday afternoon, and each one slumbered in their own beds most of the day on a dismally cloudy Sunday. The sisterly tiff between Amelia and Scarlett had subsided after a day of compromised silence. Scarlett eventually broke down Sunday evening and ended the quiet with ulterior motives. She needed to copy Amelia's history homework. Amelia accepted her apology and handed over her map of the United States, listing the National Parks.

Monday morning came early; the sun was blazingly bright as if it had taken the last two days off, recharging and regaining its strength. "Scarlett, why did you undo your hair style?" Whitney exclaimed, seeing that her work of art was back to the blank canvas it was before, straight, unimaginative blond strands of hair. No flare, no dazzle, no wow factor.

"You fixed it three days ago," Scarlett said matter-of-factly.

"Well, you could have waited until tonight to let it down," Whitney said annoyed.

"Tonight? You took it down five minutes after she left on Saturday," Amelia whispered in Scarlett's ear with a hint of a smile that matched the one on Scarlett's face.

"What's so funny?" Lucy asked as she walked up to the group of girls huddled beside their lockers.

"Nothing really," Scarlett lied as she switched topics to her boring Sunday afternoon.

The girls snickered and cackled about their sleepover memories, their mix-matched food concoctions, their truth-or-dare answers, and their infatuated crushes. Suddenly, as if it were meant to be, the herd of princely stallions paraded down the halls. The laughter silenced, their hair was quickly tossed, and their attention suddenly diverted to their heartthrobs.

Luke, the cutest boy in school, was surrounded by all the guys who wanted to be like him. Even though Luke knew that he was something special, he wasn't cocky. He wasn't the stereotypical big man on campus. He had an air of humility around him like a walking paradox.

The circle of girls formed an arc, Scarlett directly in the center with Amelia standing behind the group, unfazed.

"Hey, Scarlett," Luke smiled as he passed by the girls, scanning through the arc, politely nodding to each one. He spotted someone and quickly stopped. He turned back to the silent grouping and made his way to one individual. "Amelia, do you have a minute? I couldn't find one of the parks that was extra credit."

"Yeah, I thought it was a trick question, but I eventually found it," she said as the two headed to the classroom.

The girls stood dumbfounded before deciding their next move. "I couldn't find it either," Whitney shouted as she left their semi-circle to follow the pack of wandering guys. "Kyle, did you find all of them?"

All the girls eventually found the one they were interested in, except for Lucy and Scarlett who stayed beside Lucy's locker as the bell rang for class to begin. "Oh, I need to get my book," Scarlett said to Lucy. "I'll be right in."

Scarlett went down a few lockers and twirled in her combination number.

"Mary, how are you?" Josiah asked from a distance walking up the hall.

"Late," she huffed.

"Well, can I talk to you real quick?"

"Josiah, I need to get to class," she said as she started to walk away.

"Mary, just watch out for Lucy," Josiah said sternly.

Scarlett suddenly came to a jilted halt. "Watch out?"

CHAPTER 50

Tension filled the hallway between Scarlett and Josiah. If the lockers were moved and a tumbleweed rolled along the brown carpet, it might have resembled a gun slinging duel in the Old West.

"What are you talking about?" Scarlett huffed, opening her eyes to what Lucy had seen already.

"Mary, just be careful. That is all I am saying," Josiah tried to reason with her as he took a step closer, slowly diminishing the gap between the two.

"Careful? I think you've lost it," Scarlett said starting to raise her voice slightly.

"Mary, just calm down," Josiah continued to speak softly while taking another step toward Scarlett.

"Calm down? Calm down?" Her voice became louder and louder with each phrase. "Why should I calm down?"

"You've got to trust me, Mary," he said with sympathetic eyes, taking an additional step.

"Trust you?" She started to laugh sarcastically. "I trust Lucy."

Josiah shook his head as he came to a stop. He was still about fifteen feet away, but to Scarlett he was still too close. "Mary, how well do you know Lucy?"

"Who are you to tell me who I can and cannot be friends with?" She turned her back and started walking to her classroom, annoyed that she was already late. She reached her room and stopped before she entered. She turned to Josiah who was now a ten second run away and stated her piece. "You are just a creepy old man who stalks me."

"Mary," he said with a gentle tone of a breaking heart.

"Don't call me Mary," she said as she opened the door to the classroom. "Most of all, don't call me Scarlett either."

She walked into the room as Josiah stood alone in the silent hallway. He slid his finger down a row of lockers as he walked down the deserted hall. He found himself in the familiar lobby of the school with its high-tiered ceilings, large glass windows, and paintings of historic Bethany landmarks and figures. He knew where he was, yet he felt lost. He didn't realize that an angel could feel this way.

His mission was unraveling – one step forward, three steps back.

CHAPTER 51

Cruising down the interstate in his Lexus, he put on his sunglasses to bring relief from the morning sun's blinding rays. He wasn't a spiritual man, but this morning, prayers were being said.

The text message, the blood curdling text message, was all he could think about on Sunday. No golf was played. No *New York Times* crossword puzzle was completed. No ball games were watched. The only comfort he could find was in the arms of someone, someone other than his wife.

He knew that their afternoon rendezvous was scandalous, but he needed something to take his mind off the current problem. The best way to forget about a problem is to find solace in another. He quickly absolved himself of any wrong-doing with Karen by hiding behind the claim that most men had affairs, and the ones that didn't probably wish they had the opportunity for one.

He found a few moments of complete mental bleaching where all his doubts and fears of James were chlorinated to a sparkling shine, but they quickly tainted the busy canvas of his mind. No matter the acts performed in Karen's king-sized bed, the image of his text message kept appearing like an apparition. The chains of Jacob Marley had nothing on his binding contract with James. He knew he was playing with fire, but no matter how much water he had, he was still likely to get burned.

I will do whatever you want. Let's meet at Pharm on Monday at 9, Dan's text message read. *'I will do whatever you want.' Why did I put that line?* Dan thought. *Why didn't I just respond with, "Let's meet at Pharm on Monday at 9." Wouldn't that have sufficed?*

Sadly, he would never know. *I will do whatever you want.*

He knew those six words would come back to bite him. No matter the immunizations, he knew he was going to contract a virus of some kind; he just hoped it wouldn't kill his career instantly. A little lingering in agony was better than digging his own grave.

He came to his exit and saw the massive corporate building sitting on top of a perfectly landscaped hill. It was an architectural marvel with steel geometric curves and angles protruding through and around the glass tower. It resembled a modern art museum more than a laboratory, and with their fraudulent patent, that is what would most likely will occupy this premises in the next few years.

He parked his car and took a few deep breaths before making his way to the entrance. Walking into the spacious lobby, he was awestruck with the way the sun cascaded through the glass, reflecting off the steel rings. He had come to Pharm Laboratories, Inc. many times but never this early in the morning. He walked across the marble floor as his leather shoes clip-clopped echoing around the grand entrance. "Good morning, Michelle," Dan said as he approached the lobby attendant behind a slick modern desk. "Isn't it a lovely morning?"

"Oh, yes. Always breath-taking in the morning, Mr. Sutton," she said as she picked up the phone and smiled in his direction. "Mr. Sutton is here. Yes, sir, I will."

She hung up the phone and smiled radiantly. "Mr. Nialliv is on his way to get you. They are in the conference room."

A lump went into his throat when she said his name. "Thank you," he tried to say, but the air didn't come out clearly.

"Do you need a mint?" she asked as she opened her desk drawer to offer him a piece from her candy store – peppermints, wintergreens, butterscotches, lemonheads, and more chocolate than one should have on Valentine's Day.

"Thank you," Dan said as he unwrapped the red and white cinnamon disk. Licking his lips, he tasted the sweetness of the cinnamon, only for it to quickly diminish by the sourness of the opening of the elevator doors.

151

"Good to see you, Dan," James said as he held out his hand in greeting.

Dan politely received the handshake and stepped into the small elevator. "Good to see you too," Dan lied with a hearty laugh.

The doors closed and the two men proceeded to the corporate floor. Each was dressed to kill in designer custom-fitted suits that exhibited their best qualities. The two men stared into each other's reflection, as if judging one another in a beauty contest. They were both attractive fit men, with charisma that could charm any woman. The silence was broken by the beep of the elevator signaling the doors were about to open for the passengers to depart, followed by a proud haughty statement. "I thought you would see it my way," James said with a boisterous grin before slapping Dan on the back and clutching his shoulders as the doors opened.

Once again, the air in Dan's lungs didn't allow him to speak. All he could do was shiver at James' bullying touch.

CHAPTER 52

Stepping into the spacious conference room with plasma widescreen televisions displaying the Pharm Laboratories, Inc. logo on the four walls, each flashing images of beautiful brainy models in white lab coats, Dan felt the importance of this meeting weighing on his back. Todd Clements, CEO of Pharm Laboratories, Inc., was seated at the head of the thirty-seat conference table on the other side of the room surrounded by Karen and an unfamiliar individual.

James was walking a little faster than Dan, who appeared to have a little kick in his step. "Good to see you again, Dan," Todd said as he stood up to shake his hand. Even though Todd was CEO of a large multi-million, soon to be billion dollar corporation with a reputation of being bigger than life, he was a rather frail gentleman in his fifties.

Dan stood beside Todd during their greeting and noticed for the first time that he was at least a head taller than him. Dan was average height at 5'11", so it wasn't because Dan was a tall individual. So often people visualize or idealize presidents and leaders in the business world as tall, strong, dependable generals who built their businesses with their own two hands with little to no help from anyone else. The slight build of Todd was a little amusing.

A smile formed on Dan's face and then was immediately replaced. "Dan has agreed to handle our delicate situation," James spoke up as each person took their seat.

"Stop with the straight-laced talk, James," Todd huffed with a tone of annoyance. "No matter how well you spin the last few months, we are still in a long battle ahead."

"That is why I have asked Jud Askin, vice president of public relations, to join us in our meeting today," James said, quickly darting his eyes toward Dan and then to the man whom Dan had never seen before. "He is the one who is going to spin the whole last few months from deaths and legal suits into smiley faces and balloons."

Jud sat perfectly still looking into his lap for a few moments, while Dan wondered about the long pause. Dan stared and continued to wonder if Jud was trying to bring some cinematic climax or if he was taking a moment to bask in the glowing review. It was neither.

James tapped Jud's arm and startled him from his wide-eyed sleep. "Oh, forgive me. I was in deep thought," Jud said in a soft-spoken tone.

"As I was saying, Jud, you are the man who is going to paint a lovely landscape on the canvas that used to only show a broken-down shack in a compost pile."

"Yes, yes," Jud quickly perked up. "It may not be easy, but it really isn't as hard as it may appear. If given the opportunity I could spin Hitler into the Messiah, and after a few weeks, the world would be calling him a god."

"I don't mean to doubt your abilities, Jud, but what have you done in the past?" Dan asked as Todd wiggled in his chair like a child on Christmas Eve.

"Do you remember the sex scandal with Senator Gilmore of Virginia three years ago?" Jud asked, finally looking confident in his stature. His eyes looked alert and his body posture dramatically rose into an authoritative stance.

"Do I? It was all over the news for an entire summer," Dan announced.

"Well, what happened in the fall?" Jud asked playfully.

"I, well…" Dan started to stammer in his speech and then regained his composure. "To be honest, I don't recall."

"Well, I don't want to spill the beans, but Senator Gilmore is riding high in Washington, and in a few months, he will be announcing his candidacy for president," Jud said firmly. The room was filling with smiles. "I don't want to brag, but without me, he wouldn't even be able to run for employee of the month at Wal-Mart."

"So, what do you plan to do here?" Karen asked, since this was the first time she had ever met her savior.

"I have slowly been scouting the waters of this patent error, which no one knows about yet and never will." Jud stood up and commanded the room's attention with his charisma. He went from being the dead weight to being the living, breathing hope.

"I am so pleased to have you on board here," Todd proclaimed. "Thank you, James for finding this godsend."

"My reputation is on the line here as well as yours, Todd. If you fail, I fail," James added with a hearty laugh that seemed to be contagious as everyone joined. Everyone but Dan. James smiled an infectious smile and then glared at Dan.

Dan's stomach hit the floor. James' smile was infectious, but infectious with what?

CHAPTER 53

"I feel much, much better," Karen said as she reclined behind her desk, propping her feet on it, allowing herself to breathe a sigh of relief for the first time in a month.

Dan quickly shut the door and suspiciously examined the room. He didn't know what he was looking for, but something was throwing him off kilter. "Karen," he whispered with anxious breath, "do you really?"

The question caught her off guard. She slowly and strategically slid her feet from her desk and returned them to the floor. "Did you really ask that question?" she asked in normal tone. "And why are you being so nervous?"

"You didn't answer my question," Dan said as he paced around the room as if stopping would show a sign of surrender.

"Yes, I really do feel better." She laughed emphatically as she grabbed a bottle of water from the refrigerator behind her desk.

"Why?" Dan prodded in a mysterious tone.

"Why not?" Karen interjected, as if that question would answer all the others.

He stared dumbfounded at her lack of judgment in this pinnacle hour of her career and in the lives of possibly millions. "What did James or the great Jud say that made you feel such at ease?"

Her eyes scanned the room's ceiling as if she was going to find an answer painted there. "Look at what he did with the sex scandal," she said opening up her email to see that she had six new messages.

"Yes, he resolved that issue, but what did he say about this situation we are in now? It's easy to pick a case you won and show all the beauty and resolution, but what about other cases? I bet he has had more than one client, and I bet he has had some negative outcomes." Dan stammered through his speech with multiple long pauses while he contemplated his next words. Unlike his closings which were always

156

well-rehearsed with dramatic essence, this tirade was not going to persuade Karen.

"I bet, if we are being honest, you too have lost some cases in your past, but you didn't mention those when we approached you for legal counsel," Karen snidely remarked.

Dan stopped like a deer in the road -- an easy target. He had left himself vulnerable to that comment, and if he had some more planning he would not have opened that can of defeated histories. "True," he said as he raised his hands to show his humility. "But Jud didn't mention one thing he was going to do to spin the deaths of all the patients who are using your drugs."

"He did too," she forcefully stated as she deleted one of her emails.

"Tell me then."

Her eyes were fixed on the computer screen; apparently an important email had arrived and Dan's presence in the room had been forgotten.

"Karen, tell me what he said," he repeated with a little more tenacity. Yet his words ricocheted once again. "Karen!" he shouted as he looked over her shoulder to see the email she was reading. "Did you know about this?" Dan asked, commenting on the email on her screen.

She didn't utter any words, just shook her head. After a few minutes of silence, reading and rereading the email, she finally broke the void with her question. "What does this mean?"

"Exactly what it says, your drug is going to be shipped all over the country and even to parts of Europe," he said with a lump in his throat.

"Yes!" she exclaimed as her fist pounded on the desk.

Dan stared shocked at the happiness in her tone. "Every hospital, clinic, and doctor's office will be able to use your drug on cancer patients."

"I know! Isn't this great?" she once again belted out enthusiastically.

"It would be if the drug healed instead of killed!" He shook his head and once again read who the email was from, his friend, James Nialliv. "Why don't they wait until everything settles down?"

"Why wait when there is nothing wrong? Jud is going to solve this bump in the road," she answered innocently.

Dan proceeded to step away and found himself at the door. He opened it to leave and turned to see Karen still glued to her computer screen. He said goodbye, but she didn't acknowledge his departure. He journeyed down the hall, went down the lonely elevator, and found himself leaving the high-tech lobby. As he passed the employees of Pharm Laboratories, he couldn't offer any words of congratulations. He had another question to ask instead.

Who's going to solve the bumps in the graveyards?

CHAPTER 54

White cotton Egyptian six-hundred count threads covered Claire's lovely legs as she sat up in bed with her latest book. The stained-glass Tiffany lamp on the nightstand lit up the entire room, coloring the tan walls with a collage of reds and blues, with glimpses of violet splotches. She ended her chapter and slid her embroidered bookmark that her grandmother had handcrafted between the crisp pages before closing the hardbound book.

Reaching over to the nightstand, she grabbed her cell phone, hoping she had missed a call as she was reading. The book was one of the last things on her mind, but she was trying to think of matters other than the present. She opened her cell phone and noticed the time was 1:03 a.m., with no missed calls or messages.

Closing her phone, she clutched the device next to her chest like it was Mother Teresa's rosary. She quietly started muttering random words. She wasn't sure if she was going crazy with nonsense talk, or if this was the start of a very desperate prayer, from a very desperate woman.

"Dan, please come home," she quivered, but as she said the words, she wondered why she was saying them. The last couple of weeks, Dan had been anything but home. He still ate breakfast at home, showered at home, and slept in their bed at home, but he wasn't his normal home self. He was emotionally unavailable. He was distant. He was different.

After thinking of the last few weeks, Claire whispered a new prayer, similar in wording but with a totally different meaning, "Dan, please come back home." After a few minutes of tearful weeping, she replaced her cell phone on the nightstand. She got out of bed and roamed the hallway, checking on each of her three wonderful children. Each was soundly asleep, curled up or sprawled over their beds. She

159

smiled at their ignorant bliss, even admitting they were not ignorant. They, too, noticed a change in their home.

She turned to go back to her lonely bedroom, but the thought of sleeping alone caused her knees to buckle. She grabbed onto Charlie's doorframe to keep herself from falling hard. She gripped the paneling, almost causing her fingernails to dig into the wood. Her strength was weakening and she gently lowered herself like a rose petal to the hard ground. She felt as fragile as the plants she loved so well.

After regaining her composure, she crawled her way to her bed and between the elegant sheets. She tugged on the light's chain and the lighted room vanished into the night. She curled up and fell into a mournful sleep.

An hour passed and something startled Claire from her sleep. "Dan, is that you?" she asked, hoping her husband was home.

Nothing was said in return. She rolled over in her bed and bumped into a lump in the bed. It was too dark to see her husband, so she rolled closer to him, snuggling her head into his neck when she realized something was different. His curly locks were missing. She softly stroked his hair and realized that it was the second man of her life in bed with her. She kissed the back of his head and wrapped her long arms around his body. "I love you, Charlie."

CHAPTER 55

The aroma of coffee wafted upstairs, widening Josiah's sleepy eyes. He deeply inhaled the smell of hazelnut caffeine and woke with a dismal gesture on his face. The night had been long with plenty of tossing and turning as he replayed the look on Mary's face and her cold back as she walked away from their friendship.

He knew that if he wasn't in his situation, their bond would not have ever started. He was given a plan to gain her trust. Even though he didn't initiate the deadly close calls, he knew their possibility. He'd used her fear and insecurity to slide into her life as a hero, a confidant, a friend, and an angel.

Josiah got up out of bed and slowly dressed for the day. The morning was telling him it was time for breakfast, but his stomach was telling him that food wouldn't go through the many knots that had become entangled in the last twenty-four hours. He went downstairs to the kitchen to find Mrs. Stapleton flipping flapjacks on the bubbling griddle.

"Do you want a stack?" she smiled as she tossed a pancake into the air, allowing it to somersault and land perfectly on the spatula.

"No thank you," he calmly stated as he grabbed a coffee cup from the cabinet.

She examined his exterior and grimaced with a shaking head. "You need to eat something."

"I wish I could, but I just don't feel like it," he answered as he poured his hot drink and lifted the cup to his nose, letting the steam invade his nostrils.

Mrs. Stapleton finished cooking her last pancake and arranged three of them on her plate. Drizzling maple syrup and powdered sugar over the golden-brown circles, she tried her best to make the plate appear appetizing. "Doesn't this look good?"

"Yes, ma'am, it does," Josiah politely smiled as he took a seat, staring at his reflection in the toaster.

She cut into her sweet breakfast and took a bite. She thoroughly enjoyed the swirling of flavors in her mouth. "You are missing out."

He smiled in response as he continued to stare at his reflection. He wasn't intentionally ignoring her, but he had other matters on his mind. Matters that needed to be resolved soon, or everything that had transpired in the last few weeks would be worthless.

"Are you okay, Josiah? You aren't acting like yourself this morning."

He heard the question, but he wasn't sure how to answer. No, he wasn't okay. Thoughts were tossing around in his head like waves in an ocean. They were colliding on his skull, causing an 8.2 magnitude earthquake in his head. He needed to get back into Mary's realm of trust, but after yesterday, he knew it wasn't going to be an easy fix. At that age, a friend's opinion was always more relevant than an adult's.

"Do you need anything?"

He shook his head no, even though he desperately needed some reassurance. He needed to know that everything would somehow sort itself out. Even though he knew that everything had fallen apart, he hoped that the group on the other side of the line hadn't learned of his failure.

Sadly, he knew that if he believed he had faltered, they knew as well.

"Josiah, you don't look good."

CHAPTER 56

The week had been long, and it was only Thursday. Josiah sat and reflected on the course of the week, but as he recalled the moments of the last few days, the more depressed he became. It seemed that whatever Josiah tried only ended in defeat.

Dear Home,

I feel like such a failure. Events have conspired in the last twenty-four hours that have blindsided me more than I would have thought possible. I am unsure what to do, and the only thing I know to do is ask for help!

Please send someone here for a few days. I just need to see a friendly face and try to get my bearings back. I am going to do my best to get back on good terms with the girl, but it is going to be difficult. The only hope I have is the good standing I have with her twin.

This, too, shall pass, but I don't want it to pass before my eyes.

Can someone be here tonight?

Josiah

He watched the page with built-up anticipation, praying that the words would dissipate from the paper quickly and his request would be granted. He watched as nothing happened.

His heart began to pace like a gallop at Churchill Downs. His breathing became shorter, and beads of sweat were starting to form on his brow. *What's going on?* he thought. He had written thousands of letters using this technique and never once had it failed.

Clutching the notepad to his chest, he fell on his bed and grunted a prayer. He muffled a groan and yearned using incomprehensible sounds. The noises sounded vaguely familiar to wild animals in pain, perfectly demonstrating how he felt.

He knew he needed to look down, because maybe there was a delay in their system and the words had disappeared. He knew he needed to look, but his head wouldn't budge.

Lifting the notepad, he raised it inches above his nose as his racing heart came to a screeching halt.

Nothing had changed.

CHAPTER 57

"Mrs. Stapleton! Mrs. Stapleton!" Josiah called as he clutched the ink pen -- an ink pen that advertised *Bethany National Bank* on the casing. "Mrs. Stapleton!"

"Coming, Josiah!" she calmly shouted back as she swallowed a bite of her pancakes and slowly started to make her way up the stairs. "Coming."

Josiah jumped up from the bed and quickly hid his notepad with his letter clearly legible under his single pillow. He opened the bedroom door to find Ethel nearing the last step.

"Is this your pen?" he asked as he raised the unfamiliar pen to her face.

"Yes, but you can use it," she huffed as she was out of breath from making the journey as fast as she could. "Is that all you needed?"

"No. Where is my pen?" he asked pointedly.

She drew in a large breath and started to explain. "A few days ago I came up here to change your bedsheets, and as I was taking them off I remembered that I needed to purchase a dozen eggs since I was down to just two. I don't know why it hit me when I was up in your room, but it did." She kindly smiled as she made her way past Josiah into his bedroom and sat down on the edge of his bed. "I knew that I would probably forget so I saw your notepad and pen and I scribbled eggs on it with a few other items. I went into the bathroom and noticed you were almost out of mouthwash so I scribbled that down as well."

"But where is my pen now?"

"Well, when I went down to take your bedsheets I forgot to take my list. I came back about ten minutes later to get it. I was kind of proud of myself that I remembered the list, only I noticed that my words had disappeared."

"Disappeared?" he said shocked.

165

"Yes, I was flabbergasted," she laughed. "I remembered writing down the items, because at first I put chicken down as well, and when I realized that we had chicken just the other night I went back and scribbled it out and then added your mouthwash."

"And it just disappeared?"

"Yes, strange, isn't it?"

"Very," he said, still somewhat confused. "So the items disappeared when you wrote eggs, chicken, and mouthwash?"

"Well, I scribbled chicken out," she added, making sure that her story was accurate. "So when the ink disappeared, I wrote it again and placed it in my purse. When I got to the store for the items, the paper was blank once again. Luckily, I remembered them and wrote it down again so I wouldn't forget as I was in the store. I have done that many times," she laughed. "I have gone into the store for a can of tomatoes and have walked out with an ear of corn and a carton of milk. Old age is unrelenting."

"I know how that is," he smiled.

"Well, when I got home, I went upstairs and put away your mouthwash and threw away your pen."

Josiah's heartbeat once again started to pick up speed. "Threw it away? Mrs. Stapleton, please tell me where. It was a, um, a…" he tried to come up with an excuse on the spot, "a gift."

"Oh, Josiah, I am very sorry." She got up from the chair and went into his bathroom. "I threw it away in here, but I don't think I took the trash out yet. I was going to get it later today for the trash man tomorrow."

Josiah followed her into his bathroom and watched as she bent down and picked up a long plain black ink pen. His heart began to race with excitement for a change. "Here you go, Josiah," she said as she handed him the pen. "I'm sorry for the mistake."

"Oh, it is no mistake. I just don't want to part with it. Memories."

166

"I totally understand," she answered as she left Josiah to clutch his only true belonging.

He stared into the trashcan and noticed a wadded-up piece of paper. He unrolled it and smoothed out the crinkled edges. It was the list that Ethel had made, and just like she said, she'd added a few new items.

Cherries

Eggs

Oatmeal

Mouthwash (Josiah).

Josiah felt the warmth of a smile spread onto his face. He didn't know what was funnier, Mrs. Stapleton unknowingly sending a letter to his home, or his home receiving her grocery list, twice.

Quickly he went into his room and started to copy his letter, using his pen this time.

Message sent.

CHAPTER 58

"Dan, I'm...I'm..." Karen stuttered as he set his briefcase down and walked to her behind her desk.

"What? What is it?" he asked. "I got your message, but you weren't making any sense. I understood the comment about the threatening email but nothing else."

She picked up a sheet of paper from her printer with her trembling hands and handed it to Dan. "Just read it."

Dear Dr. Death,

Your little cancer drug didn't work. They said that without your drug she could live 6 months, and with it she would live at least 2 years and even be cancer-free. She only lasted 3 weeks. You killed my mother and now I am going to get you. I will be seeing you soon.

Kisses, your worst enemy.

"Kisses?" Dan coughed at the audacity of the closing. "Who would close the letter with 'kisses'?"

Karen stared at Dan in complete horror. "Is that really all you are going to say?" she screamed. "Kisses? This whole letter is a death threat!"

Dan took his focus away from the letter and moved it to Karen. "I'm sorry," he said as he reached over and gave her the warmest hug he could manage. He was a defense attorney that got off CEO's who had swindled their employees' retirement. He received innocent verdicts for insurance companies when they denied health claims that caused the previous insurer to suffer the financial blacklist of bankruptcy. He had been on cases where kids the age of his son were injured and would remain handicapped for life, and gave them a check for pennies of what they would have received if they had obtained better legal counsel.

Death threats were a part of his life. He kept a legal folder for the rare instance that something could happen in the future, but sadly, when he was having a lousy day, he would flip through his threats and remember days when he was doing his job extremely well. When life was peaceful, he needed to work harder.

"This is your first death threat?" he asked stunned.

"Yes, why?" Karen asked as she started nervously playing with the gold chain dangling around her neck before stopping and dropping it at the thought of being choked to death.

"Well, your drug has killed more than one person," Dan stated coldly. "And I would have assumed that more people would have been complaining to you."

"Will you stop talking about the drug killing people?" she asked, exploding like a case of dynamite. "People die everyday day. Car accidents, bee stings, lightning strikes, heart attacks. Death is just a means to an end."

"Yes, but in none of those incidents did a doctor prescribe a medication believing that it would help when only the opposite was bound to happen," he explained as if he was switching sides to be the plaintiff's attorney. From the look on Karen's face, he knew that he had crossed a proverbial line. "Karen, do not worry about this. The person was justifiably upset, but hardly anything comes out of these letters. I mean, when I'm having a good year, I get at least one death threat a week."

She gasped at the morbid notion of a death threat, but mostly at the carefree way he was handling this claim. "Death threats are not common in my industry," Karen said tearfully.

Dan looked down at the letter again and smiled as he read Kisses silently to himself.

"Well, they are now," he said flatly. "You'd better get used to getting them because I bet more will be coming."

"More?" she asked naively. "But why?"

Dan heard the words, but he couldn't believe that Karen said them. He looked at her with bewilderment as she blinked at him blankly. She truly believed she did nothing wrong. For a split second he wondered if she was as smart as all of her degrees, news articles, and reports claimed her to be.

Sadly, he knew she was a genius. He was also learning she was also very egocentric.

CHAPTER 59

The atmosphere in the school cafeteria was unlike any Josiah had felt before on any of his missions. He painstakingly watched Mary giggle and laugh with Lucy and the girls as his heart crumbled, knowing the grand plan was falling apart as well. He continued to wipe down the macaroni and cheese-crusted table edges, but from a distance, watching Mary's every move, of which she was totally aware.

"Why are you laughing?" Whitney asked Scarlett, confused as she nibbled on her cup of diced peaches. "I didn't say anything funny. Did I?" she asked once again, looking around at the gang of girls who all shook their heads.

"Sorry," Scarlett said with another forced giggle as she looked in Josiah's direction. "I guess I'm just having a good day and I cannot stop laughing!" she shouted so everyone in the noisy cafeteria could hear. "Just an awesome day!"

"What's so awesome?" Jackie questioned. "We have a quiz next period and I am clueless. I spent all night practicing my lay-ups and free throw shots." She looked around the table and found Samantha was the only one giving her eye contact. "Thanks for listening, Sam."

"You're welcome," Samantha said with a smile but quickly whispered in Lucy's ear, "What's a lay-up?"

"I was listening, Jackie," Amelia spoke up from behind her latest book. "And you have nothing to worry about for your quiz next period. It's just an essay on the steps of the scientific method."

"How do you know?" Jackie stared wide-eyed with utmost reverence, as if Amelia was reading Tarot cards and telling Jackie she was going to meet the man of her dreams under the sycamore tree on her twenty-third birthday.

"Jackie, Mrs. Pruitt told us in class yesterday," Scarlett giggled hysterically. "Sometimes you say the funniest things."

The entire table unknowingly began step one of the scientific method on Scarlett — ask questions. Scarlett's laugh started to rise higher in decibels and greater in length. Confused looks and gawks ran wild around the lunch table and soon around the entire room. Amelia even put down her book and stared at the commotion of Scarlett's obnoxious laugh.

"Scarlett, simmer," Amelia snapped as she examined the room and found that everyone's eyes were on her sister.

"Can't help a good laugh," Scarlett explained, trying to calm herself down, but she caught a glance of Josiah's eyes looking into hers. "Good times with true good friends."

"You're nuts," Amelia muttered as she stuck her nose back into *The Great Gatsby*. "You're almost as shallow as Daisy."

"I love daisies," Samantha commented as she spanned the table, "especially when they are weaved into my hair. Just beautiful."

"Wrong daisy, you nitwit," Amelia said, disguising her words with a cough so the rest of the girls wouldn't understand. Well, all but Scarlett and Lucy.

CHAPTER 60

The rosebush stretched its branches up along the trellis, weaving its vines and blooms through the small white ladder. Josiah stopped and examined the beautiful petals before he inhaled the lovely fragrance. A bee in the nostril would be just the precipice for the events of the past few days.

Josiah was in a bad mood and people knew it. Viktor asked him a few times throughout the day if anything was bothering him. He said everything was fine, but Vik didn't believe him.

Josiah stood in the front of Mrs. Stapleton's yard, and for the first time all day he was taking a moment to smell the roses. He needed a moment of refreshment because he was feeling beaten up and defeated. He trailed around the yard, examining the flowery treasures that he often overlooked, whether due to laziness or busyness. He was finally seeing the beauty in a rose garden.

Shouts of laughter were heard up the street, soon drowned out by a group of boys on their bicycles with playing cards taped on their metal bars to imitate an engine. They were hustling up and down the street, trying to get as much wind in their hair before their mothers hollered for them to come home for supper.

Josiah stood, watching the boys ride their imaginary Harley Davidsons as he started to let the events of the day fall off his shoulders. The grand statue he had been creating was now a broken heap of marble with rough edges once again. He had metaphorically chiseled a little too much causing him to start fresh again. Imagining the fresh piece of rock, he was finally beginning to see that even though his plan did not work out as he intended, it still might work out in the end. It was not the checkpoints that matter in the race, it was the finish line. This situation he was in was just a hurdle that he was going to have to either skip and be disqualified or run and leap and continue on the race. Quitting wasn't an option; he was going to leap.

Quickly he stepped up to the porch and opened the door to enter his current residence. He turned around and smiled at the landscape from this new perspective. Every rose bush had thorns. You cannot quit watering the rosebush for fear of the thorns, because then you would never get the wonder of the rose. Sometimes a thorn may snag you, but just pluck it out and start fresh the next day. Wounds heal.

"Josiah, where have you been? You have company."

Josiah heard the sweet words of Mrs. Stapleton and suddenly a spring in his step came full force. He was going to jump over his hurdle!

CHAPTER 61

The skip in Josiah's step quickly became a trip on the rug when he turned around and saw his company. It wasn't the friendly face he was expecting. They were no friends of his.

"Josiah, long time no see," one of the guests said, jumping up from the couch to hug Josiah as if they were best friends. Josiah quickly brushed his hug aside, stretching out his hand, as if meeting him for the second time in his life.

"Yes, a very long time," Josiah said forcing a smile for Mrs. Stapleton as he looked over on the couch where he found two more companions, one of which also rising for a friendly greeting.

"Now, let me get this straight. You all used to live together when you were kids?" Mrs. Stapleton asked as she beamed like a proud mom, watching as all her sons return home for a reunion.

"Yes, we go way back," said Carlos, a gentleman who appeared much younger than Josiah in his mid-thirties and without any hint of an accent. His athletic build, full thick black hair and dark Latin complexion would match the cover on any romance novel reader's dream. He smiled and patted Josiah on the back with an all boy's club feel. "Way back."

"But you look much younger, Carlos, than the rest of these men," Mrs. Stapleton added and then quickly apologized for the remark. "No offense, Josiah."

"We are used to it," Maxwell commented as he walked closer to Josiah. "Carlos joined our group after we had been there a while."

"Yeah, these three were my big brothers," Carlos said as he stood in the middle, hugging Maxwell and Josiah in a huddle formation as the other man remained seated on the couch. Carlos had a smile that was infectious, and Mrs. Stapleton couldn't help but emulate the happiness as well.

"You four visit while I finish supper," Mrs. Stapleton said as she started to hum a light-hearted tune as she left the room.

The three men stood shoulder to shoulder as Josiah removed Carlos' arm from his back. "So, coming to check up on me?" Josiah asked as he crossed his arms, trying to show the appropriate defensive body language.

"Come on, Josiah," Maxwell started as he, too, smiled. "This feud has gone on too long." Maxwell was a tall slender man standing about six-foot-six and weighing around two hundred pounds. His head was full of gray, but no wrinkles were found on his facial profile. He appeared the same age as Josiah.

"No, you come on, Max," Josiah quickly retorted with a hint of rage, realizing he needed to control his tone to not startle or alarm Mrs. Stapleton. "Are you spying on me?"

"If we were spying, would we confront you?" Jade asked stoically. He stayed completely still on the couch with his hands clasped together in his lap. "Well, would we?"

Josiah looked at the cool and collected Jade, then fixated on the cunning smile of Carlos, and lastly examined the professional exterior of Maxwell. "I'm really not sure anymore," Josiah answered as he stepped away from Carlos' reach. "The last time I saw you, you backstabbed me," Josiah said as he looked into Carlos' lucid eyes.

Carlos quickly looked down as if checking to make sure his shoelaces were tied.

"Still holding that grudge, Josiah?" Jade defended the silent Carlos. "Really? Isn't it about time to let that go?" he asked as if speaking to a misguided subordinate.

"Never," Josiah answered without wincing.

CHAPTER 62

The meal was fueled with a fiery tension that caused Mrs. Stapleton to give many sideways glances between the four supposed brothers. Ethel oozed hospitality, but Josiah wouldn't budge on his lack of friendliness. Jade and his group of bandits finished their meal and concluded their visit.

"We'll be back," Jade stated coldly to Josiah on the front porch. "You cannot beat us."

Josiah stood frigid, not from the falling temperatures of the breezy night air, but from the icy words resonating in his ears.

"Speechless?" Maxwell asked with a hoity laugh that caused Josiah's frigid veins to immediately boil with rage.

"Come on, Josiah. Join our side," Carlos said enthusiastically, breaking the fog from the mix of emotions to a lighthearted smile. "We could really use your help."

"My help?" Josiah hissed, rolling his eyes at the gumption of switching teams, of joining forces with the men he had worked tirelessly to defeat. "I should be asking you to come back to us."

"Never," Jade stated with a serious tone, stepping forward and forcing Carlos' smile to fade into the shadows of the darkness. "We will never go back. Never. But Josiah, you can do much better than what you are doing now."

"Better? Why would I want to leave?" Josiah responded in bewilderment.

"Josiah, has anyone who left ever returned?" Maxwell asked, knowing that no one who left his organization ever returned, whether due to pride or humiliation. "Don't you think that if we weren't happy we would have tried to return? Or even left our duties and went out solo?"

"No one has ever left our side," Jade answered lifelessly. "Yet, they are still leaving yours."

Jade's words cut deeply to Josiah's core because there was a little truth in them. The ones who left never did return, and there were some that were still leaving.

"If you want money, we can get you that," Carlos once again entered the conversation, trying to hide his smile from the sneering Jade. "If you want power and position, you can work yourself up. If you want less work, that is possible as well. You can have whatever you want, Josiah. Anything you want."

"Well, sounds like your lives are just fantastic," Josiah joked sarcastically. "Why don't I just sign the contract now and end my miserable existence as a slave and work the luxurious lifestyle you have grown accustomed to?" After a moment of pretending to consider their proposal, Josiah shook his head. "Nah, I will keep working for our Father."

"He's not my father!" Jade said with menacing anger behind his words. "He is dead to me. Dead." Jade walked away from the memories of his past with Josiah down the front porch to their car.

Maxwell followed Jade to their black Mercedes without saying a word.

"What about you, Carlos?" Josiah asked. "You can come back. You can always come back."

"Carlos. Now," Jade summoned with dictator-like authority.

"I can't, Josiah," Carlos said as his smile once again faded into the night. "I wish I could, but I can't," he whispered as he hung his head and walked down the porch steps alone. "It was good seeing you," he said before getting into the backseat.

Josiah watched as the Mercedes purred like a kitten then revved like a Siberian tiger. The vehicle spun its tires and raced down the empty street, passing the lamp posts scattered along the sidewalk.

He raced inside to get the keys to Mrs. Stapleton's car, and he was off on a chase. He stepped into her 1984 Buick LeSabre and looked up the street for a smoke trail, but it had already diminished. He didn't see their taillights, but he had an idea where they were going.

CHAPTER 63

The sun had descended over the freshly mowed green horizon three hours earlier. The shimmering and breathtakingly radiant crystal lobby of Pharm Laboratories, Inc. was now dark and haunting. Small glass statues aligned the glass walls that would have been ignored during the daytime but now glistened with intimidating light.

"I don't know what it is, but this place always makes me uncomfortable after dusk," Dan said as Karen walked beside him, grabbing his hand in reassurance.

"It's okay. I'll protect you," she replied before she suddenly stopped, causing Dan to also stop with her tight grip. "Did you see that?"

"You're funny," Dan smiled as Karen froze with fear.

She quickly scanned the entire lobby with her eyes and lowered her voice to a faint whisper. "I'm not kidding. I just saw a shadow."

Dan stared at her acting abilities and became enticed with her persona. He took a step forward to end the awkward moment, but once again Karen didn't move an inch.

"I'm serious," her voice trembled with uncontrollable panic. "Someone's here."

"I don't see anything," Dan commented as he tried to spin around the room, tangled in Karen's arm. He unclenched her death grip and freed himself to get a better look around the room. He trailed around the odd-shaped statues that resembled icy flames, weaving in and out, but found nothing.

"Dan!" she screamed as she pointed at the opposite side of the lobby from where Dan was searching. "There!"

Quickly, he dashed toward the other end of the lobby, running as fast as he could in his black Prada loafers as his suit jacket tail flapped in the passing wind. He stopped at the glass without any heavy breathing and peered out into the darkness. The lighted statues were making it hard for him to see out, but he knew that if someone was outside he could definitely see them. Karen started to moan as he ran into her arms. "What was it? What did you see?"

"I, I, I think I saw someone," she said as she started to slide down his body like a fireman's pole, causing him to reach under her arms to keep her up. "Dan, I'm scared."

"It's okay. I've got you."

Karen didn't feel encouraged by his words. Yes, he was currently holding her up, but she didn't know for how long. "What if he's here?" she asked with a shaking horror film voice.

"Who?" Dan asked as he once again looked around the room for a shadow, a person, or even a sign that someone was nearby. He hadn't seen any proof of anyone, and with the light reflecting on the glass, he seriously doubted she had witnessed a stranger.

"You know," she answered irrationally as her legs suddenly recovered allowing her to head back to the elevator.

"No, who did you see? I didn't see anyone," he said disturbed and confused at her sudden mental break. "What did you see?"

"A shadow outside," she answered, insulted by his unbelieving tone, and slamming her finger on the elevator button. "I saw someone walking around outside and they saw me!"

"Did you see one person or more than one person?" he asked.

The elevator door opened and Karen scurried inside, welcoming the brightly lit empty steel room. "I'm…I'm not sure."

CHAPTER 64

The journey home from the evening scavenger hunt was eerily quiet. Josiah had switched off Mrs. Stapleton's radio as soon as he got in the borrowed vehicle, so all he heard was the clamor in his own head. His thoughts were racing like a hamster wheel, spinning wildly, yet going nowhere.

The rat race began with his first inclination that they would be heading to James' temporary residence about ten miles away to discuss their meeting with him and any future plans they needed to refine. He went through the hilly winding country roads, passing herds of sleeping cows, acres of soybean fields, and an occasional bubbling creek.

After twenty minutes of driving, Josiah coasted by James' home and noticed that all the lights were off except for the front porch. He wanted to stop and step inside since the coast appeared to be clear, but that could wait for another time. Now, he was on a chase without any scent.

He thought about going to James' office, but he wasn't quite sure where it was located. James moved from town to town like a cardinal building a new nest every few weeks or months. For all he knew, James' office could be in his cold, lonely dining room.

Glancing down at the clock, he saw it was still fairly early, fifteen minutes to nine. The only other place that he could think of the hoodlums going was Pharm Laboratories, Inc. He looked down at the gas gauge and mentally thanked Ethel for her half tank of gas. He whipped the car around and took the same hilly road to the center of the controversy.

Josiah sped through the now familiar roads and found his way up to Pharm's entrance at breakneck speed. He turned off the headlights and proceeded up the path to the mysteriously darkened back parking lot. Getting out of the car, he waited a few seconds for his eyes to adjust to night vision. After a few careful steps, his sight was good enough to continue up to the headquarters at a light jog.

Climbing up a grassy hill, he found himself a few steps away from the building. He cautiously looked around in all directions, saw that the coast was clear, and rolled over and down the hill, only stopping when his back hit the glass exterior. He turned around and looked in the desolate interior and only saw an empty office with the Pharm logo swimming as the computer's screensaver.

He guided his way around the building until he found himself near the front lobby. He peered his head towards the parking lot and saw only two vehicles, neither were the black Mercedes.

They have to be here, he thought as he took a few more steps, hoping he could see more of the parking lot and maybe a few more vehicles.

Sadly, no other cars were found. He tilted his head up to the starry heavens and looked for a constellation to guide him. Even though he loved the night sky, he could rarely find the needle in the star stack, except for the obvious Big Dipper. He knew the stars couldn't tell his fate, yet when he turned around and looked into the lobby, he knew Karen's face could if he stuck around for another few minutes. It was time to flee.

He had been seen.

CHAPTER 65

"Girls, you need to start getting ready for bed!" Claire yelled from the bathroom as she scrubbed the head of her little man with his tear-free shampoo. "Eyes," she said to Charlie as she dumped a cup of water over his head, letting the soapsuds fall down to the lukewarm bathwater.

"Mommy, where's Daddy?" Charlie asked as he tried to wipe his eyes dry with his wet hands.

Claire smiled at her son as she scooped some bathwater into her cup. "Eyes," she said again as he clinched his eyes shut with deadbolt effort. She dumped the cup once again, trying to get every last soap bubble from his precious scalp.

Quickly she got another cup of water and splashed it on his head. "Mom, you didn't say 'eyes'," he gurgled as the water trickled down his open eyes and mouth.

"Gotcha," she said with a smile as she got up from her knees, drying her hands on his blue bath towel that she had laid out with his Cars underwear and baseball uniform pajamas. "You have five minutes to finish up, and then you'd better be out and dry and in your pj's."

"Where's Daddy?" he asked again as she was about to leave the bathroom.

The words went over her like the cup of water she recently dumped on Charlie, but unlike Charlie, it felt more like the force of a waterfall. "He'll be home soon. He's just working late."

"But I want him to read me my story," he said as he splashed around in the tub with his plastic boat and GI Joe's.

"Maybe tomorrow night, Charlie. Maybe tomorrow night. But I would love to read the story to you," she said as she stood in the doorway, hoping that another of the Sutton men didn't turn her away.

"Okay," he answered unfazed as he dumped a cup of water over his own head, giggling as he tossed his head around like a wet dog.

The hallway was brightly lit, housing smiling portraits of vacations, preschool graduations, and family photographs, but there was a lingering shadow over her life. She felt the chill in Dan's touch, when he would touch her, but the embraces were rare. She would even be satisfied with a bump in the kitchen or even a roll in the bed in his sleep. At least when she bumped into him, she felt him. It was the little things in life that she missed.

Walking down the hall to a room with laughter she opened the door and found two teenage girls dancing around to the latest Justin Bieber hit. "Are you his next backup dancers?"

"No, Lucy was just showing me his latest video on YouTube, and we were trying to do it," Scarlett said, laughing as she stopped her manic dancing and fell onto her bed.

"Dancing isn't a gift of mine," Lucy answered as she continued to dance around the room, moving her arms and legs chaotically.

"You two are doing fine," Claire laughed as she looked over at the video and tried to gyrate her body like a youthful teenager, flashing back to her Madonna lip-syncing days. "I used to be able to do this."

"Mom!" Scarlett huffed at her old mother since Lucy was in the room, but deep down she thought her mother was pretty cool.

"Fine, I'm leaving. You've got about an hour before lights are out."

"Thanks for letting me spend the night again," Lucy commented as Claire was about to leave.

"We usually don't allow sleepovers on school nights, but this time it's okay," Claire answered recalling her telephone call with James when he said he would be working late and didn't want Lucy to be home alone all night. Claire understood and willingly opened her home, but she didn't want this to become a habit.

"Thanks again," Scarlett said as she walked her mom out of the room and shut the door as Claire left.

"I see how it is," Claire loudly spoke as she walked to check on Amelia. She found quiet Amelia lying on her stomach in her bed, tightly wrapped under the covers. "Why aren't you in there with your sister and Lucy?"

She lifted her head from her recent novel. "I'm tired," she answered with a yawn, "and uninterested," she added with trembling lips.

Claire saw the look in her daughter's eyes that she had seen in her own earlier that night. Walking into the room, she quietly closed her lonely daughter's door. "What's wrong?" she asked as she walked over and sat on the edge of Amelia's bed, stroking her daughter's hair with tenderness and unconditional love.

Amelia felt her mother's warm love which started to melt her icy façade; cracks were forming and chips were starting to fall. "Scarlett has Lucy now."

Claire looked down and watched her strong, intelligent, and independent daughter realize that blood was not always thicker than water. She wanted to cry with her daughter, but she was trying to stay strong. "Honey, I know you hurt," she said as she scooted Amelia over in the bed and lay beside her. She didn't know what else to say. She didn't know what to do because hugs and kisses didn't heal every wound.

Amelia started to quietly sob into her book as Claire lay beside her and gave her the loving touch she wanted so badly from Dan. "She may have Lucy for now, but she will always have you."

Amelia turned her head to her mother's and they stared into each other's wet eyes. Amelia knew that Claire was her mother, but she always thought Scarlett was more like Claire than she. She loved both her parents, but she'd always felt like an outsider in the family. It wasn't anything anyone ever did, but she just felt like the ugly duckling in the Sutton flock even though she and Scarlett looked identical. Claire's eyes were wet with tears rolling down her cheeks. Amelia had

186

seen her mother cry in laugher-filled happiness, at solemn funerals, during a tearjerker movie, and from cutting onions, but this was the first time she saw her mother like this.

Fragile.

They now had a common bond.

CHAPTER 66

Inching down Sycamore Lane, Josiah finally arrived at his destination. The night had been an unsuccessful wild goose chase. He never found where his backstabbing gang ended up, but he knew that wherever they were, James wasn't too far away.

He turned off the ignition and allowed his mind to settle like the engine. Sitting in the parked LeSabre in Mrs. Stapleton's driveway, he felt eyes watching him. The hairs on his neck were rising like a sunflower at dawn, but the feeling was not as warm.

He calmly sat in the car and turned his head to the house across the street, but nothing was out of the ordinary. The same front porch light was on as when he'd left a couple of hours before. The rearview mirror didn't reflect any unsightly image except the empty street with a few flickering street lamps. He saw nothing, yet his tension didn't dissipate; it rested on his shoulders like a slimy film, oozing down his chest.

The eerie feeling was unnerving him, so he exited the vehicle and quietly shut the door. His ears were startled by the sound of clanking metal. It wasn't very loud, but it was distinct, and it was coming from behind him. He turned around and noticed the swing was barely moving back and forth on the darkened front porch. He stepped through the yard and saw a figure gliding, feet brushing against the ground with each passing movement of the swing.

"Mrs. Stapleton?" he asked as he walked up closer, still unable to see more than the figure's silhouette.

The head of the figure appeared to have moved left to right, as if signaling an incorrect answer.

Josiah, a little startled, took another few steps forward tentatively. "Are you here to see me?" he asked as he planted one foot on the bottom step.

The figure's head slowly moved up and down, building the suspense.

"Can't you say something?" Josiah asked as he made his way up the stairs until he was on the same level with the darkly dressed guest.

"Yes," the visitor spoke in a deep manly tone.

Taking another step forward, Josiah could see that the gentleman now had his head down which was covered with a black hooded sweatshirt. "Who sent you?"

"You should know." His words lingered in the air like the fragrance of Ethel's roses, but the words were not as pleasing as their sweet aroma.

"I should?" Josiah questioned as he stepped closer, only two steps away from the porch swing.

"Yes. Your boss."

"Am I in trouble?" Josiah asked with a lump rising in his throat. The guest raised his head and took off his hoodie, revealing a familiar face.

"No, Josiah. I just came for a visit like you asked for this morning."

"Ben?" Josiah asked as he recognized the voice, although he still couldn't make out his face in the twilight. The guest stood up and his sapphire eyes were inches away from Josiah's.

"Ben!"

CHAPTER 67

The two sat on the porch swing after their reunion embrace. Josiah recounted the last few weeks with all the details he hadn't mentioned in his prior letters. Ben listened with attentive ears, not dropping a single word as he stored them in his memory.

"It's so good to see you," Josiah finally said as he stopped his tirade.

"You too, Josiah. You too," Ben said as he gave his brother a friendly hug.

Ben had been raised with Josiah just like Carlos, Maxwell, and Jade; but unlike the thieves they had become, Ben was a brother who always had Josiah's back.

"Let's go inside. It's getting pretty late," Josiah said as he looked up at the moon and figured it was close to midnight. "I have to go to work tomorrow."

Ben laughed at the thought of Josiah working as a janitor. In the past, Josiah had camouflaged himself as a business executive, restaurant waiter, newspaper reporter, and even a homeless veteran, but never someone who cleaned toilets.

"What's so funny?" Josiah quietly asked as he stepped into the living room, hoping not to wake Mrs. Stapleton.

"Just the line of work we are in. With so many jobs and places to go, here you are in the small town of Bethany, pretending to be a janitor," Ben said snickering at the thought of Josiah with a scrub brush in hand. "Pride goeth before a fall."

"When have I been proud?" Josiah quipped with a smile.

"I don't know, but you must have done something to get this job," Ben commented as he walked into the well-lit living room. "Nice place."

"It's home for now." Josiah turned and saw his friend and brother finally standing in the light. It had been too long since the two of them

190

had seen one another, but Ben looked the same as he had years ago. Even after all these years, he still had a slender build and was a couple inches shorter than Josiah. In the light, Josiah could see the same pale freckled complexion with his rust-colored wavy hair that curled at the ends.

The two may have looked different, but inside they were so much alike. "Are you staying the night?" Josiah asked as he stretched his arms overhead.

"I thought I would, if Ethel doesn't mind," Ben said as he stretched out on the couch.

"She won't mind," he said. "She offered to let Carlos and the rest stay here as long as they needed."

Ben eyed Josiah suspiciously. "So, does she suspect anything?"

Josiah eyed up the stairs to where she was soundly sleeping, probably dreaming of her late husband. "Not a clue."

"Good job, Josiah," Ben said with an encouraging smile. "I mean, you really are doing a good job."

Those were the words that Josiah needed to hear more than anything else, especially after a night like tonight. "Come on," Josiah said walking up the stairs. "She has an extra bedroom upstairs."

"But the couch is so comfortable," Ben nagged as he rolled off the couch to his feet making his way to the steps. "Just because you are older, doesn't mean I have to do everything you say." The two quietly walked up the stairs as Ben glanced at the family photographs hanging on the wall. He came to a certain picture and stopped and pointed at a figure, the same figure Josiah had noticed when he first went up the stairs. "Hey, did you see his picture?"

"Yes," Josiah answered as he continued to walk up to Ben's room, flipping on the light and patting down the mattress that hadn't been used in quite some time.

"Very small world," Ben muttered as he continued to walk up the stairs. "Very small world."

CHAPTER 68

The morning dew seemed to reflect the radiant sunlight off every blade of grass. It could have been the twinkle in Josiah's smile as he walked the final leg through the school yard. *It's a new day* he kept repeating to himself with his heart pounding like a drum line playing an up tempo beat. *It's a new day.*

He had a brighter outlook since Ben was in town, and not even the greasy fingerprints on the school's front door glass was going to steal his spirit. With a spray of glass cleaner and a few wipes of a squeegee, the mess was gone, leaving only a streak-free shine. *It's a new day.*

The silence quickly ended as the sounds of screaming children and a stampede of preteen feet came crashing through the doors. Josiah watched with a smile as his spotless glass soon housed sticky fingers.

"Miss Mary," he said with a smile, but she didn't reciprocate his affection. She didn't even appear to have heard her name. Following about ten feet behind he found her look-alike. "Miss Amelia."

"Morning," Amelia said with a sorrowful expression.

"No, it's a good morning," he answered with a beaming smile, hoping that one would be planted on her face, but his hopes were ignored.

"If you say so," she said as she walked away in the middle of the bustling chaos. Her shoulders were hunched forward with her head looking down to the ground. Josiah watched as she steadily made her way down the hall as other students pushed her without any reservation or afterthought. She didn't react or spring to life, just kept walking solitarily.

Josiah watched as Amelia continued to drift down the hall, unfazed and aloof like a fallen tree limb floating with the current down an unrelenting river. She made her way to a crossroads and turned out of sight. Josiah knew Amelia's personality, but he had never seen her this unraveled. He knew it was time to take the next step.

Walking briskly up the hall he came to the point where she turned and saw her red backpack bobbing up and down with every step she took. As most of the students went to the gym or cafeteria to socialize, she made her way to the secluded quiet library.

Standing in the doorway, Josiah watched as she unzipped her book bag and unearthed a three-ring binder with *History* neatly printed on the front. He took a breath and entered the room lined with bookshelves filled with covers of every color and font. The room was empty except for Amelia sitting at a small round table that could comfortably seat four, but today only sat two.

"What is wrong, Miss Amelia?" Josiah asked as he walked up to her lonely table.

"Just got a test to study for," she said without looking up from her multi-highlighted page of typed notes.

"I'm sure you'll do great, Miss Amelia. No need to worry."

She grunted at his enthusiasm as he took a seat across from her. He stared at her rough exterior but knew that even callouses sometimes vanish with time. "Amelia, what is really wrong?" he asked as he placed his large right hand over her page, covering the section on the Alamo.

She looked up at first with a twinge of anger that slowly faded to remorse. "It's nothing," she said as she shook her head, tossing her blond hair carelessly like a mop.

"If it's nothing, I will be the judge of that. So, spill it."

She eyed him suspiciously, as if processing all reasons that Josiah would be befriending her at this time. Her mind raced with computer-like speed, finally succumbing to his politeness.

"It's Scarlett," she said with a huff as she let out a gust of air, "and Lucy."

"What has your sister done to you?" Josiah asked with loving compassion.

"Well, it is really childish, but it still hurts," she said speaking to Josiah as if he was her equal. "I overhead Lucy and Scarlett talking last night after supper, and when I came into her bedroom they quickly hushed."

"Ah, the cold shoulder treatment."

"Yes," she said with a grimace. "I left because I knew I wasn't wanted, and as I left I stopped outside her room and slightly eavesdropped."

"Slightly?" He smiled as he slid his hand away from her binder and back into his lap.

"I know it wasn't polite, but I wanted to know what they were talking about. So I listened and they were coming up with a plan about a sleepover tomorrow night at Lucy's house and they didn't want to invite me."

"Lucy didn't want to invite you?"

"Neither one of them did," she said as her chin started to quiver and eyes began to moisten. "I don't even care for Lucy, and I probably wouldn't have gone to the sleepover if I was asked, but for Scarlett to do that to me," she said as she tried to fight back an emotional breakdown, "it just hurt."

"I know about pain, Miss Amelia," he said recollecting daggers in his back from his past. "More than you know. And it does hurt."

Josiah continued to listen to Amelia and console her the best he could. He was sympathetic and comical. He told stories from his past to make her laugh; not to make her forget about her problems, but to show that this was just a phase every teenager goes through.

The bell sounded for the start of the day and they were about to part company when Josiah had an important question to ask. "So is anyone else going to be at the sleepover?"

"I don't think so," she said as she put her backpack on. "They were talking as if it would just be the two of them at Lucy's house."

"Well, don't worry, Miss Amelia. I think you are a great friend."

"Thanks," she said as she walked out of the library.

"Oh, Miss Amelia, when is your and Scarlett's test?"

"After lunch," she yelled from down the hall with a little more pep in her voice.

"Good luck," he yelled back as he started to think.

Only four hours to come up with a plan.

CHAPTER 69

The first period was over and Josiah knew he only had about three more hours until Scarlett took Mr. Turk's history test. "Josiah, where've you been?" Vik asked in his thick Russian accent.

Josiah stood shocked because Vik had never checked up on him before. Josiah looked around and realized he was still in the library. "I was just dusting around in here. There are some books that probably haven't left the shelves from when you went to school here, Vik." He laughed uncomfortably, hoping that Vik would soon chuckle at the joke.

He didn't.

"I went down to the cafeteria and it was a mess," he said, slightly scolding, but sounding much worse with his accent. "Get down there and clean it up."

"Yes, sir. Sorry, sir," Josiah quickly added as he immediately left the empty library and headed down the hall. Passing Mr. Turk's room, he peered through the glass and noticed the room was empty since it was the teacher's hour to prepare for his classes.

Turning the knob, Josiah quietly entered the empty room. He pulled down the door's blinds and locked the door. Josiah approached the cluttered desk and started fingering the stacks of paper, flipping the reams with his thumb, hoping he would come across the answer key for the girls' history test. Nothing was easily found.

Manila folders were lying on top of his lectern, and even though they were filled with ungraded essays about the War of 1812, he found no test answers. Josiah sat down behind the desk and noticed a couple of desk drawers. He opened them up and searched every corner of the tiny compartments, but once again, his search came up empty.

Josiah stood up, and suddenly a shiny silver handle in the back of the room caught his eye. Josiah ran to the three-drawer filing cabinet only to realize the drawers were locked. He racked his head with the ethical dilemma but knew it was too important to quit now. Pulling out a Swiss Army knife, he proceeded to pick the lock; fifteen seconds later, the latch popped and the drawer was open. Laying in the very front of the top drawer was a multiple-choice test covering the time period of the mid-1800s.

Flipping through the ten pages of questions, he heard an unnerving sound, the rattling of the doorknob.

"Oh, drat," an older gentleman stammered.

Josiah's heart kicked into overdrive. Thankfully, his memory was better than anyone else's he knew, and he scanned the ten pages at a breakneck pace.

Mr. Turk continued to bicker at his own ignorance about locking himself out as Josiah heard the clinking of keys leaving a pocket. Josiah threw the test back into the drawer and locked it in a flash. He scurried around the room like a cockroach, looking for a place to hide, but there was nowhere, not even an empty corner to hunker down in for a few minutes.

"Oh, dear," Mr. Turk ranted as a clank of keys fell onto the hallway floor.

Josiah looked to his right and noticed the windows were large enough for a man his size to squeeze through, and they were on the first floor. He ran over to the window, opened it up, and hung his right leg outside. Mr. Turk had picked up his keys and inserted his room key into the doorknob.

Josiah hurdled the window ledge as he fell to the ground, quickly jumping up to close his escape route. Josiah watched safely from outside as Mr. Turk opened the door and placed his keys back into his pants pocket.

Josiah walked around the building singing a new song.

"C, A, A, D, B, D, C…"

CHAPTER 70

James stood staring out of Dan's third floor office window at the lackluster commotion on the street. *Simpletons,* he thought as he watched a cordial interaction between a couple of pedestrians. *Life in Bethany, what a sad existence.*

"So," Dan broke the awkward silence from behind his desk. "What's your and Jud's next step?"

James' focus did not deter from the outside world. "You worry about the legal matters, and we'll worry about the PR."

Dan sat puzzled at James' attitude. Continuing to stare at the back of James' head, he envisioned darts being thrown at his primped and well-maintained hair. He was not a man to play opossum, but James had something uncanny about him. James did not just have a mysterious side; his entire life was one of intrigue and secrets.

Dan had gone up against some pretty tough plaintiffs in his time, but he always knew every little detail about their lives -- where they worked, if they had any siblings, if they dyed their hair, and even their favorite subject in junior high if that information could help. Nothing was off limits when it came to researching what he was up against. That's what a good lawyer did. That was until James Nialliv.

"James, can you look at me?" Dan asked forcefully. James slowly turned on his heels to give Dan his undivided attention.

"Better?" James asked facetiously.

"Much. Thank you," Dan said as James stood statuesque – no movement, no facial twitches, not even a blink. "If we are going to work together, I need to know what you know and vice versa."

James continued to stand lifeless and detached from the present conversation, as if his body language was questioning Dan's audacity.

Dan waited with bated breath for just a word from James, just a single word. Nothing was uttered or even attempted. "Will you stop being you for just five minutes?" Dan exploded. "I have put up with so much, so much…"

"So much what, Dan? What have you put up with?" James asked in a rational and condescending manner.

"For starters, you!" Dan jumped up from his chair, pounding his hands on his desk like a lion leaping onto a rock to scout out a pack of antelopes grazing in the savannah. "You caused us to get into this situation by lying on the patents."

"Really? I am the one to blame for this?" he asked coldly as his breathing pattern remained calm unlike Dan's chaotic lungs. "Why not blame Karen? Oh, that's right, because you are fu…"

Dan slammed his fist on his desk as an exclamation mark, keeping James from finishing his sentence. "Hell, James! Do you really not see that this is all because of your doing? If the patents ran their full course, they would have realized that the drug did not work as intended!" Dan stopped to catch his breath. "People are dying, James! People are taking the drugs you are promoting, and they are literally taking a kill pill."

"Well, Mr. High and Mighty, you are just as bad."

"No, I am probably worse," Dan said as he slid back into his chair, "because I know it is wrong and I did nothing because my hands are tied."

"Where do you think I'm at?" James asked looking Dan in the eyes. As if to say they were in the same boat without a paddle and Victoria Falls was just around the bend.

Dan touched his wrists together and flung them up in the air. "Hell, you're the twisted Boy Scout who tied these knots."

CHAPTER 71

The time for Josiah was coming frightfully close to lunch after the morning of dodging Vik. If he didn't jump the gun and accomplish his goal within the next few minutes, he didn't know what could happen. And that thought sickened him. Josiah looked down at his watch and noticed that he had seven minutes to get from the gym to Mary's locker, a walk that usually took three to four minutes for Josiah's lengthy legs, all while keeping out of Vik's sight.

Josiah ran from the locker room that he was supposed to be cleaning and exited the gym. He looked both ways and noticed the coast was clear. He jetted down the hall and stopped at a crossroads in the hall. He peered around the corner and saw two teachers leaving their classroom to get an early jump on the Mexican haystacks in the cafeteria. He continued to walk down the hall and then picked up his pace when he saw he was the only one in the area. He had lost only one minute, and he was almost at his destination.

"Josiah!" a voice came from behind, a voice he had been hiding from all morning. "Josiah!"

Josiah ignored the shouting and continued down the hall. He ran around the corner and sprinted down his final hallway.

"Josiah, stop!" Vik shouted as he started hobbling down the hallway, but Josiah didn't stop. He could see Mary's locker, and he was on a mission.

He started to slow down as he approached the range of lockers and stopped at locker 145. He grabbed the lock, silently thanking Vik for the skeleton key he had made on his second week of work.

Josiah slipped the key into the lock and turned, hearing the clasp open. Josiah took off the lock and pulled open the latch. He started frantically searching for her U.S. History book and folder, but his heart stopped. It wasn't in the locker. *She must have it on her.*

Only one thought ran through his crazed mind as he realized the lunch bell would be ringing in the next two minutes. He looked up the hall as he relocked her locker and noticed Vik still hadn't made it to the hall. Josiah twirled his head looking for his treasure switch, and the closest one he found was twenty feet away. He darted further down the hall and found his last resort. He knew this would cause panic, but there was nothing else to do. He pulled down on the red and white handle.

Sirens screamed throughout the school.

Fire!

CHAPTER 72

The students madly made their way down the hallway to the closest exit as the teachers were shouting, "Orderly fashion! Keep walking in an orderly fashion!" There was no order, just a crazed dash to the fire-free world outside. In a typical fire drill at Nathanial Community, the principal would announce that in the next few minutes they would be having a fire drill. Because there was no announcement, and especially since it was so close to lunch, the students assumed this was more than a drill. It was a real fire.

Josiah stood beside the alarm he pulled and watched students flee past him. He had seen Mary exit her classroom, and her lack of backpack made his heart skip. The stampede started to diminish with straggling students from the bathrooms. Josiah even caught a couple of students coming out of a utility closet from their make-out session after they figured the hallways were clear.

"Get outside," Josiah commented to the anxious teenagers. He squinted at the boy's face and noticed redder than normal lips. "And wipe off her lipstick."

The hallways were ghostly empty as the teachers hadn't yet made their way back into the unscathed school to investigate the surroundings. Josiah slipped into Mary's classroom and shut the door. He tried to remember where she sat, but he couldn't place her in the room. He walked down the aisle of chairs, looking for Mary or Scarlett's name on a piece of paper on a desk, a textbook, or even etched into the desk, but found nothing.

All he knew was her backpack was green, and there were five of them hanging on the backs of desks. When he unzipped the first one, a terrible odor escaped from the seams. He held his breath and shuffled items around, discovering a jockstrap. Not Mary's.

Jumping over two desks, he unzipped the next one like an animal devouring its prey. He flipped the folders around and saw Hannah's name neatly written on the top of each page.

Spotting the third backpack two aisles over, he pushed his way through the desks; he didn't care about the arrangement of the rows; all he cared about was the minutes ticking down. He unzipped the backpack without a care and dumped all the contents on the floor. He knelt down and dug through the mess of crumpled papers and video game magazines. Mary never played video games, so this wasn't it. He looked over at the back right corner of the room and found the next bag.

He ran across the room as the doorknob started to jiggle. His ears perked up with his keen hearing as he continued to dart toward the corner that housed a five-foot bookcase. He skidded behind the thrift store furniture and ducked his head. He watched as Mr. Turk entered the room and haphazardly scanned the perimeter. His eyesight may be fading, but Josiah wasn't taking any chances. His back was glued to the wall and his breathing stopped. Mr. Turk, known for his obsessive compulsiveness, stood in the doorway and noticed the room in shambles. He shook his head in contempt.

Josiah peered around the bookcase as Mr. Turk walked closer to the disorganized desks. The teacher, apparently oblivious to his first agenda of checking the school for fire, started to align the desks in straight rows.

Leave, Josiah thought as he watched the aging man scuff the floor as he moved the desks. *Come on, leave.*

Mr. Turk finished the desks and made it to the strewn backpack's contents on the floor. He bent down to pick them up as a funny feeling went up Josiah's nose. He looked on the bookshelf and found a collection of various flavorful potpourris, vanilla, mulberry, strawberry and cream, honeysuckle, lavender, and summer romance. By themselves, each smell would be pleasing, but in combination, it was a detriment to the senses.

A sneeze was welling up in Josiah. He bit his tongue, clinched his nose, dug his fingernails into his fists, but it was too powerful. He opened his eyes and spotted poor ol' Mr. Turk hunkered down, picking up the loose pencils and calculator. *Please, leave,* Josiah thought as he silently whimpered in fear. He had been taught many things, but holding a sneeze was just unnatural.

He continued to hold his breath, but it wasn't enough to keep the sneeze in, it had to get out. He exploded with a sneeze, jerking his head from behind the bookcase, quickly whiplashing it back out of sight. He squeezed as close to the wall as he could, awaiting the inevitable. He opened one of his eyes after a few seconds of silence and tilted his head forward, only to find Mr. Turk neatly unfolding the scraps of paper. He apparently had his hearing aid turned off.

Josiah looked down and found a green backpack dangling on the desk two feet in front of him. He stuck out his leg and kicked the backpack to the floor. Trapping the bag with his foot, he dragged it back into his corner. He unzipped it and found a soccer jersey, Mary's soccer jersey. He propped the bag on his knee and pulled out her barely used history book.

"This is for your best, Mary. You will see it one day. You won't understand it now, but He has a plan," he whispered as he carefully opened the book. Reaching into his pocket he pulled out a scrap sheet of paper with random letters written on it. He placed Mr. Turk's answer key into the book and then placed her textbook back into her backpack.

Josiah saw that Mr. Turk was trying his hardest to fit everything perfectly into the cramped backpack. Josiah tiptoed from behind the corner and slipped Mary's bag on her desk and made his way to the open door.

Josiah eyed up and down the hall as he stood in the doorway. Up a few classrooms, he saw two teachers frantically examining the school. As they each went into different classrooms, Josiah jumped out of the room and flipped up the fire alarm switch, ending the sirens.

The two teachers both came out of their rooms and stared at each other in confusion. "I guess everything is okay?" Mrs. White, the school's calculus teacher, said shrugging her shoulders.

Josiah stood relieved leaning against the wall. He hoped that everything would be okay.

"Josiah, we need to talk."

"Uh, okay, Vik."

CHAPTER 73

Lunch was light, a small salad filled with leaves of spinach and romaine lettuce, chopped up carrots and cucumbers, drizzled with raspberry vinaigrette dressing. This was how Karen kept her lean build. She ate like a rabbit and exercised like a cheetah.

"Thanks for calling," Karen said as she put the call on speaker phone while she continued to eat in her lab while the rest of the scientists were in the cafeteria.

"Are you better today?" Dan asked, remembering the trembling episode from the night before.

"Yes, I took a couple of shots of whiskey and I was out. I still think someone was out there last night, but they have upped the security in this place."

"Good to hear. So, are you making any headway?" Dan asked as he was driving from the Brock, Stallins, & Boswell, LLP office in Pascagoula. He had met with another attorney, Jason Hurt, to discuss the options of Pharm Laboratories, especially after he'd received a few more folders from some unhappy hospitals on the East Coast first thing this morning. Jason wasn't much help, but Dan finally had a legal mind to bounce off some ideas.

"Headway?" she asked as she took a bite of a cucumber, "for what?"

"Karen," Dan said with a mixture of doubt and agitation, "for figuring out the problem with the drug."

"Oh," she said as she stopped and swallowed. "No. Not yet."

Dan continued to drive on the interstate at eighty-two miles per hour and stared amazed at her lack of conviction. "You do realize the drug doesn't work."

"It's complicated," she refuted.

"You don't have to tell me that. I read all your supposed findings and the biology doesn't make sense to me," Dan said stressing the

206

word *supposed*. "But that's why I'm the attorney and you are the chemist."

"I will get to it because it isn't going to be an easy fix. It took me three years to find this, but I will get to it eventually," she said hoping to change subjects. "So, when are you going to let me meet your children?"

The words went through his ears like a shockwave. Karen knew he was married with three children, but she had never mentioned them. They were usually just brought up after Dan checked his voicemail. "Karen, that may be a problem."

"Why?" she bluntly asked as her voice started to rise with a twinge of anger. "Are you ashamed of me?"

Dan gripped his steering wheel with built-up frustration coursing through his limbs. Dan thought for a second of how to respond, but the words did not come. Nothing was coming except for a sparkle catching his eye, the sun hitting his wedding band. "We can talk about this later, but for now, you need to do all you can to find the flaw in your drug."

"Flaw?" she screamed as she ended their conversation. She threw her fork onto the steel counter, ricocheting off a beaker filled with a purple liquid. "The only flaw is your family."

Dan shut his phone and laid it on his console. *Yes, flaw*, he thought as he stretched out his fingers on the wheel. He removed his wedding ring and read the inside inscription Claire had put two days before their wedding day.

Always Yours.

CHAPTER 74

The sound of pencil erasers, the flipping of sheets of paper, the occasional huff of air from terror-filled students – these were the sounds Mr. Turk loved. He had handed out the six pages of multiple-choice questions fourteen minutes earlier, and now he rested comfortably with his hearing aid on its highest decibel, watching the students like they were a gorilla exhibit. His head scanned their habitat with the same speed and accuracy as an oscillating fan, slowly moving across the room from left to right, then returning to his starting point and starting again.

He watched a few students rub their heads, as if massaging their scalps would allow their craniums to work with more efficiency and accuracy. He often enjoyed seeing poor dimwitted Kyle Huston gnaw at his pencil's eraser until all that remained was the shiny metal piece that once housed the gummy chew toy. In his many years of testing, too many to recount, he had experienced dozens of crying fits from students, sixteen episodes of stress-fueled regurgitations, nine mental blackouts, four bladder accidents, and one coma style fainting. Most teachers would say they want all their students to pass their class, but he knew that most teachers lied. Most teachers would love to inflict pain on their pupils in an act of reciprocity for their adolescent disrespect.

Glancing down at his watch he noticed that nineteen minutes had passed since the start of his test, and he knew that in a matter of minutes the first finisher would be coming forward with a beaming smile – Amelia Sutton. On the other side of the spectrum, he knew that thirty or so minutes later he would be grabbing a test from another student with clinched hands and last second scribbles – Scarlett Sutton.

The normal test-taking sounds were interrupted with a knock on the door. The entire class shot their heads up to see the commotion;

some looked out of nosiness, while others gazed for hopes of an emergency that would ultimately cause the test session to stop.

"We're taking a test," Mr. Turk stated coolly as he stepped out of the silent room. The students strained their ears to listen, but they couldn't discern what the other mysterious voice was saying. "What?" Mr. Turk's voice raised with a hint of confusion and a twinge of outrage. The other voice continued to explain, but like before, it was inaudible. "I will look into it. Thank you for your help, sir."

Mr. Turk stomped back into his room and slammed the door, causing the students' heads to instantly drop back onto their tests with their pencils writing frantically, as if they were oblivious to the visitor. "I have just been informed that one of you has the answers to my test."

The classroom turned coldly silent. All the pencils that had been frantically moving across the test a second ago, now were held frozen in mannequin-like hands.

"Please flip over your test." The entire room was filled with the swooshing of test packets being flipped down on each of the students' desks. "Please take out your history book. Do not open it, but lay it on your desk."

Everyone grabbed their textbook from under their desks or from their backpacks and laid it gently on their desk. Mr. Turk came to the first desk, Chris Booker, and thumbed his finger through the pages. He picked up the book, held it by the hardbound cover and let the pages sway underneath to discover any loose pages that could have been hidden.

All the students in the class glanced around at one another, as if subconsciously looking for the guilty. Heads were shaking no to one another and shoulders were shrugging to each other's suspicions.

Mr. Turk continued through the haystack of textbooks until he came to Scarlett's barely used textbook. He opened the book, hearing the binding crack as if it was the first time it had been opened all year.

He twirled the book around and shook it like Claire sifting powdered sugar over one of Scarlett's favorite pies. Powdered sugar did not fall from her textbook, but a lonely loose sheet of paper that was unfamiliar to Scarlett landed on her desk. Her eyes popped as she read a listing of handwritten letters.

"What do we have here, Miss Sutton?"

"I, uh."

CHAPTER 75

"I can't believe you were caught cheating," Claire scolded as she and Scarlett sat in the school's office waiting for the principal.

Scarlett sat silently as she had already told her mother that she didn't know the answers were in her book. But that didn't work.

"I can't believe that you will not admit that you were cheating," Claire stated as the office receptionist peered around her computer monitor to see the reprimand. "It is one thing to cheat, but to lie about it, especially after they found the cheat sheet in your book. Do you have anything else to add?"

Scarlett shook her head no as she tried to unravel the knot that was being formed around her. The problem was she didn't know where to begin or where to end.

"So, the answers just mysteriously appeared," Claire said as she started to laugh sadistically. "I wish I had answers that just dropped out of thin air. Life would be so much easier if a sheet of paper with all the answers of life could just fall into my lap. What should we have for supper tonight? Where is the best price for laundry detergent? How much should I spend on a new shirt?"

"Those are the only questions *you* have to deal with," Scarlett scoffed, her heart instantly stopping after she said those damaging words.

"What did you say to me?" Claire roared, whipping her head around so she could look her daughter in her menacing eyes.

"I'm sorry, I didn't mean it," Scarlett quickly retracted, but it was too late. The words were already said.

"You may think that all I do is feed you, and clothe you, and make sure the house is clean, but..." Claire stopped as her voice started to choke, "but I do much..." Claire once again stopped to take a breath and look for a tissue as tears were forming. "I do much more and put up with more than you know."

211

"I know." Scarlett sat unflinchingly still as she continued to look ahead at the name plate on Mr. Gerald Chesterton's door.

"Don't humor me," Claire said as she stood up and walked out of the office to regain her composure.

Scarlett sat in the middle of the rubble. She was accused of a crime she didn't commit with no proof she didn't commit it, and she'd just committed a crime against her mother with the proof on her heart.

Principal Chesterton's door opened and the muffled voices were as clear as day. "Thank you for coming forward. Thank you so much," Mr. Chesterton said as he shook hands with someone before they parted.

Scarlett dropped her eyes to the ground before anyone exited Mr. Chesterton's room. She had the mindset of an ostrich that if she couldn't see them, then they surely couldn't see her. Sadly, her heart dropped when she heard the footsteps. They could see her.

"Miss Sutton," Mr. Chesterton said, "please come in."

Scarlett kept her eyes glued to the ground in embarrassment. Even though she knew she was innocent, she hated the feeling of guilty eyes on her. As she stood up, she saw a pair of dirty work boots walk by leaving a faint trail of dust behind. It was a familiar pair of boots.

She walked into his office with her eyes still on the ground when she heard two words that tensed her body.

"Mrs. Sutton."

Familiar boots with a familiar voice.

CHAPTER 76

The fingernail marks that Dan dug into his leather desk chair were slowly subsiding, but there was going to be proof of their indention for a few more days. He squeezed his telephone for the fifth time and redialed Karen's cell number. It went straight to her voicemail, just like the preceding two attempts.

"Karen, it's me again. Call me ASAP!"

He hit the receiver button, igniting the ringtone in his ear and started to dial Karen's office number for the second time.

"Pharm Laboratories, this is Charlotte," a polite voice greeted with a thick southern drawl.

"Charlotte, this is Dan Sutton again. I called a few minutes ago for Dr. Karen Anderson and she wasn't in her office. I really need to speak with her."

"I will connect you to her office again," she responded like her training manual recommended.

"No!" he demanded forcefully before retreating to a more pleasant tone. "I'm sorry, Charlotte, I just need to speak with her now. Is there any way you can page her through your intercom or see if she is in a meeting?"

"I'm sorry, sir, but we don't have any loudspeakers here. I can instant message her on her computer for her to give you a call. May I have your phone number?"

"She already has it," he muttered as he hung up his phone. Yes, he knew he was not polite or even gentlemanly, but to hell with cordial dialogues.

"Mr. Sutton," Jenna Simone, Dan's receptionist, whispered through his intercom as she hunched down behind her computer monitor to hide herself from the waiting room area. "He's still waiting for you."

Dan picked up the phone with weakening hands. "Jenna, please stall. Get him something to drink or eat," Dan demanded as he fumbled through his cell phone contacts.

"I already have. He didn't want anything," she answered, unsure of what to do next.

"Talk to him for five minutes about anything," he begged as he scrolled down his alphabetical list of names.

"Okay," she uneasily answered as she softly hung up the phone.

Dan found the name he was searching for and pressed the call button. He listened as the phone started to ring, clinging to any shred of hope that James would pick up. "Come on, pick up," he stammered as he started to clear his desk of any loose paperwork or files that could be possibly damaging.

The ringing suddenly stopped as he heard a hearty laugh. "Dan, how are you? I saw that you called just a few minutes ago, and I was about to call you back."

Dan sat frigid as he heard James' boisterous laugh. "We have a major problem," Dan whispered as he stared at his office door, praying that Mr. Yates wouldn't barge through his last barricade.

"What? Dan, I can barely hear you."

"We have a major issue here in my office," Dan said, slightly raising his tone but not his volume.

"Dan, you need to speak up. Where are you?"

Dan took a deep breath and exhaled as his patience was growing thinner by the syllable. "Get your ass to my office now!" Dan cringed at his tone, hoping that Mr. Yates, who sat twenty feet away from the door, did not hear his anxiety.

"Dan, I hear you now. What's wrong?"

Dan's fear had been growing in his stomach for the last few minutes as he scurried for telephone communication from Karen and James. He knew the truth, but it seemed like knowing the truth and saying the truth were two different things. Dan thought as long as he

214

never vocalized the words, he could keep telling himself that it wasn't real, but as soon as he said them, the words would take on a life of their own.

His insides were churning. He had been an attorney for almost twenty years, and through all the legal cases he had worked on, he had never once been taken off guard. Yes, he'd been shocked, but he knew how to react. He had even been blindsided a time or two, but a good attorney knew all the ins and outs of their client, so nothing should ever surprise them.

This case was different. No matter how hard he tried to uncover all the loose ends that could potentially strangle their closest bystander, all he found were split ends that formed new split ends. No matter the questions he asked, he never got any straight and binding answers from anyone on the Pharm team. Not even from Karen.

Sadly, he had to continue the spiral descent with James, even though he was being led blindly into a pit. Their relationship that was once trusting and friendly was now based on coercion and survival. He just didn't know how long he had until James would use him as his sacrificial lamb. The timeframe of Dan's professional future had quickly dwindled within the last five minutes.

"The FDA is here."

CHAPTER 77

Dan sipped his scotch, allowing James' response to drown in the alcohol as Mr. Yates watched without any thirst. "Sure you don't want anything?" Dan asked for the third time as he strolled back to his desk, trying to shake off the tire marks from the bus that James had thrown him under. *You're the lawyer. Earn your paycheck!* Dan sat down with his chest puffed out and his shoulders back, hoping that the Discovery Channel antics would work in his small law office.

"No," Mr. Yates firmly stated as he crossed his legs and laid his briefcase down on the end table beside him. "You are the legal counsel for Pharm Laboratories, Inc., correct?"

"Yes, yes sir," Dan nodded as he folded his hands on his desk to give his guest his undivided attention.

"We have been going over some reports that have recently been submitted to us, and we are puzzled with the effects of the new drug, Anterolistyalin. I thought it would be best if I came for a little visit and try to get to the bottom of this," he stopped for a second to communication the precise word, "this episode."

"Episode?" Dan questioned as if he was not aware of any hindrance of the so-called miracle drug.

"Episode," Mr. Yates echoed indignantly as he uncrossed his legs, leaning to unclasp the locks on his briefcase. "Are you aware of any incidents that may be damning or conclusive of the possibility of chronic or lethal side effects of the drug, Anterolistyalin?"

"I have to be honest," Dan uttered as his tongue slithered behind his teeth. "We have received a few notices of severe side effects in cancer patients after they were prescribed Anterolistyalin."

"Uh huh," Mr. Yates nodded as he began to scribble on his yellow note pad. Dan tried to stretch his neck to see the chicken scratch, but the tablet was angled away from him. "How many episodes…"

"Can you please use a different word?" Dan interrupted with a perturbed look on his face. "'Episode' just seems too catastrophic."

"As I was saying, how many episodes of severe side effects are you aware of?" Mr. Yates interrogated as he stared into Dan's eyes, fixating not on the color, but the stressful blinking.

"We have received a dozen or so claims."

"Or so?" Mr. Yates inquired. "Can you be a little more specific, Mr. Sutton?"

Dan felt like he was walking up the gallows only to find a single noose. "I do not know of an exact total off the top of my head."

Mr. Yates quickly jotted down a few notes and shook his head in courteous acknowledgement. "That's fine," he said as he laid his tablet facedown and grabbed a file from his briefcase. "I have a listing of nine names of patients who were prescribed Anterolistyalin. Shortly after they completed their round of chemotherapy, they started getting symptoms of congestive heart failure, ultimately dying three to seven days later."

"Well, I said I knew of about a dozen cases throughout the country," Dan commented, leaning back as he rested in the fact that nine deaths, although terrible, was not bad considering the number who had received the drug.

"Throughout the country?" Mr. Yates asked, eyeing him suspiciously. He strategically laid the file down on Dan's desk and opened it, allowing Dan to read the names and biographical information of each patient. "Mr. Sutton, this file is just from one hospital in Fargo, North Dakota."

Dan smoothly tilted his body back toward his desk, trying to not show the terror in his body movements as he picked up the thin file with photographs of men, women, and children who had apparently died in the last month.

"Mr. Sutton, this is just one hospital out of the thousands in the United States that have or will be using Anterolistyalin in the near future. I think you will agree that 'episode' is an understatement for this calamity."

CHAPTER 78

Scarlett sung softly and off key as she laid on her bed listening to Justin Bieber, hoping his pop music would somehow cause the day to rewind or even be totally skipped.

Her heart ached and her mouth stopped moving as Justin continued to sing. She tried to listen, but her mind was taking her elsewhere. Her scorned soul went back to the memory of the principal's office. Josiah's words not only echoed in her head, but they resounded with the force of a Boeing 777 blasting into her ears.

Bitterness swelled inside her. Mr. Turk, Mr. Chesterton, and her own mother all believed she was cheating, despite her argument for Mr. Turk to check her test and see her incorrect answers.

Mr. Turk had just sneered as he'd said, "Scarlett, you are smart enough not to put all the right answers on the test. You haven't gotten a hundred on a test all year, so you would know not to put all the correct answers on this one."

"But I didn't cheat!" Scarlett had insisted, but the proof of the answer key in her history book was as solid as a bloody murder weapon found in someone's coat pocket. "I didn't!"

Even though she felt betrayed by her mother not believing her, the real culprit, the ultimate villain and the source of all this agony was Josiah. "I wish I never met you!" she muttered out loud at the thought of Josiah stealthily slipping the answers into her book. Sitting up on her bed, she frantically scanned her memory for Josiah's whereabouts that day. She remembered ignoring him first thing in the morning and then seeing him outside of Mr. Chesterton's office, but nowhere else. *How could he have thought I was cheating when he never saw me with my history book?* she wondered. *And most importantly, how did he know that the answer key was in the book?*

Jumping off her bed, she picked up her backpack and examined the contents: unorganized folders, unread textbooks, and a soccer jersey that was beginning to smell. Nothing seemed out of the ordinary, but she wasn't expecting to find a note stating Josiah did this. She had just hoped there would be some trace of him.

Her heart dropped just like her backpack onto the carpeted floor as she watched a small cloud of dust rise as the backpack collided with the ground. Once again she bent down and picked up her backpack, finally seeing the proof of Josiah's entanglement.

A faded dirty boot print was outlined on the bottom of her backpack, dirt with a similar color to the traces outside Principal Chesterton's office. She thought about running down and showing her mother the proof, but she knew it would still be refutable from her perspective.

A devilish smile appeared on Scarlett's face as she was finally looking forward to school on Monday. *Thank God for Fridays.*

Josiah, you messed with the wrong girl.

CHAPTER 79

"I am stuffed," Ben burped, tasting the banana pudding for the second time as he and Josiah walked down the street to the downtown park.

"Mrs. Stapleton is a good woman," Josiah remarked as he rubbed his stomach to acknowledge his full belly as well. "My pants are getting too tight."

"Never thought I would hear you say those words," Ben said as he laughed. "Actually, I don't think I have ever heard those words from anyone. I didn't think we were designed that way."

"I know. I've never experienced anything like this."

"If only that was the greatest of your worries," Ben stated as they strolled down the deserted street. He glanced around the surroundings, taking in the quaint feel of the town. "Wish more towns were like this one."

"It would be a different world. A much different world."

The two men found a wooden park bench under a cluster of elm trees. They sat down to relax on the bench that seemed to have been carved in the 1800s. "So, how did it go today?" Ben asked as he unbuckled his belt to allow his stomach to expand. He, too, was feeling the unfamiliarity of fat-infused southern cooking.

"Even though it had to be done," Josiah answered staring at the illuminated fountain in the center of the park, "it didn't make it easy."

"Soon she will know the truth," Ben answered as he, too, became fixated with the gushing water as it spilled over the tiered ledges into the wading area of pennies and nickels.

"I hope it's sooner than later. Any time it involves children, I just want to fast forward through the drama and conclude the mission," Josiah spoke with a droopy chin. "What are they going to say when they find out about their dad?"

"That is not for you to determine."

"But I have grown to love these children. Can't I just tweak my mission a little?" Josiah asked as he got up from the park bench and paced around the fountain. He sat down on the concrete edge and took off his shoes. Dropping his feet into the cool water, his face expressed surprise.

"These kids are just kids. Stick with the plan," Ben answered as he walked over to the fountain and reached his hand into the water and pulled out a shiny wet quarter. "Superstitions."

"Sometimes that is the only hope people have," Josiah said as he started to splash his feet in the water like a two-year-old.

"Sad, isn't it?"

They continued to enjoy the silent company of one another until it was time for their paths to fork. "It's time," Ben said as he stood up from the fountain's ledge. The park was dark except for the fountain and the pathway lamps and the occasional flashes of lightning bugs in the far distance.

"I know," Josiah answered as he shook his feet dry. "I know."

Ben patted Josiah's back and whispered a few comforting words into his ear before he walked away. Josiah sat and watched the back of his friend slowly fade into the darkness. He knew it was time for Ben to leave, but despite this knowledge, he knew that rougher days were ahead.

Much rougher.

CHAPTER 80

Karen's office was uncomfortably silent as Dan unleashed his built-up tension from the surprise FDA visit.

Dan looked down at his Rolex and noticed that even though the time was nearing ten, the night was still young. "Aren't you going to say something?" Dan shouted as he cracked his knuckles and loosened his Brooks Brothers blue and gold striped tie, throwing the hundred-dollar silk noose beside his Armani suit coat.

"What do you want me to say?" she bickered as she swiveled her chair behind her desk like it was a ride at the state fair.

"I want you to say that this is just a coincidence."

"Fine," she groaned, "this is just a coincidence."

Dan stood shaking with rage. "Quit the bull! My life is on the line here!"

"And you think mine isn't?"

"You don't appear to realize that it is."

"Well, I'm fully aware," she quipped snatching up her double helix glass paper weight and throwing it in Dan's direction.

He dodged the flying piece of crystal and watched as it smashed into hundreds of shards of glass from the collision with the wall. He stared in surprise at this attempt on his life. Karen dumped out her monogrammed pencil holder she had received as a present after earning her doctorate, letting her cheap pens and rainbow-colored highlighters form the start of a game of Pick-up sticks. Clutching the golden cup, she examined the hardness of the metal and her distance from Dan.

"Come on! Throw it!" he shouted as he motioned with his hands for her to throw another object. "Throw it! I dare you!"

She eyed him suspiciously then glanced down at the possible weapon. Her fingers uncurled, dropping the pencil holder on her desk with a loud thud. "What are we going to do?" she questioned as her legs gave way dropping her back into her chair. "We have already spent millions of our backers' money, the company's stock went public last year, and with a news headline of deaths from our drug, there is no way that we will get any more funding to eradicate this problem."

"That is just the financial implications," Dan remarked. "The FDA will soon discover the fraudulent patent paperwork."

"But James was the one who headed up the patent procedures," she quickly answered defiantly.

"James is a crook!" he bellowed. "A weasel who will only look after his own ass." He started to pace around the room as if he was making his closing arguments before the jury. "He is smart and conniving, and he has a great way to spin crap into a beautiful compost pile. He probably has an explanation for everything, and who do you think he is going to throw under the bus?"

"He wouldn't," she timidly answered.

"By God he would!"

"What does that mean?" she asked, as if that was the first time she had thought about this being a personal crisis.

"Karen, we've discussed this!" His voice became irate again at the lack of foresight on her part. "It means big trouble!"

"Money?" she asked with a squeak in her voice.

"Prison."

CHAPTER 81

Bethany was a quiet town, day or night, but Josiah knew that underneath the montage of old fashioned southern living, a fiasco was happening somewhere in the distance. He had relished in the companionship of Ben in the last twenty-four hours, a friendly smile that knew all his secrets, a firm handshake without any fear of a knife to the back, and a brotherly pat on the shoulder as a signal of a job well done. Josiah had needed the last twenty-four hours more than air itself.

The night sounds were dissipating as the crickets and whippoorwills were apparently bidding it a night as well. The only sound heard through the dismal streets of Bethany was the shuffling of work boots on the adequately lit sidewalks. The moon was sliced in half, as if it was a wheel of cheese, while the stars sporadically peeked their twinkling lights through the blackened sky.

Mrs. Stapleton's home was dark except for the nightlight that illuminated every step from the bottom of the stairs as Josiah quietly entered his temporary abode. He gently stood on the first step, pausing as he heard it creak loudly. He continued up the stairs, gripping the railing for support.

He made it to his room as quietly as possible and started to undress and change for bedtime. As he buttoned up his night shirt, a feeling of suspicion raised the hairs on his arms. He peered around the room, but nothing seemed out of place. He made his way to the window curtains and parted them, revealing a peaceful night outside the comfort of his four walls.

He tried to shake off the uneasy feeling, but the more he thought, the more he shook. Opening his bedroom door with a slight squeak of the hinges, he poked his head out the door and examined the bleak hallway. Stepping out, he noticed Mrs. Stapleton's door was ajar; his heart stopped, knowing she always kept the door closed. Tiptoeing down the hallway, he stopped at her door to shut it, but something caught his eye in the crack. He squinted his eyes hoping they would quickly adjust to the surrounding darkness, because he thought he saw Mrs. Stapleton's slippers lying beside her bed in a haphazard fashion, which was abnormal for her routine.

Josiah's eyes finally fully adjusted as he eyed the slippers and realized they were not just tossed beside the bed. They were accompanied by a long skirt that Mrs. Stapleton would never just leave on the ground. He flipped on the hallway light switch and opened the door to let the light fall upon her darkened bedroom floor. The light swarmed the darkened room until it landed on the pair of slippers. The pair of slippers Mrs. Stapleton was still wearing.

"Ethel!"

CHAPTER 82

"You're lucky you got her here as soon as you did," Nurse Ava stated as she spoke with Josiah outside of Ethel's hospital room. "If it was any longer...who knows?" she commented as she finished writing down Ethel's vitals on a clipboard before hanging it on the door's rack.

"Who knows?" Josiah echoed as he kindly smiled, allowing Ava to check on the remaining patients in the cardio wing of the intensive care unit. Josiah entered the room filled with beeping machines, oxygen tanks, morphine drips, and a flashing heart monitor, shining a lively green line as if it was drawing the Appalachian Mountain range.

"Ethel, you probably can't hear me, but it's me, Josiah," he said as he sat down on the recliner beside her bed. He watched as her heart rate stayed steady in the mid-fifties, which was entirely too low. He looked at her pale and ghostly face, covered by an oxygen mask, barely breathing in the life-giving air. She appeared to be sleeping peacefully, but he knew sometimes there was very little difference in the appearance of a sleeping body and a dead body.

"Hang in there, Ethel. Hang in there," he whispered as he stroked her hand, caressing the bruises where they'd tried unsuccessfully three times to get her IV started. The trembling intern had breathed a sigh of relief when she'd finally hit the much-desired vein about three hours earlier. The plastic tube that filled her with morphine was both a blessing and a leash. To Ethel, it was a sheer gift.

With the touch of Josiah's hand, her heart rate increased to sixty-eight beats a minute. "I know you can hear me, Ethel. I am right here. I am right here," he continued to whisper in her ear the rest of the evening and into the early morning. A couple of different nurses came by throughout the night to check on Ethel, and each time they came in, her heart rate was improving.

"You must be some kind of healing man," Nurse Katie smiled as she wrote down Ethel's vitals at a quarter past three in the morning. "I have never seen a woman who suffered a massive heart attack rebound so quickly." Katie, a trim RN in her early thirties who wore yellow and pink scrubs on Fridays once thought about continuing to become a doctor, but life happened. She continued monitoring the medicine dosages and blood pressure as she checked off ten other things on her list of things to do.

She had been about to enter medical school when she became pregnant and decided to quit on her dream to be an M.D. and settle on becoming an underappreciated nurse instead. Most people believed that doctors were God's gifts and God's hands, but Katie quickly realized that nurses did more than they got credit or paid for. She walked around the room, throwing away her rubber gloves as she eyed Josiah. "So, is she your wife?"

Josiah continued to gently rub Ethel's hand. "No, we're just friends," he smiled with a hint of embarrassment.

"Well, you two must be close," she commented, "because she is practically smiling."

Josiah glanced down at Ethel and noticed that the fearful expression she had had four hours earlier was replaced with a relaxing smile. "Is the medicine you're giving her causing her to be this comforted?"

Katie shook her head. "No, that is all you, sir."

Josiah already knew the answer. "You're a great nurse, Katie."

She stopped and stood shocked for a moment before returning an appreciative smile. "Thank you," she said warmly. "You don't know how much that means to me."

Once again, Josiah knew.

CHAPTER 83

The alarm sounded at seven, causing Claire to smack the startling sound to a halt. Eyes crusted and breath stale, she rolled over, hoping to find Dan in his silk pajamas. The only thing she found were unwrinkled bed sheets and an indention-less pillow. She fell onto her back, staring at the wood paneled ceiling, counting the ridges as if that would erase all her anxiety.

After ten minutes of self-consoling, she stumbled out of bed. She knew that she had a solid twenty minutes to start her coffee and wake up before she would hear the screaming of birthday boy Charlie.

Her tired legs struggled down the steps, but she eventually found herself on solid ground. She couldn't fully open her eyes, but she noticed something resembling a body on the couch. She shuffled across the floor in her comfortable fuzzy neon pink house shoes and patted the crumpled blue blanket. She felt a body, long, firm, and tired. She had found her husband.

He felt her presence above him, so he forced his eyes open. "Good morning."

"I needed you yesterday," she answered as she sat down at the end of the couch, crushing his feet with her leg. "I really needed you."

"Claire, can't this wait?" he asked as he rearranged his legs so they were not squashed. "I had a bad day."

"Sorry I didn't ask how you were, but your daughter was caught cheating," she snapped as she continued to stay seated on the same couch as Dan while feeling miles away from him.

"Cheating? Why?" he shot up and threw the blanket off his legs.

Grunting and shrugging her shoulders in acknowledgement to his question was her only response.

"Did you ground her?"

"Oh, now you want to be a parent?" she snipped as she got up from the couch.

"What is that supposed to mean?" he yelled as he followed her to the kitchen wearing only his silk boxers.

"I think you know," she stated in a quiet yet confrontational voice. She flipped on the coffee machine and glanced down at her husband's sleepwear. "Nice shorts. Are they new?"

"Don't change the subject," he commanded, as he was not ready to tell his wife of the presents he had received from his adulterous flame. "What did you do to Scarlett?"

"What did I do? Are you blaming me for her cheating?" She whipped around, clutching her coffee mug, ready to throw it if it came to that.

"Claire! No, I wasn't blaming you. Did you punish her?"

"Yes, since you weren't here, I told her she couldn't spend the night with Lucy and that she will be grounded for two weeks. At least."

"Good," he stated as he took a seat at the breakfast nook. He sat in a tired trance staring at the clock on the microwave. "Do you think Lucy is a bad influence?" he asked as he continued to watch the blue digital numbers.

"Lucy?" Claire scoffed. "You think Lucy caused this? Don't you work with her dad?"

"Yes," he answered. He wanted to tell his problems to the wife who always listened to his drama, the wife who stood by his side as he worked sixty-hour weeks to climb the partnership ladder, and the wife who knew him before he was someone to be known. Sadly, he knew that if he confided in her about one piece of the puzzle, all the pieces would soon be flipped right side up, and he wasn't ready for her to know all of his adulterated secrets.

"Mom! Dad!" Charlie screamed as he came running down the stairs, almost tripping in excitement. "It's my birthday!"

"Be careful," Claire said kissing and hugging the number one man in her life now. "It would be bad having to spend the day in the ER, especially when we have the inflatables coming in a little while."

"That would be bad!" Charlie said, furrowing his brow and lips at the thought of missing out on jumping for hours inside the giant castle.

"This day is going to be lots of fun," Claire said wiping the devastated expression off Charlie's face. "Happy birthday, Charlie."

A smile quickly bounced onto Charlie's face. He was ready for his birthday party fun.

CHAPTER 84

The hospital room was deathly silent except for the tapping and beeping of Mrs. Stapleton's various machines to monitor her heart and breathing. Josiah stood staring out of the third floor of the hospital, watching the sun try to chase away the still visible moon. The rays trickled over the land as if God was repainting a landscape, adding brighter colors than were originally used.

Beyond the hospital parking lot, he saw a soybean field with a thick layer of fog weaving through the crops. He scanned the horizon, watching the foggy morning blend into the cloudy sky.

A rustling sound behind Josiah overpowered the mundane hospital noise causing him to turn around to see which nurse had returned to check on Mrs. Stapleton.

"Ethel," Josiah smiled as he rushed to her side as her legs started to wrestle and flex under the covers. "I am here."

The groggy and highly medicated eyes began to open, but only her right eye peeked through her lids. She started to move her mouth, but Josiah quickly placed his finger over her chapped lips.

"Get some rest," is all he said as their eyes connected. He smiled a ray of hope that Ethel so desperately needed. She tried to return the favor, but Josiah knew from the look of her eye that she reciprocated.

Josiah pressed the nurse button on Ethel's bed to let them know she was moving and awake. "Yes," a monotone voice shouted through the intercom on her bed before Josiah quickly adjusted the volume to a more tolerable level.

"Thought you would like to know that she's waking up," Josiah answered as he watched Ethel's eye jolt open from the loud nurse.

"Be right there," she answered as if it was a recording. He couldn't help but picture the nurse sitting behind her newspaper with a jelly-filled donut, being more fixated on the latest scandal in Washington than her patient four rooms away.

232

"Josiah" she mouthed, unable to speak due to the tube going down her throat.

"Ethel, just relax. You are doing well," Josiah answered, hoping that the calmness in his voice would bring her some comfort.

She shook her head no with a fearful expression in her eyes. His heart started to skip, but he knew he needed to be strong. "You had a heart attack last night, but they say that you are doing well."

She stopped her shaking to watch Josiah as he spoke, but she had something she needed to say. She once again tried to move her mouth, but Josiah was unable to read her lips due to the plastic tube in the way.

"I'm sorry, but I can't understand you," he replied as he rubbed her hand. "As soon as they get the tube out of you, I will listen."

She shook her head violently. She raised up her right hand and started moving it like she had a wand. Josiah tried to get her to lower her hand, but from the corner of his eye he saw that her heart monitor appeared to be in good standing. "Do you want a pen and paper?"

She nodded her head.

Josiah walked around the room, looking for some pen and paper, but all he found was a dry-erase marker and board hanging on the wall. He got it off the wall and brought it over to Ethel's bed. She smiled in appreciation and took the red marker and started writing on the white plastic board. She concentrated the best that she could, but her writing was not as good as it usually was. Her letters were sloppy and jumbled, but considering her night, Josiah would do his best to read.

"What are you doing?" Katie asked as she walked into the room. "She needs her rest."

"I know. I know. But she wanted to tell me something," Josiah kindly remarked as he stood holding the board awkwardly beside Ethel.

"Mrs. Stapleton, you need to rest," Katie forced as she tried to push Josiah away, but Ethel continued to struggle to finish her statement. "Mrs. Stapleton, please, this can wait."

Ethel grunted in frustration and shot Katie a menacing look – a look Josiah had never seen on Ethel's kind and gentle face.

Josiah stepped away with the white board looking down at the scribble as Katie performed her nursing duties. "You are very lucky, Mrs. Stapleton. It was pretty close last night for a little while, but your friend here…" Katie looked at Josiah. "What's your name again?" she asked embarrassed as she took Ethel's blood pressure.

"Josiah."

"Josiah sat by your side all night." Katie walked around and checked Ethel's IV and temperature and then injected her with a dose of morning medicines. "This is going to make you sleep because you need to get your rest."

When Katie left, Ethel looked over at Josiah demanding him to return. He immediately replaced the board inches away from her hand. Ethel continued where she left off, and after a few sleepy minutes, her hand fell onto the bed, dropping her marker onto the laminate floor. The marker rolled precisely between Josiah's feet.

"Sleep well," Josiah whispered in her ear as he bent down to pick up the pen. He walked over to the window and attempted to read the board.

He eyed the concoction of letters that was clumped into one long strand of unreadable text, but he knew that she was trying to tell him something. It was something that she desperately wanted him to read. He read and reread the conglomeration, but it made less sense than the time before.

He started to write down the letters on the board: thcrewQsomconelnmyro. As he began to write, a phrase jumped off the board, a phrase he wished he didn't see. He drew a line between the e and w, added another s beside the other one with a line between

234

them, and drew a line in front of the l, m, and r. Josiah finally realized that she hadn't finished her sentence before she dropped off to sleep. He dropped the marker onto the floor and ran back to Ethel's bed. He watched as she slept soundly, but there was somewhere else he needed to be.

Josiah quickly rushed to the nurses' station and found Katie sipping her coffee. "How long will she be out from the dose you just gave her?"

"Oh, she will be out for some time."

"Thank you," he waved as he proceeded to the elevator. He hit the down arrow and waited impatiently for the doors to slide open. As he waited alone, all he could see were the red letters. The petrified red letters.

Thcre wQs somcone ln my ro.

There was someone in my ro…om!

CHAPTER 85

The small group huddled together in James' living room. No hospitable cups of coffee or friendly greetings were offered. They had gathered together not for the camaraderie, but to accomplish a task. This was strictly business; everyone knew their place, and smiles were not welcomed.

"Is everything set for today?" the leader of the group commanded with charismatic delegation.

"Yes, I think everything is ready," Carlos feebly answered with his chin sunken down onto his chest.

"Excellent," the leader said emotionless. The room was dimly lit with a singular table lamp in the far corner; the blinds were shut, keeping the sunlight from intruding on their secret society meeting.

"Do you think he suspects anything?" Jade smugly asked as he sat rigid in the wooden rocking chair.

"I'm not sure," Carlos answered with a quiver in his speech. "Most people would assume that a heart attack was imminent for a woman her age with a lifetime of deep-fried meals."

"But Josiah isn't most people," the leader refuted with supreme dominance. "Carlos, you know him better than any of us," the leader said, grabbing his chin off his chest to see the terrified gaze in his eyes. "Why do you look so afraid, Carlos?"

"I, uh, afraid?" Carlos stuttered. "I, I'm not afraid," he spoke unconvincingly as the rest of the committee watched with bated breath.

"You can't fool us," Maxwell lectured as he loomed over Carlos' shoulder. "We know that you two were close. We know how fond of him you were before you joined us."

Carlos sensed the pressure and felt trapped and squeezed from all sides. "That was in the past," he answered with a stale glimmer of bravery. "You know where my loyalty lies now."

"You showed a little of your faithfulness last night, but I don't believe you have proven your total allegiance just yet," the leader remarked, eyeing each of the guests in the room as they returned their dedicated stare. "Carlos, if you continue to do as you are asked, you will be amply rewarded."

"Thank you. Thank you, my lord," he said bowing his head in respect as the group of men all joined in their act of submission.

"James, are you ready?" the leader asked as James sat aloof in the distant corner. "James, come closer. You have also done very well so far. Very well indeed."

"Thank you. You are too kind," James said slowly walking within reach of the rest of the members. The closer he got to his leader, the lower his head bowed in reverence.

"Look at me, James," the leader commanded with a force of barbaric proportions. "This all depends on you."

"I will make you proud, my lord."

"Carlos, what time do you make your entrance?" The leader panted with evil delight, imagining the grand victory in the extravagant plan.

"1:15 this afternoon," Carlos answered as he looked over at James, who nodded his head in affirmation.

"Very good," the leader deviously smiled as the group remained transfixed and emotionless. The tension was building. Nerves were twitching in Carlos' and James' stomachs. James had put on a good show thus far.

Beginner's luck?

CHAPTER 86

The bedroom was organized and tidy with no sign of any intruder or guest lurking in the corner. Josiah walked around Ethel's bedroom and started rummaging through her personal belongings. When he opened her jewelry box, a whimsical tune began to fill his ears as he sifted through the gold pendants and necklaces. He enjoyed the sound of the music, so he left it open as he continued to look through her nightstand.

Picking up a Bible, he saw the worn pages and tattered leather binding. He flipped the book open and saw notes neatly written along the margins. There were no blank areas on any pages. He admired her devotion in a belief of a supreme being that she hadn't met. The concept of religion had always been baffling to him because he was never taught or needed to believe in a notion of faith.

He laid the Bible down and proceeded to search every square inch of the room. He didn't know what he was looking for, or even if he would find it, but he knew that there must have been something here at one time. Ethel hadn't mentioned who was in the room, but in a quiet town like Bethany, Josiah knew it was one of his former acquaintances.

Josiah pushed clothing around in her closet, allowing him access to every nook and cranny. As he searched every pocket, he couldn't help but question what Ethel had to do with his mission.

He was not given all the information about his case, but he was starting to reason that Mrs. Stapleton's room and board wasn't just a temporary living arrangement. It wasn't just a coincidence that he was living here; it was planned that he was to stay here.

Closing the closet door, Josiah rested his back against the muted white walls. He scanned the room with keen insight, praying that something would jump off a shelf, roll off the bedspread, or even fall from the plastered ceiling. Nothing was found. Nothing was noted. Nothing was discovered.

If I were to hide something, where would I hide it? he asked himself as he began to rub his hand along the wall. He glided his palm along the smooth surface, feeling ripples and bubbles from the wallpaper under the thin layer of paint. Tapping the wall, he heard the same thud every other inch he hit. He tapped the wall beside the framed portrait of Ethel and her late husband that hung over her dresser.

He lifted the picture so he could continue to search for a secret area in the wall, causing the nail to fall out. He turned to lay down the picture when he noticed a children's nursery rhyme on the back of the frame, Ten Little Indians.

He sat down to read the childish tale as a twisted grin and hearty laugh filled the air. He got near the end of the poem as a thought struck him with lightning bolt intensity.

"Four little Indian boys going out to sea; a red herring swallowed one and then there were three."

Josiah realized who the four little Indian boys were in his life: Carlos, Maxwell, Jade, and himself. He had spent the morning being swallowed in the mystery of their red herring. Josiah got up from the bed and closed the jewelry box to silence the room. He glanced down at the clock on Ethel's nightstand and was shocked at the time, 11:18 am. The morning was wasted.

Their plan had worked.

CHAPTER 87

The house wasn't clean enough, the streamers weren't curly enough, there were not enough helium-filled balloons, and it was almost noon. Claire hustled around the house, trying to make everything look perfect, but perfect wasn't good enough.

"Amelia!" she shouted as she wiped her finger over the china cabinet, making sure no dust was found. Her finger was clean. "Amelia! Come down and help. Guests will be here in an hour."

Claire opened the freezer and saw three different kinds of ice cream: chocolate chip cookie dough for Charlie, mint chocolate chip for Scarlett, and vegan butter pecan soy cream for Amelia. Claire tried to relax in the frigid air, but it wasn't enough. She stared at the empty shelf in the cold and wished she was small enough to cram herself in and shut the door. She was supermom; she used to be able to handle a birthday party, a science project, and a three-course dinner without getting a hair out of place. That was before her suspicions.

"Mom, Amelia won't get out of bed," Scarlett said as she came from putting up her shoes that usually laid beside the front door.

"Amelia!" Claire shouted again as she slammed the freezer door. "Get your keister down here and help out!"

"She won't, Mom," Scarlett bickered as she grabbed five balloons to hang on the mailbox. "She threw her pillow at me when I walked in her room just a minute ago."

Claire stomped up the stairs and proceeded down the hall. "Amelia, if you are not out of bed by time I get to your room, so help me God, I may just lose it!" With each step she took, her rage grew. This day was not turning out the way she had wished. Her blood was boiling, and she knew that even though Amelia was being lazy on her brother's day, the reason for her anger wasn't Amelia. It was Dan.

"Sorry, Mom," Amelia said as she stood slumped over trying to get on a pair of jeans. "I just don't feel good."

240

"Amelia, please, just get some clothes on and help us. Your dad went to go get the cake and he should be back in fifteen minutes." Claire turned out of Amelia's room and jumped down the stairs. "And brush your hair."

Claire looked at her watch and knew they were cutting it close on time. "Charlie, is your room clean?" she yelled as she saw her son lounged on the couch watching *Sponge Bob Square Pants*.

"Yep," he answered without looking away from the television.

Scarlett's hands were free from putting up the balloons. "Why does he get to sit around while I have to help you?"

"Scarlett, please don't start," Claire moaned as she entered the kitchen to get the bags of chips down from the cabinet and vegetable tray out of the refrigerator. "Charlie, come help me make your veggie dip."

"I don't want any veggie dip," he moaned as he got up from the couch.

"Fine, you can just help me make it for Amelia!" Claire yelled, losing her temper.

"Okay," Charlie said walking into the kitchen, looking up at Scarlett for protection.

"I got you little buddy," Scarlett said. "We got this, Mom."

CHAPTER 88

"So, am I invited to your daughter's birthday party?" Karen asked as she lounged in her pajamas, sipping a cappuccino and watching her recorded *Modern Family*.

"I don't think that's the best thing right now," Dan responded as he eyed the birthday cake in his front seat. "And it's my son, Charlie's birthday."

"Yeah, good ol' Charlie," Karen snickered as she was half listening and half watching her latest addiction.

"I hate to bring this up all the time," Dan said as he was interrupted.

"Then don't. It's the weekend."

Dan ignored her comment. "Have you spoken with James this morning?"

"James?" Karen asked confused.

"Karen, you said last night you were going to call him and see what he was doing with the PR. The FDA is onto Pharm, and it's only a matter of time before anyone that has had any history with this pill is going to go down."

"I'll go down with you," she said seductively. Dan would have smiled in any other situation, but due to the circumstances he rolled his eyes in aggravation.

"Karen, stop!" he billowed, slamming his fist on the steering wheel. "I have to get off the phone, and you need to call James!" Dan ended the call and threw his phone into his empty cup holder.

His world was unraveling. His career was getting too close to the line. His marriage was teetering on the edge, and Karen was on the verge of manic narcissism. He looked down at the cake and wondered what would make him the saddest to lose.

He wasn't sure.

CHAPTER 89

"Put the presents on the dining room table," Claire said to Scarlett, blindly handing her the perfectly wrapped presents in odd-shaped boxes as she continued to welcome her party guests.

Scarlett carried three presents that were stacked, forcing her chin to hold the top present down. She put on a pleasant smile because so far today, her mother hadn't mentioned the cheating scandal. Today was all about Charlie.

"Amelia!" Scarlett snapped as she entered the dining room to find her sister sitting with her head down on the table, using one of the softer presents as her pillow.

"I can't help it. I just feel so tired," Amelia said as she looked up defenselessly at her sister. "Please let me stay in here a little while longer."

Scarlett laid down the presents and thought for a second. *What should I ask for? To do my English report or my history paper?* "Hmm, this is an interesting situation."

"Scar, I'll do whatever you want, just let me go upstairs to my room during the party."

"Whatever I want?" Scarlett grinned like a cheetah about to pounce on a wounded gazelle. "I have two papers I need to finish."

"Done," Amelia answered as she struggled to get to her feet, clumsily making it to the door.

"Are you going to make it?"

Amelia let go of the table and headed out of the room. "I'll be fine. I just need a little more sleep."

"You shouldn't have stayed up so late reading one of your books," Scarlett said as she heard her mom yelling for her and Amelia.

"You promised. Make up an excuse to Mom. Tell her I'm organizing the presents or outside with Charlie or something."

"Amelia, really? You're telling me how to lie?" Scarlett laughed at the thought of her tight-laced sister trying to teach her how to sneak around their mom. "You're covered, Amelia."

The house was filling with guests, and Scarlett knew that given a few more people, her mother wouldn't even notice that Amelia wasn't around. This was going to be the easiest way to earn her free papers. "You needed something, Mom?"

"Can you check on your dad outside with the grill and make sure he doesn't need anything?" Claire asked as she stood around a group of moms half listening to one of the proud mothers brag incessantly about her daughter's wizardry skills on the violin.

"Will do," Scarlett said, turning around with a look of gratitude for leaving the boring conversation.

She started to walk away when her mother stopped her, "Where is Amelia?"

Just as Scarlett was about to choose one of the five excuses she had up her sleeve, the doorbell rang. "I'll get it, Mom," Scarlett said, allowing her mom to visit with the other forty-year old women. By the look on Claire's face, she would have rather gotten the door than listen to another play-by-play of the whiz kid's recital.

Scarlett opened the door to find another present held in a pair of arms. "Hey, Scarlett," Lucy said as she and her father, James, entered the living room.

"Hello Lucy, Mr. Nialliv," Scarlett said taking the present out of Lucy's arms. "Dad is in the backyard if you want to see him," she said to James as Lucy followed her in the dining room to drop off the present.

"We got him a board game," Lucy groaned to Scarlett. "I didn't know what a seven-year-old boy would want."

"Me neither and I live with the twerp."

CHAPTER 90

"The flame is really getting your burgers," James commented as he watched Dan slave over the grill, trying to cook twenty-five hamburgers and hotdogs. "You better watch them so they don't burn."

Dan nodded his head in agreement but continued to let the burgers get surrounded by the fire.

"I don't want to tell you how to grill," James said as Dan thought, *Then don't.* "But that is too much flame."

"Do you want to do this?" Dan asked with a forced laugh as he pressed the burgers with the spatula. The grease squirted out, causing a skyscraper flame to build inches from Dan's hairline.

"No," James answered as he inched closer to the flaming grill with a hypnotized smile, "you are doing just fine."

"So, did Karen speak with you this morning?" Dan asked as he rolled the hotdogs around on the grill.

"Yes. Yes, she did," James answered as he picked up a hotdog from the grill, guiding his arm through the burning flames. He retrieved it unscathed and proceeded to eat it without any bread.

Dan closed the grill and lowered his voice to a muffle, "So, what did you say?"

"Oh, I told her that she should get a red one."

"You told her what?" Dan questioned, confused by the off-hand statement.

"Yeah, she was asking about what color she should get for her new Beemer."

Dan flipped open the grill and maniacally tossed the burgers onto his metal platter. He took a deep breath and clung to a thread of hope that James was being his typical self – an ass. "Did you two talk about my visitor yesterday?"

"Oh, yes, she started talking to me about that, but I told her that you should have it all handled," James said, taking another bite of his charred hotdog.

When the last burger and hotdog were on the platter, Dan took the lunch over to Claire, who was now sitting under a rented canopy with room for forty-five, watching the children play on the inflatable bouncy castle. "Here you go."

"Just lay it over there by the buns," she said waving him off as she continued to watch her son smile while he jumped and collided with kids from school. At first she was nervous when he was falling and bumping into the others, but when she heard laughter and not blood-curdling cries, she relaxed.

"Thanks," he smugly answered as he laid the food down and motioned James to follow him into the house.

The two men walked into Dan's office, where he hadn't worked for a few weeks since he had been spending so much time at his downtown office and with Karen. "Let's get this straight!" Dan ignited his fuse and it was now time to blow since everyone was outside at the party. "I cannot handle your lies! When the government comes to me, wanting my head on a platter because of all the deaths that you have caused, that is where I draw the line!"

"But Dan, you promised, remember?" James asked cunningly, as if forming a web around their conversation.

"Yes, I remember I promised, but you didn't tell me everything!" he answered firmly and decisively. "You manipulated me!"

"I did no such thing," James remarked with a facetious tone.

"James, you basically coerced me by saying that my career would be over if I didn't do this for you!"

"Yes, and your point is?" James sneered.

Dan took a moment to find the right words. "My point? My point?" he shouted with aggravation. "My point is that I am just an attorney that got blind-sided. I have legal privilege to get out before it is too late."

"Really? You think I would let you do that?"

"Is that a threat?" Dan rebutted.

"If you walk away, I will make sure that you are burned more than your hotdogs!" he scoffed with arrogance. "I will make sure that you never work again. I will use my connections and get the Bar Association to look into all of your past cases and they will dissect you. After you lose your clients and your job, how will you pay for this lovely house?" He walked around the room like it was a theatric production. "I will call every lending institution in the country, if need be, and blackball you so fast that you will be out on the street!"

"You wouldn't dare!"

"Oh, dare me, pretty boy!" James stood a few inches from Dan's face and patted him on his check. "You are fairly handsome. At least I assume your wife thinks so since she married you, but I'm definite about Karen. If you think that you will keep your pretty little family after you lose everything, consider how you will keep your wife after she knows that you are slipping it to your co-worker!"

"You are crossing a line between business and personal!"

"Oh, Dan, with me, there is no line. Always remember that. I will never give a second thought about your minuscule existence if it betters mine." The heated argument ceased as the two men heard the doorbell ring. "I think you have a visitor," James smiled wickedly, "and she's right on time."

"What are you doing?" Dan's words trembled off his tongue.

CHAPTER 91

"Where is the birthday boy?" Karen asked as she handed Dan the Wal-Mart plastic bag she was carrying. "I didn't have time to wrap it since *you* didn't invite me, but when I spoke with Jimmy, he told me to come on over."

"He did, did he?" Dan feebly smiled, his stomach curling up into knots as he looked at Karen, who was wearing a holster top and a mini-skirt, revealing almost more skin than someone in a bathing suit.

"I didn't know what to get your son, so I picked up a movie," she said, slurring her words as she entered the house and spun around the room, taking in every little detail. "This is a lovely home. Your wife has some excellent taste." She winked as she undressed him with her eyes. "Excellent taste indeed. Yum."

"You didn't need to get Charlie anything," Dan said as he looked into the bag. "*The Hangover?*" Dan asked with a surprising tone.

"Yeah, does he already have it?" she asked as a frown appeared on her face. "I really wanted to get him something he would like, so he would remember me," she said, flirting inappropriately, not just because it was Charlie's birthday, but because she was in his home.

"No, he doesn't already have it," Dan quipped, but apparently Karen didn't hear the condescending tone since her face lit up. "He's seven. He doesn't need to watch this movie at his age." He handed her back the bag, "Here, put this in your purse."

"Jimmy!" Karen squealed as she noticed him standing in the hallway.

"Good to see you, Karen. You're looking good," James said, greeting her with a kiss and acknowledging her skimpy outfit.

Dan pulled Karen by the arm to get her attention. "Are you drunk?"

"What if I am? What if I'm not?" she asked with a sinuous smile. "But what if I am?" She laughed like a freshman sorority girl getting caught by her older handsome room advisor.

"I can't have a drunk woman at my son's birthday. It just wouldn't look right."

"Oh, Dan, come on," James interrupted. "What harm will it do?"

Dan could list a number of possible harmful situations that could arise with her alcohol-impaired personality. "I think it would be best if you just leave."

"But I haven't even met Carl yet," Karen said depressingly.

"Charlie," Dan corrected, getting more perturbed by this situation orchestrated by James.

"And I haven't even gotten to talk to your wife." She frowned a puppy dog face, trying to gain some sympathy, but Dan wasn't going to give any.

"No, you need to leave," Dan demanded. "I have to go be with my son, but when I come back in here, you better be gone."

"Dan, why aren't you outsi--," Claire asked and stopped her sentence, unaware of his company. "I'm sorry, I didn't know you had company in here."

James took command of the situation. "This is Dr. Karen Anderson. She is the creator of the drug we are working on."

"Nice to meet you," Claire said with a little shock in her tone as she stuck out her hand to greet her new visitor. "So, you are Dr. Anderson."

"That would be me," Karen giggled like a teenager in an awkward situation.

"Well, my husband never told me that Dr. Anderson was so attractive," Claire smiled, leaning into Dan's ear and whispered, "or a woman."

CHAPTER 92

The driveway of the Sutton's home was filled with a plethora of vehicles including minivans, SUVs, and luxury sport cars. Josiah's ride was an eyesore compared to the lifestyles of the Sutton's circle of Bethany's rich and famous.

Josiah heard the sounds of a birthday party: the laughter, the early childhood screams of excitement, and the drowning conversation of middle-age adults coming from behind the house. He wondered about ringing the doorbell but thought it would be better to come to the backyard unannounced.

He looked around the house as he walked through the yard. The last time he had made this journey was with only the light from the moon. He came to the back of the house and peered his head around the corner to see the red, yellow, and blue inflatable castle that was larger than some of the homes in the projects. He scanned the crowd for the Sutton clan, but he didn't see any of them.

The party was lively, the children were enthused, and the atmosphere was lighthearted. Josiah continued to stand at a safe distance and watched the smiles flash as the kids jumped up in the air on their trampoline-like castle. He knew all the kids that were enjoying themselves, but he was searching for just a choice few. Suddenly, a head popped out of the Velcro gate with a loud contagious laugh. Charlie was the life of the party.

Lurking around the corner, he slowly looked for the other Sutton children, but he could not find the twins.

Sadly for Josiah, he was spotted.

CHAPTER 93

"How dare he come to my house!" Scarlett yelled, shaking in fury with the notion that the man who planted evidence in her book was now hiding beside her house.

"What is he doing here?" Lucy asked as the two of them sat in the shade of the trees, a few yards away from the peaceful river.

"I don't know. To tell on me for taking a finger of icing before the cake was cut?"

The two girls watched Josiah and giggled at the different ideas of revenge they were forming. "What if I spray him with the water hose?" Scarlett asked.

"No, he would probably just enjoy it. Getting all wet in front of these kids; it would probably be a turn-on for him," Lucy said with a disgusted attitude. "He would probably like it. Pervert."

"Yeah, he probably would," Scarlett agreed with a grotesque grin. "What if we call the cops on him for spying on us?"

"Nah, he would get out of it," Lucy said unconvinced. "Your sister would probably say she invited him."

"Dumb Amelia."

"Yep," Lucy agreed annoyingly.

Their minds were spinning as Scarlett continued to spout out ideas, but none of them seemed easily attainable or brutal enough from Lucy's perspective. They stopped mocking the kids in the play castle to fixate solely on Josiah's demise.

"I got it!" Lucy exclaimed as she dropped her plate of half-eaten hamburger.

"What?" Scarlett asked as she finished drinking her Sunkist.

"It's good," Lucy mischievously gazed, "but…" she stopped.

"But what?"

"I don't think you have the guts to do it," Lucy jabbed wickedly.

Scarlett was taken back by the remark. She wasn't sure if it was a friendly josh, or if her friend was truly questioning her bravery. "Test me."

"I don't know. It's pretty bad," Lucy said, figuratively dangling a carrot in front of Scarlett's face.

"Lucy, tell me!"

"Okay," Lucy surrendered, whispering the menacing idea into her best friend's ear. Scarlett's eyes widened with intrigue as Lucy continued to lay out every little detail of her plan.

"That is good," Scarlett smiled cruelly. "Let's go."

CHAPTER 94

The women parted ways. Claire returned to the birthday party disgruntled, while Karen drunkenly drove home. "Do you see how easy it would have been for your life to fall apart, with just one word out of my lips," James bullied. "BOOM! Your life would be toast."

Dan internally crumbled as he watched the smile slowly fade from James' face. He was not ready for everything to blow up, but was anyone ever ready for a disaster? "Can you just leave?" Dan choked on the words as they came out of his mouth.

"Dan, is that how you are going to treat me?" James snidely asked. "Look at our history."

Dan built up a figurative barrier so he wouldn't feel damaged by the cunning words. "History? History? The only history I recall is infamous."

"Dan, if you fulfill your promise, your future is limitless." James wickedly smiled, as if the words were leaving a delicious tingle on his taste buds.

"Just leave," Dan commanded once again, walking to the door to let out his unwanted guest.

"Dan, just slow down for a second," James said changing his manner to a more flattering and friendly tone. "Think about what you are doing. If I walk out this door, all hell will break loose on your career, your family, and your life." James stepped toward Dan until their noses almost touched. James stood undaunted, while Dan's breathing was starting to quicken. "Dan, I think you need some time to think about what you are doing."

The two men stared with primal instincts coursing through their veins. No words were said, no smiles were exchanged, nothing but a force field of tension was standing between them.

"If that is how you want to end this Dan, that is fine by me," James said as he walked away heading to the backyard. "I can always find another attorney, but you will never be able to find a new life."

"Where are you going?" Dan followed. "The front door is where you need to go."

James got to the back door and turned. Dan looked into his fiery eyes and was startled by the intensity. "Yes, but I have an announcement to make first." James turned the knob and slowly cracked the door open.

The image of his life falling to shambles was too much for Dan to stand by idly. "James, wait!"

"Too late, Dan. Too late." James stepped out and took command of the playing field. "Excuse me, excuse me, I have an announcement to make!"

"James!"

CHAPTER 95

"I am going to go get some sugar free ice cream!" James shouted, turning around to see Dan slump as his tension deflated out of him like a birthday balloon.

"We'll go with you," Lucy said as she came running up with Scarlett slowly walking behind with an incredible smile grazing her face.

"Fine with me," James said to Dan as Claire came walking up to them.

"Thank you so much, James. I totally forgot about Christian being diabetic," Claire said as she politely tapped his arm. "Sure you don't mind?"

"No, not at all," James said with a polite smile.

"Can I go with them?" Scarlett asked, begging her mom and dad to leave with them, even though she knew she was grounded.

"I don't know," Dan said as the frightening conversation between him and James echoed in his mind from just minutes ago. "You are grounded."

"Oh, Dan," Claire let out, "she is just going to get ice cream."

"Please!" Scarlett begged once again. "Please!"

"Well, hello Mr. Sutton, Mrs. Sutton," Josiah said, nodding as he spoke to each one of them.

"Josiah, how have you been?" James asked as he stuck out his hand like a gentleman.

Josiah politely stretched out his hand and returned the gesture. "Mr. Nialliv."

"I think he asked you a question," Scarlett spoke up, making sure he was aware of her presence.

"Yes, I'm afraid I am not doing very well," Josiah answered quickly staring back at James. "Mrs. Stapleton had a heart attack last night."

255

"Oh my, how is she?" Claire asked as she clutched her chest with the surprising words.

"She is, she is doing…" Josiah was about to answer, but suddenly stopped as he saw James continue to smile. "She's doing."

"I will say an extra prayer for her tonight," Claire kindly remarked.

"Yes, I will too," James said, as he continued to smile and look intently at Josiah. "Well, we need to get the ice cream."

"I need to speak to you," Josiah said as he looked down at Scarlett.

"Well, I don't want to speak to you!" Scarlett shouted.

"Scarlett, stop that!" Dan sternly stated as he glanced over to Claire who was shocked as well by Scarlett's outburst.

"I just need to speak with you. James, you can go and get your ice cream," Josiah systematically pointed out.

"I don't think Scarlett wants to speak with you," James said stepping forward in between Josiah and Scarlett, forming a human shield. "Let's go."

"Mary, please," Josiah requested with a heart-felt plea.

"Should have thought about that before you accused me of cheating!" Scarlett snapped as she looked over at her parents.

"I'm sorry, Mary, but I had to," Josiah feebly replied.

"You had to?" Dan inquired with confusion. "When you say you had to, does that mean she cheated or that you accused her of cheating?"

"I'm sorry," Josiah said in need of forgiveness so he could once again regain her trust. "Mary, I'm really sorry."

"But they found the answers in her book, didn't they?" Claire asked bewildered as she looked at her husband and then to Josiah before turning once again to Dan.

"Josiah, I am not sure what is going on here, but I think it's time for you to leave," Dan said as he watched his daughter's eyes light up. "Please leave. We can talk about this when it isn't my son's birthday."

"But Mary," Josiah begged as James pushed Scarlett and Lucy into the house.

"Bye, Josiah," James waved childishly behind the glass of the backdoor. Josiah's demeanor dropped from hopeful to devastated as he watched Mary turn and go side by side with his enemy. "Goodbye," James silently said with a grimacing smile, nailing shut all of Josiah's wishful thinking.

CHAPTER 96

"I cannot believe him!" Scarlett ranted as she tried to buckle her seat belt in the back seat. "Um, Mr. Nialliv, I can't get my seat belt to work back here."

"Oh, I'm sorry, Scarlett, they haven't worked in a few months, but since I never have anyone sitting in the back seat, I have never gotten them fixed. If you just sit back, I'll be careful."

"Okay," Scarlett said, whipping the restraining belt away from her chest. "I never like wearing them anyways because they always choke my neck."

"Me either," Lucy said, as she unbuckled her's as well.

"You're going to get me in trouble if a cop sees us," James laughed as he started to back out of the driveway. He passed Josiah's ride and chuckled at the old lady vehicle.

They drove down the lonely country road, surpassing the speed limit easily with his sports car's engine. He watched the needle dance around eighty miles per hour as he continually glanced out the rearview mirror. Oblivious of the circumstances, Scarlett began to giggle wildly, followed by Lucy joining. "What is so funny, you two?"

"Nothing, Dad."

"Come on, you can tell me," he said, trying to act like the coolest dad in the world as he glanced at his rearview mirror again, seeing a distant vehicle behind him. "You've never kept anything from me before."

"Well," Lucy remarked.

"We can't tell you," Scarlett added enthusiastically, "because if you knew what we did, that would make you an accomplice."

"An accomplice?" James' voice heightened in suspicion as he pressed the gas pedal to hit ninety. "You can't leave me hanging after you say that."

"Dad," Lucy groaned, stretching the word into two syllables.

"Fine," he mumbled, keeping watch on his rearview mirror.

Scarlett peered out the window and realized that they weren't near downtown Bethany and that the car was going faster than she had ever ridden before. "Cool, Mr. Nialliv."

"Scarlett, call me James."

"Okay, James," she said as she started to laugh.

"What's so funny?" he asked.

Scarlett rolled her eyes at her thought. "It's just that you are driving me and I'm in the back seat and your name is James."

"You're not the first one to say that," he smiled, catching her eyes in the rearview mirror.

"Well, anyways," she tried to control her laughter, "where are we going to get this ice cream?"

"Yeah, Dad. Sam's Market is the other way."

James smiled as he drove forward where the fields of soybeans gave way to a forest of trees. "There's a small gas station down this road. I just thought we would drive this way to get out of the house for a little bit after the whole Josiah incident."

"Thanks," Scarlett said as she moved to the center of the seat and inched forward so her head was in between the front seats.

Looking into his rearview mirror, a smile stretched wider on his face. The car he had been watching seemed to have disappeared in the distance. He looked down at the clock and saw that it was 1:02 p.m. He started to lower his speed to forty-five miles per hour, even though the speed limit was fifty-five. As he rounded a curve, he noticed that a silver Toyota Camry had its emergency lights blinking on the side of the road. "Looks like someone is having some car trouble up ahead. Should we be nice and ask if they need help?"

"Fine by me," Scarlett answered. "I'm in no rush."

"Help we shall then," James answered as he glanced over at Lucy in the passenger seat.

CHAPTER 97

Josiah calmly walked away from the tension-filled atmosphere, while the eyes of every parent were taking mental photographs of his appearance. As he turned beside the house, out of view from the party guests, he took off at a sprint. He saw James' M6 go the opposite direction of Bethany.

Panic filled his body at the thought of the endless possibilities that James' demented mind was capable of accomplishing. He jumped into his car and did a U-turn to retrace his path. He slammed his foot on the gas pedal, squealing his tires and leaving tire marks on the flawless road.

"Come on, come on!" he yelled as he saw a red dot fleeing down the road ahead of him. He knew that he needed to get closer, but Mrs. Stapleton's vehicle was little competition for an M6. He pressed the pedal all the way to the floor and felt the steering wheel rattle and shake from the mounting speed. "Please get there. Please!" he prayed as he watched the red dot become a larger red dot. He was starting to make out the image of the car when the unthinkable occurred.

A horrendous loud pop resounded outside his vehicle, and the car suddenly began to decelerate. "No! No! No!" he screamed as he felt an uncomfortable jarring from the car. He tried to ignore the damage and continue forward, but it was too much. He pulled over to the side of the road as the car hobbled to a stop.

Stepping out of the car, he saw what he expected. A flat back tire. Bending down to examine the rubber, he realized that this was no accident. "You little!" he shouted as he ran his finger along five slash marks on the outside of the tire.

He was being sabotaged by the very person he was supposed to protect.

CHAPTER 98

James slowed his car, coming to a stop beside the stalled vehicle. Rolling down his passenger side window, James leaned down to see a rugged-looking man. "Excuse me, do you need any help?"

Scarlett sat nervous as a man in a pair of worn out blue jeans with holes scattered up and down the legs looked up from under his car hood. He wiped his grease-covered hands on his thighs, leaving a black smeared handprint. She watched James as he heroically offered his assistance without dropping a syllable from a quivering lip. He was perfectly calm with a warm smile.

"Well, I'm not sure," the stranger answered as he stepped away from his vehicle and approached their makeshift shield of protection. Scarlett looked in his direction, but she couldn't see his face behind his aviator sunglasses and his Florida Gators baseball cap.

"I'm not a handy man," James laughed as he looked at his manicured fingernails, "but I can call someone for you."

The stranger took a step away from the sports car and shuffled his feet on the road deep in thought. "I don't want to be of any inconvenience." He stooped down to examine the inside of the BMW. His fingers crossed the safety parallel of the rolled down window, feeling the soft leather of the car's interior.

"No inconvenience," James said as he pulled out his cell phone from his shirt pocket. "I'll call you a tow truck."

"That is awfully kind of you, sir."

Scarlett's breath was taken away as she looked at his face, seeing her image in his reflective sunglasses. Her family had never stopped to help a total stranger, and being on a deserted country road made the situation feel more uncomfortable.

"You got some mighty pretty girls here," the stranger commented with a boyish smile.

"Thank you," Lucy said, giggling and blushing at his remarks.

"Yeah, thank you," Scarlett whispered as her eyes darted into her lap, hoping that her childish ostrich philosophy would suddenly become dogma.

"I think so," James said as he waited for someone to pick up at the twenty-four-hour roadside recovery. "Yes, I have a man here who is having some trouble..." James continued with his conversation as Scarlett tuned him out. All she wanted was to drive away from this goosebump-worthy moment.

"This is a really nice ride you have here, little girl," the man said as he stuck his hand into his coat pocket. "Much better than my worn-out rice burner."

Scarlett watched with frightened eyes as she saw a pointed object protruding from his lightweight jacket.

"What are your names?" he asked, looking only at the two girls.

He fumbled his hand around as Lucy answered, "I'm Lucy and this is Scarlett."

"Lucy and Scarlett," he said with a mysterious smile. "Those are some cute names. I like them," he said as he stared directly at Scarlett. "I love the color scarlet," he moaned sensually. "It's just so deep and rich in beauty." He stopped and took a deep breath. "Do you two live around here?" He looked up and down the empty road. "I mean, there are no homes around here."

Scarlett looked into James' rearview mirror, staring into his compassionate eyes, hoping that his kindness would cease and they would drive off safely.

"It's not safe out here. You never know who you might meet," the stranger said with a creepy smile.

"Uh huh," Scarlett answered as she watched his hand move, gripping an object in his pocket. He started to pull out his hand, and Scarlett's heart began to beat uncontrollably. She stared as the top of his hand became visible. He slowly continued to unearth his hand, clearly gripping something in his clenched fist.

"James!" Scarlett screamed at the top of her voice, screeching with terror-filled lungs. "He's got a..." she watched as he opened his hand, showing his cigarette lighter.

"I'm sorry, that is not polite of me to smoke in front of you," he said as he stood up straighter and put away his lighter. "I'm sorry, Scarlett."

James put up his phone and apologized for Scarlett's outburst while looking down at the time on the clock radio. "They just taught them about drugs in school the other week," James quickly spoke. "We have to be off and get some ice cream. Harvey's Garage said they would be here in twenty minutes."

"Thanks a lot," the stranger said as he tipped his ballcap to the young girls.

James put the car into drive and sped away, kicking up dust from the tires into the stranger's face. Well, a stranger for Scarlett, but not for James. He looked up into his rearview mirror, watching Maxwell stare in their direction.

Only a few more minutes, James thought.

1:13 p.m.

CHAPTER 99

Scarlett turned around in her seat and watched the creepy man grow smaller and smaller as they drove away. "That guy was scary," she said as she could still make out his outline. Even with the growing distance between them, she felt like he was still watching her.

"Oh, Scarlett," Lucy said as she looked into the backseat, "you're just a chicken."

"Well, there's nothing wrong with not feeling good around a stranger," Scarlett said as James took a turn, causing her to fall onto the seat. "You could have warned me about that." She laughed as she rolled off the seat onto the cramped backseat floor as he made another quick turn, zigzagging his way through the country roads.

"Sorry about that," James said as he hit the gas when the road became straight again, inching his speedometer to seventy miles per hour. The car was zipping past the end of the forest and entering into a dark golden-colored grain field. "Can you get up?" he asked as he turned his head around for a better look.

"I'm getting there," Scarlett huffed, struggling up to the seat behind Lucy, her butt stuck by the front seat. "I guess I'm not as small as I thought I was. Can you scoot your seat up?"

Lucy reached under her seat for the lever. "I can't find it."

"Come on Lucy, reach for it," Scarlett said, grunting as she tried to grab a hold of the front seat console, but it wasn't enough for her to budge.

James looked down at his clock as it blinked 1:15. A haunting smile enveloped his face, one similar to Charlie's as he watched all his friends unloading their birthday presents.

"I can't, I can't," Lucy said as she reached one last time and then waved the white flag in surrender. "We're almost there, right?"

"Yes," James said wickedly.

Scarlett looked overhead and saw the handrails on the ceiling over the passenger side window. She stretched her long athletic arms up like she was blocking a shot and clung onto the secure grips. She pulled her upper body, allowing her butt to move off of the floorboard. Her legs were able to bend, giving her arms some leveraged support.

James turned his head around and saw that she finally made it up. He opened his mouth, but Scarlett stopped him. "Deer!"

CHAPTER 100

There wasn't just one deer that galloped across the deserted road, but a mob of them. They were traveling in their herd at full speed, camouflaged by the swaying grain field which blended with their brown coats. The first buck that leaped on the road was a massive sight with twelve points on its antlers. His muscles rippled with each jump, showcasing his beauty like a chiseled statue. Sadly, the male was no competition for the speeding sports car.

James hit his breaks, colliding into the gorgeous creature that would have been worthy to be mounted in any hunter's cabin. The tires squealed as Scarlett screamed, holding onto her handle. She was thrown into the back of Lucy's seat, ricocheting back to hers and then pounding onto the thick glass window of the backseat. She saw her life flash, but she wasn't ready for it to flash to the end.

She tightened her grip as the car started to spin like a hazardous merry-go-round. The deer stampede continued to pounce over the car; some were being bucked off as Scarlett dizzily watched the car circle. James tried to control the fiasco, but the car was not obeying. He strongly jerked one last time, and Scarlett's head crashed into the ceiling, knocking her unconscious and causing her to release her clutches from the handle.

As she fell onto the seat, Lucy's body soared through the broken glass landing crumbled like a rag doll in the grass fifteen feet away from the stream of deer.

Scarlett's eyes closed and she couldn't feel the summersault of the M6. She couldn't see James' face pressed against a portion of the remaining driver's side window. She couldn't smell the earthy aroma of the deer coated in the grain. Her legs were dangling over the seat's edge while her body collapsed, tumbling along with the rolling car in the chaos.

The car soon ceased its rolling, but the deer were not startled by the heap of metal in the road. It was just another rock to trample over, a rock that was sinking under the pressure of the four-hoofed animals. The collapsing car ceiling was coming close to the same level as the front hood, which looked as if it was tightened by a vice from both ends of the vehicle. Fragments of glass sprinkled over the pavement like powder sugar on a homemade cherry pie. The sky was cloudless as sunshine fell upon the wreckage with a sunny attitude -- nature carrying its own bag of irony.

The last deer slowly crossed the road in a prance, undaunted by the massacre. It was unfazed that there were a dozen dead deer lying on and off the road. It walked by, its hoofs clapping against the cement road, scraping the glass with each step. The deer entered the tossing waves of grain to catch up with the other members of its herd, its hoof stomps fading as the rustling of grain diminished as well. It was the silence after the storm.

A tragic storm.

CHAPTER 101

"Charlie," Claire yelled under the canopy tent to her son who was across the yard still flipping inside the inflatable castle. "Let's cut your cake."

A cheer of screams erupted inside the castle as if someone was being knighted by King Charlie. The kids darted out of the castle, running in their socks across the grass. Many parents were yelling at their children to run and get their shoes on, but the children could only hear one thing: "Cake!" They were not fazed by the idea of grass stains.

"Dan, go and get the ice cream from the freezer."

"But Scarlett isn't back yet," he commented. "Don't you need the sugar-free ice cream?"

"I have some fruit for Christian to eat until his ice cream comes," Claire answered undisturbed. After all, it wasn't Christian's birthday, but Charlie's.

"I just think it's rude," Dan muttered under his breath, but it must have been loud enough for Claire to hear as she dropped her knife on the ground.

"Since you are being so kind, can you get me another knife, honey?" she asked in a polite voice lined with pure sarcasm and hatred.

"Anything for you," Dan returned insincerely as he entered the kitchen through the back door. "Anything for you." The house was silent but still held the tension from his conversations with James and Karen. He pulled open the freezer with all his strength, slamming its door into the wall. An indention from the handle cracked the paint and drywall. "Great!" he yelled at the top of his lungs, knowing the screams of the children would drown out his own. "Just freaking great!"

He grabbed the two cartons of ice cream, clutching the cold to his chest, and kicked the freezer shut. "Here's the ice cream, sweetie," he said superficially as he scanned the crowd of midlife crises. Half the men staring at him probably had an affair and the other half most likely wished they had one.

"My knife?" Claire snorted in disgust. "I just asked for two things, is that too hard for you?" She laughed unconvincingly with showboat attitude. "My husband, the big time lawyer."

"One second," he huffed as he went back to the kitchen to find the freezer door open again. "Shit!" he growled as he slammed the door shut. "What do I have to do to keep this door closed?" Opening the cutlery drawer, he saw many blades but knew that a small one would suffice.

"Sorry, Dad," Amelia said, whimpering in the breakfast nook, curled up with a bowl of her soy ice cream. "Sorry."

CHAPTER 102

Josiah sped down the lonely road, trying to catch up to James and the girls, grasping at straws of lost hope. He turned a curve, digging his nails into the steering wheel, straining to stay on the road. The road straightened out and his stomach flipped at the sight of chaos. He pulled up to witness a swarm of emergency vehicles surrounding a solitary area on a two-lane road in the middle of a farmer's field. The red lights circled the top of the ambulance and police cars as EMTs were running to the center of the action.

He strained his ageless eyes for any sign of commotion, but saw nothing except for the St. Mark's Hospital logo emblazoned on the side of the ambulance that was parked diagonally, halting any possible traffic. Josiah parked the shuttering car and jumped out, rushing past a deputy staring hypnotized at the standing crops of grain, dancing in the wind.

"Stop!" the young deputy shouted to Josiah as he passed. He hitched up his pants and started chasing him until Josiah came to a sudden halt. "Sir, stop!"

Even though Josiah stopped, the deputy's words were not heard. The scene resembled a hunter's dream as bucks and does lay lifeless in various red puddles of blood. The blood from the deer surrounded the vehicle like a gruesome moat of fallen soldiers protecting their castle's fortress. Sadly, Josiah didn't see a fairytale scene.

The knights in shining armor were replaced by police officers with golden shimmering badges. The ferocious guardian dragon was recast as the barely legal deputy. The ever helpful fairy godmother was the life-saving medical technicians. Though the images resembled the modern-day characteristics of the classics, Josiah knew that there was indeed a villain and an innocent princess.

His eyes were magnetized to the metal heap in the middle of the road. "You've got to step back!" a twenty-two-year-old version of

Barney Fife screamed as he signaled Josiah back behind the line with his flashlight, only slightly illuminated in the early afternoon sun.

"Is she, is she alive?" Josiah asked as he tiptoed his way back, glancing at Terry's police badge.

Deputy Terry turned off his flashlight and put it in its holster like it was his gun. "I'm not supposed to say," he whispered as he swayed beside Josiah, "but it was a girl and a man." He stopped to take a brief moment of silence. "They have already been placed in their bags."

"Weren't there two girls?" Josiah asked as he took a step forward to the wreckage.

"Not sure," Terry shrugged, grabbing the back of Josiah's shirt to keep him from proceeding another step.

"No, there were two girls," Josiah erupted, jerking Terry's hands from his back.

"Sir, you've got to stay back!" Terry shouted, but Josiah wasn't listening to him. Josiah silenced Terry with a menacing look that caused all of Terry's blood to plummet. Josiah looked away from Terry and stayed still.

He watched as the EMTs used the Jaws of Life to cut through the heap of massacred steel. Hoof prints were scattered throughout the exterior, making the red sports car look like a crushed aluminum Coca-Cola can ready to be recycled.

"Don't know how anyone could survive that," Terry grimaced as he turned back to look at his watch post. Josiah's car was still the only one that had come down the desolate highway.

"But someone could," Josiah hoped. "Couldn't they?"

"I don't know," Terry answered sadly.

Josiah watched anxiously, knowing that he could help, but protocol wouldn't allow him to interfere with events unless given the command. Tears were starting to fill his eyes as he softly spoke.

"What was that?" Deputy Terry asked, stepping forward to Josiah.

Josiah took a breath and softly repeated his phrase with stuttering words, "The girl in the backseat is Mary Scarlett Sutton. Her parents are Dan and Claire Sutton. You need to call them."

"You know the girl?" Deputy Terry said shockingly.

"I know all three." He stopped and let the words linger in the air. "I know all three, very well."

CHAPTER 103

Following the thirty-minute parade of emergency vehicles to the hospital was agonizing for Josiah. The ambulance hustled along the highway, darting down sideroads and through neighborhood communities, finding the quickest route to St. Mark's Hospital.

Following closely along the route, Josiah couldn't help but flashback to the sight of Mary being gently pulled out of the destroyed vehicle. His eyes watched intently as they placed her on a stretcher with no deathly black bag around her. She was unconsciousness and limp with contusions around the face, blood-splattered hair, and an arm twisted unnaturally, highlighting its brokenness.

The speed of the procession was above the limit, but when the sirens wail, they trump the limit. Josiah watched the police car ahead of him, but he couldn't help but see kids riding their bicycles in a few suburban areas wearing baseball caps and smiles. The various small groups of boys watched with amazement as their quiet locale became the center of excitement. They waved frantically like typical adolescents as they turned their bikes around to follow the chase on their safe sidewalk.

Josiah wished that Mary would soon be riding her bike, letting the wind run through her hair. It was a lofty wish.

As they took a final right turn, St. Mark's Hospital towered into view. Josiah continued to follow the line of vehicles to the emergency entrance, finding a familiar family clutching one another. A small boy with a dollop of icing in his hair hugged a preteen girl clutching an older woman's arm with tears dripping down her face as an older man clung onto the woman's hand. The Sutton family had made it to the hospital. This was not the ideal birthday memory Claire wanted for today.

CHAPTER 104

"Why can't you tell me how my daughter is?" Dan shouted, pounding his fist on the nurse's waiting station. "We've been here for fifteen minutes and no one has told us anything except for our daughter was in a wreck!"

"I'm sorry Mr. uh," the nurse stammered, glancing down at her computer for his name.

"Dan Sutton. My name is Dan Sutton!" he exclaimed, coming unglued.

"Yes, Mr. Sutton," she responded. "I will get someone to go see if there are any updates."

Dan turned away to rejoin his family frustrated by the lack of knowledge. "Thank you," he said unconvincingly, even as he knew that it wasn't the nurse's fault. He just wanted some answers.

"I can tell you a little," Josiah said as he sat across the room since he wasn't welcomed to come any closer.

"Why on earth would you know?" Dan snarled. "Why is a measly black janitor always around my daughters?"

Josiah ignored the vicious remark and forced a smile on his face. "Mrs. Stapleton is at this hospital, so after I left your home I was coming here. As I was traveling I came upon the wreck."

Claire looked up from combing away the icing in Charlie's hair. "Josiah, please, tell me. How was the wreck?"

He shook his head, unable to describe in words the horrid sight he walked upon. "Mrs. Sutton, I am not going to lie to you, it didn't look good."

"Why? Why did you have to say that?" Dan shouted as Charlie sunk deeper into his mother's loving arms. "I mean, what good did that do? I don't even know if I should trust what you're saying right now!"

"It's going to be okay, Charlie, it's going to be okay," Claire whispered into her trembling son's ear.

"Yeah," Amelia stammered from the other side of Claire, "Scar's going to be okay, right Josiah?" Amelia winked, dropping a tear from her lashes.

Josiah saw the grief already in the family's faces. Even though Josiah's words were not promising, he knew the statement he needed to say. "Yes, she is going to be okay." He watched as three members of the family huddled together, sitting silent except for the occasional sniffling.

Dan paced around the room, unable to sit still during this tumultuous time of unknowing conclusions.

"Dan," Claire said as he looked at her. She mouthed, "Sit down," and gave him a dirty look. She looked down at Charlie, as if telling Dan to grow up and be the man in this situation.

Sulking, Dan walked over to his family and sat down. He looked over at Claire and smiled facetiously.

The waiting room's doors swung open as a doctor in green scrubs removed his medical mask. "Are you Mr. and Mrs. Sutton?"

Josiah watched from across the empty room as the family's world was either about to spring to life or fall into the dismal pits of death.

CHAPTER 105

"Yes, I'm Mr. Sutton," Dan said as the family stood up with shaking legs and walked together towards the doctor in his early thirties.

He motioned for them to return to their seats. "I'm Dr. Clinton. Please sit," he said as he took a deep breath to collect his thoughts. He was a skilled professional, who could perform any medical procedure at the drop of a hat, but this was always the hardest part of his job.

Claire felt her world spin as she sat down. *Those are the words that are spoken when bad news is about to come*, she thought. "Oh, God!" she panted as she squeezed Amelia into her chest. "No! No! Oh God, no!"

"Mrs. Sutton, your daughter is alive," he said with a small smile, hoping that those words would bring some relief, "but she has had some extensive damage."

"What kind of damage?" Dan interrupted.

"Your daughter has a broken arm, a few fractured ribs, bruising on her thighs, some deep gashes that needed ten stitches above her right eye..." Dr. Clinton said as he continued to read through his chart of injuries.

Claire felt relieved the moment she heard that Scarlett was alive. She knew that she was going to be able to handle anything else, no matter how long the injury list.

"Now the serious part," Dr. Clinton continued.

"That all sounded pretty serious," Amelia said with a snarky tone.

Dr. Clinton nodded in agreement. "Well, one of the ribs has punctured her lung and her breathing is minimal. We are going to need to do emergency surgery to repair the damage."

"Mom, is that bad?" Charlie asked as he looked up at his feeble mother.

"It's going to be okay, Chuck," Amelia said as she clasped his hand. "Surgeries happen here all the time."

CHAPTER 106

The two Sutton ladies followed the nurse down the winding hallway until they reached a room with padded tables along the exterior. "If you don't want to do this, Amelia, you don't have to," Claire said as they walked into the medical room with clear plastic tubes funneling into plastic bags.

"I want to, Mom," she said squeezing her mother's hand for some encouragement. "Anything to help Scarlett."

"Just lie down on one of the tables and someone will be with you in a minute," the nurse said as she walked towards the door. "You are a very brave young girl, but there is nothing to be scared about here."

"If you say so," Amelia stated as she plopped down on the closest table as Claire sat beside her. "I hope so."

The nurse stopped and turned around before leaving the room. "And for doing this, Amelia, you'll great a treat!" The nurse had an overly cheery tone as her voice heightened in excitement at the word treat.

"Oh boy," Amelia mumbled sarcastically.

"Bye now," the bubbly nurse said as she strolled out of the room.

"What planet is she from?" Amelia asked her mother.

"She's just trying to be warm and friendly," Claire said with a smile. "You should try it."

"Maybe another day," Amelia said unconvincingly. "I can only try one new thing a day and today is giving lifesaving blood."

They sat in silence as they waited for a nurse to come and take Amelia's blood. Claire rolled up her sleeve and started to shake her arms around.

"Are you hot?" Amelia finally asked, breaking the void.

"No, are you?"

"You're the one who rolled up her sleeves."

Claire got up and went to the nearby table. "If you're giving, I'm giving."

"You don't have to, Mom. I'm fine," Amelia said putting on a brave front.

"They said they are low on blood. I don't think they will reject mine."

"No, we won't," a nurse in pink scrubs said flatly as she entered the room with an expressionless face. "My name is Tara and I am going to be taking your blood in a few minutes," she said as she grabbed her clipboard. "I have to ask these questions. Some of them may sound dumb, but I have to." She started asking the questions and Amelia answered no to the majority of them. Suddenly the questions became more relatable.

"Have you been tired lately?"

Amelia scrunched her face, trying to decide how to answer the question. "I haven't felt great lately."

"You haven't?" the nurse asked. "It may be best if you don't give."

"No, I need to. My sister is having surgery and she needs my blood," Amelia erupted. She was suddenly filled with energy that commanded the room. "I can do it."

"What do you think, Mom?" Tara asked in a monotone.

"You're the medical expert," Claire answered. "But Amelia, if you don't feel like it, you don't need to do it."

"No, I can do it," she said as she rolled up her sleeve.

Tara got her medical equipment set up and grabbed Amelia's arm. "Looks like you have good veins," she said routinely. "That will make my job easy." She rolled Amelia's sleeve up a little more so she could tie the rubber band around her bicep. "I need to do this so I don't hurt you very much."

"Sounds good to me," Amelia remarked.

The nurse began to tie the band and noticed a mark on Amelia's arm. "When did you get this bruise?"

"I don't know, a few days ago," Amelia answered.

The nurse stopped and her brain spun with more questions. "Do you have any other bruises?"

"A few."

"Amelia, what have you been doing?" Claire gasped as she saw the bruise on her arm. "Where are the other bruises?"

"Oh, Mom, it's nothing. I'm just a klutz, unlike Scarlett."

"You need to take better care of yourself," the nurse commanded as she stuck Amelia in the arm. "There you go; just try to relax."

"That's all?" Amelia asked shockingly.

"For you, but my veins are harder to find," Claire laughed. "Be gentle, Tara."

"Should I, Amelia?" Tara said with a forced laugh as she tied the band around Claire's larger bicep.

"Nah," Amelia said as she closed her eyes.

"Thanks a lot!" Claire squealed in laughter. "Ouch."

"Your veins are hard to find," Tara said robotically.

"Ouch."

"Sorry," Tara said. "Okay, there you go," she said after she pricked Claire a few times to find a vein. "I will be back in a few minutes to check on you. Just lie back and relax."

Amelia opened her eyes when she heard the door close signaling that Tara was gone. "She's freaking awesome."

"Really?" Claire groaned. "She didn't seem friendly or warm at all like the other nurse."

"I know," Amelia moaned. "Isn't she great?"

"I sometimes wonder if you're my daughter," Claire laughed.

"Yeah, you got the wrong set of twins from the hospital," Amelia laughed. "That happens all the time."

"Oh, Amelia, you are too much sometimes."

281

CHAPTER 107

A PGA tournament was playing on the waiting room television as Charlie searched the room for the remote control. Dan sat frigid with his arms folded and his head bowed down, unaware of the mad scavenger hunt. The room's walls were almost bare; a single magazine rack, housing half a dozen news magazines leaned against one wall and a portrait of a man, presumably an artist's rendition of St. Mark, hung on the opposite wall. The painting accentuated a caring servant with arms extending out resembling the posture of a hug.

The television was muted, but Josiah could see that the telecasters were cheering about a golfer's tee shot landing on the green. He looked over at the large faced clock and watched the secondhand spin around like it was on a race by itself. It was going to be three o'clock in nine minutes.

"Dad, where's the remote?" Charlie asked as he popped up from behind the makeshift toy box of four toddler gadgets.

Oblivious to the question, Dan continued to stare at his feet, racking his brain with the complexities of the surrounding circumstances. He knew that surgeries happen daily, but they don't happen daily for his daughter.

"Charlie, where are you Buddy?" Dan asked, waking up from his solitary thought. Charlie walked over to his dad with a frown. "Scarlett's going to be okay, Buddy. She's going to be fine."

"I know that," he sulked. "I can't find the remote."

Dan slightly laughed as Josiah continued to watch the father and son interaction. "Do you know what we were doing the last time we were here?"

"Nope," Charlie said.

"Well," Dan widely smiled, "it is probably one of the best days of my life."

"Really?" Charlie asked shocked. "Here?"

282

"Yep. Do you have any guesses?" Dan asked picking up his son and holding him in his massive arms, hugging his tiny body.

"Nope."

"Well, the last time I was here, was on this exact day, seven years ago."

Charlie's eyes widened with a twinkle of realization. "I was born here?"

"You sure were. And did you know that Amelia and Scarlett waited in a room like this one for four hours with your grandma Naomi? They were so excited when they came here after school. They couldn't wait to see you."

Charlie looked up at his dad and his head fell onto his muscular chest. "I can't wait to see Scarlett, Daddy."

"Me too, Buddy. Me too."

The two Sutton men sat in each other's arms. Dan wiped a few tears away from his eyes as he heard a few deep breaths from Charlie. He looked down at his son and noticed that he was no competition to the bouncy house. Two hours of jumping and flipping was more than enough for this seven-year-old.

Josiah got up and walked across the desolate room and took a seat next to Dan. "Do you need to talk, sir?"

He shook his head no as he wiped another tear away from his cheek.

The two sat side by side, staring up at the television that neither man was watching. "If you need to," Josiah said, "I am here."

"Dan! I just heard the news and I couldn't believe it!"

CHAPTER 108

"Karen, what are you doing here?" Dan softly asked, startled by her second appearance in one day.

"I was at home checking Facebook, and I saw an update from one of my girlfriend's Melissa Upstein, whose aunt works here, and her aunt posted a message about a wreck and to pray for the Sutton and Nialliv families. So I called her to get all the details I could get and then I just had to drive here and see if it was all true." She rambled with words flying out of her mouth, faster than ever before. "I called Melissa on my way here, but she couldn't tell me much, but just to say a little prayer. I blew her off because I'm not a prayer, I'm a doer."

"Can you lower your voice?" Dan asked as he pointed to his sleeping son.

"Oh, is this little Chuck?" she squealed like a teenage girl seeing a cute puppy dog without lowering her voice at all. "Isn't he a doll? Just an absolute doll."

"Please, Karen, he's had a hard day. Just lower your voice a little."

She sat down beside Dan and motioned with her hands that she would speak a little softer. "Well, tell me what you know."

"I don't know much, just that there was a wreck and Scarlett is in surgery."

"Who?" Karen asked, baffled at the unfamiliar name.

"Scarlett, my daughter."

"Oh, yeah, that's right." She giggled at her self-centered memory. "Well, Melissa gave me the number to her aunt, Geraldine, and she told me that it was a horrible wreck."

Dan quickly clasped his son's ears so he couldn't hear the graphic details that he was sure that Karen would not leave out.

"James apparently hit about a dozen deer and got dinged up on every side as his car spun out of control."

"I haven't heard how they are. They won't tell me since I'm not family."

Karen made a crackling noise with her mouth and swooped in without any empathy. "Dead."

"No!" Dan gasped at the word. "And his daughter?"

"Dead as well," she answered undisturbed by the loss of life. "They said she probably died first." She started to raise her voice up again and suddenly realized her increasing volume by Dan's facial expressions. "She told me that the two girls were not wearing seatbelts and that they found James' girl…"

"Lucy," Dan commented.

"Yeah, her," she continued. "They found her on the side of the road. Dead at the scene."

"This is devastating," Dan said, shaking uncontrollably as emotions were starting to overflow. A mixture of emotions – sadness, anger, disbelief, unrelenting heartache. They were commingled and his body couldn't hold in all the chemical reactions bubbling up.

"But," Karen said brightening up with a sadistic smile, "now that James is gone, we can pin all the FDA stuff on him. Right?"

"Karen, that can wait!" Dan belted out at her disrespect for the dead. "People have died and my daughter is hurt, and all you can think about is your pill."

"Is that a problem?" Karen asked impervious to anyone else's issues. "I mean, this will solve everything."

"Not everything," Dan murmured.

CHAPTER 109

"What do you mean, not everything?" Karen leaned into Dan's ear. Dan looked over at Josiah who instantly got up and walked away during the uncomfortable situation. Josiah headed towards the hallway then decided that it would be best to go check on Mrs. Stapleton.

"Can you quit thinking just about yourself?" Dan pondered out loud. "I mean, just for one moment, can you acknowledge that I am holding my son and waiting to hear if my daughter's surgery went well?"

Karen straightened her posture away from Dan's cold shoulder. "Of course I can!" She huffed as she crossed her arms and legs. "I came down here to check on you, didn't I?"

Dan shook his head in sad realization that he gambled his life on the person sitting next to him, and right now he wished she was half a world away. "You didn't come to check on me," he said as he glanced over in her direction, gazing into her eyes for any sign of a soul. "You just came to check up on yourself."

"Myself?" she asked bewildered, puffing up in exclamation.

"Yes, you and your career."

The response back from Karen was void, just a breath of exasperated air leaving her infuriated hot lungs. Dan went back to cuddling his little boy in his arms, rocking his body while caressing the brown curly locks dangling slightly above his neck. They were similar to his own that Claire twirled and fingered when they first started dating.

His first and main priority was the well-being of his children, not Karen's career. His heart sank at that thought, because it didn't include the protection and welfare of his loving, devoted wife. He had irreverently skidded her on a fizzled backburner and revved up the flames of his adulterous affair.

"Is that really how you perceive me?" Karen asked as she kept her head up, staring intently at the periodic bubbles in the wallpaper's border along the ceiling.

"Mr. Sutton?" The same nurse from behind the counter walked up. "I just got word that they have taken your daughter back for surgery."

"How long?" he stammered with his unfaithful tongue. "How long will the surgery take?"

The nurse shook her head and rubbed Charlie's rosy cheeks. "I wish I knew, sir. It could be thirty minutes or it could be a few hours." She watched as Dan's eyes glazed over without any emotion. There was no fear or even any hope that was being shown through the windows of his soul. All she saw was the expression she had seen too often in this waiting room. Disconnect.

"Mr. Sutton, we have some really good surgeons here, and if the surgery takes less than an hour, great, but if it takes longer, that doesn't mean something is wrong. It may even be a good sign that they work on your daughter for a couple of hours so they can mend her properly." The nurse started to walk away, questioning herself like she did every time she had to speak to patients' family members. "If you wish to wait in the surgical unit's waiting room, I can take you there."

"Thank you," he mumbled. "I think I will just wait for my wife and daughter to return."

"Very well, sir," she said giving him a friendly smile of hope -- a smile that she knew couldn't solve his problems but was all she could give at this time.

CHAPTER 110

The hallways were winding mirror images of each other with florescent light bulbs overhead and unhelpful directions to the various units of the hospital. Josiah wandered for fifteen minutes, trying to find Mrs. Stapleton's room, walking down the same path of hallways three times before succumbing to ask for help.

Foolishly, he was only two hallways away from the ICU area that Mrs. Stapleton was resting in comfortably. "Good evening," he said as he walked into the room to find Mrs. Stapleton reclining in her bed, enjoying a cherry Popsicle and an old episode of *All in the Family*.

"Josiah, you didn't need to come check on me," she said as she motioned him to come closer into the room.

"I would have come back sooner, but…" he was about to explain the situation, but didn't want the news of the wreck to delay her recovery.

"But what?" she questioned, ignoring the comedic genius of Carroll O'Connor.

"There was an emergency at the school that I had to take care of," he quickly lied to spare her additional heartache. A lie is a terrible thing when it is said to someone you love, Josiah thought, but a lie is sometimes also an essential aspect of his duties.

"Did you get it taken care of?" she asked as she bit off a piece of the cold treat, crunching on the softening ice like it was candy.

"Oh, forget about that. How are you feeling?"

"I think I am going to make it." She smirked without her dentures in place, which caused Josiah to smile as well. She laid down her Popsicle stick that had one bite left and pushed away her tray, reaching for his hand. "Thank you, Josiah, thank you."

"No thanks needed," he replied. "None at all."

Stretching her arms overhead, she tried to readjust her pillow, but Josiah quickly jumped into action. "Thank you. You are too kind."

288

"You have been very kind to me as well, Ethel."

Her pale cheeks blushed redder than the rouge she normally would dab on her face each morning. "This medicine really does a whopper on me," she laughed. "The nurses were telling me that I was talking about going to meet some soldiers at the local dance hall."

"You didn't!" he exclaimed as he slapped his knee with laughter.

"I did! They said that I was moving and a grooving in my bed," she said, giggling like a young woman. "When I get out of here and feeling better, will you take me dancing Josiah, just to make an old lady feel young again?"

Josiah wanted to do nothing better than pick her up and twirl her in the air, but he knew that he couldn't make such a promise. He didn't even know where he was going to be in the next few days. He looked over at her piercing eyes, fluttering with the idea of swaying to the music. She was charming with old age elegance, while her youthful heart was as pure as gold. He wanted to unburden himself and relinquish all the secrets that he had kept from her, but he knew that it wasn't the time. He wondered if there was ever going to be a time. There were many missions in his past when he would just walk away and disappear without any explanations given. No 'Goodbye', no 'See you later', no 'Until we meet again'. Those were always the hardest days of his mission.

"I would like nothing better, Ethel," Josiah said with a smile.

"Josiah, you won't believe me if I tell you, but last night I could have sworn that someone was in my room," she said picking up her Popsicle and finishing the last sweet bite. "I mean, I just felt like someone was in here watching my every move."

Josiah watched Ethel as she ended their dialogue and continued to take harbor in the safety of classic television. "I believe you, Ethel. I believe whatever you say." Josiah walked around the bed and found his seat on the recliner beside her bed.

He listened to her giggle at Archie Bunker's rant on Meathead's liberal ideals. "They don't make good shows like this anymore."

"No, they don't," he agreed as he watched a familiar man walk past the doorway, waving mysteriously as he went by. Josiah jumped up from his chair and walked across the room, "Please excuse me, Ethel."

"Anything wrong?" she asked, raising herself up to see what had caused such a commotion for Josiah.

"Nothing," he answered as he followed the man who periodically would look back so Josiah could see his stone-cold face down the sanitary hallway. Josiah couldn't help but question, was this a façade? With every step he took, he felt that the path was leading to an untimely demise, but he had to follow through with it, even if it led down a darkened pit. He had to keep following the white rabbit.

He had to keep following Jade.

CHAPTER 111

Josiah continued to keep close to Jade's heels who was surprisingly not trying to lose Josiah through the maze of hallways. Jade turned into a hospital room with a patient in the bed and a visitor with his back turned. Josiah peered his head into the room and found Jade staring out the window. Josiah passed the patient's bed and realized that it wasn't a patient at all.

"Why did you lead me here?" Josiah asked as Carlos uncovered himself and sat up on the plastic hospital mattress.

"We thought you needed to talk after the accident this afternoon," Maxwell remarked as he continued to stay seated comfortably beside the bed.

"Talk? You thought I would want to talk to you?" Josiah asked sarcastically, keeping his tone somewhat calm.

"Josiah, you need to know that this isn't your fault," Maxwell schemed menacingly. "You can't help it that you are an absolute failure."

"Max!" Carlos scolded as he quickly turned to give a friendly smile to Josiah. "He didn't mean that, Josiah."

"No, I'm pretty sure he wishes it was true," Josiah responded unwaveringly. "But I know better than to listen to him."

"My name is Maxwell." His arrogance filled the room. "I am right here, and you two are speaking as if I am a wee little boy."

"Max, we are not," Carlos kindly refuted with a pleasant smile.

"Maxwell! My name is Maxwell, you twit!"

"Sorry," Carlos sulked, sinking back into the flimsy mattress that wrapped around his body as he laid back down.

"So, why am I here?" Josiah abruptly asked, hoping to speed up this unwelcome meeting.

"Josiah, we have an offer for you," Jade said as he continued to watch beyond the glass to the outside world. "An offer you better consider."

"An offer?" He rolled his eyes and laughed at the lunacy of the idea. "From you?"

"Josiah, you need to listen to him," Carlos begged as he curled his legs up into a fetal position. "You really need to open up your mind and think about the proposition."

He looked over at the man-child, curling up, wrapping himself with the blue knit blanket and couldn't believe the standards that Carlos had sunken to. "Carlos, really? Look at yourself?"

"Silence!" Jade commanded as Carlos trembled under the covers. "Josiah, if you join our side, we will allow the girl to live." He turned and piercingly stared into Josiah's eyes, stabbing at the innocence Josiah tried to hide behind. "If not…you know what will happen."

"You can't guarantee who lives or dies!" Josiah erupted as he left the conversation and walked over to the door to leave the confines of the room.

"Why can't we?" Jade asked ghoulishly. "Times are changing, Josiah. The times are changing."

CHAPTER 112

The silent walk back to the waiting room was lonely as Josiah passed by hospital rooms that looked bleak and depressing. Nurses were not friendly; they didn't converse with the patients, and there were not any visitors in any of the rooms. It was as if this was the unit where people just went to die.

Josiah turned down the wing to go through the neonatal unit and hear the sounds of life, even if it was the cries of innocent children. He glanced up and saw Nathanial leaning against the wall halfway down the hall.

"I really needed to see you," Josiah said, hugging him as if he hadn't seen him for years.

"Peace to you," he smiled as he embraced his comrade.

"I feel like..." he started to say, but didn't know how to finish.

"Don't say anything. Don't think anything either," Nathanial said as they parted, starting to stroll up the remainder of the hallway.

Josiah thought for a moment of how to respond, but even after the chance to think it over, he still wasn't sure how to move forward in the conversation.

"So, they came by?" Nathanial asked nonchalantly, stuffing his hands in his back pockets and continuing his careless stride.

Josiah continued to look down at his feet, shocked at Nathanial's knowledge of the event that just happened a few minutes earlier.

"Josiah, they always come by," Nathanial remarked effortlessly. "If they don't come by that only means that they're not afraid of you."

Josiah's vocal cords instantly became untangled. "But..." but one word was all that Nathanial allowed him to say.

"No buts, Josiah. No buts at all." The two men stopped in front of a window and pressed their noses to the glass, examining the sleeping newborns. "You are just like these babies, but in the same breath you are nothing like them."

Josiah's face twitched at the comparison and Nathanial must have seen his awkward reflection.

"Josiah, you came down here alone on this mission without anyone else guiding you along your way, and they are trying to pull you down when you are at your weakest." A stifled cry came out of a sleeping baby boy, swaddled in his blue blanket and sock cap. The boy's face suddenly became flushed. A healthy-sized woman in her late forties picked up the crying child and started to sway the newborn in her arms. Josiah couldn't hear the nurse, but he could tell that she was singing him a lullaby. "You see, Josiah, when you are down, there is always someone who will come and help you up."

"How am I nothing like a baby then?" he asked, trying to find the correlation between Nathanial's comparisons.

"Josiah, look at you! You are not a baby." He patted him on his back. "I saw you in battle. You are a fierce warrior. Be that warrior now!"

The two men watched as the baby's cries subsided, and somehow Josiah felt the same relief. There was a peace that flowed through the hospital wing during that moment. It was like a cool gust of air found its way inside and sought out Josiah.

"Oh," Nathanial said as he stepped away from the glass, nearing the door, "and He wanted you to know that everything is working out as planned."

Josiah turned his face away from the glass. "As planned? How is this as planned? Scarlett is hurt."

"I don't know," Nathanial said as he shrugged his shoulders and flung the swaying doors open to leave. "I just say what I am told to say. You will see." The doors closed behind Nathanial as he walked away. As they continued to open and close in their pendulum motion, Josiah could see Nathanial quickly walking away.

Planned? Josiah thought. *Who would have planned it this way?*

CHAPTER 113

The plastic tube tunneled down Scarlett's throat as an incision was made opening her chest. They had stitched up her facial wounds, which were now slightly hidden under the surgical tape used to seal her eyes. An RN stood to the side of the table and watched the heart rate of Scarlett peak and plunge, taking notes at every little change from the previous graph.

The masked group huddled around the patient as if they were discussing the next down of their football game. Each was dressed in surgical attire; they didn't have shoulder pads or jock straps, but each was equipped nonetheless. Scarlett, for the first time in her athletic life, was not a part of the team. She was the sudden death goal to score. She was figuratively the touchdown to make, with only seconds to spare. She was essentially the last and final buzzer shot.

"What movie did you go see last night?" Dr. Renee Kox asked as she delicately removed one of the fragmented ribs from the pierced lung.

"Didn't go," Dr. Ishmael Raman said as he started to drain some excess fluid from Scarlett's skull. "My son had a late baseball practice."

"Isn't it early for baseball?" Dr. Kox asked as she meticulously started doctoring the first hole.

"It gets earlier and earlier each year," surgical tech Robin Walters stated as she assisted Dr. Raman. Dr. Kox and Dr. Raman were the lead surgeons on these two operations, but they each had plenty of help to aid them in their successful procedures.

If Scarlett knew that a dozen people, five doctors, six nurses and one endoscopy technician, were in one room and she was the center focal point, she would be crawling into the corner, especially with the knowledge that each of the medical personnel had seen her naked body. They were medical professionals and the human body was just their career, clothed or unclothed.

"How are you doing?" Dr. Raman asked as he examined the x-rays for a second time to find the origin of the bodily fluid.

"Kathy, how's her breathing?" Dr. Kox asked.

"Steady, Dr. Kox. She is stable," Kathy answered as she turned to watch an unfamiliar man clothed in scrubs with only a sliver of skin around his eyes showing, approach the patient and assist Dr. Raman.

"Good. We are doing well down here, Dr. Raman, how is your end?"

"Doing," he exhaled. "I'm doing."

"Let me try something," the guest physician spoke startling Dr. Raman, who wasn't aware of his presence in the room.

"Dr. Jade?" Dr. Raman asked as he continued to concentrate on Scarlett.

"Yes."

"I am sorry to be meeting like this," Dr. Raman politely smiled under his mask. "So this is your first day here?"

"Yes," he answered quickly. "May I?" he signaled with his hands to take over in Scarlett's brain surgery.

"How about you examine the x-rays and charts and get familiar with the patient's condition," Dr. Raman said trying to slow down his rushed hands.

"I am familiar with her condition," he answered robotically. "May I?"

"You may, Dr. Jade." Dr. Raman relinquished his power as lead surgeon and allowed Dr. Jade to have full control.

Scarlett continued to stay in a drug-induced sleep, unaware that she was being cut in two different locations of her body. Before this day, she hadn't had any real medical problems. In her past she'd only had minor childhood ailments and injuries, ear infections, chicken pox and the occasional sprained ankle from various daredevil falls or heroic feats. This was more than any one person would want in a lifetime, let alone a year, and definitely, not in one day.

"Her pulse is dropping," Susan, an RN, announced as she started to see the numbers gradually decline.

"Dr. Bennett," Dr. Raman's voice raised a few keys in surprise, "I need you up here now."

Susan watched the pulse continue to fall as the green heart rate monitor was barely moving. "It's still dropping."

"We're losing her," Dr. Raman yelled as the team kicked into overdrive, taking their life-saving positions. "Dr. Jade, please let me."

CHAPTER 114

"How are things going?" Josiah asked, sitting beside Dan who was still holding Charlie who had started to sweat from the additional body heat.

"The nurse hasn't come by in the last forty-five minutes," Dan nervously answered with pent up aggravation in his voice.

Josiah patted Dan on his shoulder. No words were said. The three of them sat in an empty waiting room with the sun shining brightly through the glass windows. "Where's Amelia and Claire?"

"Amelia had a little spell as she was giving blood since she didn't eat much for lunch, so they are forcing her to eat something and relax."

"Poor Amelia," Josiah commented sympathetically. "Poor, poor Amelia."

The hospital's intercom system paged for a few janitors to proceed to ICU, as the television in the waiting room showed a *Cheers* re-run. The unknown rattled through Dan's head, causing terrible thoughts of funeral preparations, picking out coffins and the horrible sight of having to tell his children that Scarlett would not be coming home. He shook, as if shaking would cause his thoughts to vanish like an Etch-a-Sketch. It didn't, and his torturous contemplation sprung up to the forefront of his brain once again.

Josiah sat uncomfortably beside Dan, dismissing the afternoon's commotion and rant between him and the Sutton family. He couldn't help but feel Dan's eyes burning a hole in his head inches above his ear, but every time Josiah turned, Dan quickly turned away.

"I don't know what I'm going to do," Dan said emotionally, breaking the awkward silence with an even more foreign purge of feelings.

"Don't think like that, Mr. Sutton," Josiah consoled, turning to examine every inch of Dan's face.

"But how can I?" He sniffled as his eyes began to water. The hard façade of emotional steel was breaking like a dam of toothpicks. "How can I not?"

"Don't be jumping to that conclusion, Mr. Sutton. All that will cause is needless pain," Josiah answered convincingly. One look at Dan's face proved he didn't buy the psychological advice.

"Those are just words, Josiah," he said, shocking himself to utter Josiah's name. "No offence, but I need more than an opinion from you."

"I wish my words could soothe you and bring you some sort of comfort," Josiah started as a figure passed by the door. It was a handsome lean masculine figure wearing a black suit and black tie. Josiah watched suspiciously as the familiar figure continued to walk away until he was out of sight. The moment only lasted two seconds, but those two seconds seemed like an eternity.

"Josiah?" Dan nudged his arm to grab his attention, but Josiah was more focused on the gentleman than their conversation. "What is it?" Dan quickly looked over at the direction Josiah was gaping, but all he saw was a closed glass door showing an empty hallway.

"Um, oh," Josiah stammered for lack of words. "I need to, um," he continued without making any coherent speech. "Need to go check on someone."

"Yes, how is Mrs., oh, I can't think of her name?" Dan asked as he clinched his eyes to think of the long-forgotten name.

"Who?" Josiah asked, still not focusing on Dan. His focus was a million miles away. "I'll be back."

CHAPTER 115

Josiah quickly memorized the map that hung on the wall of the hospital's entrance lobby and he knew the desired path to take. He mentally photographed the interweaving hallways of this giant medical facility. He quickly trotted through brightly lit hallways, entering areas that were supposed to be locked and secure from non-hospital employees. Josiah knew how to get through the high-tech system of pass codes and sliding nametags, and within a few minutes he made it to the elevator and hit the bottom floor.

The atmosphere of the basement was depressing with singular light bulbs on the ceiling every fifteen feet, surrounded by metal makeshift chandeliers that were not visually appealing. They were giving enough light to see, but there were some parts of the hallway that seemed to be nothing but a shadow. The hallways were narrow and damp, like a secret tunnel for runaways to escape through to obtain their freedom.

Closing his eyes, he remembered the location of the room where he was headed. He was to go straight until he came to a crossroads, take two lefts and then it would be the last room on the right. He dashed down the hallway and came to another set of heavy steel-plated doors. He pulled on the handle, but the door was locked. He looked around for a number pad to enter his skeleton code, but the basement floor wasn't high-tech enough to have that type of security. Pulling out his pocketknife, he succumbed to the old fashioned way of picking locks.

He slid his tool into the lock and started gently rattling it until he heard a click. His eyes widened when he realized that he was not the one who unlocked the door. He looked back in the hallway and found a shadowed spot along the wall to sink into as the door creaked open.

"Strange," a male attendant in black scrubs uttered as he passed with another man with blue scrubs.

300

"I could have sworn they were in there an hour ago," the other man croaked with vocal cords heavily coated with years of nicotine. "This isn't good for us," he coughed, hacking up what sounding like a portion of his lung.

The two men continued to fade away, disappearing and then reappearing under the random shorted out lights as their conversation slowly became just a slight muffle. Josiah watched as the door slowly creaked, reaching his hand in the crack to allow him through to the final area of the basement.

He sped down the hallway as the words of the two men echoed in his head. *I could have sworn they were in there an hour ago.* His heart pounded as he turned left and then quickly turned left one more time. He sprinted down the eerie cement channel and found himself standing in front of the last room on the right.

Turning the doorknob, he entered the room with a wall full of freezers and a column of four-square doors stacked on top of one another, with a row of ten doors running down the side. Opening the first door, a burst of cold air slapped him in the face as he pulled out the rack. It was empty. He looked over all the doors and knew that he didn't have enough time to examine every container.

Spinning around, panting with anticipation, he noticed a clipboard on the desk and prayed that this was his hidden treasure. It was. He noticed that it had forty slots to be filled in. He scanned down the column and found what he was looking for.

He ran over to drawer 23, flinging the door open to find a black plastic bag on the rack. Pulling out the drawer he knew that he shouldn't be surprised. Drawer 23 – James Nialliv. Empty. Slamming the door shut he grabbed drawer 24's handle and lingered for a few seconds in the quiet mystery. After his expectation got the best of him he swung it open. Drawer 24 – Lucy Nialliv was empty as well.

Leaving the empty morgue, he sunk back into the darkened shadows of the hallway, retracing his path to get back to the first floor.

He longed to get back into the daylight and the communion of individuals, and he jumped with adrenalin to get back to his mission.

Mission is a go.

CHAPTER 116

The hospital was strangely calm for a Saturday afternoon as Josiah walked through the many identical hallways on a manhunt. The nurse's stations were empty, all the patients were in their rooms, and the intercom system was uncannily silent. Josiah had his way with the hospital, but he didn't even know what his way would be.

He poked his head in patients' rooms, peered through windows, and placed his ears against doors to hear the dialogue in various rooms. He examined every janitor closet, break room, doctors' lounge, and bathroom, hoping to find his traitors. They were nowhere to be found on the first floor, so he climbed the rectangular stairwell to the second floor to once again try to corner his previous comrades.

Thankfully, this floor had a few nurses that he could question for assistance in his search, but neither of them had seen a small group of men in black suits. "Are we in trouble?" the youngest nurse asked as her lip started to quiver. "Black suits, is that like FBI people?"

"No, no, nothing like that," Josiah quickly reassured them, but this group of men was worse than the FBI. He quickly parted company, leaving their minds in a state of confusion. He didn't have enough time to discuss the circumstances; he just needed to find them. The old wives' tale was certainly true: keep your friends close and your enemies closer.

The frantic search continued as he passed a medical lab with the door locked, but when he spied through the window, all he could see was part of an empty room full of beakers and test tubes. Josiah spanned both sides of the hallway and noticed no one was watching. He punched in his skeleton code and the door automatically unlocked.

He entered a world of medical testing; sophisticated liquid droppers were lying over the spotless white marble countertops beside various sized glass door refrigerators to house bodily fluids and liquids. Josiah walked down one of the two aisles and inquisitively studied all the contents on the counters. He turned to get to the last aisle when he heard a muffled scraping sound across the room.

He stopped and the noise stopped. His heart began to skip a beat with wishful thinking. Turning the corner he found his way walking down the last aisle seeing nothing out of the ordinary, except one of the refrigerator doors was ajar. He looked through the glass and saw a lone red test tube that was barcoded with Sutton, Claire taped on the side. He eyed the open door suspiciously when the same muffled sound came from the other side of the aisle. Quickly walking toward it, he peered down the first aisle but saw nothing. Taking a step back, he looked back down the second aisle but saw nothing there as well.

An idea struck him. He walked over to the door, turned off the light, and opened the door and let it shut. Sinking into the corner, he let his ears heighten in the blinding darkness. The muffled sound became louder and he distinctly heard footsteps in the room.

As he flipped the light switch, he knew his instinct was correct as Maxwell's eyes darted over to Josiah in terror. Maxwell's right hand clinched shut, trying to hide an object that was bigger than the width of his hand.

"Don't do anything crazy, Maxwell."

"Crazy?" Maxwell laughed at the thought. "What would be crazy?"

"I know what's in your hand," he said as he took a step toward Maxwell, who was less than twenty feet away.

"I don't know what you're talking about. You really need to get some rest," he remarked, trying to be sly, but his eyes were forth telling. He did know what Josiah was talking about.

"Put the test tube down!" Josiah commanded as he took a few more steps toward Maxwell, erasing the gap between them.

"Stop where you are, or I will destroy it!" Maxwell screamed, holding his fist up in the air, as if he was going to drop the glass and let it break and leak out all of its contents.

304

"Maxwell, do you think that I couldn't get another sample?" Josiah grinned playfully. "I have her wrapped around my finger."

"You do not, or you wouldn't even be arguing with me," he answered without any intimidation, while his grip was getting looser. The test tube was becoming more visible.

"Drop it then," Josiah remarked. "Drop it and run to the others."

Maxwell looked up at this hand and then smiled back at Josiah. "I think I will." He threw the test tube into the air as he ran toward the door, colliding with Josiah as he passed. Josiah fell to the ground just three seconds before gravity caused the vial of blood to hit the floor.

"No!" Josiah cried as he tried to crawl over to the falling object. He heard Maxwell laugh in hysteria as the two men heard the thud of the test tube on the floor. "No!"

"Bye Josiah," Maxwell looked back to see the aging man wiggling on his belly before he stormed out of the room. Maxwell walked with great respect for himself for doing his duty brilliantly.

Josiah lay patiently on the floor, waiting for the door to shut before making his move. He turned behind to make sure the coast was clear. He smiled at the thought of Maxwell's haughty attitude as he picked up the unbreakable test tube. His laughter began to fill the room as Josiah stood up and twirled the red vial in his fingers before placing it beside Claire's blood sample in the refrigerator.

He walked out of the room with a little more confidence than a few minutes before. Amelia's blood was now safe.

CHAPTER 117

The hotel motif of the hospital waiting room was drastically different from the classy décor of the Sutton's family room. Their grandfather clock that chimed on the hour was replaced with a blue worn out plastic one. The luxurious sofas and loveseats purchased from Pottery Barn were substituted with uncomfortably padded chairs from a wholesale store. The atmosphere was not a homey feel, and Claire prayed that this room would not become a familiar sight.

Charlie had regained wide eyes after his afternoon nap, but his body now sat beside his father, limp and sluggish while his eyes were in a hypnotic state at the television showing reruns of *The Suite Life of Zach and Cody*. "Amelia, how do you feel?" Charlie kindly asked with a raspy voice from all the screaming of the afternoon party.

"Better," she answered as she sat up, propping her feet in a nearby chair.

"Are you sure?" Claire asked, echoing Charlie's concern.

"Don't worry about me," she shrugged. "Scarlett's the one you need to worry about," she countered without any thought of how she sounded. At the sound of Claire's runny nose, Amelia realized the pitfall of her words, "I'm sorry, Mom. I didn't mean it. Really, I didn't."

"I know..." Claire said, grabbing a tissue from her pocket. "I know you didn't."

"Does anyone need anything to drink or eat?" Dan asked as he got up to stretch his arms and legs. Everyone shook their head no. "Well, I am going to get some coffee." He asked if Charlie wanted to go for a walk, but he wasn't in the mood. All Charlie wanted was to be at home enjoying his birthday presents with his big sister.

Dan left the waiting room as the remaining family members sat fixated on the childish show, yet none of them were laughing with the show's laugh track. They each felt like this was a horrible dream. A dream that they each wished they could wake from feeling refreshed and energized. Occasionally, Amelia would pinch herself and her mother. "Just checking," she would mumble as Claire would kiss her on the cheek.

"Thanks for checking. I was wondering too."

The waiting area doors opened and in walked the school's heart throb, Luke. "Amelia," he said as he sat down beside her. "I just heard the news. How is Scarlett?"

Amelia did her best at explaining the situation, because truthfully, she didn't know how Scarlett was doing. The nurse hadn't been over to see the family in the last thirty minutes, and the last time the nurse came over, it was just to tell them that Scarlett was still in surgery. She didn't comment on the procedure. She didn't remark on if the surgery was almost complete. She didn't give any sign of the outcome. She was just relaying the message she was told to say, and that was very little.

"How are you doing?" he asked as he looked into her bleak, darkened eyes.

"As good as one could be doing," she answered, turning her head to look back at Charlie who sat in a catatonic position. "Just waiting."

"I'll wait with you," Luke said, leaning back into the chair and staring up at the television. He didn't say anything else. There were no fake words of "I know how you are feeling" or "Everything is going to be okay." Amelia enjoyed his silent company as she too leaned back into her chair, resting her hand on the armrest beside his.

Luke moved his arm, accidentally touching Amelia's hand, but he didn't apologize. He slid his hand down to hers and softly patted and caressed it. Neither one looked at each other; it was just a kind touch that Amelia needed at just the right time.

"The surgery's finished," the nurse said as she walked up. "Dr. Kox will meet with you in a few minutes in the consultation room."

"Is she okay?" Claire asked with tearful eyes.

"Dr. Kox will go over everything with you."

"Is that a good sign?" Claire asked again, hoping to get some hope before the doctor's meeting.

"All I can say is your daughter was in good hands."

CHAPTER 118

Three hours and seventeen minutes after Dr. Clinton had come to speak with the Suttons, Dr. Kox made her journey from the operating room to the consultation room. The Suttons sat together in the cramped office, waiting breathlessly for Dr. Kox's announcement.

"Mommy," Charlie whispered while he sat in her lap as Claire clung to him like he was a life preserver.

"It's going to be okay, Charlie," Claire whispered back optimistically, but inside she was fragilely unsure. "It's going to be okay."

They waited in the silent square box for ten minutes as the torturous time built mountains of brick towers on each of their backs. The unknown was bittersweet, because they currently believed Scarlett was alive; they hadn't given up on the hope of her life. In one fatally quick word, all the hope could be dashed away like a wave wiping away a playful sandcastle. They were not ready for such a crashing tide.

Dr. Kox entered the room with a cordial smile as the entire room inhaled one painful breath, knowing the possible tide was about to come. "Mr. and Mrs. Sutton, I am Dr. Kox, and I was one of the lead surgeons for your daughter."

"Yes, doctor, please, tell us, how is Scarlett?" Dan asked, his words tumbling over each other.

Dr. Kox gave another polite smile, "Scarlett is recuperating after the surgery…"

"So, she's alive?" Claire clarified with mixed emotions. Tears were streaming as she beamed a radiant smile, with an irrepressible giggle filling the room's gloomy atmosphere.

"Yes, Mrs. Sutton, your daughter is alive…" Dr. Kox announced, but her tone wasn't uplifting. "But…"

The entire family halted their commotion at the dreaded word.

"But what?" Dan questioned as he clenched Claire's hand tighter than he thought capable.

"But we had some complications in the surgery," Dr. Kox answered flatly.

"Complications?" Claire interrupted feeling her stomach twist and convulse, "What kind of complications?" she uttered as the room felt like it was on a tip of a pen, tossing and swaying to balance itself.

"As I was repairing the punctures to her lungs, Dr. Raman was trying to alleviate some of the pressure and built up fluid from the internal bruising in her brain." She concluded her sentence, believing that she would once again be interrupted, but she continued. "Everything was going well, and then her pulse started dropping. We thought we had her stabilized and then her blood pressure bottomed out. Dr. Raman did everything he could do, but her vitals were not recovering."

"Oh, God!" Claire screamed as she sobbed on Charlie's shoulder.

"Mrs. Sutton, I am sorry, but Scarlett is in a coma. We are going to watch her very closely throughout the night and we may try another surgery soon, but we don't want to risk it at this time."

"So, you are telling me that our daughter is in a coma? For how long?" Dan said trying to regain some composure. "How long?"

"I wish I could tell you a time frame," Dr. Kox empathically answered. "I wish I could. Your daughter may wake up tomorrow, or next week, or…"

"Or never?" Amelia chimed in.

"I am sorry, but that is a possibility," Dr. Kox stated compassionately. "They are moving her to a room, so you can go up and see her shortly." She stood up and offered her condolences. "Just don't give up hope. We will do everything possible to try to get Scarlett to wake."

Dr. Kox left as the Sutton family held onto one another in a giant bear hug. Tears were flowing effortlessly, noses were running faster

310

than tissues could catch them, and hearts were breaking into thousands of fragmented pieces.

"She's alive." Dan tried to console everyone the best that he could. "She is alive," he muttered once again as he started to lose control of his masculine emotions. "That's something, right? I mean, she's strong. She is really strong."

No one said anything as they clutched each other tighter, nodding their heads emphatically.

The sun was setting and the moon was rising, alerting all the tides to come farther up the shore. The doctor's words had brought a wave crashing on part of their castle. The only thing was, how much of their fortress was left standing? The moon's reflection didn't cast enough light for them to see all the damage. They were going to have to wait until sunrise to see the extent of nature's wrath.

"What's a coma?" Charlie coughed as he sat in the middle of the tight embrace, getting hot from being surrounded with so much body heat.

Ignorance is truly blissful sometimes.

CHAPTER 119

The nurses lingered in the uncomfortable room, examining the patient's vitals as the Suttons sulked in the corner, too afraid to come any closer to the bed.

"They say that people can hear you when they're in a coma," Amelia whispered to her mother who stood motionless beside her.

Claire glanced over to her daughter comfortingly, but didn't verbally respond.

"Dad, why don't we just wake her up?" Charlie asked as he tugged on his father's pants pocket. "Can't we just shake her?"

"I wish that is all it took to wake her up." He looked down at a pair of naïve eyes that looked up into his jaded ones. The thought-provoking comment formed an instant confused gesture on Charlie's face, but he didn't ask any more questions. He didn't want to see his dad's depressing eyes again.

Amelia took a step closer to the broken Scarlett's bed, coming within a few feet of the nurses who sympathetically smiled and motioned for her to come forward.

"It's okay, honey," one of the nurses said as she gingerly rubbed Amelia's shoulders. "I think it would do her some good to hear a familiar voice."

Amelia looked around the room, taking in the various machines allowing the bandaged-up Scarlett another heartbeat, the IV administering numbing morphine into the arm with the cast, and the musical beat of her respirator granting another breath for the somewhat stable lungs. She clinched her hands and felt the dampness of a cold sweat forming. Closing her eyes, she tried to forget the surrounding environment. She tried to erase the horrid picture of her athletic sister, lying lifeless with visible stitches on her delicate face and even more frightening surgical scars underneath the layers.

She could feel the eyes of her family drilling into the back of her head, waiting with bated breath to listen to every word that her mouth dribbled out. Opening her mouth, she had so much she wanted to say, but she felt herself crumbling under the pressure.

"I can't," she said, turning to her family and then running out the door, fleeing the scene as if it were a crime she just committed by being mute to her comatose twin sister.

"Amelia," Dan hurriedly followed, catching up with her at the entrance of the ICU doors.

"I just couldn't, Dad. I just couldn't speak to her." The mortar of her fortress wall was chipping away. It was just going to be a matter of time before the tearful moat would be crashing down the drawbridge. She sank against the wall, falling to the ground as her legs gave way.

Dan took a seat on floor beside his healthy daughter and a startling thought crept into his mind. *Why am I comforting Amelia when Scarlett is the one who is truly suffering?* He looked over at his daughter crying, watching the teardrops fall onto the newly mopped floor and the perplexing thought drifted away as if it had never stopped for a visit. "I couldn't either, Amelia." He leaned closer to her, wrapping his arms around her shoulder and squeezing her into his side.

As Amelia had her head on her father's chest, a vibration resonated from his shirt pocket. He carefully moved her head and unearthed his cell phone, "Incoming call – Karen Anderson."

Looking down at the top of his daughter's head, he gently kissed the crown of her brow. Ignoring the phone call, he silenced it and laid it beside him on the ground. He had other more pressing matters to fill his attention.

313

CHAPTER 120

"I'll be back," Amelia sniffled as she stood up and walked away from her comforting father.

"I'll be here," Dan said as he slowly uncoiled his legs and stood up, bracing the walls for support.

The hospital looked different from Amelia's current dimension, the leaving from the coming. Looking back when she entered the building of technical surgeons, care-giving nurses and incomprehensible medical equipment, there was a feeling of warmth and optimism. Funny, she thought, the past always seems better when you are suffering in the present. The past is the past no matter which way you look at it. It never changes. The only thing that changes is the emotional ties that are wrapped around events. She shook the fantasy of happily waiting in the dismal waiting area and recoated herself in the authentic agony of the precipice of the unknown.

She continued to walk around and philosophically debate herself between the true identity of the past and the grandeur that people tend make the past out to be. She was no Socrates, Voltaire, or Confucius, but her mind was able to wrestle with the moral dilemma like the best of them.

"Amelia!" Josiah called as he saw her from across the third-floor lobby.

"Oh, Josiah," she ran into his arms. "Have you heard the news?"

"I just found out." His embrace encompassed her entire frame. "I'm sorry to hear it, Amelia. How are you doing?"

"I'm, I'm…" she started to say fine, but her heart wouldn't let her. "Not good."

"Amelia, just let it out."

She lowered her head and her wall, allowing the emotions that she once again tried to hold back to run havoc. "That's good, Amelia, just let it out." Her strong demeanor subsided, and she squalled like a child, pounding her fist into his chest, and crying like a mighty waterfall. Her dam had been broken; now it was time to let nature run its sometimes destructive, yet healing course.

"I....I....I just....just can't stop...stop cry....ing," she panted between syllables, trying to catch her breath during her emotional eruption. "Scar...Scarlett is....is in a co...she's in a co....co..."

"I know," he stopped her from saying the dreaded word. "I know."

"How could....could this happen?" she asked with snot running down her chin. "She hasn't done anything wrong."

"Oh, darling, this isn't a punishment."

"And I haven't been too nice to her lately," she bawled without relenting. "I was so...so...so mad at her the other day."

"She knows you didn't mean it," Josiah emphasized. "She knows."

"But what if...?" she asked, trembling with the idea that her mind would ask such a gory question.

"What if she wakes up tomorrow?" Josiah smiled. "Life is full of what-ifs. It's not that you ask what if. It's that you believe your what-ifs are possible."

"I don't know what I believe," she muttered as she unwrapped herself from his grip. She looked up at Josiah with solemn eyes. "I just don't know what to believe."

"Hope is something good to believe."

"It's good, but I don't know if I can believe in it."

She left Josiah standing alone to go back to Scarlett's disheartened room. Her comment destroyed his faith in her.

Without hope, what is there?

CHAPTER 121

Jud Askins had lain on the couch all evening after hearing the news of his public relations guru's death from Karen. He couldn't get the words out of his head. They seemed to echo like a thousand personalities swirling around inside himself, stalking his every thought so that its path would round back to the death of James Nialliv. He tried watching his favorite movie, *Vertigo*, but the masterpiece didn't have the same glimmer of mystery.

Looking across his entire studio apartment from the view of his couch, he found his favorite pair of blue jeans crumbled beside the box of Pharm Laboratories, Inc. work. He walked over to the box and opened the lid, but he didn't feel right working on a project that James specifically handpicked him to lead, out of respect for the evening. He looked into the paper-filled box, but memories of James were embedded on each sheet.

He placed the top back on the box as a symbolic burial for the night. "Rest in peace," he whispered quickly in his empty apartment. He bowed his head and took a moment of silence for the passing of his dear friend whom he had only met a few months before. James had taken him under his wing and demonstrated the tact and charismatic charm that was needed in public relations. He had learned more in the last three months than in all his political years in Washington.

Walking back to the beckoning couch, he heard a chirp rise from his cell phone that he had charging on the kitchen bar. The screen showed, "Message."

"Hey Jud," James voice appeared optimistic, yet eerie to Jud's ears. "Hope you are having a good Saturday so far. I really wanted to talk with you about Dan, because I feel like he is starting to backslide on us."

Jud's mouth dropped open in shock listening to James speak as if this message came from beyond the grave. "You really need to stay on top of Dan and follow up with him. He seemed a little rattled with the surprise visit yesterday, but you need to persuade him to follow the course."

He stood frigid, his hand gripping the cell phone with so much pressure that it was likely to crush into pieces, while the other hand grasped the bar for support. "I don't want to pressure you, Jud, but this is your time to shine. Show the world what Jud Askins is made of. And if you don't know, for hell's sake, make it up! Don't let Dan start to waver on his contract with Pharm. If he does, remind him that he is a member of the crew, and if the ship goes down, he will drown in the aftermath as well. Make him realize the horrible outcome of his selfish decisions," James said with a voice of booming authority. He initiated so much presence that Jud's knees were getting weaker as the message continued.

"Lastly, this is on your shoulders, Jud. If you cannot turn Pharm around, you were not as special as I once thought you were."

"End of message," a computerized voice echoed in Jud's ears.

Jud took a seat on a bar stool, letting the words sink into every empty space in his soul. He felt the weight of something grander than the world on his shoulders; he felt canonized with the responsibility that stared him right smack dab in his face. Fumbling around with his cell phone, he looked at when the message was received. 1:03 p.m.

He stared at the time and then remembered the estimated timing of the accident per Karen's reports. His heart ceased to beat. "This was probably the last call James made," he thought. Suddenly the frailty of his body was replaced with confidence. "If James believed in me," he thought, "then I believe in me too."

CHAPTER 122

The family separated for the night as Claire sat by Scarlett's bed, praying for any movement. She gazed hoping for her fingers to twitch to signal a thumbs up. She pined and pleaded for a blink to awaken her from her timeless sleep. Stretching out her arms timidly, she brushed Scarlett's frail cheek. The porcelain skin that used to be untainted and blemish free, now housed blotches and cuts. Claire closed her eyes and felt each wound. She felt the glass that carved into her daughter. She sensed the curvature of her broken nose that now sat unsymmetrical, teetering slightly to the left.

Her feeble hand trembled as she counted the stitches over her right eye, catching the outline of the swaddled bandages which were wrapped tightly around her entire head. She traveled her hand down to her shoulder that was jolted from her socket as Scarlett clung onto the handle. She crossed over the newly hardened cast, wishing that in a few days she would have graffiti of names scribbled up and down her arm. Her journey ended as she carefully stroked Scarlett's hand, which laid like marble, with three splints for the broken fingers.

Amelia watched from the darkened corner, taking in every touch. She couldn't move any closer, because when she looked at Scarlett, all she saw was herself.

The boys were at their dreadfully silent home after Claire and Dan decided that it would be best to take Charlie home for the night. Dan tried to persuade Amelia to join them, but she felt it would be more appropriate to stay with her mother. Claire didn't refuse the company, and she didn't try to avert Amelia from her decision.

Charlie fell asleep during the moonlit drive home, dismissing the twinkling stars that he usually wished upon. If ever there was a night for wishing, this would have been the night.

Dan packed in his snoring bundle and placed him on his king-sized bed. He carefully undressed him down to his Spiderman underwear without waking the dreaming child and then rolled him onto Claire's side of the bed. He stooped down beside the bed and watched Charlie's chest rise and fall with each breath he took, praying that Claire was watching the same from another child.

Sleep was the furthest thing from Dan's mind, so he curled on the bed beside Charlie and wrapped his arms tightly against his son's bare chest. "Daddy," Charlie groggily said without opening his eyes, "is Scarlett home?"

Dan slid his face into Charlie's hair and wiped his tears away. "Not yet." He listened as his son ended their conversation with a loud snore.

A vibration filled Dan's pants pocket. He pulled the phone out hoping that it was Claire telling him of a modern-day miracle. It wasn't Claire. It was just the eleventh time Karen had called him today.

"Hello," he answered perturbed at the number of calls and the six missed messages he listened to on the way home. Each saying the same thing.

CHAPTER 123

"I thought you were never going to pick up," Karen scoffed as she bit into a chocolate-covered caramel candy. "Glad you did."

"Karen," he sighed, "it hasn't been a good day."

"I know, I know," she said carelessly. "But I really need to talk with you."

"Can't this wait?" he asked, unwrapping his arms from his soundless little boy.

"I don't think that it can," she answered shortly with a tone of command, only to be erased with a childish giggle. "You turned me on today."

"What?" he stammered with disgust walking out of his bedroom.

"When I saw you holding your son, I couldn't help but want you to be holding me like that. After I left you I drove to Victoria's Secret and bought you a little present to unwrap off of me."

"Karen, his sister was in a car accident. I was trying to console him."

"Well, you can console me any time with those manly hands of yours. Better yet, you can do it right now." She bit her upper lip, getting excited at the thought of a romantic rendezvous under the full moon.

"Stop that!" he barked from the stairwell. "Just stop!"

"What is wrong with you?" Karen asked defensively, smoothing out her silk negligee.

"Really? That is what you ask me?"

"Are you still upset over the FDA meeting yesterday? Just throw James under the bus. I mean, he's already dead; there's not much he can say about it now."

"You are some piece of work!"

"Thank you," she smiled, taking the insult as ravishing flattery.

"That's not a compliment!" he yelled at the top of his lungs. "Is that all you think about? You, you, you? You never take anyone else's feelings into account."

"I think of your feelings when we are making love," she bantered erotically.

"You don't think of me. You use me."

"Is anything wrong with that?" she asked childishly.

Dan could not believe the conversation he was having. He marched around the family room, getting angrier and fiercer with every uncaring word she spoke. She was dispelling droplets of self-centeredness while Scarlett was sleeping on life support.

"Are you still there?" she asked not waiting for a response. "Because I don't know about you, but I am more turned on now than ever just thinking about you…and thinking about me…and thinking about us doing whatever you want me to do to you and your delicious body." She licked her chocolate seductively, mentally picturing Dan as the chocolate treat. She was enjoying every taste, while savoring the pent-up tension until she could meet with Dan.

"Do you want to know what I want you to do?" he asked as he stopped in front of his mantle, examining the family portrait that was taken a year ago.

"Anything for you," she moaned. "Nothing is too dirty."

"Anything?" he teased her, dangling her wildest desires within her reach.

"Anything."

"I want you to leave me alone!" he yelled. "I am finished with you."

CHAPTER 124

The restless night eventually faded and the dawn rose as always, but nothing changed in Scarlett's favor. Claire remained by Scarlett's side as the sunshine enveloped the room with cheery warmth, but it wasn't enough to melt the icicles dangling off of Claire's cold heart. Dark circles rounded her eyes, appearing as if she was wearing a raccoon mask for Halloween. She wished that it was only a mask and that Scarlett was celebrating All Hallow's Eve by dressing as a mummy. Halloween was still five months away.

"I brought you a donut," Charlie grinned to Amelia sitting beside the window where she had been throughout the night, watching the nightlife rustle through the field of crops. She watched as the sun rose, oozing its colors effortlessly over the horizon. She pondered the vastness and the wonder of such an event, and given any other day she might have even felt the hand of a superior intelligent being taking the reins of such a performance, but her atheistic belief was solidified yesterday. To her, intelligent design was just a cop-out for scientists who tiptoed into the grassy fields of theology.

"Did you get this at the Seven-Eleven?" she asked, knowing that the convenience store didn't sell organic donuts with soy milk and that the only place in Bethany that sold her delicacies with all the wholesome goodness was Delta's Bakery. Delta's Bakery didn't specialize in healthy options, but Delta realized the growing attraction to vegan diets and had started to dabble and experiment in this new cuisine.

"No," Charlie huffed, "we went to your place."

Her eyes lit up like she just struck a match. "You like Delta's too," she said turning to grab the bag out of his hands to find her dad and mom standing over Scarlett's bed, holding each other up. The emptiness in her stomach vanished as the tormented feeling of being alive weighed her down. "Thanks, but I'll eat it later."

She watched as her dad and mom stood whispering into each other's ear. Neither said much because nothing worthy of telling occurred through the night. Charlie licked the sugary glaze off his donut that was worn like a ring around his index finger. He nibbled around the edges, spinning the breakfast treat so each side was even. "It's really good," he mumbled, munching with a glob of glaze sticking on his chin.

"I believe you," Amelia responded still peering at her parents, wondering if they would ever acknowledge her in the room. She knew that her parents loved her, but the night was uncomfortable and too quiet. Her mother would speak to the nurse, but she never said a word to Amelia. She recalled the events of the evening, and she couldn't even remember a time that Claire looked at her. Not one time did Claire turn her head to check on Amelia.

Claire's main focus was Scarlett, which Amelia understood, but she also thought that since she was Scarlett's identical twin, her mother might not be able to look at her without feeling more remorse. That idea was concocted at three twenty-four in the morning when the nurse asked if Claire needed anything and she plainly stated no. Being any other circumstance, she would have asked Amelia if she needed anything, but Claire didn't ask or even turn around to see if anything was needed. It was as if Claire was ignoring her healthy daughter.

Amelia wanted to walk over and hug her family and let them know that she loved them. She wanted to speak a word, but what word? She wanted Scarlett to wake up from her dream state, if people dream in comas, but she knew that belief was a far cry from reality. She wanted to do so much, but yet, she didn't feel able, so she just turned back around and stared out the window, watching the crops move in the wind.

CHAPTER 125

Ethel Stapleton was feeling much better than she was twenty-four hours earlier. She was sitting up and eating her scrambled egg whites and wheat toast with sugar-free and fat-free blackberry jelly. "Looking good this morning," a nurse said walking in and then turning back out when she saw Ethel enjoying her breakfast.

"Do you want some, Josiah? I can order it for you," Ethel asked as she took another bite of her dry toast.

"I don't feel that hungry," he said, stretching his body from a long night.

"I didn't want to ask, but I saw you come and go a couple of times through the night," Ethel commented. "Why didn't you just go home? I'd be okay," she said smiling through the lie because she didn't want him to go home. The comfort in knowing someone was nearby sometimes has better healing power than modern prescriptions, she thought.

"I just needed to move around." He looked concerned, wondering if she had started to put some of the puzzle of his existence in Bethany together. She didn't respond, causing him to breathe a little easier despite not finding what he was looking for through the deserted twilight hospital hallways.

"Well, I hope you found what you were looking for," she said, nodding her head at him suspiciously.

"Why do you say that?" he automatically questioned hastily, quickly apologizing for his rashness.

"Oh, I didn't mean anything by it. It's just that when I get up it isn't always just to stretch."

"Well, I'm not being completely honest," he spoke up, shocked that the words escaped his locked lips. He'd been taught to keep secrets and mysteries silent, even for years. He'd been trained to withstand enemy interrogations and torturing techniques. Yet, it took just two nights in a hospital for him to almost release all that he kept hidden.

"Josiah?" she asked uneasily, sitting up straighter in her bed with her pillows propping her up, while laying her fork down onto her swiveled bed tray.

"It's not what you are expecting," he quickly answered, trying to calm her fears and not disinherit her trust, all while trying to tame his tongue from saying what he swore not to say.

"What is it?"

"Well, you see, this isn't easy to say." He stood up and walked around the room, grasping at any random thread dangling in his brain to cling to and start to weave a story. He looked around the room and caught a glimpse of a newspaper with a headline of an unnatural pilgrimage of deer in the county this season. "It's about Mary, Mary Sutton."

"That young girl that you saved?" she asked, rearranging herself to sit more comfortably.

"Yes, that is her." He regained some ground which was slipping away from him and the rest of story rolled off his tongue without scheming for an easy way out. "She was in a very bad wreck yesterday."

"Oh, dear."

"Oh, dear is right. It was because of some deer." He continued with the story, not giving all the details or the seriousness of her condition for fear that it may slow Ethel's recovery. He finished the portions of the story he was inclined to tell and then exited her room. He came too close to messing everything up after coming this far. As he walked down the hall, he wondered if it would really be that bad to tell one person the true purpose for his coming to Bethany. He slowly began to question and doubt if it would really cause everything on the playing board to shift if one extra person, an elderly woman at that, came to know the truth.

325

He stopped halfway down the hall and turned back to see Ethel's door open as her nurse announced that it was time for her bath.

At this time, yes.

CHAPTER 126

The nurse's station in the ICU was hopping with patients' rooms buzzing to signal time to check their vitals, give medication, or family members who have once again misplaced the television remote. Josiah entered the unit as the nurses scattered as if they started a game of tag, each moving in a different direction. He watched the nurses and noticed that none of them went near Mary's room. A strange feeling overcame him, and he instantly felt the need to get into her room.

He hurriedly walked toward the elevators and bumped into someone dressed in scrubs with a white mask over his nose and mouth. "Sorry, excuse me," Josiah said as he looked up into the nurse's eyes.

"No problem," the male nurse responded, quickly looking down.

Josiah stood in the hallway and watched the nurse leave his sight. He steadily walked down the hallway, passing the nurses' station to head to the elevators. Closing his eyes he replayed the two words the nurse said. The voice was vaguely familiar, but he couldn't place it. He looked back into his memory and peered into the man's eyes, which had also seemed vaguely familiar.

Stepping into Mary's room, Josiah saw the Sutton family scattered around. "Good morning," he said warmly as the family each greeted Josiah kindly. "Has it been a good morning for Mary?"

"No improvements," Claire said, frowning discouragingly.

"But no drops either," Dan optimistically interrupted. "It's been pretty quiet this morning, which hopefully is a good thing. Maybe the more she rests, the more she...." He stopped in mid-sentence as the alarms on her machines started screaming.

"Nurse! Nurse!" Josiah shouted as he stood at the door, looking up at their station to see that no one was available.

"Scarlett!" Claire squirmed in her seat as she watched her daughter's pulse flat line.

Josiah rushed out of the room and remembered that one of the nurses was four rooms down. He ran to the room and grabbed a nurse who was talking to an elderly man about fishing on the riverbanks, "She's dying!"

"What room?" The nurse asked jumping up.

Josiah didn't answer, but ran back down to see the frightened family. Dan and Claire were staring frantically at Mary who continued to lie unconscious as Amelia tucked Charlie's head into her armpit so he couldn't witness the chaotic scene.

The nurse started administering her life-saving procedures as Josiah took off to the next room to get another nurse. "Room 3015!" he screamed as the next nurse fled the room, dropping the patient's breakfast tray back onto her table.

Josiah didn't want to settle for two nurses; he wanted everyone who was available. As he was running wildly through the halls, he heard an announcement on the intercom system, "Code Blue, Room 3015!" That was all it took, and all the medical staff on the floor was rushing to Mary's side.

Following the pack of scrubs, he saw the family standing out in the hall, embracing one another as sobs were rising among them. The doctors and nurses had closed Mary's door and they were trying to bring her heartbeat back.

"Can we pray?" Josiah asked, and everyone nodded in agreement. Even Amelia's eyes now showed hope of a powerful being that could help her dying sister. Josiah started praying as everyone else wailed in heart-gushing pain. He continued his earnest prayer when he remembered the nurse he had bumped into earlier. It was no nurse.

Carlos.

CHAPTER 127

The waiting room was gut wrenching as they waited for the news. There was a fifty-fifty chance of what the doctor would say when they walked through the doors, either death or life. This was not a coin toss that anyone wanted to make.

Twenty minutes and forty-three seconds later the door opened and Dr. Tom McArthur walked through with a tired look in his eyes. The family jumped up as if they had been released from their chained shackles. "How's Scarlett?" Dan prodded as Dr. McArthur stepped closer to the family.

"We are unsure of what happened, but we did revive her. Her pulse is beating steadily right now, but we are going to be keeping a closer watch on her."

"You don't know what caused this?" Josiah asked, wanting to give his input on the situation.

"She may have had a reaction to some of the medicine, but when we looked at her charts, nothing had been given to her recently. The last time they had given her anything, it was the same dosage and medication as we started yesterday," Dr. McArthur commented, mentally scratching his head.

"But," Amelia spoke up, startling herself that she was speaking.

"What is it?" Claire asked.

"But, someone was just in there and I thought I saw him give her something," Amelia feebly said.

Dr. McArthur opened up her chart of her recent medicines. "The last time she was given something was by her head nurse, Sally, at 7:56 a.m."

"I don't know, but someone came into the room about thirty minutes ago and I would have sworn I saw a syringe in his hands as he took her pulse on her right hand." Amelia continued to spill every little detail of the visit.

"Sally is her nurse, so I do not know who you saw," Dr. McArthur stated, dismissing the claim coming from the twelve-year-old. "You might have thought you saw something, but we document everything, and there aren't any male nurses in the ICU this morning."

"Could it have been a doctor?" Dan asked, defending his daughter's questioning. "I wasn't paying much attention, but I did see a male nurse come into the room this morning, just a few minutes before Scarlett…just before Scarlett, well, you know."

"I am sorry about that, but I will look into it," Dr. McArthur answered. "Very confusing, but I seriously doubt that what you saw had anything to do with your daughter's scare."

"Really?" Amelia rhetorically asked, scoffing his belittling attitude.

"I believe you, Amelia," Josiah whispered in her ear as he stooped down. "We have to watch out for her. Anything can happen here."

Amelia nodded her head as Josiah winked, sealing their contract. The family returned to Scarlett's room and Josiah realized that he had to step up his protection. They were not going to be backing down, and it seemed like they were doing much more than he expected. His insides were churning, wondering when all the drama was going to be over and the lingering cloud of responsibility was going to scatter from over his head.

Even though Nathanial said things were going as planned, Josiah was seriously on the verge of doubting the plan, no matter who orchestrated it long ago.

CHAPTER 128

The women went back to see Scarlett sleep, with Amelia keeping a watchful eye on her sister's well-being. Josiah eventually made his way back after giving Claire and Amelia a few minutes alone with her.

Charlie was down on the ground watching *The Flintstone's* while playing with the waiting room's sparse toy collection as Dan took a few minutes for a much-needed laugh. "I thought I would find you here," Karen said, sultrily sauntering into the dimly lit ICU waiting room.

Dan jumped up before Karen made it halfway into the room, catching her by the arm and heading to the door. "Didn't I make myself clear last night?" he murmured angrily, allowing Karen to catch the tone without a doubt.

"Yes," Karen answered jadedly, as she half-heartedly tried to remove her arm from Dan's grip. "But I spoke with Jud this morning, and he is on his way here," she hissed, grinning menacingly. "He should be here soon."

Dan released his hand from Karen's bicep as Jud stepped through the elevator doors. "I'm sorry to hear about the accident," Jud politely started, but the gentlemanly introduction quickly fled. "Karen informed me of your conversation last night." Jud stood commanding the conversation with his newly discovered testosterone. He stood back straight, chest out, butt in, as if he was going to salute the president of the United States if he walked into the room. Glancing over at Karen, who smiled at his new charm, he continued to drill into Dan the importance of the next few weeks.

"I don't care about Pharm anymore!" Dan exploded with volcanic energy. "I don't care! My daughter is on life support right now, so you two can carry on without me!"

"Dan, Dan, Dan," Jud ticked his tongue like a displeased parent scolding his child. "We have a contract with you as our legal counsel."

"Attorneys quit cases and clients fire attorneys all the time and they hardly sue them for breach of contract," Dan roared.

"We won't need to sue you, Dan," Jud laughed deviously. "All we will have to do is put your name in every negative document we submit to the FDA and state that you are the one who fraudulently submitted patent documents. It won't be hard to forge your signature."

"That, that's illegal and unethical!" Dan stammered.

"Oh, Dan, Pharm's drug is accidentally killing people, no offense Karen," Jud said, quickly patting her hand approvingly. "So forging documents will not make me lose any more sleep. It will probably help me sleep. I use a sound machine and take…" he continued as Dan interrupted Jud's sleeping regime.

"You, you are evil," Dan scolded with new vision of his lacking soul. "How can you do this? Not to me, but to the patients taking the pills?"

"How could you do it last month?" Jud quipped back without dropping a breath, or his smile. "Don't make me out to be a beast, Dan. You are just as liable as everyone else. You either stick with us to the pot of gold," Jud said, pulling Karen to his side to signify their unity, "or you can be buried alive and pray for a quick death."

"I, I need to see my daughter," Dan said, fleeing their coercion and pulling Charlie off the ground to make their getaway to Scarlett's room. "Don't follow me!"

"We'll be in contact," Jud waved. "Soon."

"So," Karen started, eyeing Jud like a piece of candy. "Where have you been?"

CHAPTER 129

Tuesday morning was a day of both highs and lows for Josiah. The last couple of days he had spent almost every minute of the day watching Mary sleep. When he knew Amelia would take over his watchman shift, he would occasionally make his way from the ICU to visit Ethel who was on the second floor in the recovery unit.

Ethel was in good spirits with each of his visits, mainly because her friends from church had started a cycle of visits, so Ethel wasn't alone except to get some rest. "So, am I going to be able to go home today?" Ethel asked Dr. Johnson, the head cardiologist on staff at St. Mark's.

"I think it would be a good idea to let you go home today, Mrs. Stapleton," Dr. Johnson remarked as he continued to go over the finalization of his medical procedures. He assigned her a long list of multicolored pills to take with each meal to help stabilize her blood pressure, cholesterol, and to just help her relax and start to feel as good as new.

"Oh, thank you, doctor, thank you," she grinned like a teenager being asked out to her senior prom. "When can I go?"

"Well, as soon as the nurses get everything ready for you to leave, I guess, we can let you return home." Dr. Johnson smiled at her good humor and personality. He wished that all his patients were as kind and loving as Mrs. Stapleton. She did have a good recovery, which could account for her cheerfulness, but he had known Mrs. Stapleton for quite a while in this small town, and he never once had known her to be a problem.

"Dr. Johnson, when I get home, I'm going to have you and your family over for supper one evening."

"I might just take you up on that offer," he smiled kindly.

"I wasn't offering, I was telling," Ethel laughed heartily. "You'll come to my house for supper one evening."

"Well, good to see you so lively, Mrs. Stapleton," he said with a laugh as he finished his final checklists and made his way to the next room to possibly release another patient.

Ethel sat in her recliner, basking in the feeling of a clean bill of health, counting down the minutes until she would be back home in her own bed. She didn't want to make a fuss about herself, but all the church ladies had already assigned a timesheet of shifts for people to be with Ethel during her recovery. Since Ethel didn't have any children or any family nearby, the church was her family. They were the best support Ethel would ever need.

"Glad you are doing so well, Ethel," Josiah said as he entered into her room, exchanging pleasantries with Cathy Reynolds, a dear friend of Ethel's who had been up at the hospital most of the morning.

"Me too," she giggled, unable to control her happiness.

"I'm glad to see you smile," he said taking a seat beside Mrs. Reynolds hoping to feel lifted up in this room of lovely women. "I haven't seen a smile in the other room in some time."

"She's still in the coma?" Cathy asked sincerely. She had been informed by Ethel of the horrible accident. "We have her on our prayer list at church."

"Thank you, Mrs. Reynolds. I think the family would appreciate that. But yes, she's still in the coma."

"Sad, just so sad," Ethel said, bowing her head for a moment of silence. "Almost rude of me to be giddy this morning about getting out of the hospital with that poor child still like that." The room was silent. No one knew how to respond. Josiah and Cathy glanced at one another, waiting for the other to say something, but Cathy bravely broke the ice.

"God is much wiser than we are, Ethel. We may not understand why things happen or don't happen, but that doesn't mean that we shouldn't rejoice when God grants mercy and healing." Cathy ended her testimony, and even though the words were true and heartfelt, Ethel still felt the unfairness in the situation.

"I'm an old fat lady, Cathy," Ethel thoughtfully remarked, trying not to dismiss or refute Cathy's miniature sermon. "That girl is so young and precious. It just doesn't make sense sometimes and I guess it never will make sense to me."

"Me either," Josiah responded with a hearty tone of amen. "Me either."

CHAPTER 130

In the twenty-four hours since Ethel Stapleton returned home, there were not any changes in Scarlett's condition. Charlie was taken to school each morning while Claire and Dan took turns spending the night at the hospital with the ever-present Amelia in the room nightly. The nurses were now bona fide family members. The Suttons had a family reunion every five years and there were more than a hundred and fifty relatives that arrived for the weekend adventure. Amelia recalled that every time she went, she met new faces with the knowledge that they would most likely never meet again until the next reunion.

She had come up with stories with the daily nurses and their make-believe relationship, whether it be "Aunt" Cecilia, "Second Cousin" Tammy, "Third Cousin" Abigail or Abby, and finally "Uncle" Terry. Aunt Cecilia always had a joke for Amelia, while Cousin Tammy had the latest gossip about the off and on-again relationship between Abby and Terry. This is what Amelia's day came to now, waiting to see her loving relatives.

Dan had spent the night with Charlie the night before, allowing him once again to sleep on Claire's side of the bed. Charlie didn't ask to, but Dan still didn't like the feeling of being alone. His mind was jumbling with the remorse of Scarlett, the tragedy of James and Lucy, the animosity of Karen, and the rage of Jud. The emotions were colliding with one another, forming hybrids as if the feelings were being smeared like paint on a palette. He tossed and turned most of the night again with very little sleep. The legs of his sheep were getting too toned for their own good.

After dropping Charlie off at school to keep him in some sort of normal routine for a seven-year-old, Dan's cell phone rang. He picked up the phone before looking at, thinking that it was most likely Claire, "Hello?"

"Hello," he heard the sexy greeting from Karen, and he immediately wanted to end the call, but something was nudging him to once again try to get Karen to see his side of the situation. It was a far leap in faith, but that was currently the only jump he was able to take with her. "How are you doing this morning, sexy beast?"

"I am on my way to the hospital," he answered coldly, hoping the iciness was felt on her side of the phone. It wasn't.

"Again?" she moaned as if annoyed by his constant commitment to his daughter's health.

"Yes, again."

"Does she do anything when you are there?" she asked rudely, and Dan suddenly felt the urge to throw the phone out the window and roll over it with his vehicle.

"No! She is in a coma!" he yelled, angered by the constant disrespect that ran profusely from Karen's poisonous lips.

"So, why go?" she playfully asked. "You can come and see me. I am all alone in the office today."

"You should be trying to resolve your drug problem."

"I don't do drugs," she giggled. "I just do you."

"Karen, will you just listen to me for a minute! You need to quickly find a reason for the defects in the drug, so it can be ratified by the FDA legitimately. They may only slap you on the wrist if you can solve this issue," he said, knowing that would not be the case. Too many innocent lives had been taken by her disregard of their health. He just wanted her to move forward with the drug research.

"No, Jud said for me to do nothing until you get everything settled."

"I have repeatedly told you and Jud that I quit. You can try to pin this fiasco on me, but I did not do anything but give you legal counsel. I was not aware of the trouble that James caused until it was too late. I should have resigned from the case sooner, but I let my personal feelings for you take the front seat in my decision-making process. Not anymore."

"I think that is probably the sweetest thing anyone has ever said to me. You risked your career for me?" She gushed, missing the whole point of his conversation.

"Really? That is what you got out of the last thing I said?" He rolled his eyes, wondering what made him fall for her to begin with, but sadly he wasn't thinking rationally or with his heart. "This is your problem. I quit! I will call Todd as soon as I get off with you."

"You can't."

"Why can't I?"

"Because he is gone. James apparently contacted him over the weekend and warned him about the meeting you had on Friday. Since James is no more, Jud is currently heading up Pharm during this time."

"What?" Dan pulled over to the side of the road, allowing his mind total focus to process this outlandish flowchart. "That is crazy! Jud is just a PR man. He's not president potential."

"I don't know, but James had it all figured out Saturday morning. So, you can try calling Todd, but he won't answer. He is probably off on an island somewhere, enjoying the sun."

"So, Jud is in charge. Perfect. He already knows I quit. No need in calling anyone. Good luck!" He slammed down his phone and watched the traffic pass him on the two-lane road. He didn't know what to do, but he knew that it wasn't his primary concern anymore.

CHAPTER 131

After the morning conversation with Karen, and eleven missed calls and three messages later, Dan assumed that Karen had gotten the hint that he wasn't going to deal with her problems anymore. The morning passed with no changes on Scarlett's condition. Dr. Raman spoke with Dan and Claire about the possibility of another surgery to try to alleviate the pressure as Josiah left the room to give the family time to be alone with the doctor.

"Could this work?" Claire asked with a glimmer of hope, more than she had shown since Saturday.

"It could and it could not," Dr. Raman frankly stated. "We have waited and there has been no change, so it won't hurt to go in and investigate. The procedure is risky, so it is ultimately your decision."

Dan and Claire sat mulling over the decision as Amelia interrupted, "I think Scarlett would want it done."

Dan and Claire both looked up at Amelia, unaware that she was in the room or even listening to the conversation for that matter. "It's risky," Dan pointed out while Amelia nodded in agreement.

"I don't know of any time in Scarlett's life that she just sat around and waited for something. She's a doer. Not a waiter."

"But," Claire tried to respond, but she didn't know how to reject Amelia's point, because in her heart she agreed. "I think you are right," she said, smiling at Amelia for the first time since Saturday. Amelia rushed over to her mother's side and the two finally connected after four days of sitting in the same hospital room. "I am afraid," she cried, wiping away Amelia's tears instead of her own. "But Scarlett is stronger than all of us."

"She is," Amelia agreed, trying to control her crying. But her mother's embrace was too much for her to hold it together; she had longed to feel her mother's love and not her resentment.

Dan looked at Claire for a final answer and a nod was all he needed. "Do the surgery," he said, shaking Dr. Raman's hand with a feeling of appreciation. "Take good care of her."

"I will, Mr. Sutton."

The family said their short goodbyes to Scarlett, whispering in her ear that everything was going to be okay, and that they would see her soon. Abby started to tear up, watching the emotional scene as if it were a Hallmark movie. "I'll be right there with her," she said before hugging everyone in the family, sinking deep into their arms, and seeing the desperation in their eyes.

"Thanks, Cousin Abby," Amelia said as she left the room, shutting the door behind her for Scarlett to be prepped for another surgery. "Be strong, sister," she muttered walking down the hall beside Josiah.

"She will," he smiled with a wink. "She will."

CHAPTER 132

The nurses wheeled Scarlett's bed to the operating room as the family watched their sleeping daughter and sister be taken away behind closed doors. They each had a flurry of butterflies in their stomach. There was nervousness for the outcome of the surgery, but there was also optimism at the same time. It was a powerful concoction, like that of a Long Island iced tea.

They once again were huddled in the surgery area's waiting room as a friendly hospital attendant introduced herself and stated that she would keep them informed on the surgery. She warmly smiled and turned to go back to her desk where she was studying the newspaper's crossword puzzle and trying to find a six-letter word for Hitchcock's shower masterpiece.

Ignoring the hunger pains in his stomach, Dan looked down at his watch; 11:34 a.m. "The surgery shouldn't take as long as the last one."

"I will wait for days if it will help Scarlett," Claire announced enthusiastically. "Days." Claire knew that Dan was trying to console her and Amelia, but she didn't want to focus on the time or the thought that they were once again cutting into her daughter's head. Some thoughts did not need to be voiced.

"Does anyone need anything?" Josiah asked, trying his best to help in any way possible.

"I could use a coffee," Dan mentioned. "But I can get that. Anyone else?" he asked, but they each shook their head no. He stretched his wobbly legs, which started to work normally after the third step and headed to the familiar cafeteria.

"I haven't told you," Claire said as she looked over at Josiah. "Thank you for staying here with us, but I know you are busy."

Josiah reached out his hand and held hers. It was just a touch, but it seemed to miraculously ease Claire's fear. "I'm not that busy."

Claire smirked at the kind statement and patted his hand in appreciation. The three sat and waited for the nurse to come and tell them the surgery had begun, but they would have to wait some time before that phone call would be made due to the preparation time.

"How's Mrs. Stapleton?" asked Amelia, trying to find a different avenue to tread down this morning.

"Very, very well," Josiah answered with a light-hearted grin. "She is still tired and sore, but the doctors say that in a few weeks she will be back to her old self."

"That is good to hear," Claire responded, hoping that they would be having the exact conversation in a few weeks when someone asks how Scarlett is doing. "So good to hear."

The attendant picked up the ringing telephone and appeared confused on the telephone. She scribbled down a message and then repeated the information back into the phone. Claire watched and tried to listen, but her chair was too far away from the attendant's desk. She hung up the telephone and grabbed her note and started to walk toward them with a strange expression on her face.

"Is one of you Amelia Sutton?" she asked, reading her neon pink Post-it note.

"I am."

"Dr. Lisa Pottinger needs to see you and your family in her office. It is on the fourth floor in Room 4024."

"What is this about?" Claire asked bewildered. "Why Amelia?"

"I'm not sure ma'am, but the doctor is expecting you."

"Probably just want more of my blood," Amelia moaned as she looked down at her arm where they stuck her last time.

CHAPTER 133

Claire and Amelia went up one floor and waited outside Dr. Pottinger's office while Josiah stayed in the waiting room to tell Dan where they went. Claire examined the room, but there wasn't anything that gave any kind of hint about their reason for this unexplained visit.

A woman opened the door, "Amelia Sutton?"

Claire and Amelia stood up and walked to the door just as Dan and Josiah turned their last corner. "Right on time," Dan smiled as he took a hot sip of his French vanilla coffee.

"Please, come in. I am Dr. Pottinger. Have a seat," she said as she walked around her desk and sat comfortably in her ergonomic office chair with firm padding and neck rest. A trickling of water was coming from a relaxation fountain in the corner, surrounded by her Zen sand garden. The walls were coated in a neutral almond shade which mingled with the bamboo plants growing on top of her antique mahogany desk that had golden accents on the legs. Dr. Pottinger's office was more than a workspace, it was a retreat for her soul with the type of work she dealt with daily. She had taken half a dozen trips to Japan for conferences and seminars, and during her second visit, she fell in love with the decorating styling of Feng Shui.

"I'll wait out here," Josiah said as the door shut.

"You all may be a little confused why I have called Amelia up here."

"Want more of my blood?" Amelia asked with an awkward expression of annoyance covering her face as she watched the water cascade over the modern metal art deco tower.

"About that," Dr. Pottinger remarked. "Yes, you had some blood taken a few days ago."

"Yes, when my sister had her surgery," Amelia stated as Claire hushed her from speaking anymore. A chill went up Claire's back and she prayed that her instincts were telling her wrong. The calming serenity of the room was not doing its purpose.

"You are a good sister," Dr. Pottinger replied warmly. "Well, when you donated your blood we ran some standardized tests to check your blood type and to make sure you don't have any contractible diseases. Then we ran some other tests to double check you."

"Double check?" Dan asked as he held his coffee on his thigh.

"Yes, the nurse who took your blood noticed some bruises and asked a few questions, and when you answered her, your responses didn't seem normal or appropriate."

"Is this just about my bruises?" Amelia asked thinking that this was a counselor who was investigating abuse. "I was not beaten and I have not been beaten. My parents love me and I love them."

"That is good to hear, but I am not here to speak about that," Dr. Pottinger assured.

"You're not?" Amelia asked, confused once again while her eyes darted across the room to the Japanese scroll with red lettering that looked like little houses.

"I don't know how to say this delicately, but when we tested your blood, we tested your red blood cell count. And your count was very low for a person of your age."

Claire heard the worst words she could imagine, and she knew what those words meant. She had a daughter who was going through an emergency surgery, couldn't this just be a mistake, she thought? But it wasn't a mistake. Amelia listened to the doctor with fascination of the human body without fully understanding what the doctor was implying.

"Dr. Pottinger, are there more tests we can do? Maybe they are wrong. Maybe you got the wrong person's blood. I mean, mistakes happen," Claire responded, dodging the situation with possible excuses.

344

"We will do more tests to make sure, but I am pretty sure with the results," Dr. Pottinger sighed with empathy.

"So, are you telling me what I think you are telling me?" Claire gasped, squeezing Dan's hand for a pinch to wake her up from this nightmare.

"I'm afraid I am, Mrs. Sutton," she responded and then looked down into Amelia's innocent wide eyes. "Amelia, we are going to do everything to beat this, but it looks like you have leukemia."

Amelia's eyes widened as they turned to look at her father's that had started to dribble tears. She then turned further to see her mother crying frantically, grasping at Amelia's hand to pull her into a hug. The word was heard, yet it was suddenly drowned out by the noise, not of wailing, but of the bubbling of the meditation-inducing waterfall.

CHAPTER 134

"We've got to stay strong," Dan whispered in Claire's ear as he clung to her fragile body, beaten and battered from the punches and blows that seemed to be never ending. "For Amelia."

The two parted, Claire returning to the waiting room with Josiah to check on Scarlett's surgery as Dan almost carried Amelia to Dr. Pottinger's medical exam room for more tests. Dr. Pottinger was an oncologist who graduated from the University of Chicago and completed her residency in Loyola University Chicago. She loved her school and training but hated the frigid cold winds of Chicago, so she took the first position that came available in the South, thus making her exodus to Bethany.

"It's going to be okay," Dan optimistically spoke, hoping that the words would somehow break through his wall of doubt and convince himself. "They could be wrong. More tests will show that."

Amelia didn't respond. Her legs were moving forward, but she didn't feel the ground. She looked around, and it appeared that everything was going in slow motion. The nurses were walking like flexible zombies, limber and able to move their joints, but at a decreased speed. Staring down the hallway, she wondered if her vision was tunneling with the shock, but she realized that the hallway itself was tunneling. "Dad, I'm scared," she mumbled as they followed Dr. Pottinger to the last door of the hallway, her exam room.

Dr. Pottinger flipped on the florescent lights, brightening the darkened room to illuminate several medical gadgets and similar-looking torture devices. "Amelia, we are going to take really good care of you, and you have nothing to be afraid of. There are new medical advances every day to help beat leukemia, but we are going to have to do some tests and run some x-rays. Ten years ago leukemia was a scary word, but today, today it is different."

Amelia flinched every time Dr. Pottinger rolled the word leukemia off her tongue like she was merely saying chocolate chip cookie. She felt a punch in her gut every time the l-word was said. *Not scary*, she thought. *Not scary for who?*

"See Amelia, we just have to stay positive," Dan replied, offering his two cents of medical experience and knowledge, which only led him to being bankrupt. His response didn't ease Amelia's fears because it was the typical phrase to say at the time.

"That's right," Dr. Pottinger smiled. "Attitude has an enormous impact on the treatment of leukemia."

"Um, Dr. Pottinger," Amelia spoke up while taking a watchful seat on the examination table after she stopped flinching.

"Yes."

"Can you do me one favor?" Amelia asked.

"I will try," Dr. Pottinger smiled as she closed the door.

"Stop saying that word."

CHAPTER 135

The Suttons were scattered through St. Mark's Hospital, being cut open in an operating room, being photographed in an x-ray tunnel, and waiting in the radiology and operation waiting rooms.

Scarlett was the only member of the family who was totally oblivious of the circumstances, lying like Dr. Frankenstein's monster, ready to be prodded and shocked. Just like the monster, she wasn't aware of what the doctors were going to be doing to her. She was like their experiment, and each was hoping for the same result as Dr. Frankenstein.

Amelia, thankfully not claustrophobic, was in a state of shock and wonder. This was the first time that she had been x-rayed and she was taking in all the senses. As she was being pulled into the majesty of science by her love of knowledge, she was starting to slide into the tunnel. She watched as the scenery of the room vanished into a pasty plastic white wall resting five inches above her nose.

"It's going to be loud," the radiologist technician said through the headphones that Amelia placed over her ears. "Your music should be coming on."

Amelia's ears were flooded with the sounds of soothing violins and cellos. She closed her eyes and envisioned the musicians' fingers dancing over the strings effortlessly. A loud humming sound surrounded her. The machine had begun.

Dan dug out his cell phone from his pocket and opened up the internet so he could Google leukemia and become a well-informed parent. He knew that with his research he would see marvelous advancements in the medical field, but he would also see the black cloud looming around each webpage. He clicked open an article from St. Jude's Children's Hospital detailing the leaps and bounds that researchers have hurdled triumphantly in recent years. The bald heads of the smiling children caused a knot in his stomach. He saw the

348

jubilation on their faces, but he saw their battle scars as well. He wasn't ready for Amelia to face this war.

Claire sat beside Josiah, who did his best to sympathize with her raw emotions. She swayed in his arms, frail and delicate from Amelia's bombshell. "Why is this happening to us?"

"Some things we are not meant to understand," Josiah replied as he continued to hold her.

"You're a religious man. Why would *God* do this?" she questioned, emphasizing God's name as if she was wishing that He didn't exist and at the same time praying that He was big enough to fix all her problems.

"I wouldn't say I'm religious, but I have seen the power of God," he poignantly commented. "I cannot say why things happen, but I can say that everything happens for a reason."

Claire stopped and slowly removed herself from his grasp, sitting up straight and ignoring his close vicinity. Those were not the words that she wanted to hear. How could someone say that a coma has a reason or cancer has a reason? Who could look at a young married couple who loses their newborn child from SIDS and say that everything happens for a reason? "I don't buy that."

"I know you probably don't right now, and I'm not sure if you will ever believe that. I just have to believe that if God is all powerful in the good things in life, He must also be all powerful in the bad times. It isn't an easy concept, but that is the only thing I have to cling to."

"Josiah, it's nothing personal towards you, but I just need something more than a story of this God that you believe in. I need to know that everything is going to be okay. I just need a touch."

Josiah listened to her heartfelt cry and wanted to say that our plans are not God's plans, and that our faith should not be based on what God can do for us, but that is not what she needed to hear at this time. Josiah reached out his hand and placed it on hers. "God uses more things to reveal Himself than you could possibly know."

349

CHAPTER 136

The hardest thing in life is not the pain of enduring the hardship; it is not the fear of coming face to face with the demons one wrestles with; it is not even the ultimate foreseen conclusion of death. The hardest thing we have to handle is the period before these events. The hardest time is the season of waiting.

Claire scribbled these words in her journal that the hospital psychiatrist gave her three weeks ago, during her first visit after her emotional breakdown from the weight and stress of Amelia's and Scarlett's conditions. The journal had become her outlet for her frustration, her psalm in her depression, and her loyal confidant always willing to listen to every word she wrote.

Scarlett's condition was the same as it was four weeks ago. She continued to lie in the same bed, hooked up to the same machines, beeping the same sounds every minute of every day. There had been no improvement, but there also had not been any complications. Claire had learned to take each day as a single experience. She didn't lump sum them together and see the grand scale of a week or a month anymore. She didn't peer into her illusionary crystal ball to see what the next season entails, but she waited day by day.

The hospital employees knew Claire, Dan, and Charlie better than some of their own relatives. The women in the cafeteria knew all about Charlie's love for chicken and they always had a few legs available for him the days that he visited.

Claire and Dan moved from floor to floor in shifts; one spent the morning reading with Amelia while the other conversed bedside to Scarlett. It seemed that the only time the two of them met some days were in their commute between daughters at the elevators.

Amelia's leukemia was further along than Dr. Pottinger had hoped. They immediately started a regime of chemotherapy and advised Amelia to stay in the hospital for the next couple of weeks. She didn't expect to be stuck for a month, but her condition was quickly deteriorating, and Dr. Pottinger didn't feel that it would be safe for her to return home, especially with Scarlett's condition and the lack of attention from her parents.

Amelia was already feeling tired, so the first chemotherapy treatment wiped her out. "Daddy," she would moan throughout the night as she threw up everything that she had eaten in the past few days.

"I know, honey," Dan cried with her, stroking her head and feeling the softness of her hair. "I know it hurts, but this is going to make you feel better." Amelia continued to lean over the toilet and spit up all that jarred around in her stomach as Dan held her hair back, realizing that in a few days or weeks he wouldn't need to hold her hair back anymore.

Every once in a while, she would look up with red eyes into Dan's tear-filled eyes, but their glances would only last a few seconds until she would have to cough something else up.

Three weeks of chemotherapy had passed and Amelia was not delighting herself in the science that was surrounding her. She didn't smile with her twinge of sarcasm to the meddling nurses. She had even stopped reading. All she wanted to do now was rest in a darkened room. Once a week she was taken to Scarlett's room for her sisterly visit, which usually lasted fifteen minutes because that was about as long that Amelia could stay sitting up without feeling tired or sick. She spoke to her sister about the nurses on her floor and asked if Scarlett's nurses were as crazy as hers. She always waited for a response, but with each question, her heart drooped with the unresponsiveness.

"See you later, Scarlett," she would say to her sister before leaving, and then she would lean down next to her sister's ear and whisper so only she and her sister would know, "I love you."

A lone tear fell gently down Scarlett's cheek, signaling to Amelia that she heard her.

351

CHAPTER 137

"Dr. Karen Anderson, were you aware of the hazardous effects of your drug, Anterolistyalin?" Mr. Yates with the FDA interrogated as Mitch Harrelson, the new legal representation for Pharm Laboratories, Inc., sat coolly beside Dr. Anderson with his legal pad in hand, scribbling down every detail.

"No, I was not aware," she lied with a criminal smile, hiding behind her flawless beauty.

"You were not aware of the deaths associated with Anterolistyalin?" he responded professionally, belying his internal shock.

"That is correct, Mr. Yates," she answered warmly, crossing her legs to reveal her perfectly toned calves. "I was not aware."

"Mr. Daniel Sutton never mentioned to you the reports that he was receiving from hospitals across the United States, detailing the flawed effects of Anterolistyalin?"

"Really, does she have to be here?" Mitch asked, annoyed with the line of questioning bombarding his client. "I think she has answered your questions. No matter how you try to say it, she was not aware of any 'flawed effects.'"

"It's okay, Mitch," Karen patted him on his knee to cool off from his outburst.

"Yes, Mr. Harrelson, I have to ask these questions to Dr. Anderson. Since you are her legal counsel, you do have the right to speak for your client, but at this time, I need to continue with my line of questioning to Dr. Anderson," Mr. Yates stated dutifully, articulating every point with detailed precision.

"Carry on, Mr. Yates," Karen remarked, playing the role of good cop that she and Mitch had scripted out the previous evening while basking in the sweaty afterglow of sexual release. Karen had moved on from Dan with her sexual prowling to a much younger and unattached male specimen that didn't have any reservations in the bedroom. Every once in a while she still thought about Dan, causing a flurry of heat, but unlike Dan, Mitch jumped at the opportunity to fulfill every wish she dangled in front of him.

Mr. Yates opened up a manilla filing folder, pulling out a stapled document of about a dozen sheets of paper. "Dr. Anderson, will you please turn to page six?" he asked, passing her the presumed legal document. "Is that your signature?"

Karen flipped through the legal jargon until she saw her signature plastered on the bottom of the page. "Yes, but I, but I don't know what this is," she lied once again, forgetting the day that James had brought in the drafts of the patented legal documents.

"So, that is your signature?" Mr. Yates drilled forcefully, ignoring her quivering succulent lips.

"It is, but I did not sign this," she trembled, just like she practiced the evening before while lying beside Mitch underneath his satin sheets.

"You did not sign this patent on September 29th before the notary, Barbara Clarmont?" he proceeded to ask, as a flutter of doubt entered her brain.

"Have you spoken with Barbara Clarmont?" she asked, vaguely remembering an elderly frail woman notarizing the document.

"Please answer my question."

Karen felt trapped in her lie. *If Barbara is given a picture, could she recognize me? What if they already found her and she has already pointed me out?* Her heartbeat started to race at the speed of her fingernails tapping against the wooden chair arms. She looked down at Mitch's notepad, hoping for a sign of what to say, but all she found were doodles of arrows and stars. "No, I did not sign the patent," she proclaimed with newfound resilience, straightening her demeanor and regaining her composure as she looked Mr. Yates directly into his lie-detecting eyes. "I never met Barbara Claymart."

"Clarmont," Mr. Yates corrected as he brought out another file folder with more of her signatures to examine. He passed document after document to Karen, and each time she blatantly falsified her statements. She was getting on a roll with her lying, and even started to gasp at the number of times her signature was being added to these documents.

She played her role convincingly. "This is horrible," she surged with controlled hostility. "Absolutely outrageous. Who forged my name?"

Mr. Yates sat comfortable in his chair, leaning back as if about to start regaling an old tale. "I am not sure, Dr. Anderson, but if what you are saying is the truth…"

"It is," she interrupted with schoolgirl innocence.

"Yes, well, we will do our best to settle this matter," he stated as he received the legal documents back from Karen's guilty hands. "Who would you suspect would be the culprit with these fraudulent documents?"

"I, I couldn't say," she said, trying to appear surprised by the maliciousness of one of her business partners. "If I had to say…"

"You don't have to," Mr. Yates commented, trying to make Karen feel more at ease.

"James Nialliv. He handled the patent process," she answered quickly, maybe a little too quickly for Mr. Yates' ears. "But there is no way of finding out because he died a month ago in a car wreck."

"Do you have any other questions?" Mitch asked as Karen fought hard not to roll her eyes, annoyed that now he was showing some gumption as her attorney.

"If I do, I will be in contact with you or Dr. Anderson," Mr. Yates answered, handing the two his business card. "If you have any new insight, please give me a call."

"Will do," Mitch replied as the three of them stood up and walked Mr. Yates to the door of Karen's office. "Can you see yourself out?"

"Yes, I think I remember how to get out of here. Thank you for your time," Mr. Yates said.

A rush of emotions were rising in Karen's stomach, and she needed to do one more thing to unleash all the baggage onto someone else. Someone who caused her so much pain with little thought to her feelings. "Daniel Sutton."

"I beg your pardon?" Mr. Yates asked confused.

"Karen, stop!" Mitch whispered in her ear, trying to control her client. "It's nothing, Mr. Yates, have a good evening."

Karen whipped her malicious eyes at Mitch, causing him to take a step back with his invisible tail between his legs. "Daniel Sutton could have forged my name. I didn't want to say anything, since he worked so hard with me at the beginning and especially with the tragedies he has faced the last month with his two daughters, but he could have."

"Thank you," Mr. Yates nodded as he turned and walked down the hallway to the elevator.

"Why? Why did you do that?" Mitch asked when they were behind Karen's closed door. "He is still technically your attorney. I am just here while he is away on personal leave."

"If it gets the Feds to stop looking at me, that is all I care about," she smiled as she started to unzip her dress, letting the black silk fabric slide down her legs like a fireman's pole. "Should be all you care about too."

"I see your point," he beamed as she unbuckled his belt. "I see it now."

"Really?" she whispered in his ear as she slowly unzipped his pants, letting her hands feel him. "Are you going to charge me for this visit?"

CHAPTER 138

"You are looking very well today," Josiah announced as he brought Ethel her supper that he picked up from Patty's, a local diner specializing in southern home cooking.

"What did you bring us today?" Ethel grinned to her friend, Constance, who had been taking care of her since Josiah was always at the hospital.

"Baked chicken and rice, scalloped potatoes, green beans, and wheat dinner rolls."

"Lovely," Constance drooled as Josiah opened the cartons and a wave of aroma-filled steam rose from the delicacies.

"So, how has she been today?" Josiah asked Constance, making sure everyone had their proper utensils and plating.

"Very well, very well, indeed," Constance replied as she spooned Ethel some green beans. "We went grocery shopping today."

"You didn't get anything you're not supposed to have, did you?" Josiah quizzed, watching Ethel's face beam like a criminal caught red-handed.

"No," she answered. Then realizing that her guilt was written on her face, she added, "I know how much you like Doritos, so I bought a bag."

"You didn't have to do that," Josiah grinned as he politely scolded her. "Do not worry about me. We have to get you feeling as good as new."

"At our age, you shouldn't aim so high," Constance chimed in as she grabbed a piece of baked chicken for herself. "Let's try as good as not dead," she said as the three of them laughed heartily.

"So, how are the girls doing today?" Ethel asked, changing the spotlight from her to someone else.

"About the same," he shook his head in slight disgust. "I thought Scarlett would be doing better by now. I just thought she would be better."

"Don't lose hope," Constance reminded. "Tomorrow is a new day and God's wonderful mercies are new every morning."

"Amen," Ethel elated. "Amen. How are the parents doing?"

"The same. Just tired and on their last thread of hope."

"Well, Josiah, you've got to be their thread of hope. When you go there looking like death warmed over, that doesn't give them any encouragement. You need to go there with the love of God radiating from you," Ethel preached with conviction and authority.

"Uh huh," Constance agreed as the group continued their little circle of Christian testimony.

"You need to go with a refreshed and renewed smile on your face. A smile doesn't heal all wounds, but it does spread. When you know that our Lord is holding everything together and it's not about what we do, but all about what He will do, what is there to frown about?" Ethel asked while pointing at Josiah's face with her fork.

"Thank you, ladies. I needed to hear that."

They said their blessing and commenced eating their heart-friendly feast. Josiah felt a little out of place for their first time in his role. He was the messenger from God. He wasn't used to be the recipient of His message.

Sometimes even an angel needs to hear a good message.

CHAPTER 139

Amelia's hospital room was quiet, allowing the puny little girl to rest. She didn't have any chemotherapy today, but her body was still trying to recover from the last dose a couple of days ago. Dan sat in the recliner and texted Claire who was sitting with Scarlett for the evening.

So, are you hungry?

I'm never hungry anymore.

Me either.

How's A?

Sleeping. Dan looked over at his pale daughter with her skin tightly pressed, allowing him to see every bone in her body. Today she was wearing a rainbow sock cap that Luke brought five days ago. It was a hat that hadn't left her sight since. His phone buzzed again.

That's good.

Any report on your end? But there wasn't a reply. *Claire?*

I'm here. It's just so sad to say 'no.'

I know. I love you. He sent the last message and he truly meant it. He sat in a state of self-searching and he was saddened by the fact that it took sitting in a hospital room one floor away for him to fall in love with his wife again.

I luv u 2.

He closed his phone and reclined as he watched his lovely daughter sleep. It was a joyous scene. There were no moans of pain, no wheezing, and no tears running down her face. When she slept, she was free of pain. He started to smile, feeling a comfort in her bliss that only a parent could understand.

His cellphone started to vibrate, signaling an incoming call. "Hello," he whispered, trying not to wake up Amelia.

"Hello, you," Karen said seductively, as if nothing had happened between them in the last month.

"Karen, I can't talk right now. Call Mitch."

"Call Mitch. Call Mitch. That is all you say to me these days," she moped as if his words shattered her world. "Mitch was a dud today."

"What happened?" he asked, slowly getting pulled into the Pharm scandal that he had been whittling himself away from.

"Mr. Yates with the FDA came by again today and questioned me. He caught me in a lie, but I just lied again."

"Karen, don't tell me that. Talk to Mitch about this. Not me."

"But Mitch isn't as good as you," she whined, hoping to gain an inch of sympathy that could possibly lead to another inch and another. "I looked to him for an answer today and he was just drawing pictures."

"I'm sorry, but I cannot talk about this right now."

"You seem to never want to talk to me."

"Karen, we are through. You have Mitch to handle your case, and I am in the past."

"I don't know about that."

"Huh?" Dan asked confused.

"Well, I kinda said something today," she winced.

All the bells and whistles of alarms were going off in Dan's throbbing head. "What did you say?"

"It's probably nothing," she lied.

"Tell me!" he barked, instantly hoping that he didn't wake up Amelia.

"Well, he asked who could have forged my signatures."

"Forged? No one forged your signatures."

"Well, I kinda told him someone did."

Dan's blood started to boil at the thought of what Karen might have said. "Who did you say forged your signatures?"

"James. I said James probably did it," she responded defensively.

"So, what does that have to do with me?"

359

"Well, when he left, I kinda blurted your name out too," she said as she heard nothing but dead air. "I'm sorry Dan. I'm really sorry, but I didn't know what else to say." Dan still did not respond, but sat dumbstruck with the notion of him forging her name, even before he became their legal counsel. "I know I shouldn't have, but I was stuck. I don't want to go to jail, so I thought the more names I mentioned the better. Dan, say something," she cried. "Dan, just say something. Anything."

Dan sat with the phone to his ear, listening to a backstabbing, self-centered little devil sob uncontrollably at her own scheming.

"Dan, please, talk to me. I'm sorry. I'm sorry, but I was hurt. You wanted to quit being our attorney and then you wanted to stop seeing me. You're cruel, Dan. Very cruel. You knew that I loved you and you just tossed me aside when you were done with me. Well, I was angry and it just floated out of my mouth before I could stop it. Mitch was bad today and that made me mad, because if you were beside me, you would have taken care of me. Dan. Say something."

Dan thought long and hard at what he wanted to say, but words could not convey his emotions. "What should I say? You would rather sacrifice me than hold yourself accountable for your error."

"Error? Why do you keep saying that? And you're not all that innocent."

"Karen," he walked into the bathroom and closed the door. "Your pill is the one that has killed a lot of people. You have a problem bigger than someone forging your name, and it's up to Mitch to end it. My flaw was hiding the deaths while I thought you were trying to fix the pill. I was not the one who pushed the patent through without the proper process. I came in after everything was pretty much done."

"Whatever! I don't want Mitch," she commanded like a three-year old. "I want you!"

"Sorry, this discussion is closed."

360

"How about I discuss it with your wife, what's her name? Claire?"

"Don't you dare!"

"Oh, did I strike a nerve with you?" She laughed wickedly at the thought of his marriage falling apart. "What's wrong Dan, scared?"

"If you speak to her, so help me!"

"So help you what? I don't need you anymore. You've already said to leave you alone. What is keeping me from sitting down with her over a cup of coffee? Does she like French vanilla like you?"

"Stay away from my wife!"

"Oh Dan, your buttons are hidden well, but once you find one, it is so easy to push it again and again and again."

"Karen, not now. Please, my daughters are sick."

"I'm sick about losing you, but you don't care about me." She hung up her phone, leaving Dan to stand silent in the bathroom to process the rattling conversation. In just a few minutes his career was once again on the line along with his marriage. He looked into the mirror and figuratively flipped the coin on which was more important.

He stepped out of the bathroom confident to make amends to his past mistakes. He loved Claire. He didn't love his job anymore.

"Dad, who were you talking to?" Amelia asked weakly with a crackling voice, as she rolled over in her bed.

"No one important, darling," he said as he bent down and kissed her forehead. "No one important."

CHAPTER 140

"Thank you for seeing me this afternoon," Dr. Pottinger said as Claire and Dan sat in the same chairs as they had a month ago when they got the tragic news about Amelia. The tolerable springtime weather bid ado as the wave of summer heat covered the southeast with its blanket of humidity. Sadly, Scarlett was not able to say goodbye to the cool evenings and welcome the beach season afternoons. "I'm sorry to have to say this, but Amelia's condition is worsening. Her blood counts are falling faster than we anticipated, and the chemotherapy doesn't seem to be helping her very much."

"What do you suggest?" Claire asked as she and Dan clutched each other's hands.

"Well there are a couple of options. The first is a new drug that has been in circulation for just a few months that targets the cancer. The test results show a significant increase in recoveries in cancer patients, but it is a new drug. I have not used the drug or personally know of any doctors who have, but from the reports that I am getting from medical journals, it is a remarkable drug that speeds up the remission process."

"That sounds wonderful. Do you think it will work for Amelia?" Claire asked with newfound optimism. A glimmer of hope streaked like a rainbow across the sky, and she was ready to find this tangible pot of gold.

"What's this drug called?" Dan questioned as he held his breath with the response.

"I'm not sure. Let me look it up," Dr. Pottinger said as she pulled up something on her computer.

"Oh, that doesn't matter. If it will save her life, I don't care what it's called," Claire said with some renewed hope in her voice.

Dr. Pottinger shook her head in agreement with Claire's positive response. "It is called Anterolistyalin, and it is produced by Pharm Laboratories, Inc."

Dan's fears were realized. "I need to speak with you," Dan whispered in Claire's ear with a tremble in his voice.

"Okay," Claire smiled, dismissing his concern. "When can you start this medication on Amelia?"

"We can start it tonight."

"No!" Dan shouted, shocking himself and the two ladies with his sudden outburst. "Claire, I think we need to discuss this."

"Yes, you two need to talk, but the sooner we start this, the better," Dr. Pottinger said pointedly.

"Is this what you would recommend?" Claire asked, getting Dr. Pottinger's insight since she was the oncologist while neither she nor Dan had any medical knowledge besides band-aids and cough syrup.

"Yes, I think at this current time, this is the best option," Dr. Pottinger smiled. "I can give you the printouts of this drug for you to look over."

"Do you hear that, Dan?" Claire asked, rubbing his hand enthusiastically as she smiled as big as when she was celebrating Charlie's birthday. "What's wrong?" she asked as she noticed his dismal expression.

Dan sat in contemplation. How could he allow his daughter to take a drug that is killing people? He saw the excitement in his wife's body language, her personality brightened up, and all of a sudden she was once again the bubbling woman he had fallen in love with twenty years ago. His heart began to break, realizing that couples all across the country had similar responses to this miracle drug when their oncologist announced it to them. They saw the light of hope radiating from the drug's name with the possibility of it saving their brother's life. They caught a glimpse of the hand of God releasing His healing power to give their mother another thirty years to live. They felt the

363

adrenaline rush through their bodies with the belief that their child would see his next birthday.

He sat at a crossroads and faced a moral dilemma. How could he have sat on the sidelines of this scandal for so long and put it on the back burner? If the cancer patient's family members knew the truth, would they still have wanted their dying relative to take Anterolistyalin? Why was he blessed with the knowledge of this so-called life saving drug? He stared up at the ceiling, hoping to see a sign. Hoping to catch a break, but he didn't. He just saw blank and confused stares from Claire and Dr. Pottinger.

He looked down at his hands and noticed that they were not just trembling, but he could see the blood of hundreds to thousands of innocent victims.

He didn't want to see his daughter's blood on his hands too.

CHAPTER 141

"Hey Amelia," Luke said as he strutted into her hospital room with a present behind his back as if they were at school and nothing was wrong. "Where's your mom or dad?"

"I don't know," she said with a raspy voice as she raised up in her bed, but she was struggling with her frail arms.

"Oh, don't bother moving. Just relax," he smiled.

"Okay," she obliged as she lowered back down, adjusting her body so she could see Luke. "Did you go see Scarlett?"

"Not yet," he answered shyly. "I brought you a new hat."

"You shouldn't have. I love the one you brought me last week," she said, continuing to lie on her side as she delicately unwrapped the paper. Luke watched with great anticipation as a smile spread across his face. "Sorry I'm so slow."

"Don't worry about it."

Amelia opened up the hat box and pulled out a new black sock cap with mathematical equations scribbled like chalk writing all over the garment.

"Do you like it?" he asked beaming.

She twirled the hat around on her finger, examining each formula as a grin started to spread across her face. "Like it? I love it!" She went to pull off her rainbow hat, but then stopped. She stared at Luke who was looking at her. She felt self-conscious with her bald head and she didn't want to scare him off.

"Go ahead, put it on," he said, grinning as he pulled out his camera phone. "I want to take a picture of you wearing it."

She started to frown slightly because she didn't want to scare him off with the sight of her hairless scalp. She reached up and tugged on the hat, but she couldn't take it off in front of him. "Can you, can you close your eyes?"

"If you want me to, I will, but you don't need to hide anything from me," he said, lowering his phone.

"Still, can you just close them?" she asked politely and fearfully.

"Yes. Will this do?" He laughed as he held his hands over his eyes like a four-year old hiding from someone.

"Thank you." She removed her rainbow sock cap and as quickly as she could put on her new one. "How does it look?"

He removed his hands and noticed that part of the hat was crooked. Getting up from his chair by her bed, he reached over and gently adjusted her hat. "I always hated it when my hat was crooked."

The words jarred Amelia as she heard him say hated instead of hate, meaning past tense. "Hated? Do you not hate it anymore?"

He quickly sat back down and looked around the room, realizing that his tongue slipped revealing a little more of himself than he wanted.

"Luke, did you hear me?" Amelia asked, trying to grab his attention.

"Well, as you can tell, I still hate it when a hat is on crooked," he laughed as he quickly looked up at the television that wasn't on. "Want to watch some TV?"

"What's wrong?" Amelia asked. "What are you hiding from me?"

Luke swiveled his head away from the blank television screen and stared directly at Amelia. "I've never told anyone before, but before we moved to Bethany, when I was five years old, I had leukemia."

CHAPTER 142

Luke and Amelia talked for over an hour discussing everything she had wanted to speak to someone about, but didn't feel comfortable. She was able to unleash all of her fears onto the shoulder of someone who carried her weight once before. He survived, and it gave her hope to see that he was a strong, healthy young man.

Meanwhile, Dan and Claire were walking back to their vehicle to discuss the cancer treatment since Dan didn't feel comfortable speaking with her about it where anyone could hear.

They entered their Lexus and sat on their leather seats in silence. Claire posed the question into the void, hoping to get an answer out of Dan. "Why do we need to talk about this? And out here?"

"Claire, I need to be completely honest with you, and I was afraid of doing it in the hospital."

"Dan, what's wrong?" she asked, feeling the fear in his voice, causing her intuition to sucker punch her.

"The drug, Anterolistyalin. Have you heard me talk about Pharm Laboratories before?"

"You might have, but I can't remember," she said as her thoughts had been jumbled the last month. She had lost her ATM card twice, her sunglasses four times, and even forgotten the hospital room numbers of her daughters half a dozen times. Currently, her mind was not reliable to remember technical details.

"I have been working for Pharm with their patents and the distribution process of Anterolistyalin."

"That's wonderful, so you know all about the drug," she swelled with joy.

"Yes, I know all about the drug," he relinquished. "I know too much about it."

"What? Dr. Pottinger said the FDA approved the drug."

"Yes, they did approve it, but they approved fraudulent patent documents." He took a breath as he watched Claire's eyes begin to grow cold. "Claire, the drug doesn't work. It even kills people who are taking it."

Claire shook her head violently in disagreement. "This must be a mistake. That drug, that Anterolistyalin, it has to work or doctors wouldn't be giving it out to their patients. What doctor would give medicine that would kill their patients?"

"Doctors who don't know the truth. Claire, we can't let Amelia take the medicine. There has to be another way."

"No! No! No!" she screamed. "No! Don't be telling me that! Don't say that it can't work!" Her screaming quickly turned into wailing. "How could you? How could you do this to us?" Dan turned to hold his distraught wife, but she wouldn't let him. Her fists were punching him in his chest, but he deserved it so he continued to try to hold her. "Why?"

"I know," he too began to cry as he watched his wife fall apart. He saw the hope that she had a few minutes ago be swept away as if she was caught up in a tidal wave. "There's more."

"More?" she whimpered as her stomach twisted and churned with the idea of more bad news.

"I quit working for Pharm because I couldn't do this anymore. They are not worried about the deaths of the victims. All they care about is the profits."

"What? What are you going to do?"

"I have tried to quit, but they are going to blackmail me. They are saying that I forged signatures and documents. And you've got to believe me that I didn't do it. James, James Nialliv, Lucy's dad, he's the one that caused all these problems. If he didn't fake the patent process, the tests would have shown that the drug didn't work and it would have never made it into hospitals."

"Blackmail?"

"Yes, Claire. I am sorry for all this. I am really, really sorry. You know I love you, don't you?"

"Dan?"

"Claire, you know I love you? Just answer me."

"Yes, but you're scaring me," she said, her voice cracking with fear.

"Well, I have something else to tell you." He looked over at his wife, his lovely wife who was still as beautiful as when he met her twenty years ago. "They are going to blackmail me by saying that I had an affair."

"Did you?" Claire spit back. "Did you sleep with another woman?"

Dan started to tremble as he broke down emotionally. "Yes."

Claire sat silently, hugging herself as she looked into the distance of the hospital entrance doors. The parking lot light poles were turned on and the hospital was well illuminated all over their grounds.

"Please, Claire, say something. Anything."

"I suspected something was going on," she stated coldly without making eye contact. Her heart had been trampled, backed up and run over again and again. "I hope you feel better."

"Feel better?" he cried. "I didn't want to tell you. I never wanted to hurt you or the kids, but…"

"But your conscience was too much to carry so you wanted me to help carry it?"

"I know this is a lot to take at once, but we've got to think about Amelia right now. I love you, I really do, but it's life or death for Amelia."

Claire shivered at the words of affection, and quickly slid them off her back. "What do we tell Dr. Pottinger? 'We don't want to use the drug you recommended because my husband says it is killing people. Thanks for the advice, but no thank you.'"

369

"There has to be another option," Dan said, wiping his eyes dry. "She even said that, but the drug was the best option. We just need to meet with her first thing tomorrow morning and discuss the other options."

They sat in their car in tension-filled silence. Dan watched his wife quietly cry, as tears tumbled down her cheeks. He tried to brush them away, but she only pushed away his affection. Dan wanted to say something, but he didn't know what else to say to convey his heart. He wanted to show his wife the brokenness and remorse of his ill-fated actions, but he didn't know what else to do.

Dan reached out his hand, hoping for just a touch of hers, but he was the only one who reached out.

"Good bye, Dan," Claire said as she opened the door and slammed it shut.

CHAPTER 143

Dan looked over at Amelia who was smiling as she slept in her new hat. He needed to see the joyous grin on his daughter's face. He needed to see it now more than ever. He leaned over and kissed her on the forehead, reading the unknown mathematical equations and wondering where 2 + 2 was on the hat. He tiptoed to the door since he needed to pick up Charlie from the babysitter's and get him into bed for the night.

He went down a floor to say goodbye to Scarlett and once again he kissed her on the forehead and told her that he would see her tomorrow. He turned to see Claire in her chair, but all he found was a blanket and a few used tissues, with a light coming from the bottom crack of the adjoining bathroom. He tapped on the bathroom door, but there wasn't any response.

"I'll see you tomorrow and I love you," he said, but there were no screams of anger, no shouts of threats, no cries of grief, and no breaths of relief.

He picked up Charlie from the babysitter, who was the mother of one of his friends, Emanuel, and they headed home for night. Dan bathed him and they talked about Scarlett and Amelia, but Dan sugar-coated the situation. He didn't want to be brutally honest to another member of his family.

Charlie crawled into Dan's bed and he followed him under the covers. He was exhausted, but he wondered if after all the drama if he was going to be able to sleep. Surprisingly, he drifted into a quick dream.

Dan sat in a small metal chair in an all-white empty room. He peered around the room, but he couldn't see where the floor ended and where the walls started. The room could have been the size of a coat closet or it could have been as expansive as the universe.

Suddenly he heard something. Something that startled him. "Hello?" he asked, "Is anyone there?" He tried to stand up, but his body was unable to move. He felt as if he was glued to the ground and the chair.

"It's just me," a voice resounded. "I'll be right there."

"Who's there?" he asked again, as the sound of faint footsteps started to get louder, signaling a person approaching.

"We need to talk, Dan."

Dan circled his head around the room, but he still couldn't see anyone. He felt blind, with only the ability to see himself. "How do you know my name?"

"Dan, don't you remember me? Or have you so quickly forgotten me?" The voice whispered into Dan's ear, as if the guest was standing right beside him.

Dan quickly turned his head to the right, but there was nothing but just the vastness of white. He turned his head forward and found the guest leaning inches away from his face.

"James?"

"Good job, Dan. I'm glad you remember me. I was starting to think that our friendship meant nothing to you." James stood up and circled Dan in his chair like a cat prowling an injured mouse.

"What do you want?" Dan screamed at the top of his lungs. "You have made my life into a living hell!"

"Well, then, I did a good job," he said, laughing wickedly. "I guess I did it better than I could ever have imagined. But enough about my accolades. I have come to talk about you and Pharm."

"Why? That is over! I have resigned as their legal counsel."

"Tsk tsk, Dan. We have a contract with you," James said from behind Dan's back, patting him on his shoulder like a disapproving parent. "When you sign a contract, you have to follow through with it until completion."

"Come around here so I can see you," Dan commanded, but James didn't follow through with his orders. "Fine. You have no bounds to hold me to the contract."

"Danny, come on. We're friends."

Dan shook his head in disagreement. "We are not friends. Friends don't coerce one another."

"Oh, Danny, I was just trying to prod you to see my side of things."

"I saw your side of things. I didn't agree with it!"

"You didn't agree with it!" James growled with fiery breath while his eyes reddened with intimidation. "You will!"

"You can't make me!"

"Oh, I can do things to you that you will not believe," James smiled menacingly. "Do you want Claire to forgive you? Done. Do you want Scarlett to wake up? Done. Do you want Amelia to be healed? Done. All you have to do is work with me. Is that so hard?"

The words were swerving Dan's ideals of right and wrong. He had been an attorney for many years and he was used to bending the legal bar to best suit his clients, but now, now, he saw things as black or white.

Slowly the white ground around Dan's chair started to change to a darker color, but the black was oozing out of James' feet. "What's going on here?"

"Oh, nothing Dan, don't worry about the room," James calmly answered.

Dan continued to watch as the white started to swirl with the black, forming a light gray floor. "Stop! I will not side with you!"

"Looks like I am convincing you. You can't fight me!"

"You are dead! You are dead! DEAD!"

"Oh, Dan. Did you go to my funeral? Did you ever see my dead body? How can someone like me die?" James asked, leaning down to look in Dan's eyes.

"What?" Dan questioned with a terrified feeling in his body. He clinched his eyes shut, hoping to make James disappear or even wake up from this nightmare.

"You can't get rid of me by closing your eyes!" James yelled in his face. "You can't get rid of me! I own you! I own you! If you want your family to live, you will do what I want you to do!"

"Come on, wake up! Wake up!" Dan screamed to himself as he opened his eyes, seeing that the room had once again become pure white.

"It's okay, Dan," a voice announced. It was an unfamiliar voice that soothed his fears and anxiety. "It's going to be okay."

"Daddy, wake up!" Charlie shouted as he punched his dad in the ribs, then proceeded to jump on the bed. "I'm going to be late to school."

CHAPTER 144

Claire and Dan sat silent in Dr. Pottinger's office, waiting for her to arrive to discuss the other options available to Amelia. Dan desperately wanted to chip away Claire's icy exterior, but knew that it would not help the situation. It could not erase the past mistakes he had made.

"I had the strangest dream last night," he commented, but speaking to Claire was just like speaking to the bamboo plant on Dr. Pottinger's desk. "It was so lifelike."

Claire watched the fountain dribble down the silver wall, closing her eyes to focus on the soothing sounds to drown out Dan's toxic voice. She sat, daydreaming of the future with Scarlett and Amelia as young ladies with families of their own. She began to smile as she witnessed the limitless possibilities of life past the coma and leukemia. She was starting to see a light of hope.

"Good morning Mr. and Mrs. Sutton," Dr. Pottinger said, entering the door, quickly sitting down behind her desk while examining Amelia's files. "So, are we going to use the new drug?"

"I, I don't think so," Dan answered, wiggling in his chair with discomfort.

Dr. Pottinger leaned back in her chair suspiciously. "Can I ask why?"

"Dan works for Pha..." Claire started to speak as Dan quickly took control of the conversation.

"I have worked in the area of drug patents in the past, and I don't feel comfortable subjecting our daughter to a new drug that has not been tested by the masses just yet."

"Mr. Sutton, the drug passed the FDA's grueling tests and guidelines. I understand your concern, but currently, this is the best option."

"Not the best for us, but there still are some others, correct?" Dan questioned, exhibiting his legal skills with his line of questioning, as if Dr. Pottinger was on the stand of a criminal court case.

"Yes, there are a few other options." Dr. Pottinger resigned for the moment in trying to sway their minds to the new drug and started discussing the other possibilities. "First off, we can continue to do chemotherapy, but this is not currently working. We have not tried radiation with Amelia, but I believe that radiation will make her worse instead of better.

"There is biological therapy, but our hospital does not have the capabilities to perform this adequately. I can give you a list of other hospitals that have specialists in this field of medicine.

"Lastly, allogenic transplants, which are commonly referred to as stem cell transplants."

"Yes, yes, I heard a lot of good things about that," Dan buzzed in enthusiastically. "Lots of good things."

"Yes, stem cell or bone marrow transplants dramatically increase the recovery percentage, but there are some risks that go along with this procedure. Her body could reject the new cells, could destroy her old cells, and she could develop a very severe and life-threatening infection."

"Isn't it hard to find a match?" Claire asked skeptically, not trying to dash Dan's hopes, but knowing realistically that matches don't happen every day.

"Yes, first we would ask for family members and friends to undergo the test to see if they match. If no one does, we could put her name on a database and wait for someone with a match."

"A match. What about an identical twin? They would match, wouldn't they?" Dan posed.

"In theory yes, but due to Scarlett's current condition, it may not be in her best interests. I talked with her physician yesterday before I met with you, because I was wondering about the likelihood of donating her bone marrow, but they want to keep her as comfortable as possible to increase her chances of waking up." Dr. Pottinger looked at the struggling couple and wished that her words could solve all their problems, but words are just words, and there is no guarantee that anything will work. "This is a tough spot you are in. If Scarlett was not in a coma, she would be a likely candidate for a bone marrow transplant. However, there is a chance that she may also get leukemia since she is Amelia's twin, even though she doesn't have it right now. I have checked her blood levels and they appear healthy."

"Huh?" Claire asked. "Scarlett could get it?"

"Yes, they have the same genetic code, and since Amelia got leukemia, there is a risk for Scarlett now. There is no way to determine why people get cancer. Different people may have their theories, and everyone has mutated cells in their bodies, but not everyone will get cancer. I don't want to scare you, but I want you to be aware of the chances."

Claire slumped over, placing her arms and head on her legs. She had not realized that Scarlett could also face this same fate. "She's going to make it." Dan patted her on the back. "Our daughters are going to make it."

"Right now, we need to come up with a decision on what to do with Amelia's health. Do not worry about Scarlett's possibilities of cancer, because that is useless. Anything could happen. You need to let the doctors focus on bringing her out of her coma and keeping her as comfortable as possible during this time."

"When can I be tested?" Dan asked.

"In this case, they will most likely be able to do it within the hour. Time is crucial right now, so I will get a test set up."

CHAPTER 145

"Where are your parents?" Josiah asked as he took a seat beside Amelia's bed. She was relaxing comfortably after spending the last hour sitting in Scarlett's room, before leaving for her sister's daily checkups.

"Talking with the doctor," she answered unhappily. "Again."

"What's wrong Ms. Amelia? You have a spiffy new hat you're wearing this morning."

"Yeah, Luke dropped it off to me last night." She continued to recline, snuggling a little more with her stuffed penguin that Charlie gave her during her first round of chemotherapy.

"Luke, he's a good boy; stay close to him." Josiah winked as he scooted his chair closer to Amelia's bed. "Really, how are you doing?"

She breathed a sigh of annoyance as she looked up at the tiled ceiling that had glow in the dark stars spread out forming various constellations that her father pinned up. "Look at me, how do you think I am doing?"

"I think you are getting a little depressed, to be honest," he answered without any reservations. "You have a family that loves you, friends who come to visit you, and the best medicine in the world." His words had little impact on her attitude by the way she continued to stare up at the non-illuminated stars. "What do you want to be when you grow up?"

"Why think about that, Josiah?"

"No, come on, tell me. If you could be anything, what would you want to be?" He pressed as he leaned closer, resting his elbows on her bed. "I'll tell you what I want to be when I get older." He smiled at his joke, as her cold surface finally broke with a hint of a grin.

"Well," she thought as she looked around the room then finally settling her eyes on Josiah. "I used to want to be a marine biologist or a zoologist."

"I can see that in you."

"Yeah," she beamed. "I would love to live in Australia and spend a few months interacting with the kangaroos and koala bears, and then take a boat down to Antarctica and witness the life of penguins. I think penguins are the most underestimated animals there are. And they are pretty cute as well."

"Australia? I never pegged you as a world traveler."

"I have a few surprises up my sleeve." She held up her stuffed penguin and gave it a little kiss on its forehead. "That's how my dad kisses me each night. He doesn't know that I'm awake when he does it, but I am. The last few weeks he hasn't been shaving as often and his whiskers tickle me a little. I have to bite my tongue not to laugh, but you can't tell him that."

"Oh, I'm good at keeping secrets." He relaxed for a moment in his chair, getting the confidence to speak his message, praying for the right words to say. "Amelia, I think you would be great at working with animals, but I think God has something bigger in store for your future."

"Really?" She eyed him with bewilderment as she rolled over onto her side, making sure that her IVs didn't come undone.

"I do. I really do. Call it intuition. Call it a gut feeling. Call it whatever you want, but I believe there is something monumental ahead of you, but you have to have faith in yourself to know that it is possible."

"I'm not the best one with faith. I'm not like you, Josiah," she commented, not with disrespect, but with the attitude that they differ in their philosophical paradigms.

"Oh, you have more faith than most people do, Amelia. I wish more people were like you. You test things. You don't just believe things because people say to believe in them. You're not a follower, and that takes a lot of faith. It's easy to be led by someone who knows where they are going, but you…you lead your own way to places you have never been.

"Call it stubbornness, but I call that searching. Some people spend their entire lives searching for something when they don't even know what they are looking for. Sometimes they never find it, but most of the time…," he leaned back down and spoke in a soft whisper that drew Amelia deeper in the conversation, "it is found in the easiest place to look.

"We always think that life is complicated and diverse and hard to understand, but if we just take a step back and reexamine our current surroundings, the answers will be found. God didn't give us a brain for it to not be used. Most people are afraid to use their God-given gifts," he said as he patted her on her head. "Don't be afraid to use yours."

"So, you see big things in my life?" Amelia smiled, looking back up at Orion's Belt directly overhead. "What kind of big things?"

"Well," he scratched his chin as if deciding what to say, "if I told you that, you would miss all the fun in God's little scavenger hunt. It's hard, but life is in the journey, not the destination."

CHAPTER 146

Josiah squeezed Mary's hand, kneeling beside her bed, praying for God's perfect timing to intervene. Even though he was an angel, he didn't know all the details. All he knew was his duty – protecting Mary.

He watched as she laid unresponsive to his touch and flashed back to their first encounter. She was on death's front door due to the mysterious collapse of the old rickety bridge, but it was not a mystery to Josiah. He didn't know that she was going to fall into that river that day, but he knew that any time Lucy was nearby, trouble wasn't too far to follow.

He closed his eyes and replayed the horrific scene, watching Lucy dash ahead of Mary out of sight down the street and then navigate her way through the wooded area that Mary had mentioned during soccer practice. Josiah saw the streak of a blond-haired girl running through the woods and started to chase after her. He was trying to catch up when he suddenly heard the fearful screams and splash of the water. His chasing of Lucy had ended, but it would continue the next day.

Opening his eyes, he scanned the room and saw balloons of all sizes scattered around the window, and the one that stood out the most was the one of the soccer ball. Lucy's first plan was spoiled, so Josiah knew that another one would be coming. He became the school's janitor so he could always be nearby, and he especially wanted to be around when Lucy was in close proximity. He continued to rub Mary's hand as he remembered the second close call in the parking lot.

Josiah closed his eyes once again and recalled the powerful kick by Lucy that led Mary chasing the speeding ball through the crowded parking lot. Reaching out his hand, he once again saved Mary's life when James was supposed to run into her with his blazing sports car. Who would have suspected foul play when a kid darted in front of a speeding vehicle?

Waking up from his vision, he tried to shake off the terrible memories, but he knew that he needed to continue on his mental journey. He wasn't in the home when Mary choked, but he knew that Lucy was the one who placed the game piece into Mary's supper. A tear began to run down his cheek as he remembered how close he came to ruining his mission and all humanity. With that small plastic piece, the outcome of the entire future could have been terribly altered. "You are such a fool!" He murmured to himself. "Such a fool to drop your guard!"

Finally, he reached the last week of Mary's vibrant life. He had to get her grounded so she couldn't spend the night with Lucy at James' home. If Mary had entered the house, there was no way she would return home safely. He did what he had to do. He hated it, but it was in the call of duty he had to get her grounded.

Lastly, the incident. The final incident that led Mary to be in her current state. He tried to stop Mary from going with Lucy and James, but it seemed like the entire world was against him. He could have revealed his true identity, but it was not the time. The police had labeled the accident an act of nature, but nature couldn't send a hundred deer storming through the crop field and across the road at that exact moment when James was speeding down the straight country lane.

Josiah got up from his knees and proceeded to speak, to speak the message that he was called to speak before he ever knew the Sutton family.

"Mary, I know you can hear me. I know you can. You may not understand why this is happening to you, but you will one day. God has a plan for your life. God has a great plan for you to live a long, healthy life, but first you have to go through this trial. You may not understand the purpose of the pain. I myself don't understand that. All that I know for certainty is that you are going to be okay.

"You may be screaming right now and you don't think anyone can hear you, but He can. He can hear you. He has always heard you when you scream in pain. He hears you when you cry in fear. He will hear you when you laugh in the coming joys. Always remember that you are heard, even when you think you are alone.

"This may sound strange to you, but God has a plan. Did he intend for you to go into a coma? No. He did not intend for that, but God, in his infinite wisdom allows things to happen. He allows people to get cancer. He allows people to get in car accidents. He allows economies to dive and people to lose their jobs. He allows loving spouses to cheat on a cheap thrill. He allows people to get hurt over and over again. He allows all that could go wrong in the world, so He can allow you to feel His unbelievable love.

"Mary, without evil we would not know what good really is. The same can be said with pain. Sometimes you have to go through the darkest valleys in life to finally see the true sun.

"Just as God allows all these things to happen, God is big enough to mend wounds, heal chronic diseases, bring peace to war-torn communities, and unify broken hearts. The actions people make affect other people, but God is a God of action. He does not live in a state of chaos, but he composes an orchestrated symphony. What we sometimes see as a mess, He sees as a masterpiece.

"Mary, you may feel like you are a mess, but you are His masterpiece. All the things in life that seem to be crumbling and falling apart around your feet, those pieces can be picked up and used to create a breathtaking mosaic. Never underestimate His power. Never underestimate yourself." Josiah bent down and whispered one last thing into her ear and turned around to leave the sleeping child.

Standing in the door was Claire, eyes reddened and trembling.

"Do you really believe all that?" she asked as her legs started to give way and Josiah caught her in his arms.

"I do. I really do."

383

CHAPTER 147

Resting in the recovery room after his bone marrow test, Dan laid in his bed and second-guessed all the decisions of the past six months, most of which, he wished that he could do over. But no matter the decisions he made or didn't make, he would still be lying in the hospital bed, nursing a swollen hip.

There was a knock on the door, quickly followed with it being opened, "Mr. Sutton, may I come in?"

Dan laid with his back to the door, twisting his head to see the new visitor, but his vertebras weren't agile enough to see the gentleman. "Yes, that is fine."

"Good, I am sorry to see you in this condition," the familiar voice sounded as he walked across the hospital room to face Dan. "But I am on a deadline," Mr. Yates with the FDA stated as he pulled up a chair from across the room and sat down near Dan's feet at the end of the bed.

"Mr. Yates, I am sorry, but I am no longer the legal counsel for Pharm Laboratories. My daughters…"

"Yes, I have heard the tragic news, and I cannot help but see the irony in your daughter," he looked at his iPad, fingering the screen to get the correct information, "Amelia's recent bout with leukemia."

"Irony? I wouldn't say that the circumstances I am in would warrant the term ironic."

"You don't?" he asked patronizingly. "Not to sound cruel or unsympathetic, but I was told by Dr. Pottinger that her condition is not good."

Dan stared at the well-groomed governmental employee in his black suit and watched as he continued to glide his finger through various opened documents. "That is why I am here, hoping to be her bone marrow donor."

"How courageous of you," he facetiously replied as he didn't look up from his iPad. "Have you considered other options, or is this your last resort?"

"It's our last…" Dan spoke too quickly, seeing the conundrum in his response.

"Last resort? Why not try Anterolistyalin? From your patent reports that I am reading, it does remarkably well in the same stage of cancer as your daughter is experiencing."

Dan tried to adjust his body, to not appear as a wounded gazelle ready to be killed, but he cringed at the pain that was starting to prevail through the numbness.

"Don't move, Mr. Sutton. Just relax," Mr. Yates said without remorse.

"Relax?" Dan became infuriated with the lack of bedside manner. "Relax? My daughters are seriously ill, and what am I doing? I am being questioned and probably investigated by you for something that I did not do or was even a part of until the very end when they hired my firm. I am sealed by attorney-client privilege from discussing with you why I felt that it was in my child's best interest to not undergo Anterolistyalin."

"I bet Charlie is grateful that his dad worked with Pharm. I know that Bruce Williams in Denver, Colorado would have loved to be privy to the same 'privilege' as you were before he decided to give Anterolistyalin to his wife and mother of two."

"Mr. Yates, I have more pressing matters than Pharm right now."

"Mr. Sutton, the way I see it, all three of you have a shorter lifeline now."

CHAPTER 148

Nurse Kathy sat in the nurses' station, bobbing her head to the music on Pandora barely playing through her computer speakers. She flipped a few pages in her bridal magazine, praying for the day when her boyfriend, Peter, would finally propose to her and stop dragging his playboy feet.

A beeping noise sounded beside her desk as she looked at the room that it was coming from. "Mrs. Sutton, I'll be right there."

"No rush," a faint voice sounded with a congested cough that seemed to be on the verge of laryngitis.

Kathy stood up, still eyeing the white bridal gown worn by a five-foot eleven model that fit her frame perfectly. She looked down at her round five-foot four figure and realized that the dress would not look the same on her. She had been dieting, nibbling on carrot sticks most of the time, but every once in a while, a donut stick would sneak into her purse.

She left her desk when another patient buzzed her, "I can't get the television volume to work."

"I'll be right there, Mr. Sadeni," Kathy answered as she turned to go to the first room of the hallway beside the waiting room area since Mrs. Sutton didn't sound like she was in any hurry. She went towards Mr. Sadeni's room and noticed that Josiah was hugging a female out in the waiting room. A strange feeling went up her spine. She couldn't put her finger on it, but any time Josiah was around, she had an unexplainable emotion that filled her. It wasn't happiness or sadness, or anything in between, it was just something unknown to her.

She walked into Mr. Sadeni's room and quickly found his remote control between the guard rails of his bed and his mattress. She raised the volume, allowing him to watch the news, even though she knew that in five minutes he would be asleep.

"Do you need anything else, Mr. Sadeni?"

"No, thank you," he answered as he held tightly to the corded remote control.

Kathy walked out of the room and glanced over at Josiah and Mrs. Sutton talking. "Sorry, I didn't get to you quick enough," Kathy said as she walked over to the two as Claire quickly wiped her nose dry.

"Oh, I am fine, Kathy," Claire said. "Just chatting with Josiah here."

"Well, I'm glad you sound better now than you did a few minutes ago."

Claire looked up at Kathy with a terrified look on her face. "Oh, I'm sorry Kathy, I didn't mean to be so loud. Josiah was trying to calm me down," Claire said patting his leg like an old friend. "Thank you, Josiah."

"Loud?" Kathy laughed, "I could barely hear you when you buzzed me. I'm glad your voice is better. It sounded like you were catching a cold a few minutes ago. Allergies, I guess."

"Buzzed? I never buzzed you," Claire said with a confused look in her eyes.

"Well, if you didn't buzz me, who did? Was there another woman in the room?"

"No, only Scarlett," Claire answered casually, as the words didn't register at first. "Scarlett!"

CHAPTER 149

"Mom?" a fragile voice spoke up as she raised her tangled arms from the IVs and blankets holding her down.

"Thank you, God!" Claire cried as she ran into the room, throwing her arms around Scarlett's neck as Kathy announced over the intercom for Dr. Raman to come to their room. "Thank you! Thank you! Thank you!"

"Mom," Scarlett said roughly, as if her vocal cords were stripped raw.

"What, Scarlett?" Claire brushed Scarlett's cheeks with loving tenderness, "Anything."

"I'm thirsty."

Claire looked up at Kathy who frantically ran out of the room to get a cup of ice water. Suddenly, the room was filling up with various doctors and nurses to witness the remarkable awakening. Dr. Raman wasn't available due to a surgery he was performing, so one of his partners rushed down to examine Scarlett. He smiled and tried to make Scarlett feel at ease with the sudden attention by trying to be a doctor comedian with what he was about to do to her.

Claire clung to her side as Josiah watched from the back corner, basking in the affirmation that he desperately needed, especially after the last two hard weeks of watching the strain on Dan and Claire.

"I'm going to call your dad," Claire said as she looked down at Scarlett who didn't let go of her mother's hand. "Dan! Dan! She's awake! Scarlett's awake!" she screamed, tugging on her daughter's hand with untamed excitement. "Yes, she's wide-eyed and talking! Yes! Here she is!" She lowered the phone to her daughter's ear as the doctor continued to do a quick examination.

"Hi, Daddy," Scarlett choked out.

The feeling of Mary's recovery surged through Josiah, like he was going to start flying. He watched as she looked around the room, taking in the surroundings, the fresh cut flowers, Charlie's toy stash, and the plethora of multicolored balloons dangling from the ceiling. Her head moved closer in his direction and passed him by, still moving around the room to see the pieces of equipment that beeped every few seconds.

Josiah wanted the past to be the past. He wanted Mary to forget about all the bad blood between them and the division to be bridged. He took a step toward the door to tell Amelia the wonderful news as he continued to watch Mary stare around the room. The doctor was trying to get her to look at him as he asked her questions, but she was too fascinated with the atmosphere to stop and look at him. She moved her head in Josiah's direction again, about to pass him by a second time, but this time, this time she stopped and backtracked her movements.

She looked back at Josiah and stared him in the eyes. He waited for her to do something, but she just continued to watch his movements. Josiah felt like a sideshow attraction in a freak show booth, when his baggage suddenly drifted away with one smile and a nod from Mary.

He returned the smile and a nod as he left the room to announce the news to Amelia.

"How many fingers am I holding up?" the doctor asked, and Josiah heard Mary answer sarcastically as he started to walk down the hallway.

"Is a pinky a finger?"

CHAPTER 150

The room became overjoyed as Josiah shouted the miraculous news to Amelia. "Take me down there!" she commanded, and Josiah quickly obliged as he helped her into her wheelchair as the nurses watched with tears running down their cheeks.

"I'm going to see my sister," she waved as Josiah proceeded to the elevator. "She's awake!"

The two journeyed down the hallway to Scarlett's room as Dan was being wheeled shortly behind.

"Amelia!" Dan shouted last in their parade-like procession.

"Dad!" She turned her head around as Josiah stopped, allowing Dan with his attendant to catch up. "Have you heard?" She started to cry. "Is it real?"

"We're about to see," he beamed as he stretched out his hand to hold onto hers as the two were pushed the final distance side by side.

"Scarlett!" Amelia cried as her tears began to stream down her sunken face. "Scar!"

"Hey, A," she answered faintly, yet her eyes spoke louder than any volume. Her eyes shone brighter than any star in the cloudless sky as they twinkled with moist tears. "How you doing?" she asked, seeing her sister in a wheelchair and sock cap for the first time.

"I'm, I'm doing really good now." She continued to cry as she got within reach of her twin sister. "Really good."

Dan entered the cramped room and the head doctor asked all the nurses and physicians to leave so the family could be alone for a little while. "Scarlett, all I can say is you are a miracle," Dr. Phillips added as he wrote down his last comment on his clipboard. "I'll be back shortly."

"Thank you, doctor," Claire said, running over to give him a hug. "Thank you!"

"Sorry doc," Scarlett grinned. "She does that a lot."

The room exploded with laughter as Dr. Phillips closed the door so the family could have some privacy. "I'll come back later," Josiah announced as he stepped away from Amelia's wheelchair.

"Hold on there." Dan grabbed his arm as he passed him. "You're family to us."

"Right," Claire grinned as she kissed Josiah on the cheek. "Yes you are."

"Where's Charlie?" Scarlett asked, noticing the little tyke wasn't in the room.

"Charlie!" Claire gasped. "I forgot about Charlie. He's been at Emmanuel's house. I better call him." Claire whipped out her cell phone and proceeded to call him.

The family was all together, maybe not in location, but they were in heart. Charlie squealed with contagious enjoyment with the awesome news. "Let me talk to her," he panted. "She's up! She's up!" he screamed to Emmanuel and Gloria, Emmanuel's mother.

"Get your shoes on, Manny," Gloria yelled from the background. "Fast!"

"Hi Scarlett, I've missed you," Charlie said tenderly and sincerely.

"I've missed you too, boy."

Charlie giggled at the sound of his sister's voice over the telephone. "We're leaving, so I'll be up there. Don't do anything without me."

"I'll be waiting," Scarlett said, passing the phone back to her mother who tried to say something to Charlie, but he had already hung up. His adrenaline was pumping too much to sit around and talk.

CHAPTER 151

Amelia struggled to keep her head up as she visited with Scarlett even in her noisy room, due to the commotion and visitors. "Tired, honey?" Claire asked as she stroked under Amelia's chin.

"It's been a good day. Just a little too much for me," Amelia said as she yawned once more.

"Do you want to go back to your room?" Dan asked from the recliner that he was lounging in, still holding onto his hip.

"I'm fine," she answered, trying not to deter everyone's attention from Scarlett.

"I'm tired too," Scarlett lied, watching her sister's eyelids grow heavier as the conversation proceeded.

"Out. Out we go," Dan beckoned to everyone. "Josiah, will you push Amelia, and Charlie do you want to push me?"

"Do I?" Charlie grinned with childish intrigue.

Dan waved at Claire, who surprisingly walked over and kissed the four of them on their foreheads. "I'm going to stay here for a while."

"Come on, Charlie, you got to be strong," Dan said, giddy-upping like a jockey. Charlie may have had the strength, but Dan needed to steer with his feet and hands. "Ouch!" Dan shouted then started to laugh at the collision with the janitor's cart on the side of the hallway.

"Sorry," Charlie sighed, reversing the wheelchair and very carefully maneuvering around the cleaning supplies.

"Amelia, you better be glad you have Josiah and not Charlie," Dan said with a chuckle, while looking back at his daughter who was oblivious to the hazardous journey. She had already slid her head slightly to the left, mouth gaping open and eyes sealed shut.

"Shh. She's sleeping," Charlie whispered in his father's ear.

"Well, when we get back to her room, you can take a nap as well," Dan said with a smile.

"Oh, Dad," Charlie said as he rolled his eyes.

The group finally reached the elevator and waited for the doors to open. Josiah didn't know what was slower, their procession down the hall or their ancient elevator that seemed to be stalled on the first floor. The only thing he knew was Amelia needed to get her rest because her roughest days were still ahead.

"Sleep well," Josiah softly spoke in her ear. "Sleep tight."

CHAPTER 152

Josiah looked down at his watch and realized that Amelia, Charlie, and Dan had been asleep, resting soundly, for about an hour. He had more important issues to fill his attention than a desired nap. Sitting in a waiting room chair he brought into her room, he watched as her pulse and blood pressure started to slightly drop. He didn't make a sound to startle Charlie or Dan, but just continued to stare at the green and red numbers on the monitors.

A few minutes passed and each number fell another five digits. He got up and examined the clipboard hanging on her door that listed her vitals. Her pulse and blood pressure was steady this morning when it was recorded at 7:30 a.m., but now, now they were descending slowly like a jar of molasses. He knew that nothing would happen for the next few hours, and he had another piece to place into the puzzle of Amelia and Mary.

Josiah left the room with the sleeping Sutton family and warned the nurse at the center station to not let anyone enter the room unless they had clearance. The nurse nodded in suspicion, but assured Josiah that no one would enter the room.

He made his way back down to Mary's room and found her resting while her mother was sleeping in the recliner, probably peacefully for the first time in a month.

"Josiah," Mary whispered as she looked over at her mom, hoping that her scratching voice didn't wake her up.

"Shh," Josiah said as he quietly scooted a chair closer to Mary's bed.

"Mary, it's good to see you."

"Yeah, good to see you too," she grinned as she let out a heavy sigh. "Strange, isn't it?"

"I've seen stranger things," he smiled warmly, trying to bring her some peace and comfort during this tumultuous time. "How are you doing?"

"I don't feel normal," she said as she wiggled around in her bed. "Doctors say that it may be weeks before I get my strength back."

"You will be back as good as new before you know it."

"I hope so," Scarlett said, stretching out her good arm, but sadly, the healthy frame she had a month ago had disintegrated in that short time. Her muscles were now masses of flab from the lack of movement and calisthenics.

"Mary, I don't know if you know, but your sister isn't doing too well."

"Yeah," she frowned as she watched Josiah. "Strange. I remember hearing her talk to me and I knew that something was wrong, but I wasn't expecting to see her so, so, sick."

"I don't know if your parents want you to know, but I feel like you need to know." He leaned in to a whisper distance. "The chemo isn't working for your sister."

"No!" She huffed as her lips started to tremble slightly at the sound of the negative words.

"Her doctor is running out of medical procedures, because the leukemia was further along than they expected. She had been sick for quite some time, but they didn't realize it. She had been tired for months, but she assumed that she was a typical teenager always wanting to sleep more."

"So, what's going to happen?"

"If they don't find something quick, it doesn't look good," he said, patting her hand to show some compassion. "I don't think your family truly realizes that when the doctor said they need to do something soon, she was meaning within the next few weeks."

Scarlett started to quietly sob with the depressing news.

"I probably should not have told you since you are still recovering yourself, but there is something," Josiah said soothingly.

"Yes, what?"

"It involves you."

"Me? How?" Scarlett questioned, looking around the room suspiciously.

"Well, a way that she could recover is called a bone marrow transplant. Your dad got tested this morning, but his results are going to come back unmatchable and he won't be able to help Amelia."

"How? How do you know this already?"

"You just have to trust me," Josiah pleaded. "I know that is hard for you with some things that I have done, but I only did them to help you."

"Josiah, you are crazy!"

"Mary," he said as he looked around the room noticing that Claire was still asleep. He got up and closed the door, so he could have some privacy.

"What? What are you doing?" Scarlett asked nervously, trying to raise herself up, but she couldn't.

"Mary, please," he said, placing his hand on her arm to guide her gently to her bed.

"You're scaring me," she whined as she looked over at her mother, sleeping deeper than she had ever slept.

"Mary, please, just listen to me."

"No," she squirmed. "No. Lucy was right about you."

"Mary, Lucy lies."

"Lucy's my friend," she said as a feeling of remorse filled her being with the memory of Lucy lying on the side of the road during the traumatic accident.

"She is not a true friend."

"Says who?" Scarlett questioned, becoming irritated with their conflicting accounts of Lucy.

396

"Mary, you may not believe me, but," Josiah breathed out and knew that this was the time. "Mary, I'm an angel."

"You're a what?" She stared amazed at the ludicrous statement. "Where's your wings and halo, Mr. Angel?"

"Mary, the notions and pictures of angels you see are not how we really look."

"Well," she grinned menacingly. "If you're an angel, prove it! If you are who you say you are, you could do something. Fix Amelia!"

"Mary, that's not how it works."

"Sure. Sure it isn't," she said unbelievingly as her fright quickly faded to sadness for the confused black janitor.

Josiah stood up and quietly walked around the room, trying to decide his next step on this hair-width tightrope. "Mary, I could do anything, but if you don't believe me now, you will never believe me."

"Try me!"

Josiah sat back down and leaned once again toward Mary. "Just look into my eyes."

"Why?" she asked with a belligerent tone.

"Just do it, Mary. Just do it."

She rolled her eyes at the thought of looking intently into Josiah's eyes. The idea made her stomach slightly nauseous, but she followed his orders. "Okay. What am I supposed to see?"

"Just wait. You will see it," he said coolly. "You will see it."

CHAPTER 153

A light summer breeze passed through Scarlett's hair, tossing it freely as she stood examining the luscious colors of dandelions and African violets scattered throughout the meadow. She frolicked through the grassy field, basking in the freedom of the weightlessness.

She skipped over a brook on a path of protruding flat rocks, tossing a few small pebbles into the water to watch the splash and dozens of ripples down the peaceful stream. She closed her eyes and inhaled the sweet aroma of honeysuckles that were not visible, but she somehow knew were within walking distance.

The scenery was a dream, or even better than a dream. It was a form of utopia with all of her favorite natural surroundings. The lively meadow where soccer would be played while witnessing a family of rabbits. The gentle rushing of a small creek bed to explore the livelihood of turtles or wade up to her knees. The tasteful decadence of honey that would made anything much sweeter.

This was her ideal locale. This was her vision of joy. This was her meditation state. She turned away from the brook and noticed a grand oak tree that was swaying beautifully with the wind. The limbs were moving, causing the leaves to rustle musically with one another, as if composing their natural symphony.

The tree's base was thick, with about five wingspans of Scarlett to circle. She rested in its shade, sitting down and leaning up against the solid fixture. Her fingers started to trace the roots that had seemed to explore the surface, but then retreated back into the familiarity of dirt. Suddenly, the earth shook. She jumped up to her feet and ran out into the vast open field to get away from the towering tree.

The quake lasted for about a minute as Scarlett began to circle, watching the outer horizons to see the damage done. The brook was splashing wildly, but as the movement ceased, it soon regained stability and settled itself to a smooth current. The green field was untouched, no cracks or divots. She saw a huddle of clutching rabbits soon hop away on their merry journey.

All was back to normal, all but the grand tree. The quake's epicenter must have been directly under the tree, because it was split down the middle. In a matter of minutes the tree started to quickly shake, tossing and turning in agony. Suddenly, the tree stopped. Half of the tree laid on the ground to the left and the other laid on the right. Scarlett couldn't take her tear-filled eyes off of the wreckage. She stood safely from a distance, but she heard its cries. She felt its pain. She saw the unrelenting destructive power of one incident.

Something was beckoning her to come closer to the tree. She was fearful of the steps, yet she felt a surge of bravery. She wiped away her tears as she took a few steps closer. One side of the tree twitched. She waited for the movement to cease before she continued, and it eventually died down again.

She unflinchingly took a couple more steps forward, and one side of the tree started to move again. It looked like the tree limbs were trying to push the tree back up. The other side remained still.

Odd, she thought as she was witnessing a freak of nature. *Very odd.*

She continued her journey, and with each step forward, the tree seemed to get stronger and stronger. The tree was gaining momentum, inching further and further to stand erect.

She got within touching distance of the fallen side and felt the leaves that were starting to already wither as if rigor mortis was taking the tree captive so quickly. She peered through the fallen branches, but there wasn't anything that she could do.

Investigating the strange sight, she saw the light color wood of the inside of the base with its jagged edges down the middle caused an eyesore, but the tree seemed to be fully rejuvenated. Suddenly, the sturdy portion of the tree leaned down toward the lifeless segment on the ground.

Scarlett ran back into the safe pasture, thinking that the tree was about to collapse once again. She gasped at the sight of the strong tree, as its thousands of limbs and leaves started to wrap around the branches of the fallen half. She watched in awe at the willingness to help the fallen member. Once again she started to feel the earth shake, but when she looked around, she didn't see anything terrifying happening. Whipping around to the tree, she realized that the tree, itself, was causing the quake.

Its roots were buckling to the ground, trying to grip onto anything that was firm enough to hold. She felt the pain in the strong tree as it was trying to carry the weight of the lifeless half back to its original position. Branches were cracking with a few breaking and falling to the hard ground below. The strong tree looked tired and weary, on the verge of giving up when something happened. Something unexplainable occurred. It lurched back one last time with a grunt, and the dead looking half stood beside it.

Scarlett watched from a safe distance, as a few tree limbs unlatched from their grasps and swung down and started wrapping around the base of the tree like rope to tie the halves together.

Quickly, the light started to fade overhead and darkness covered the sky. Within a few seconds, the light returned. Then once again, the sky started to turn black, revealing the moon and stars, only for the sun to return quickly yet again. The cycle continued until it seemed like a month had days and nights of a few seconds. With each burst of light, Scarlett saw a glimpse of the tree, and each time, there was less withering and more growing.

Instantly, the night ended and the sun started to slowly rise over the horizon. Scarlett turned around to watch the sun rise, waiting for the speed to ignite once again, but it didn't. The sun continued it glorious and steady climb.

She turned around and saw the miraculous tree. The limbs were freely swaying. They were not clinging onto one another for dear life anymore. She moved in closer. The base of tree had a huge scar down the middle, but that was the only reminder of its ordeal.

She looked back at the sun that was still halfway hidden from the horizon, but something was begging her to turn around. She looked back at the tree and saw its base suddenly had some new markings. She walked closer and was startled by the etchings.

The healthy half had her name carved into the wood, resembling her sloppy signature. She stared unsure of the meaning, when she glanced over at the other side of the tree base, the side of the tree that was the weaker of the two. The once dead tree had "Amelia" on the surface.

"It's time to lift her up," Josiah whispered. "Only you can lift her up now."

Scarlett woke up from her vision, looking over at her mother who was still resting soundly. Sweat poured off of Scarlett's brow as Josiah wiped the chilled beads away.

"You were rooted the same. Share with her," Josiah said softly.

"Share what?" Scarlett asked, believing in Josiah. "What do I have that she needs?"

"Just remember, the best presents come with great sacrifices."

"Please, tell me," Scarlett begged. "Please."

CHAPTER 154

"Take me to Amelia's room," Scarlett yelled to her mother as Josiah wouldn't answer her echoing questions.

"Huh, what?" Claire answered, groggy from her much-needed nap, but also slightly rattled from the sudden outburst from Scarlett.

"I need to see Amelia," Scarlett commanded as she tried to fling her limp legs to the side of the bed.

"Scarlett, she's resting right now. You need to rest as well," Claire answered as she started to move around the room with her body twisted like a question mark from her curled-up position.

"No, I need to see her," Scarlett said, trying to lift her body to the nearby wheelchair, struggling with her weak and casted arm, but humility was a too big of a pill to swallow. "Fine, I will go see her myself."

"Scarlett, you need to just lie back." Claire walked over to the Scarlett's bed and pushed her gently back onto her bed.

"Mom! I need to see her. I need to see her now!" Scarlett's headstrong attitude was piercing through her fragile exterior, and she felt the hole in her strength. "Please, Mom. Please help me." Scarlett looked up into Claire's compassionate eyes and started to tear up. Claire knew that Scarlett could pull the tear card, but now, the tears were honest.

Claire's motherly instincts peaked as her heart started to melt when she wiped away Scarlett's warm tears. "Let me go get a nurse and see if it is okay." She walked out of Scarlett's room and began to second guess herself. She was the mother, she was the one who made the decisions. She was the one who had sat beside her daughter's bed for the last month, not her daughter. She stopped in the hallway wanting to turn around and tell her daughter no, but she also wanted to give her daughter anything she wanted.

"Mrs. Sutton?" Nurse Kathy asked. "Do you need something?"

"I'm, uh, can Scarlett go, well, she can't go see her sister, can she?" She fumbled her speech as if she had split personalities speaking in the same sentence.

Nurse Kathy stared confusedly at the incoherent rambling, but taking into account of the threads that the Sutton family had been clinging onto for the last month, she had grown accustomed to Claire's communication skills. "Does your daughter want to see her sister?"

Claire feebly smiled, acknowledging the correctness in the question, while thinking that the journey would be halted. "Yes. I've tried to tell her to rest, but she's on a mission."

"Let me go ask someone, but I don't see that it would be a problem."

"Really?" Claire answered shockingly.

"I'll be right back."

Claire walked back to Scarlett's room but waited outside the door. She was grateful that Scarlett was feeling able to move around, but apprehensive in disturbing Amelia. She knew the truth in Amelia's condition, but she didn't want to stress out Scarlett. She didn't know if Scarlett could mentally and physically handle the wrecking ball of Amelia's chronic condition at this time, especially her first day after a very long month of a comatose state.

Scarlett noticed her mom standing outside the door. "I'm ready," she barked as Josiah tried to calm her down. "Push Josiah, push!"

"Wait a minute, Scarlett," Claire said, stepping in front of her wheelchair like a boulder on a railroad track. "We have to wait to see if it is okay to leave."

"We can wait in the hallway," Scarlett huffed with stubbornness.

"Scarlett, no!" Claire commanded.

The room was anxiously tense, waiting for a simple word of yes or no from the nurse. Scarlett begged her mom to allow her into the hallway, but Claire didn't budge. She didn't want her daughter to get her hopes up anymore for it to be swept away under her like a bridge in a swollen river.

"It's okay, Mrs. Sutton," Kathy said walking up. "They said it would be okay."

"Push away, Josiah! Push away!" Scarlett commanded like the captain of her iron ship. The three moved along the hallway as Josiah slowly pushed the wheelchair and Claire tried to reason with Scarlett while tiptoeing around Amelia's delicate illness.

"I know, Mom," Scarlett grunted. "I know she's dying."

CHAPTER 155

The mostly empty room was silent except for the occasional giggling of Scarlett sitting up in her wheelchair as Amelia laid on her back propped up with a mountain of pillows. Scarlett had asked everyone in the room to leave so she could talk to her sister alone.

"How are you doing, A?" Scarlett asked sincerely.

"I'm tired. Really tired," Amelia said wearily. "Not sleepy, but tired."

Scarlett closed her eyes and remembered the last image of her sister, with her skinny, yet full face, her long brownish blond hair, and her inquisitive and curious eyes. Now, she had lost her innocence. The twinkle of her sharp-witted sarcasm had fallen into the black hole of chemotherapy.

"Is there anything I can do?"

"I don't think so," Amelia smiled. "I guess. I guess I need to say thank you."

"Thank you? For what?" Scarlett shot back with utter shock.

"Well," Amelia started unsurely, "I, well, when I donated my blood for you to use during one of your surgeries, the nurse noticed something and had my blood tested. That's why they found this. Who knows," she coughed with droopy eyes. "Who knows where I would be if…" she stopped and looked into Scarlett's eyes.

"You're welcome," Scarlett said confusingly, as if she answered an in-class discussion question correctly without knowing the answer. "Just fate, I guess."

"Maybe," Amelia said, leaning her head back to examine her plastic night sky.

"Are you sure there is nothing I can do?" Scarlett asked once again. "Think hard. I feel like you know something."

Amelia closed her eyes and a tear started to form, trickling down the side.

"A, what is it? What are you not telling me?"

"It's just that Dr. Pottinger came in and talked with me this morning when I was alone, and she thought that she needed to be honest with me." Amelia looked over at her sister and tried to bravely announce her words, "I'm dying."

"I know," Scarlett said, beginning to cry as Amelia's shield started to crack under the pressure. "Don't ask me how I know, because you won't believe me, but I know."

Amelia raised her body up, stretching her arms toward Scarlett who mirrored her actions. "I don't want to die, Scarlett. I don't want to die." The two sisters tried their best to hug, but with Amelia's tangled IV's and Scarlett's shackled wheelchair, they couldn't wrap arms around one another.

"I don't want you to die either. What can I do? I know there is something I can do, and I will do anything for you. Anything!" Scarlett let go of Amelia and tried to fling her body up into the bed.

"Scarlett, don't hurt yourself."

"Oh, Amelia, stop worrying about me." Scarlett smiled as she once again tried to get closer to the bed. "But I could use a little help."

"I don't know how much I can give you," Amelia coughed as she held onto her sister's good arm and pulled with all of her might.

"On the count of three," Scarlett stated as she took a deep breath. "One....two....three." The two girls grunted and they pushed and pulled each of their fragile bodies to the extreme.

Scarlett was able to get one of her legs onto the bed as Amelia continued to pull, allowing half of Scarlett's body on the bed. "Watch out," Scarlett waved as she shimmied her way closer to Amelia, trying not to roll on top of her.

"Ouch," Amelia snapped as Scarlett's leg fell onto her leg.

"Sorry," Scarlett apologized sincerely as she continued to move closer to Amelia's side. "I think. I think we got it."

"I hope so," Amelia said, leaning back as Scarlett too leaned back and rested her head on Amelia's shoulder, wrapping her arms around her sister's body and squeezing her tightly.

"We are in this together, Amelia," Scarlett whispered in her ear. "What do you need?"

The two sisters held each other for a few minutes in silence, each breathing heavily as their tears diminished and their smiles grew wider. Amelia turned her head to see her sister staring right at her.

"Well, Dr. Pottinger said that there is one other thing that they can try."

"What is that?"

"A bone marrow transplant."

"Take mine." Scarlett kissed her sister on the cheek. "Take as much as you need."

"I'm not sure it's that easy," Amelia said, closing her eyes. "I'm not sure about anything anymore."

CHAPTER 156

The peaceful room quickly became filled with controversy as the entire Sutton family discussed the possibility with Dr. Pottinger and Dr. Phillips.

"I want Amelia to have my bone marrow!" Scarlett started to yell over Dan and Dr. Phillips' talking. "It's my bone marrow."

"Yes, it is your bone marrow, Scarlett," Dr. Phillips agreed. "But there are some underlying factors that we need to look into first."

"Underlying factors?" Scarlett huffed. "Underlying factors? My sister needs it. I don't care about these factors."

"Scarlett," Dan sat in Scarlett's wheelchair while patting her arm. "I know you will do whatever you can for your sister, but the doctors do not feel that you are in a healthy enough state to perform this procedure. You need your bone marrow to help yourself get better for now."

"Help myself?" Scarlett cried. "Help myself? Mom, didn't you always teach us to share?"

"Yes, Scarlett, but this, this is different," Claire answered as her voice wavered at the remark. Her heart was aching at the thought of losing one of her daughters, and then a possibility of losing both of them with a risky surgery. She couldn't allow it.

"How is this different?" Scarlett asked in a back-talking manner.

"Scarlett, just drop it," Amelia begged. "Please, I will be okay."

Scarlett looked over at her sister who was putting on a heroic façade. "No you won't. You need it." She looked around the room. "She needs it."

"Yes, but," Dr. Pottinger tried to refute, but she was quickly silenced.

"But what?" Scarlett responded, begging for a fight.

"Scarlett, I know you love your sister, but there are more things needed to do this procedure than a little love. There are side effects. Deadly side effects."

"So, isn't cancer a deadly side effect?" Scarlett retorted boldly and confidently. "We cannot pick or choose; if we do, it is like choosing life or death. This procedure may bring death, but it can also bring life." She started to cry as she looked into each pair of eyes staring at her and her sister. "How can you deny her this?"

"We are not denying her anything, but if we rush into things, we may rush incorrectly. A better candidate for a transplant may be found," Dr. Pottinger strategically and methodically stated as she looked towards Dr. Phillips for back-up.

"What better candidate does she have than me?" Scarlett asked. "Her twin?"

"Scarlett, you just woke up this morning. You have a long road of recovery ahead of you. You need to focus on your own recovery and let Amelia focus on hers."

"We came into this world together," Scarlett held tightly onto her sister's hand as Amelia tried to wiggle from her grip, but Scarlett was too strong. "And by golly we will leave togeth…," she stopped.

Amelia leaned into Scarlett's ear, "Please stop, Scar. Please."

"I will not stop until we are both out of here," Scarlett whispered back. "It's all or nothing."

"Can I talk with you two?" Dr. Phillips asked as he looked over at Claire and Dan. "You too, Dr. Pottinger."

"Can't talk in front of us?" Scarlett snarled disrespectfully as she watched the procession out of the room to shut the door so the three Sutton children couldn't hear the discussion.

"Amelia, quit surrendering," Scarlett bickered. "If you back me up, it may mean more."

"Scarlett, I know you mean well, but," Amelia closed her eyes and just let her words spill from her lips. "I don't want you to die trying to save me."

"Amelia, listen to me," Scarlett said as she snapped her fingers in front of Amelia's face. "Look at me. I'm not going to die; this is why I am still alive."

Charlie ran across the room and jumped up onto the bed and curled beside Scarlett. "Hey, Buddy," Scarlett said, rubbing his hair haphazardly.

"I love you, Scarlett," he whispered. "I love you, Amelia."

"I love you too, Charlie," they both replied like an echo of one another.

The three Sutton children leaned their heads back and flipped on the television to watch anything to get their thoughts away from their current situation. They flipped the television for ten minutes until they landed on The Weather Channel when nothing else seemed to appeal to them. Suddenly the door creaked open and the grand marshal of the parade, Dan, entered first.

CHAPTER 157

"Well, we have decided," Dan started as Scarlett tried to interrupt. "Will you please stop for one minute, Scarlett, and listen to me? We have decided that if you are feeling well in a few days and there is still no donor match, you can donate your bone marrow. Dr. Phillips has gone over the problems that may arise, and we are certain that you won't listen to them, so I won't say them." Scarlett grinned as she shook her head no. "I don't know why we are doing this, Scarlett, but I know you will eventually wear us down, so why not do it?"

"Really?" Scarlett screamed with enthusiasm. "Do you hear that, Amelia?" Scarlett looked over at Amelia who was sound asleep. Scarlett nudged her arm, but she didn't wake up. "Amelia...Amelia..."

Dr. Pottinger rushed to Amelia's side, glancing down at her blood pressure that had bottomed out. "Everyone needs to leave," she commanded as she buzzed the nurses to come into the room.

"What's? What's going on?" Scarlett cried as Josiah walked in from sitting out in the hallway and carried her out of the room.

"It's going to be okay, Mary," Josiah reassured her as he whispered into her ears, wrapping his loving arms around her jittering body like he did when they first met. "Get ready, the surgery is going to be very soon."

"I'm scared," she cried. "Promise me, Josiah, promise me."

Josiah continued to walk with the trembling little girl in his strong arms. "God is watching over her, Mary. There is no need for me to promise, when He is the one who is holding her now."

CHAPTER 158

"This is happening too fast," Claire said, rocking herself in the surgical waiting room while through the doors and down the hall Scarlett was donating her bone marrow. Amelia had passed out from her falling blood pressure and the doctors quickly stabilized her the best that they could, but they all realized that she needed the bone marrow transplant as soon as possible. "She just woke up this morning. I didn't get to spend enough time with her today. What if something happens? She isn't healthy enough to donate her bone marrow. What if she needs it and then it doesn't work for Amelia?" Claire started to whimper. "What if I lose both my girls?"

"She's had many near-death experiences this last year and she survived them all," Josiah pointed out as Dan paced around the room. "She is going to pull through this one as well. And Claire, the new bone marrow is going to work! You just have to believe it."

"I wish you knew for sure," Claire mumbled as she bowed her head in prayer. "I wish you knew." She closed her eyes and she heard a familiar voice, but it was one she hadn't heard in many years. There was something different about this voice. It sounded as if it was coming from overhead.

"She's going to be okay, Claire. I am with her."

"That's a good thought," Claire replied as she opened her eyes and noticed that no one was around her. Josiah was now walking beside Dan as Charlie sat on the floor coloring.

"What did you say?" Dan asked as he came running to her side. "What, honey? What is it?"

A smile stretched across her face as a strange sensation started to filter through her body like the purest source of water. "Nothing," she smiled as she leaned over to her husband and kissed him. "It's going to be okay."

"I hope so," Dan replied, as he hoped that her words were not just surrounding Scarlett and Amelia, but around their marriage as well.

"It will." She looked him in his eyes. "It will." She stood up and walked over to Charlie, "Do you want to go get a cookie with me?"

"Sure," he answered as he clumsily got to his feet.

"Do you two need anything?" Claire asked.

They shook their heads no as Claire and Charlie walked out of the room. "You have a good wife," Josiah said, patting Dan on the back.

"I know," Dan agreed. However, his heart fell to the ground seconds later as he watched Karen walk through the doors.

"We need to talk!" she grunted as she pressed her finger into his chest.

"Yes," he nodded. "We do. Excuse me, Josiah?" Dan and Karen walked out of the waiting room and stepped in an empty white bleak stairwell with white railings circling the walls down the steps.

"Mr. Yates informed me that you turned over all your files to the FDA," she said, laughing schizophrenically. "He's kidding with me, right?" Right?"

Dan looked squarely into her eyes and boyishly grinned, "I wish he was, but no."

"No?" she hollered while gripping the railing to catch her weakening legs. "No?"

"How can I allow you to kill more people?" he calmly proceeded, stepping away from her reach. "I kept this case at arm's length away from my heart, but when Dr. Pottinger said that my daughter's greatest chance of survival was your fake drug, I realized how all the families of your victims felt. I saw the light of hope on my wife's face, but I knew the truth. I couldn't let that drug kill my daughter."

"Oh, you are something!" She growled like a lion on the prowl. "All you think about is you!"

"No, I am thinking about everyone. Even you."

"It doesn't look like that! You sold us out!"

413

"No, you sold your souls to the devil when you signed the patent documents even when you knew that it hadn't passed, and I have proof."

Karen's eyes that were filled with rage suddenly began to fill with tears. "You have no proof."

"Karen, it is in your best interest to go to Mr. Yates and tell him the truth."

"The truth?" She laughed. "Never! I am not a timid, spineless little flake like you."

"That is fine, but he told me that you told him that you didn't know about these *accidents*."

"Um...yeah," she answered, growing more annoyed by their conversation.

"Well, I have emails from and to you stating something else."

"You didn't! You didn't give those to him, did you?" Her calloused exterior started to scrape off with each word she muttered. "You couldn't have."

"I did." He shrugged his shoulders. "And he knows you lied. That isn't looking good for you. Lying to federal officials is not highly appreciated in court."

"Screw you!" she screamed in his face, almost spitting the words. "I'll tell your wife about us!"

He looked down at his feet ashamed of the last few months. "I already have."

"You little twerp," she said, scolding him. "You are such an ass!"

"I may be, but I couldn't live with all that on my mind."

"You are so weak! I don't even know what I ever saw in you!" Dan turned to walk away as Karen continued to scream and ridicule him. "You are a loser! You are dead to me! Just walk away!"

"Good luck, Karen." He waved as he got to the door. "You're going to need it!"

"Go to hell!" she screamed as the door shut behind Dan.

414

CHAPTER 159

The sound of Charlie's snoring was louder than any of the machines or nurses' conversations on Scarlett's entire floor. He slept on the couch under the window as Dan continued to rub his back, like he had been for the last two hours.

"Is she, is she okay?" Scarlett woke up groggy back in her hospital room. When she moved her body, she instantly felt the soreness in her hip as she grimaced in pain.

"They have her tube in her to receive the bone marrow, but they have to do some more chemo to make room for your good bone marrow. But," Claire answered from her recliner as her emotions started to flood up. "She's going to be okay, Scarlett. She's going to be okay. How are you feeling?"

"I'm, I'm okay," she answered as she widened her dazed eyes, looking around the spinning room. "What time is it?"

"It's a little after two in the morning," Dan answered as he walked over to her bedside looking back at Charlie to make sure that he didn't startle the sleeping bear. "We've been waiting to see you wake up."

"How much longer is it going to be?" Scarlett asked.

"I'm not sure," Claire replied. "A couple of days? Maybe a week? They are doing everything they can to make sure that your bone marrow is received with open arms."

"Who's with her now?"

"Josiah, but we'll go get him. He wanted to see you when you woke up," Dan said as he motioned for Claire to follow him out of the room.

"I'll stay here with her until Josiah gets here," Claire said.

Dan turned around and kissed Scarlett on the forehead. "You are so brave! I love you, my darling."

"Love you too," she yawned back as she tried to adjust her tired body from all the commotion in the last twenty hours. "Love you too, Mom."

"Oh, honey, I love you." Claire kissed Scarlett's forehead and ran her fingers down her rosy cheeks. "You are sometimes as stubborn as your father, but you are braver than any of us."

"No I'm not," she sighed. "Anyone would have done it."

"You may think that, but not everyone would have. Do you need anything?"

Scarlett shook her head as she rested it on her pillow recalling the unpredictable events of the day. A grin came to her face and she just let the joy of the excitement gallop all over her. "Can Amelia and I be in the same room?"

"What?" Claire laughed. "You two wanted separate rooms at home and now you want to room with her?"

"I know, right?" She smiled tiredly as her eyelids started to slide down.

"Right now you both need to get some rest, but I will ask tomorrow."

Josiah entered the room and beamed his bright smile at both of the women in the room. "Miss Mary, you are looking mighty well this evening."

"You too, Josiah."

He blushed at the thought of his aging body looking well, especially after the last few months of running all over the place trying to keep watch over Mary and Amelia.

"I'll leave you two alone, but I'll be out in the hall," Claire said.

"Thank you, ma'am." Josiah hugged her as she went by. "See, it's all going to be okay."

She smiled warmly with his assured optimism as she walked out of the room with a new pep in her step.

"You wanted to see me?" Scarlett asked, moving around in her bed.

"Yes, Mary, yes I did. You did a very good thing this evening."

"Why do people keep telling me that?" She moaned like a typical teenager who feels like no one understands her point of view.

"Because *you* are the one who pressed the issue, Mary. The doctors didn't want to do this, but *you* wouldn't quit. Without *you*, who knows what would happen to Amelia?" He stopped and looked intently into Mary's eyes. "Or the rest of the world."

"The rest of the world?" she mocked. "Josiah, I know you said you are an angel, but what does Amelia have to do with the rest of the world?"

"It is not for you to know right now, Mary, but you do need to know that your sacrifice, your perseverance to save your sister's life is the reason I am here. I've been watching you because you had a very important part of a very important life."

"Huh?" she asked, wondering if her brain wasn't able to understand his rambling due to the drugs she was on.

"Mary, your life saved one, but that one life will save *millions*," he whispered with dramatic flair, and suddenly she felt the importance of her selfless act.

"I'm not sure how me helping Amelia is going to then help millions, and I really don't care, but if Amelia is going to be okay, then it is worth it."

"Well, it's worth it then," Josiah grinned. "It is definitely worth it."

"So, you were sent to watch over me? Watch over me from what?"

Josiah kindly smiled and shook his head in wonder at the blindness of the child's eyes for the last few months. It wasn't important for her to know that she had a target on her and all those

417

coincidental near-death experiences were not as random or run of bad luck as she hoped.

CHAPTER 160

"She's asleep now." Josiah sat down beside Claire who was flipping her fingers through the Gideon Holy Bible that had sat unopened on the waiting room magazine table since the day of Scarlett's accident. "Good book."

"I think it is time to see what this is all about. These last few months of crazy could not just happen. There has to be a reason behind it all." She spoke with affirmation and clarity, as if for the first time in her life she realized the complexities of life and fate isn't just a poetic word.

"I believe you are on to something, Claire. Stick with it." He got up and walked away to check up on Amelia. With each step he took, a scene of the last few months flashed before his eyes. He didn't even know how everything would come together, but he had faith in the one who did. He started to smile bigger than ever as he started to see the random memorized photos that at the time seemed like just a piece of a jigsaw puzzle; but now, finally, he was seeing how the pieces were coming together. There is no incident in life that isn't important. No person in one's life who is meaningless. From a nighttime stroll to a dinner with a friend, everything in life has a purpose. Even an angel needs to see proof that it isn't a random game of pick up sticks, but it is more like a strategically and perfectly planned and timed lining of dominos. One event leads to another, and without one domino, who knows what would happen?

"Josiah." James entered into the hallway from an empty darkened room. "Good job, but it isn't over."

"Well, I'm pretty sure that you can't do anything about it now."

"What are you going to do? Watch her the rest of her life?" James folded his arms as Josiah continued to stride with his joyous smile. There wasn't anything that James could say or do that would cause him to doubt God's power.

"Yes, well, maybe not her entire life, but until it is accomplished," Josiah answered confidently without any acknowledgement of fear or discomfort in his voice. "She's going to change the world for the better."

"You may think so, but she hasn't yet," a little girl's voice commanded from behind.

Josiah turned to see Mary's little friend, Lucy. "I was wondering where James' boss was at? Did he do well? Is he going to get a promotion? Or did he fail because both girls are going to live?"

"Shut up, Josiah!" James barked as his remarks struck a loosened cord. He took a few steps forward growling his wet breath inches from the back of Josiah's neck.

"James, that is not how we talk to one of our old friends, is it?" Lucy smiled innocently, playing with her fingers childishly, as she swayed in her pink and white poke-a-dot dress.

"You may trick the world, Lucy, or should I say Lucifer, but I know who you are."

"Trick the world?" She giggled playfully, while her cold piercing eyes would not have a problem gutting an innocent baby without a second thought. "It's no trick, Josiah. I'm just here to show the world that your way is not the one and only way. There are other ways, and I believe mine is more fun."

"If the world only knew what you really looked like, they would," Josiah stopped.

"They would do what? Be scared? I'm just a little girl. What could I possibly do?" She interrupted snarling her words like a venomous snake, ready to poison its next victim or strangle them like a toy doll.

"Just a little girl," James whispered in Josiah's ear melodramatically. "She doesn't have horns or a red cloak. She doesn't have a pitchfork. She doesn't even look like a scary old man, like yourself. You look more like their images than she does."

420

"I know. She's played them well." Josiah's smile faded as his warm exterior suddenly went ice cold. "Lucifer, you may be cute in their eyes, but one day you will get what is coming to you!"

"Oh, the whole Revelation prophecy!" She hissed as she and James laughed mockingly at the ludicrous thought. "How does *He* know what is going to happen? It hasn't happened yet!"

"He knows, Lucifer. He knows just like He knew that you would be sending your men to kill Mary so Amelia couldn't grow up to become a well-educated and influential woman. He knows you better than you even know yourself."

"Keep repeating His brainwashing, but if you ever want to join me, Josiah, I have a great spot for you. I have a place for you to think for yourself and be as powerful as you wish to become. It is possible." She negotiated with a businesslike approach as she took a few steps forward with her hand held out to shake on the agreement.

"Never," Josiah said, bending down to look her square in the eyes.

"Fine by me," she laughed childishly. "It's been fun, Josiah, but you'll be seeing us again soon." She waved goodbye and blew Josiah a kiss. "Come on, James!"

"Coming," James replied before giving Josiah a snarling look.

CHAPTER 161

The pot on the stove was bubbling and spilling water over the edges, causing a scorching sound as it hit the simmering hot stove. "Josiah, are you having any trouble?" Ethel asked from the couch in the living room as she propped her feet up and watched the evening news. "Sad, sad, sad," she thought as the newscaster was telling a breaking story about Pharm Laboratories, Inc. and the fraudulent medical scheme that had killed one hundred and thirty-two innocent victims so far in Mississippi with more hospitals around the nation coming forward daily.

"No, no trouble," he laughed as he stirred the pot of mixed vegetables, lowering the heat. "Almost done."

"Good!" she exclaimed as she flipped off the television set and strolled into the kitchen. "Smells good."

"I thought we would have supper in the dining room tonight." Josiah spun around to check on the tilapia in the oven. "I have the table all set."

"Do you need anything from me?"

"No, just go sit down and I will have it in there in a minute."

Ethel entered the dining room and witnessed a beautiful layout of her crystal goblets and porcelain china, crisply ironed linens, two tall lit candelabras, and a bouquet of freshly cut roses. She sat down in her chair at the end of the table and noticed that there was an extra place setting. She racked her memory of Josiah's comment of a guest, but nothing registered. Josiah walked into the room carrying a silver platter with his exquisite fish, decorated with lemon wedges on a bed of rice and colorful vegetables.

"Lovely, Josiah. Just lovely, but is someone else coming?"

"It was a surprise, but my guest should be here in just a few minutes."

422

"Can you tell me something about this guest?" she prodded. "I'm old and I don't like surprises. Do I know this person?"

Josiah smiled cunningly. "I think you will recognize this person." Suddenly their conversation was interrupted by the ringing of the doorbell. "Here's our guest now." Ethel got up from the table but Josiah motioned for her to sit back down. "Wait here."

Her ears perked up as she heard the door open and Josiah greet another man with a hearty laugh and a few pats that she assumed were from a friendly hug.

"Did you tell her?" the visitor asked as they made their way back to the dining room.

"No, I wanted it to be a surprise." Josiah stood in the doorway and looked over at Ethel who was squinting, hoping to see through Josiah to see the visitor's face behind him. "Ethel, I think you will recognize my friend." Josiah stepped out of the way and there stood a young man that looked to be in his middle thirties. He was very handsome, dressed in a white suit with a dazzling turquoise tie. His eyes were the same gorgeous color as his tie and his smile seemed to glow brighter than the candles lit in the room.

"Mrs. Stapleton, it's so good to see you again."

"Gab," she choked as a tear started to run down her face. "Is that really you?"

"Yes, Mrs. Stapleton, it is." He went over to where she was sitting, kneeling down to give her a welcoming hug. "I hope you have taken as good care of Josiah as you took care of me many, many years ago."

"She has," Josiah smiled. "She has indeed."

"I....I...I have?" She fumbled her words as she looked into Gab's warm eyes and melted into his hug. "I've missed you, Gabriel. You saved my life."

"That is what I was sent to do," Gabriel smiled. "If I didn't stop you, who would have Josiah lived with during the last few months?"

"Josiah, you're an angel too?" Ethel asked amazed.

"Yes ma'am," he said from across the table with his hands folded under his chin. "Funny, isn't it? You thought you were just a woman taking in random strangers these last forty years, when really, Gab, your first guest lived in your house to give you the idea to take in guests so I could stay in your house now."

Ethel broke from her hug and stared over at Josiah and then back at Gab. "That is why you came? For Josiah to stay here today?"

"Well, we needed you to not take those pills. You need to remember *His* timing is different than yours. What seems like years to you, well, it's nothing to *Him*."

Ethel sat bewildered staring at Josiah in awe. "So, my life had a purpose?"

Josiah smiled warmly with a few tears beginning to fall. "More than you will ever know."

"So, do you all want to eat?" she asked and then a thought ran through her brain. "Are you two here..." she smiled with great anticipation. "Are you two here because I am dying?"

They both shook their heads no. "No, your time isn't finished yet. There are still some things you are supposed to do," Josiah answered calmly.

"I'm an old woman," she laughed. "What else am I supposed to do?"

"We can't tell you that, but don't ever let your age determine who you can be. Nothing is impossible. People still need you here," Gab explained the best that he could without going into details.

"So, did you just come to eat Josiah's good cooking?"

Gab shook his head and smiled. "No, I came because Josiah said that you requested to dance with him back in the hospital and I wanted to dance with you tonight as well."

Ethel began to blush like a young schoolgirl. "I guess we could dance now."

"After I slaved over this cooking?" Josiah remarked with an insult that soon was followed by a roar of laughter and the sound of happily dancing feet through the night.

CHAPTER 162

The desk was cleared off where towers of files and damning evidence once used to reside under the same roof as his three children. Dan sat back in his leather chair in his home office and sipped his coffee, taking in the last moments of freedom for a short while.

"Hello Claire," he said picking up his cell phone with a cheerful tone. "How is Amelia?"

"Well, her stomach is sore this morning, but her mouth sores are going away, she says."

"Is she eating?"

"A little, but she is afraid to eat because she will probably throw it up right now. I just cannot believe that it has already been a week from the transplant. We still have a long road ahead of us, but the doctors told us this morning that her cell counts are already improving." Claire's nose started to run as her eyes began to water. "Did you hear that, Dan? She's improving."

Dan dropped his cell phone on his desk and slumped over, crying uncontrollably at Amelia's miracle.

"Hello, Dan? Are you there?" Claire asked.

"Yes. Yes, I'm here," he said, picking up the phone as he wiped away his tears. "And Scarlett is doing well also?"

"Oh, Scarlett is here just laughing away with Amelia, Charlie, and Luke." Claire got up from the couch in their room and stepped into the hallway. "It's so good to hear them all laughing again. Dan, I'm going to miss you."

"I'll miss you too."

The phone went silent as neither knew what to say. They had gone through a lot the last few months and it looked like the mountain climb was going to continue for some time. Dan continued to breathe and casually wipe away a few tears as he thought about the valleys his family had gone through. From his viewpoint there were fragments of sunlight, but still it was dark.

"I love you," Claire finally said with a slight quiver of her voice. "I love you, Dan."

Those words were so sweet to his ears. He knew that somehow all the lumps of coal he had around him would eventually become diamonds with time. "I love you too, Claire. I guess it is true what they say that it is always the darkest before the dawn."

They ended their call and he sat his cell phone back on his desk. He swiveled around in his chair, seeing his clutter-free office pass around him. His chair started to slow as he came face to face with the portrait of his family on his desk. It was two years old, but everyone was smiling and healthy. He prayed that the same family would be photographed again soon.

He stood up and proceeded down the stairs when he heard the doorbell ring.

"Good morning, Mr. Sutton, we are here to pick you up," Mr. Yates smiled as a pair of FBI officers appeared on each side of him.

"Am I the last one?" Dan tried to joke to lighten up the awkward situation.

"As a matter of fact, there is one other person we have yet to get, but we will eventually track him down. We have Jud Askin flagged, so he will not be leaving the country, and it is just a matter of time before he runs out of cash. We'll get him."

"Excellent." Dan winked as he placed his hands behind his back for the officers to cuff him.

CHAPTER 163

Summer soon ended and autumn approached for the majority of the country, but in the South, there wasn't much changing of seasons. Scarlett was still going through rehab to strengthen her body three times a week, and Amelia was finally able to exit the hospital and sleep in her own plush bed. She still had to go in for chemotherapy, but she didn't know how much she had missed her home until she slept soundly in her bedroom with Scarlett by her side. The bed was cramped, but since they shared a womb for nine months, a twin-size bed was nothing to worry about.

Dan turned over all his information as state evidence in the various court cases that Pharm Laboratories, Inc. was involved in. Jud Askin was finally found living on a farm working as a hired hand in Illinois, but before the FBI could arrest him, he hung himself from a limb of an elm tree behind the farmer's barn.

Autumn rolled into winter, and Dr. Karen Anderson's and Todd Clements' attorneys, Dan's previous partners, did their best to place all liability and blame onto James Nialliv and his rising star, Jud Askin; however, the jury didn't see that they were blameless. They even tried to demonstrate that Dan was one of the main culprits in their fraudulent scheme, but there were too many holes in their hypothetical theory, and since Dan was once a partner in their law firm, the jury didn't believe them.

Spring sprang into action as Karen and Todd were found guilty on charges of corruption and involuntary manslaughter and were sentenced to twenty-five years in prison. Due to the legal system, they would be up for parole in twelve years. Pharm Laboratories, Inc. settled out of court with an undisclosed amount, but the newspapers estimated that it was over a billion dollars to the victims' families. It was a large settlement, but since the death toll from the drug eventually reached over three thousand individuals after the FBI compiled all of the hospitals' data, no family received a just amount for an innocent death.

Dan sat in a prison cell for thirteen months as the trial was being heard. He signed a plea agreement with the FBI, and Mr. Yates gave him a very good deal of time served. He still continued to have guilt and remorse for the lives that he unknowingly stole at the time, and some said that as Pharm's attorney he should not have served any time in jail, but his conscience wouldn't allow it. Every time he listened to his daughters talk over the phone from prison, he knew how close the drug that he once defended almost tore his life apart.

Dan thought that his legal career would be over and his license would be revoked, but Mr. Yates wrote into his agreement that Dan would still be able to practice law after his time was served. Some people throughout the country scolded Dan on talk shows and news programs for his lack of ethics, but he knew the truth. Yes, he did some morally corrupt things and the spiral sucked him in further, but he eventually grabbed onto a life preserver before wrecking his entire life. Of course, some things would never be the same.

CHAPTER 164

Dan laid in the grass, resting under the shade of a towering oak tree as he worked on his newest passion in life, writing. He started to develop characters and a plot in prison, and now he felt like that his legal career was behind him and his writing profession was his future.

"Dad!" Scarlett yelled from the back porch of a much smaller house than the one that they resided in a year ago. The southern style plantation home with spacious rooms and lovely décor was now a cramped three bedroom home next to Ethel Stapleton's home.

"What?" he asked, rolling off of his stomach and walking up to the stairs of his wooden whitewashed back porch.

"Amelia wants to know what kind of ice cream you want."

"Surprise me." He grinned as he laid down his yellow notepad of random drawings and a few sentences here and there. "Cake batter would be nice."

"I think he said strawberry," Scarlett laughed and hung up the phone.

"You little…"

"Uh, I know." She let go of the soccer ball that was under her arm and kicked it around in the kitchen and proceeded to head outside as her father followed along. "Want to play a little?"

He started to sit down on the porch, but immediately stopped, gripping the handle to help him back up. "Sure, why not? I still got it, don't I?"

"When did you have it?" she remarked wittingly.

"You've been around Amelia too much," he said. "Maybe I need to get another house with an extra bedroom so you don't have to share anymore."

Scarlett kicked the ball towards her father who stopped the ball and kicked it back proudly. "Wow, that's good for an old fellow."

Scarlett stopped his ball and took a step backwards. She aimed her ball to go five feet to the left of her father like a bullet. "Stop this!"

"Whoa, killer!" He missed the ball completely and it hit Ethel's fence and bounced back within a few feet of Dan.

"Nah, I like sharing my room with her now," Scarlett smiled as she brushed her hair out of her face.

The two proceeded to kick around the ball gently. Dan was breaking a sweat as Scarlett glowed in laughter at his trickling beads.

"So, is she coming to get you two today?" he asked while kicking the ball back to Scarlett.

"I think so," she said concentrating more on the ball and less on the conversation. "We'll leave around five."

"So early?" he playfully whined. "But it's Saturday and you were with her last night."

"I know. Sorry, Dad." Dan looked down at his watch, missing the ball that Scarlett just kicked to him, "Dad!"

"Sorry, but it's twenty till five now. Are you ready?"

"I guess I need to get ready, but we have to wait for Amelia. She and Luke should be back in a few minutes. It doesn't take that long to walk down to the store to get your, I mean my, ice cream."

"Nice one. So, she and Luke...is it serious?"

"Oh, gross, Dad. I'm not going to talk about her love life. You have that talk with her." She laughed as she ran into the house to change clothes while Dan kicked around the soccer ball to himself. He kicked the ball over into the shade and eventually relaxed under the sheltering limbs. He closed his eyes and remembered the fun times they all had at their old house. Fishing on the river, swinging on the swing set, grilling out and playing badminton, it was a lovely ideal family. He opened his eyes and he saw a much smaller and older home. This was not what he pictured when he decided to go to law school.

Claire stepped through the back door and stood on the back porch and shouted at Dan, "Where's Scarlett, it's almost five?"

431

"She's getting her stuff."

Claire turned around and went back into the house to help Scarlett with her belongings. Dan took a deep breath and got enough energy to get up. He stomped up the back porch and met Amelia, with her long brown hair and healthy figure, and Luke in the kitchen. "So, back with the ice cream?"

"Yes, yes sir," Luke respectfully answered as he proudly displayed the strawberry ice cream in his cold hands.

"I asked for cake batter." Dan stared unwelcomingly at the trembling boy's eyes.

"Whatever, Dad. Scar said 'strawberry.'"

"Yeah, she did." Dan smiled jokingly at Luke, who stood unsure of what he should do. "I was kidding, Luke. Lighten up."

"Yes, yes sir," Luke once again responded as he put up the ice cream.

"Is Scarlett ready?" Amelia asked as she glanced over at her father who sat down at the kitchen table.

"About." Dan smiled as he leaned back and stretched his arms overhead. "Come over here and talk with me, Luke."

"Yes, yes sir."

"Well, I guess I have to do everything. And Dad, be nice," Amelia said, pointing her finger at him before leaving the kitchen.

"Nice?" he laughed. "I'm always nice, aren't I, Luke?"

"Yes, yes sir." He sat down timidly across the table from Dan and the two just looked around the room, but not at one another.

"Scar, are you ready?" Amelia shouted as she walked up the hallway.

"Yes," she said putting on her backpack and meeting Amelia in the hallway as Claire followed the two girls into the living room as they were about to leave.

"Um, don't you need to tell your dad goodbye?" Claire asked.

432

"Oh, yeah, and Luke too," Amelia realized as they turned and walked back into the kitchen. "Bye, Dad," she said giving him a hug and a kiss. "Come on, Luke, you're going with us," she said, tugging his arm up from the chair to follow her outside.

"Love you, Dad," Scarlett said, leaning over and kissing him on the cheek.

"Love you too!" He got up from the table and followed the procession out the front door. "What time will you be back?"

"About seven-thirty," Amelia answered as they walked across the yard into Ethel's yard.

"Good evening ladies. Ready to go to the nursing home?" Ethel asked as she got out her keys from her purse as Josiah stood beside her like a bodyguard.

"Yes, what are we doing there tonight?" Scarlett asked as she took off her backpack and pulled out a few games. "I brought bingo and a couple of other games to play."

"Wonderful idea." Ethel replied. "Now let's get to the car. Here you go, Josiah, lead the way," she said as she handed him the car keys so he could be the group's chauffeur. The five of them huddled into the car and waved goodbye to Claire and Dan on the front porch.

"We have some good kids, don't we?" Claire asked Dan as they hugged and waved goodbye.

"We do," he agreed as he tilted his head to kiss his lovely wife. "We really do. How many teenagers would agree to volunteer at a nursing home on their weekends?"

"Well, that Ethel is a lively woman," Claire laughed. "She seems to be getting more and more energy every day. I heard she is going to start a soup kitchen."

CHAPTER 165

Mirabile Dictu looked eerily empty as the small group huddled around the centered roundtable. It was ornately decorated with black plates and flatware with matching dark crystal goblets. The lights were dimmed with only six tall black candles flickering their fragile light, casting ghoulish shadows on the wall. The gentlemen each had been invited into this place as a means of celebration at least once. They ping-ponged their eyes around one another knowing that this occasion didn't have a celebratory feeling.

The door opened as a pair of slipper-covered feet softly entered the room, as if tiptoeing across the hardwood floor.

"I wish to see Chef Renner," Lucy said to the hostess who was fixated by her lectern. "And then you can leave."

"Yes, as you wish," the hostess bowed before scurrying off to the kitchen.

"I'm so glad that each of you accepted my invitation," Lucy said, waltzing over to the table of grown men. "I have always commended you on your loyalty to me," she started as she stopped and patted Carlos' chairback. "You didn't have to follow me, but you knew the truth. You knew the limitless possibilities of freedom and I will be eternally grateful for that understanding."

Carlos solemnly nodded, but never looked Lucy into her piercing eyes. It was as if he was mesmerized by the empty plate before him.

She proceeded to the next gentlemen and stopped beside Jade. "Yes, I am grateful for each of your allegiance. Some are not as brave as you. Bravery is never easy because it requires a drastic situation to be shown. And each of you has shown it at one time."

Jade turned his head away from Lucy, looking at Maxwell seated to his left. Jade pursed his lips in contemplation and held his breath, waiting for the tension to pass.

It passed as Lucy strolled past Maxwell. "You have each amazed me at one time with your tenacity and skills as well as your dedication and willingness to accomplish the mammoth tasks I have given each of you." She stopped and clutched her heart. "It has been awe-inspiring to see the depths each of you has discovered in yourselves. Depths that you have carved out in order to achieve what I have asked you to achieve. And for that I thank you."

Maxwell turned his head and smiled up at Lucy, but his smile quickly faded when she didn't return the grin.

She proceeded to the last guest at the table, James. "Some of you embarked on new roles that I had never given before and I allowed you the opportunity to shine in the spotlight." She looked directly at James who started to quiver in his chair.

"And we thank...," James started to speak before Lucy silenced him.

"Did I say you could speak?" she rhetorically asked as he childishly shook his head no. "That is correct, James. I didn't ask for your wasted breath. And that is all you have done since the start of this."

James lowered his head in defeat as Maxwell reached out his hand to pat James on his knee as a sign of compassion.

"I wouldn't do that, Maxwell, because you don't have any solid footing with how you handled your tasks," Lucy hissed, whipping her head in his direction at breakneck speed.

"I wish I could say that tonight will be a feast we would all enjoy, but a feast of congratulations isn't what any of you deserve. No, tonight is a feast for only me."

Suddenly the door parted and Chef Renner slowly walked to the table. "Good evening," he smiled timidly before bowing to Lucy.

"Chef Renner, will you tell this fine group of men what you will be serving us tonight?" Lucy smiled wickedly.

He stood, wringing his hands as he looked around the depressed table and then up at Lucy. "You told me you would be requesting something special, so I am unsure what I will be preparing tonight."

Lucy's wicked laugh echoed around the room. "You are correct, Chef." Lucy slowly walked around to the empty seat between Carlos and James and sat down. "You may not believe it, but the main course is already here, Chef Renner."

"But I don't see it," he said astounded.

"You will," she winked. "Please head back to the kitchen and get your preparations ready for a feast that we will never forget. Well, some of us," she giggled as she looked around the table.

"I assume each of you has discovered that due to your failures, no one is safe. No one. Are you ready?"

Carlos looked wide-eyed and blurted out before he could stop himself, "You're not saying what I think you are saying?"

"What do you think I'm saying?" Lucy asked confusedly, cocking her head slightly.

Carlos scanned around the table at the other gentlemen, looking for a sign of encouragement, but each one stared at Lucy. Suddenly, Jade stood to attention, then followed by James, and then Maxwell.

"You can't be serious?" Carlos said, remaining seated.

"Oh," Lucy nodded in a superior attitude, "I'm serious, deadly serious." She basked in the atmosphere, closing her eyes to savor the fear in the air like a sweet rose. She slowly opened her eyes and smiled at Carlos. "Begin."

Chaos erupted as each of the soldiers grabbed anything they could use to harm another. James grabbed a goblet and whacked it against the table leaving jagged edges of glass. Maxwell grabbed a candle and quickly grew the flame by grabbing an antique torch hanging on the wall. Jade clutched a knife that he had been eyeing since he sat down, because this wasn't the first time he had failed.

Sadly, for Carlos, it was his first time. He jumped up from his chair and ran in the opposite direction toward the exit door.

"Oh, Carlos, the doors are sealed," Lucy remarked nonchalantly.

"You can't do this!" Carlos screamed as he turned around, saw Lucy, and felt a punch to his chest.

"I can do anything I want!" Lucy screamed as she stood up.

Carlos looked down and saw a black handle sticking out of his chest. "Jade?"

Jade slowly walked over as Carlos' knees buckled at the shock of his pending death. "It's nothing personal, Carlos," he said as he bent down and tenderly brushed Carlos' face. "But I don't lose," he whispered as he twisted the blade.

CHAPTER 166
Twenty Years Later

The years flew by as Scarlett and Amelia grew into womanhood. After graduating from high school, they each went to Ole Miss University where Scarlett studied early childhood development education and Amelia turned to her love of science. They each received their master's degree in five years.

Scarlett moved back to the town of Bethany and started working as a first-grade teacher and fell in love with Chapman Littleton, the former school bully who was now the seventh grade history teacher. He may have been rude and distasteful when he was younger, but he grew into a kind and compassionate soul. They were married sixteen months later and had their first of three sons two weeks after their fifth wedding anniversary.

Scarlett loved her life, a stay at home mother of three fearless boys. They were not wealthy, existing on a small town teacher's salary, but they had enough to survive and live happily.

Amelia got her master's in chemistry and then went on for her doctorate in biochemistry at Vanderbilt University. She continued to date the love of her life, Luke, who also received his doctorate in biochemistry, until they married the summer after they both wrote their dissertations. They both got a job with an up and coming pharmaceutical company, Klyne, Inc. in Charleston, South Carolina, and they worked day and night on their research.

They decided that it was best to wait for children, because their stressful and time sensitive jobs might be too much for them. They came up with a plan to get an aquarium to see if they could sustain life, but after their school of fish died in three weeks, they knew that children would be further down on their list of things to do.

That is, until now.

CHAPTER 167

"Hello?" Scarlett picked up, barely able to hear the static on the phone from all the commotion of cowboys and Indians being played in her old west living room. "Hello, I can't hear you. You will have to speak up."

"It's me, Amelia!" She raised her voice, almost to the verge of screaming.

"Boys, quiet! Aunt Amelia is on the phone."

"Hi, Aunt Amelia," the three young boys said in unison almost like a song. "How are you doing?" Scarlett asked as she made her way down the hall into the bathroom so she could talk in peace and quiet.

"Fantastic!" Amelia squealed. "We did it!"

"You did it? What did you do?"

"We did it!" she screamed at the top of her lungs. "I wasn't allowed to tell you a couple of months ago, but we got the results back today and it was positive!"

"Really? It is positive?" Scarlett sat down on the toilet to let her legs regain some composure, as she suddenly wondered out loud, "What is positive?"

"Scarlett, really? What have I been working on for the last ten years?"

Scarlett felt all the air leave her lungs. "You...you..." she tried to speak, but the words were not coming from the lack of oxygen.

"Yes, we did it!"

"Oh, Amelia! That is fantastic! Really great! Tell Luke for me. Have you called Mom yet?"

"No, not yet, but there is one other thing."

"What, what is it?"

"Is it okay to name it after you?"

"What? You want to name it after me?" Scarlett became speechless at the thought. "No, Amelia, this is your drug. You need to name it something to symbolize you."

"Scarlett, without you, I would never have found this drug. I would not even be alive without you. How can I not name the drug that will save the lives of leukemia patients with the name of the one that saved mine?"

Scarlett sat speechless as tears began to fall down her cheeks. She reached for the toilet paper, tore off a few sheets, and blew her nose. "I am…I am truly honored, but if you change your mind, I will totally understand."

"I will not. Luke and I decided the name a month ago when we sent in the information. We got the letter back from the FDA stating their findings and it passed. The drug will be used in hospitals in the next six months. I am so excited, Scarlett. I am so excited!"

"I am so happy for you, Amelia!" She screamed and stomped her feet on the bathroom tile. "I am literally stomping my feet in joy for you."

"I love you, Scarlett," she said and then paused as her voice started to crack. "Thank you for what you did for me. Thank you for your sacrifice. Now, hopefully, no one will have to die from this disease."

"I love you too, A. I love you too."

Amelia breathed deeply as she tried to control her running tears. "I need to call Mom now. I love you."

"Dad would have been so proud of you, A. We will be visiting you soon to celebrate."

The two hung up their phones. They were states apart, but each sunk into their chair and joyously bawled like a happy child.

Scarlett wiped away her tears and got up. Glancing in the mirror, she saw her running black mascara. As the black skidded down her

440

face and darkened her cheek, she flashed back to Josiah's hopeful words.

Mary, your life saved one, but that one life will save millions.

God bless you, Josiah, she thought, *God bless you.*

CHAPTER 168

Amelia blew her nose as she wiped away her mascara. She picked up her cell phone when Josiah entered the room. "How did Mary take the news?"

"Um," she stared in shock at the familiarity of the voice and features. "I'm sorry, but who are you?"

"Don't you remember me?" He playfully frowned as he stood in her doorframe.

"Josiah?" She sniffled, grabbing another tissue. "Is, is that you?"

"Have you called your mom, yet?"

"I'm about to. What are you doing here?" she asked, confused at his lack of aging and his sudden appearance in her office.

"Tell her hi for me, but I need to talk to you real quickly before you call her."

"Okay." She reached her finger down to her alarm button but didn't press it yet. Her heart started to pump faster. *This must be a joke, this has to be a joke. Josiah has to be dead* she thought as she looked the gentleman up and down, and every bit of him matched her memory of Josiah.

"I am so proud of you, Amelia for sticking with this. It hasn't been easy, but I knew you could do it. You are going to change the world." He stopped as he noticed her expressionless face. "You found your answer and it was right in front of you the whole time, wasn't it?"

"Thank you, Josiah," she replied. "Yes, it was staring right at me, but how did you know, and how are you here?" He looked down at his feet and shuffled them around like a bashful child. "What is it, Josiah?"

"It's time for me to leave you. You don't need me to protect you anymore."

"Protect me? Josiah, what are you talking about?" she asked baffled. "How were you protecting me?" Her finger was frantically twitching on the alarm button as the word protect started to sound strangely familiar to stalk.

He looked at her with a soothing smile that seemed to ease her worries. "Just ask your sister. She'll tell you."

"My sister? What does Scarlett know?"

"More than you think. Take care, Amelia. Oh, and by the way, you can handle a child if you want. You are going to be a great mother too. Twins." He turned and walked out the door and suddenly vanished. His mission was over.

Amelia jumped up from her desk and ran out the door, but she couldn't see anyone or anything that resembled Josiah as she spun around in the hallway. Her hands were shaking wildly as she pressed 2 on her cell phone speed dial.

"Hello?" Scarlett answered.

"Scarlett, it's me again. You are never going to believe who I just saw!"

Scarlett began to smile as she heard the shock in her sister's voice. "Was it Josiah?"

"Shut up!"

Scarlett laughed down the hall as she ran back to the bathroom so she could tell the story of Josiah to her sister.

"He said that he has been protecting me." Amelia gasped at the unusual circumstance as she walked back into her office and closed the door. "So, he has been watching me?"

Suddenly, as if her brain was being guided by a higher power, she recalled a conversation years ago between her and Josiah in her hospital room. *It is found in the easiest place to look,* he had said. *We always think that life is complicated and diverse and hard to understand, but if we just take a step back and reexamine our current surroundings, the answers will be found. God didn't give us a brain for it to not be used. Most people are afraid to use their God-given gifts.* Amelia stood with her back against the door, gradually sliding to the floor as her legs were weakening from the

443

monumental weight that had been unknowingly on her shoulders for the last twenty years.

"Hello?" Scarlett stated at the lengthy silence on Amelia's side of the conversation.

"Yeah, I'm still here," Amelia said, waking herself up from her flashback. "I just remembered a strange conversation I had with Josiah years ago. It just came to me out of the blue. So, I wasn't listening to you. Can you tell me what you said again?"

"Oh, A," Scarlett started to laugh behind the closed doors of her secluded bathroom as she began her true tale, no matter how outlandish it appeared.

ADDITIONAL BOOKS

Solomon's Dreams: The Hunting at Huntington

Solomon "Solo" Davis is a man of faith, but even for him not all things are believable. How quickly his life is turned upside when he comes face to face with one of his doubts. Can he believe in something that is so impossible?

What if your dreams of last night…

"Top story tonight," read the senior news anchor. Solo held his breath, waiting to hear about the kidnapping or the death of the older couple. He had already had two of his dreams strangely come true with frightening detail, and he couldn't help but wonder if it was some cosmic coincidence; a million to one chance that all his dreams actually occurred. Could this really be happening?

Became your realty for today?

"Oh God! Oh God! Oh God! What do I do? What do I do? What do I do?" Solo prayed hoping the perfect answer would drop out of the sky at his feet. The thought sickened him that if his dream with the preschool students with their laughter and singing was real. Then the ruthless kidnappers and serial killers must be real. And the crying, terror stricken kidnapped girl must be real too.

How can you do nothing when you know something is going to happen?

Watch out Washington D.C. The Carbon Monoxide Killers are on the loose.
"Are you ready for this?" she asked her father who slowly nodded, taking in a deep breath.
"It's now or never."

We all have a dream
We all have a purpose
It's time to use your dream to fulfill your purpose

We were created to dream, but so often we lose the childlike innocence of dreaming of things to come. The Bible is filled with stories of people following their dreams – walking to freedom through a sea, defeating giants with mere pebbles, or watching loved ones be healed. These people dreamed big dreams, but not from their own imagination or merit. No, God ordained these great men and women of faith to chase their dreams, just as He still does today. In this captivating book, mystery and inspirational author, Eric Suddoth engages dreamers to begin a journey they were destined to walk.

First steps are always scary, but we are on this journey together. It's time to be Dream Chasers.

Unsung

Within these pages is a deeply intimate work of praise-filled poems, heartfelt prayers, reflections on hard lessons learned and hopeful reminders of God's infinite love and mercy. Each of these writings may not have been intended to become songs, but somehow found themselves, sometimes years later, sung behind my piano or guitar. The majority of these songs have only been sung from the safe confines of my home. Until recently, I believed these writings were just cherished moments between me and God. That is until now.

This book is decades in the making.

A book I never intended to publish.

Come and prayerfully meditate over these words. I pray that this book will bring a blessing to you and that God will sing over you as He originally sung them over me.